PENGUI

Women

Louise Morrish is a librarian whose debut novel won the 2019 Penguin Random House First Novel Competition. She finds inspiration for her stories in the real-life adventures of women in the past, whom history has forgotten. She lives in Hampshire with her family.

Women of War

LOUISE MORRISH

PENGUIN BOOKS

PENGUIN BOOKS

UK | USA | Canada | Ireland | Australia
India | New Zealand | South Africa

Penguin Books is part of the Penguin Random House group of companies
whose addresses can be found at global.penguinrandomhouse.com

Penguin Random House UK,
One Embassy Gardens, 8 Viaduct Gardens, London SW11 7BW

penguin.co.uk

Penguin
Random House
UK

First published 2025
001

Copyright © Louise Morrish, 2025

The moral right of the author has been asserted

p. vii: Coat of arms of the United Kingdom (1837–1952)
by Sodacan, via Wikimedia Commons

Set in 12.5/14.75pt Garamond MT Std
Typeset by Jouve (UK), Milton Keynes
Printed and bound in Great Britain by Clays Ltd, Elcograf S.p.A.

The authorized representative in the EEA is Penguin Random House Ireland,
Morrison Chambers, 32 Nassau Street, Dublin D02 YH68

A CIP catalogue record for this book is available from the British Library

ISBN: 978–1–405–96774–7

Penguin Random House is committed to a sustainable future
for our business, our readers and our planet. This book is made from
Forest Stewardship Council® certified paper

MIX
Paper | Supporting
responsible forestry
FSC® C018179

For my daughter Ellen.

And in memory of all the female doctors, nurses and orderlies who helped save lives in the First World War.

Your King and Country Need You

A CALL TO ARMS

An addition of 100,000 men to His Majesty's
Regular Army is immediately necessary in the
present grave National Emergency.
Lord Kitchener is confident that this appeal will
be at once responded to by all those who have the
safety of our Empire at heart.

TERMS OF SERVICE

General Service for a period of 3 years or until the
war is concluded.
Age of enlistment between 19 and 30.

HOW TO JOIN

Full information can be obtained at any Post
Office in the Kingdom or at any Military Depot.

GOD SAVE THE KING

I

Edie: August 1914

She fights them with everything she has, tooth and nail. So much wild energy fuelled by terror. For a short while she manages to resist them, begins to hope she might make it. But the trio of wardresses, all strong of limb and hard of eye, are too much for Edie in the end. They soon have her pinned to the plank bed, and now the prison doctor's face looms into view.

'It will go easier if you just submit.' The doctor, a young man with deep-set eyes, wipes perspiration from his brow, then rolls up his shirtsleeves in a manner Edie has come to dread.

Sheened in sweat, skin itching beneath her coarse serge dress and thick black stockings, she is slowly suffocating in the stifling cell. The doctor wields his bottle of bromide, flourishing a tin spoon dented with the bite marks of Edie's teeth.

'Hold still now.'

A dull, persistent ache throbs at the base of Edie's skull. Three days without a crumb of food has left her too weak. The doctor's vice-like grip prises open her jaws, and she is helpless to prevent the cloying sedative sliding down her throat.

Choking, she renews her desperate struggle for release,

earning herself a knee in the groin from one of the wardresses. 'Give it up, girl!'

Why are you doing this? Edie wants to scream at the woman. *Why aren't you helping us fight?* She's never understood why so many women seem content with the status quo. Some of suffrage's biggest detractors are fellow females, which Edie cannot fathom.

As her strength wanes, a part of Edie's lucid brain is coming to the fore. If she wants to survive, she will have to play the doctor at his own game. She lets her body slacken, shorn head dropping on to the wooden bed with a thud, arms and legs completely inert.

The wardresses continue to grip her ankles and wrists, breathing heavily, until the doctor tells them to step away. 'She won't give us any more trouble.'

Won't I?

At last, they leave her, the cell door slamming. Edie drags herself up, then over to the slop bucket in the corner. A practised finger down the throat, and a moment later she's vomiting up a thick brown mixture of bromide and stomach bile. Her tongue burns, but she feels cleansed. She lies down on the bed, turning her face to the wall.

Two weeks, Edie.

Two more weeks and then you're out.

She stares at the flecks of dried porridge, the remains of her rejected breakfast stippling the whitewashed wall, her tongue worrying at the ragged edge of a broken molar.

Resilience has always been her strength, she tries to remind herself. She must draw on all her reserves now, suppressing the bite of animal hunger in her belly, turning her thoughts from her raging thirst, her stiff and aching joints.

She inspects the bracelets of mauve bruises encircling her wrists, tentatively rubs the bridge of her nose. It's still tender and she can breathe through only one nostril.

Where there's breath, there's hope. Her mother's mantra comes to Edie now, and it lends her strength. Her body might be little more than bone, sinew and skin, but it's whittled to an iron core.

If the prison doctor hopes she'll weaken and break her hunger strike in here, he sorely underestimates her. She'd sooner lick the inside of her slop bucket.

They're waiting for you to break.

The doctor, the governor of Holloway, the wardresses, they are all enjoying watching her strength drain like water from a broken pail. As soon as she's deemed to have reached the limits of her endurance, they'll release her under the Cat and Mouse Act, the government's latest attempt to suppress the suffrage cause. The imprisoned women are pushed to the very brink, then released to be nursed back to health and imprisoned all over again. Edie thinks of the rest home she'd briefly stayed in during the spring after her last stint in prison. The place near Notting Hill was known as Mouse Castle to her fellow suffragettes, and Edie pictures the handsome female doctor with the kind eyes who'd treated her there, dosing Edie on strychnine to 'brace you up'.

The lady medic's name eludes Edie now, but she's never forgotten her words: *Courage calls, Miss Lawrence, and it finds you ready.*

She wonders what the doctor is doing at this precise

moment, but her brain is too sluggish with the heat, her imagination stifled. She closes her eyes, and for a time there is blessed peace.

Muted voices filter through the thick cell door, overlaid by the clip of boot heels on stone, the sinister jangle of keys. Edie's eyes snap open, her breath growing shallow. She's mostly learned to ignore the constant noises of the prison, the cries and screams and curses of the inmates. Yet her pulse still bounds at the approach of a thick-armed wardress, or the threat of the doctor with his instruments of torture.

A smouldering ember of fear is trapped under her breastbone. Each slow day that passes in this cell is a painful reminder of all that she risks losing: her job at Mr Stead's paper; her sanity; Nate.

Nate.

Why hadn't he visited?

Don't think about him.

Her misted gaze travels from the dank cell wall over the filthy stone floor to the stinking waste bucket in the corner seething with flies. Listening to the sounds of the prison, the weeping and moaning of other women in neighbouring cells, the incessant drone of a bluebottle circling the grimy slit window, she tries to calm her breathing.

A familiar metallic clatter at the cell door ruptures Edie's fragile composure. The door swings open to admit the tall figure of the chief wardress. Before Edie can react, the woman is looming over her.

'*Up*, 241.' The wardress's glass eye fails to move quite in synchronicity with her real one, so Edie is unsure exactly where the woman is aiming her beady gaze. Rumour had it that the wardress removed her false eye each night and polished it with a duster. The thought makes Edie shudder, as she slowly rises.

'Move, 241.' The wardress hauls Edie to her feet. 'Get your cap and apron on.'

Lightheaded, Edie reaches for the wall to steady herself. What was happening? The lunch bell hasn't sounded yet, and it's too early for chapel.

The wardress thrusts Edie's cap and apron at her. 'Put them on.' She yanks Edie away from the wall, causing her to stumble. 'Where are your shoes, girl?'

Edie forces herself to meet the wardress's real eye. 'You took them.' *After you attacked me, you bitch.*

The assault two days ago is seared into Edie's memory; her throat bears the scratches from the woman's fingernails, and her nose still hurts.

The wardress glares at Edie. 'Put those on,' she orders, gesturing to a pair of men's slippers in the corner of the cell. They are dear Nate's, donated to Edie on his last brief visit, and too large for her feet. Slowly, she obeys the wardress: if she refuses, she will no doubt be beaten again.

The wardress grips Edie's arm and propels her towards the open door. Crossing the threshold, the world tilts on its axis and Edie sways.

'Don't you dare,' the wardress snarls, yanking Edie alert. 'I'm not scraping you off the floor no more.'

Edie bites her tongue as she's propelled along the corridor, past the open doors of neighbouring cells, glimpsing other women being dragged from their beds.

'Edie!'

She hears her name, turns to see her friend Maud, a fellow suffragette from the Society, staggering in the grip of a male warder twice her size.

'What's going on?' Edie calls to Maud, stubbing her toe painfully as one of her slippers comes off. The wardress drags her on, the lost slipper left behind.

'They're letting us go!' Maud shouts back hoarsely. 'Prime Minister's called an amnesty!'

Edie staggers on, none the wiser, her remaining slipper torn from her foot by the wardress's large boot.

She's hauled along echoing corridors, past the prisoners' visiting rooms, the doctor's lair, the governor's office, until at last she arrives at the reception hall. At the desk, she's reunited with her meagre belongings – her misshapen straw hat and Sunday best blue dress, which she was wearing on admission, and her confiscated shoes.

'Where's my purse?' Edie stammers. It had a precious few pennies in it.

'That's the lot,' the reception clerk snaps, picking his ear with a bent finger.

'I had a purse.' Edie's empty guts clamp, as the man shrugs.

'That's the lot,' he repeats.

'But –'

Edie feels hot breath on the back of her neck. 'You heard him,' the wardress says, with soft menace. She shoves Edie into a tiny cubicle off the main room and orders her to change out of her prison-issue clothes.

Back at the desk, Edie relinquishes the yellow badge she's worn, bearing the number of her cell, 241. A nauseous headache is building behind her eyes, and she barely has the strength to stand. With an unsteady hand, she signs the form granting her freedom.

Dismissed by the clerk, she wills herself not to faint. Moments later, she finds herself outside the walls of Holloway, breathing in the humid, dusty air of the city, and she's free.

A small crowd of suffrage supporters are demonstrating in front of the prison, waving flags and singing 'The Women's Marseillaise', their voices high and tuneless.

> *Arise, ye daughters of a land that vaunts its liberty!*
> *Make reckless rulers understand that women must be free,*
> *That women* will *be free!*

Someone catches sight of Edie emerging from the gates, and a shout goes up: 'Here she is! The first!'

'Come here, my dear! Come!'

Edie falters, but the women soon surround her, blocking her escape. She submits to their embraces, endures strangers' hands stroking her shorn head. To receive so much enthusiastic affection from these people, after bearing such violence, makes Edie tremble.

'You're free, Miss . . .'

'The amnesty, it's true . . .'

A man with a camera on a tripod pushes his way through, and deftly sets up his contraption. 'Photograph for the papers, Miss.' Too stunned to refuse, Edie submits to her picture being taken, while around her people talk of McKenna, the suspension of all militant suffrage activity, and how the suffragettes, regardless of their crimes, are being freed from gaol.

So much has happened since war was declared, only a week or so ago. Edie has missed more than she ever imagined, locked away in her cell. Realization is dawning: she's stepped out into a changed world, and the knowledge makes her head swim.

A girl hands Edie a mug of tepid tea and an oat biscuit as more women are released from the prison, staggering through the gates, blinking in the sunlight.

The sweet tea revives Edie, and after a short while she's able to stumble away from the crowd, towards a boy pasting a black-bordered poster on a nearby gas lamp. 'EAT LESS BREAD AND VICTORY IS SECURE,' the poster proclaims. The boy finishes his task, and as he hurries off, Edie fights the urge to rip down the government poster and throw it into the gutter. The fact that she doesn't even have sixpence for a loaf of bread infuriates her.

Has she still a job? At his last visit, a week ago, Nate had promised Edie he'd speak to his father, but Mr Stead's support of the Cause had its limits, Edie knows. He'd turned a blind eye to his maidservant handing out flyers at suffrage meetings, but when Edie was arrested this last time, charged with assaulting a police officer, even though she'd been trying only to defend herself, he hadn't wanted to know.

Well, she won't find out the fate of her job by wasting time here. She'll return to the newspaper offices, clean herself up, and hope Mr Stead's in a good mood. If her luck holds, she might even be reunited with Nate.

As she threads her way through the crowded streets, the prospect of seeing Nate again sends a flicker of energy through her veins, inuring her to the tumult of horses' hoofs and carriage wheels, the stench of petrol fumes issuing from an idling motor-car. She flinches as a drunken beggar lurches across her path, aware of several passers-by giving her second glances, a few eyeing her with open suspicion.

Head down, she forges on, conscious of her damaged nose, her bare arms tattooed with bruises. As her feet pick up speed along the dusty pavements, her wary eye snags on more government posters stuck to shop windows, walls and lamp posts.

THE EMPIRE NEEDS MEN
WOMEN OF BRITAIN SAY 'GO'!

As she nears the newspaper offices, another thought occurs to her. Perhaps Mr Stead's reporters, Mr James and Mr Arnold, have joined up. On its heels comes a far darker concern: will Nate volunteer to fight too?

Pushing the thought to the back of her mind, Edie lets herself in through the unlocked back door, removing her hat. She hears Mr Stead call from his office along the passage: 'Who's there?'

Edie finds her employer seated at his desk, pen in hand, habitual cigarette smouldering in a saucer at his elbow. Mr Stead's eyes widen behind his steel-rimmed spectacles, as Edie steps through the door.

'I'm back, sir,' she stammers. 'Released early, on amnesty.'

'So, it's true, then.' Stead gropes for his cigarette, waving at Edie to sit down in the chair opposite. 'They've let you all out?'

'Yes, sir.' Edie regards her boss across the expanse of

mahogany, and only now does it occur to her that the offices are unusually quiet. No sign of Mr James or Mr Arnold, no messenger boys flitting in and out of the place.

'You've come straight from Holloway?' Stead asks.

'Yes, sir.' Where else does he think she'd go? This has been her home for five years, nearly. Ever since she left the only other place she's known: the workhouse.

Stead gestures with his cigarette, scattering ash on the desk. 'What on earth happened to your face?'

'Fell, sir.'

The editor regards Edie for a long moment, cigarette forgotten in his hand, and she half expects him to challenge her. Instead, he mumbles to himself as he stubs it out, half-smoked, in the ash-filled saucer.

'I'm back to do the cleaning, sir.' Edie's mouth is so dry she can barely get the words out. The last time she'd copped a short spell in Holloway, Mr Stead had been supportive and had kept her post open. *Please*, she thinks, *don't sack me now.*

Mr Stead clears his throat. 'There won't be any cleaning required, Edie.'

'Pardon, sir?'

Mr Stead sighs deeply, not quite meeting Edie's eye. 'I'm closing the offices.'

Edie's stomach plunges. 'Closing them? Why, sir?'

'I can't run this place on my own.'

'But what about Mr James and Mr Arnold?' *And Nate? Where is Nate?*

'They answered the call last week.'

Edie takes a breath. She has to know, but she can't speak Nate's name. 'Your son, sir?'

'Nathaniel too. The Rifle Brigade.'

A charged silence thickens the air. Edie's mind is in freefall, and all she can think is, *Why didn't he tell me?*

After a moment, Mr Stead rises from his desk and moves to a bureau, rooting in a drawer. 'I can only give you a fortnight's severance pay, I'm afraid.' He hands Edie a brown envelope, heavy with coins. 'I'll provide a reference, of course, that goes without saying.'

Edie knows this is more than generous of him. Not only had she forfeited her freedom in prison but also her right to employment.

'You've been a good worker, Edie,' Mr Stead says. 'I'm sorry to let you go.'

Five years I've worked for you, she wants to scream, panic blurring her vision.

'I can help you, sir,' she hears herself say. 'I can help you run the paper.'

'Without reporters?' Mr Stead replies. 'Impossible.'

'I can write reports for you, sir,' Edie stammers. *It's all she's ever wanted to do.*

Mr Stead regards her for a moment, blinking behind his spectacles. His expression speaks volumes: her suggestion is ludicrous. She's not one of his freelance reporters. She's a workhouse-educated maidservant.

If only Nate were here: he'd seen potential in her, and they'd sometimes worked on stories together, in secret.

Mr Stead lights another cigarette, and Edie's eyes begin to smart. She's finding it hard to breathe.

'I know you like to write,' Mr Stead says. Edie stiffens in surprise. 'Nathaniel told me how you helped him with his copy sometimes.'

Nate had told his father? But they'd been so careful to

keep their illicit writing sessions a secret, meeting late at night after the offices were closed and Edie's chores finished for the day. But Mr Stead had known all along.

'Good luck, Edie, wherever you go.'

'I have nowhere to go, sir.' Her voice is little more than a whisper.

Mr Stead nods sadly. 'I wish I could help you, but . . .' He spreads his hands, palms upwards, on the desk, a clear message that his duty as Edie's employer is over.

She drags herself up to her room in the attic. After so long holding herself together, her strength now fails her, and she collapses on to the bed. She waits for the tears to come, but instead she's filled with a sickening terror.

What the hell was she going to do? Where else can she go? She has no family left, nothing to her name apart from a few clothes and Mr Stead's pay packet.

She turns on her side, and her cheek meets the edge of something hard beneath her thin pillow. Forcing herself up again, she lifts the pillow to find a small notebook bound in dark blue leather. Someone has left a book in her bed. But no one ever came up to the attic.

Except . . .

With hands that tremble, she opens the cover of the notebook. On the first page, written in a script she instantly recognizes, are the words:

Keep writing, Edie

with love,
N

A tear drops on to the page, smudging the N. Edie closes the notebook and hugs it to her chest. Nate is gone, taking Edie's hope with him.

She curls into herself, the notebook clutched tight, and now the tears come.

She is all alone again.

2

Lucinda: August 1914

Monday's post brings yet another parcel to Lucinda's breakfast table, sent all the way from rural Somerset. It's the third this month, and Lucinda holds her breath as she cuts the string, eager to discover the bizarre and wondrous contents within. What on earth has Mama sent this time?

She lifts a corked specimen jar from its nest of news-paper, and reads the label: *Rattus*. She angles the glass in a shaft of early-morning sunlight, studying the walnut-sized brain suspended in murky preserving fluid. Lucinda smiles to herself, picturing her dear mother lovingly wrapping the bottle, not for a moment considering its contents an odd or macabre thing to send to her daughter.

The rat's brain floats benignly in its liquid, and Lucinda finds herself wondering how her own equivalent grey matter can contain thoughts, emotions, intelligence. Would the mysterious workings of the human brain ever be understood?

She thinks of her textbooks full of anatomical sketches and diagrams, remembers the cadavers she'd once dis-sected during her medical training, the skulls sawn open to reveal their grey-jelly contents. Ten years ago, studying for her medical degree at the London School of Medicine for Women, she'd been particularly fascinated by the mysterious workings of the human brain. But, frustratingly, her ambitions in that regard couldn't be pursued. The only hospital to accept her once she was qualified had been the New Hospital for Women, founded by her own dear mother, which treated only the physical health problems of women and children.

With her cup of tea growing cold, her toast and marmalade uneaten on the plate, Lucinda stares at the rat's brain, pondering how Broca and Wernicke had established the different parts of the human brain, the components of thought and speech and suchlike. Last week, she'd read a paper on nerve cells, the so-called building blocks of the brain, how they spark and connect, the mechanism as magical and intriguing as electricity. Discoveries were being made all the time, yet so much remained unknown about the most important organ in the human body.

A truly fascinating mystery.

'Good morning, Lucie.' Florence's soft Scottish burr breaks Lucinda's reverie.

She looks up to find her friend and colleague already dressed for work, her dark blonde hair neatly coiled and pinned. Florence smiles affectionately as she approaches Lucinda, bending to place a kiss on her cheek.

To her dismay, Lucinda feels her face grow warm. This involuntary, unsettling reaction has been occurring more frequently of late. She's worked happily alongside Florence for years, ever since they trained and qualified as doctors together. Firm friends since their first day at medical school, it was a natural progression for them eventually to set up in business together. For the past two years, they've run a successful women and children's clinic in the

East End of London, treating the very poorest patients, their partnership built on the strength of true friendship.

But lately Lucinda's feelings for her friend have shifted, deepened. She tells herself it's only because Florence is so vibrant and intelligent, the antithesis of the stuffy, patronizing, overbearing male colleagues she has so often suffered in her line of work. Yet this knowledge doesn't help her; why is it that when she looks into Florence's clear hazel eyes, she finds it so hard to draw a full breath?

'What's that you've got there?' Florence asks, taking a chair opposite and pouring herself a cup of tea.

Lucinda collects herself. 'A rat's brain,' she replies, setting the jar carefully on the well-polished oak. 'From Mother.'

Florence stirs her tea, arching an eyebrow. 'Another gift? How thoughtful.'

Lucinda smiles. Anyone else would be horrified by the sight of a rodent's body part at the breakfast table, but not Florence. She's the only other woman Lucinda knows who is as dedicated to the medical sciences, as fascinated by the workings of the human body, as un-squeamish as herself.

'Mama's having a huge clear-out, it seems.'

'Your dear mother.' Florence unfolds a napkin, spreads it on her knees. Lucinda can't help but admire her poise and grace. 'When will she accept she's retired and slow down?' Florence takes a sip of tea and grimaces. 'This is stone cold. Where's Mrs Fairweather?'

'I sent her home,' Lucinda replies. 'She was coughing and looked wretched, and you know how she complains at the best of times.'

Florence's eyes glint, in the mischievous way Lucinda finds so disarmingly endearing. 'Only Mrs Fairweather could catch a cold in the middle of a heatwave.'

'Indeed. She said she'd be back this evening to make dinner. I tried to dissuade her, but you know what she's like.' Lucinda shrugs, takes a bite of her toast. Their housekeeper has been with them since they moved here and opened the clinic, and was, to all intents and purposes, one of the family. Like a cantankerous elderly aunt, who means well but is almost insufferable.

'She walks all over you, Lucie. If I'd been down earlier, I would have told her to stay at home for a week,' Florence says. 'We're quite all right on our own, aren't we?'

A toast crumb catches in Lucinda's throat, and she coughs. To be entirely alone with Florence in their cosy little terraced house, undisturbed by anyone, especially Mrs Fairweather, is something Lucinda has found herself fantasizing about recently. She gulps a mouthful of cold tea.

'Are you all right, Lucie?'

'Hmm? Oh, yes, quite all right, thank you.'

'What are you going to do with your wee pickled onion?'

'My what?'

Florence nods at the rat's brain.

'Oh, I was going to leave it in the kitchen for Mrs Fairweather to find.'

Florence laughs, and Lucinda's heart flips. She loves to make Florence laugh.

'Have the papers arrived?'

'Only the *Woman's Dreadnought*,' Lucinda replies, passing it across the table. 'And the *Express* just now. I haven't read them yet.' She rises, taking up the teapot. 'I'll make us a fresh brew.'

'Have a look at this,' Florence says, on Lucinda's return from the kitchen. On the front page of the *Dreadnought* there is a blurred photograph of a crowd gathered in front of the gates of Holloway prison with, in the foreground, a slight young woman in a plain dress, her hatless head shorn. Her expression is hard to discern, but her face looks vaguely familiar to Lucinda.

'AMNESTY FOR SUFFRAGETTES,' screams the headline.

'*Mr McKenna has advised the King to remit the remainder of the sentences of all suffragettes,*' Florence reads from the paper. '*His Majesty is confident that prisoners will respond to the feelings of their countrymen in this time of emergency, and be trusted not to stain the causes they have at heart by any further crime or disorder.*'

'This war has rather put the Cause on the back burner,' Lucinda says, pouring fresh tea into Florence's cup. The clock in the hall chimes eight. She swallows a sigh. Is that the time already? They'll have to leave for the clinic soon.

'Listen to this, Lucie,' Florence says. She continues reading from the paper: '*Sir, now is the moment for the suffragists to prove their worth. Let them defend their country, guard the stores, nurse the sick and wounded, help the poor. Let them do something big for the good of the country, and gain the admiration of the world, and the love of the people, and eventually the vote . . .*'

'Prove their worth,' Lucinda mutters. She takes the newspaper from Florence and scans the article for herself, reading of Miss Nightingale's endeavours in the Crimean War, how she saved the government of the time from eternal disgrace. 'What this fails to mention,' she remarks, the newsprint smudging beneath her fingers, 'is that when the same government dealt with the franchise question, they decided that while a male criminal should be entitled to regain his voting right as soon as he'd served his sentence, we women still couldn't exercise the vote on any terms whatsoever.'

'It's maddening,' Florence agrees, pushing back her chair and rising. 'When will this damned government see sense?'

Lucinda drops the paper on to the table, mildly thrilled to hear her friend curse. Together, they swiftly clear the dining room of plates and cutlery, moving in fluid synchronicity honed over years of working together in operating theatres. As she washes up in the kitchen, Lucinda's mind churns. The newspaper article has sparked an idea, and she turns to Florence, busy drying the dishes. 'I know what we should do, Flo.'

'Hmm?'

'Offer our services.'

'What are you talking about, Lucie dear?'

'To the War Office. We must put ourselves forward, offer our skills.'

'How do you mean?'

'Volunteer our medical expertise.'

'Like Miss Nightingale, do you mean?' Florence leans against the kitchen dresser, brow creased in thought. 'I suppose if we accepted wounded officers at the clinic, the government would be obliged to grant us larger premises.'

'No, I didn't mean that.' Lucinda dries her hands on a tea-towel. 'I mean doctoring in France, treating soldiers at the front.'

Florence regards Lucinda for a moment. 'But they'll never let women anywhere near battle.'

'We won't know unless we ask.'

'Oh, Lucie,' Florence says, smiling as she lays a hand on Lucinda's arm, 'you do know I *wasn't* named after Florence Nightingale?'

'I'm not suggesting we *nurse*,' Lucinda says, Florence's touch sending a warm tingle up her arm. 'We're qualified doctors, are we not? Ready to lend our medical expertise for the good of the country . . .'

'. . . thereby gaining the admiration of the world, and eventually the vote,' Florence concludes, with a wink that softens Lucinda's knees.

'Let's do it today, Flo,' Lucinda says, meeting Florence's steady gaze. 'Sister Bryony can cope with this morning's clinic. We haven't any surgeries until this afternoon, have we?'

'My impetuous wee Lucie,' Florence teases. 'You can't just launch into this. We need to think things through.'

'We have the brains for it,' Lucinda half jokes, waving the rat's brain in its jar. 'I think it's a wonderful idea.'

'I don't know,' Florence replies, moving to the door. 'Anyway, you're not even properly dressed yet.'

Lucinda glances down at her slippered feet. 'Why put off till tomorrow what you can do today? As dear Mama would say.' She grins at Florence.

'I hope at least you're going to brush your hair before we leave,' Florence says.

Daily Herald

No.672   Friday, 10 July 1914   One Halfpenny

FIGHT AT RALLY IN HYDE PARK

PANIC IN PARK
Police Arrest Women

A suffrage rally in Hyde Park yesterday was the scene of disturbances remarkable for their violence. Fighting took place between men and women, bottles were thrown, clothes torn, faces scratched and pummelled. The disorders lasted about an hour. Fifty or sixty persons were ejected, and several arrests were made.

The rally was advertised as a 'peaceful demonstration' of suffrage supporters, and was held in the grounds of Hyde Park. Mrs Honora Jones and Miss Mary Sykes were the principal speakers. The audience, which was considerable, included a majority number of ladies.

Suffragettes were among those arrested, and several are currently in police custody awaiting sentencing.

FRACAS

Fights took place between men and women, and police were employed to deal with the fracas, but it was found that they were unable to cope with the disorder created.

For more than an hour there was a scene of wild confusion, with people tearing one another's clothes and scratching each other's faces until they bled, and rolling about on the grass in a confused mass.

In the midst of it, one of the press reporters, Mr H. Levinson, climbed on to the stage and attempted to gain order, but he was seized by police and removed from the area.

3

Edie: August 1914

The midday sun burns through the attic skylight, gilding the dust motes floating in the muggy air. Edie packs her meagre belongings with a heavy heart, cramming everything she owns in the world into a battered holdall. Among her few items of clothing are a man's shirt, a brown flannel suit, a pair of patched long johns and a soft cap, all foraged from Nate's room downstairs. If he were here, she'd tell him she means only to borrow his clothes. Would he understand the reasoning behind her plan, though, or would he think she was being stupid and reckless?

She's also pilfered a spare pair of his shoes, the leather scuffed, the heels worn down. Wrapping them in newspaper, she hides them at the bottom of the holdall. Lucky that Nate isn't a big man, she thinks. When he returns from fighting, she'll give everything back, she promises herself.

Her mind drifts, her fractured thoughts warping into a memory of the first time she'd met Nate. She'd been trying to coax a fire to life in Mr Stead's office hearth early one morning, soon after she'd started working for him. There'd been a stack of old newspapers next to the grate, and Edie had taken one, intending to twist the pages into firelighters, but instead her eye had been caught by an article written by a female doctor. She'd read with bated breath, heedless of the minutes ticking by, the fire unlit, her work forgotten. The article had described the doctor's experience of being arrested for her involvement in a suffrage protest, and imprisoned in Holloway. Her courage had sparked the first flame of interest in Edie: perhaps she, too, could fight the good fight?

She'd been so engrossed in the newspaper article that she hadn't heard the office door open or the steady footsteps approaching.

'Anything interesting in there?'

The voice had startled Edie, and she'd dropped the newspaper with a gasp and fallen back on her bottom. Scrambling to her feet, she'd found herself facing a young man not much older than herself. She'd swiftly lowered her gaze, as she'd been trained, but not before registering the man's sweep of dark hair and arresting green eyes. Nathaniel, Mr Stead's precious son and heir: she'd recognized him instantly from the photograph on Mr Stead's desk.

'The old man's finally hired some help, I see,' the young man said, eyeing Edie's dusty apron. 'What's your name?'

Edie's voice had entirely deserted her.

'It's all right,' Nathaniel had said. 'I won't tell the old man I caught you slacking.'

At that, Edie's head had snapped up, and Nathaniel had met her sharp look with a grin, his expression gently teasing.

'Edie,' she'd managed to croak. 'It's my first day.'

'Edie.' Nathaniel Stead had rolled her name around his mouth as though it was a boiled sweet. 'Is that short for something? Edwina, perhaps?'

Was he mocking her? She bit back a retort, and he smiled at her then, the warmest smile anyone had given her in such a long time, a glimmer of sunshine on a winter's day.

Fleeting as a ghost, the memory dissipates. Edie is left feeling strangely drained of energy, yet the day is barely half begun. Her only hope is to appeal to her friend Sylvia Pankhurst at the Society, a kind woman known to help her fellow suffragettes in times of distress.

She needs somewhere to stay for just a few days, until she works out her next move.

And what then? a voice demands in Edie's head.

She's homeless unless her fortunes change, and what chance is there of that happening?

Yesterday evening, she'd appealed to Mr Stead again, pleading with him to let her stay and skivvy for no pay, just the roof over her head. But the editor had remained adamant: he was shutting down the weekly paper, at least for the duration of the war. But that will only be until Christmas, Edie thinks, the New Year at a push. By January, it will be over, surely.

She sinks down on the edge of the bed, the leather notebook on her lap, flicking through the blank pages. The dream she's nurtured ever since she can remember, the dream she's never shared with anyone but Nate, now returns to the forefront of her mind. Nate's parting gift is more precious than he could ever know.

Hefting her bag, Edie descends the stairs, wondering what she will say if she encounters Mr Stead again. But there's no sign of the editor in his darkened office. Perhaps he's gone to his club for lunch. A stab of hunger has Edie slipping into the deserted little kitchen, where she quickly cuts herself a slice of stale bread and a chunk of cheese. She devours the makeshift meal in a few bites, then carefully clears away the crumbs, taking one last look about the room. It still hasn't quite sunk in that she no longer works here. Finally, with her straw hat pulled firmly down over her head, shorn in prison as punishment, Edie lets herself out of the newspaper offices for the final time.

She sets off towards the East London Federation of Suffragettes offices in Roman Road, half an hour's walk away. Thoughts churn in her mind as she negotiates the foot traffic clogging the pavements. What if Sylvia Pankhurst can't help her? What if she can't find another placement? How long before she ends up on the streets? Nothing on this earth will compel her to return to the workhouse. She would rather die in the gutter than set foot in that godforsaken place again.

An elderly woman is tottering towards her along the pavement, draped in layers of black lace from head to toe. She must be steaming under all that material, Edie thinks. She offers the woman a nod of greeting, and receives a wary frown in return.

It takes Edie a moment to realize she must present an alarming sight. Her skinny, bruised arms poke from the sleeves of her frayed summer dress, and her nose, broken by that bitch in Holloway, remains crooked and swollen. She hurries on, negotiating busy streets filled with young men in straw boaters, girls in calico dresses, people scurrying here and there, like ants. Union flags, slack in the heat, hang from windows. Soldiers in khaki are everywhere

Edie looks. On the surface, the summer scene appears benign, yet Edie's skin prickles at the undertone of tension permeating the air.

By the time she nears the suffragette headquarters on Roman Road, Edie is sweating. She makes her way through the bustling market, assailed by the smell of hot pies and freshly baked bread, the sing-song shouts of stall keepers trailing after her. At last, she arrives at her destination, a narrow building nestled between a sweet shop and a haberdashery, and pushes open the door.

Edie's heart sinks at the sight of Joyce Millard, a stout woman of mature years and a founding member of the Federation, on duty at the front desk. She hasn't the energy for the woman's snide remarks. Joyce Millard has never concealed her dislike of Edie, treating her like a skivvy whenever their shifts in the office coincide. It's taken Edie a long time to pinpoint the source of Joyce Millard's animosity: the fact that Sylvia Pankhurst occasionally chose Edie to contribute short pieces for the *Woman's Dreadnought*. Edie also assists Mr Arber, a fellow suffrage supporter, in his shop down the road where he prints the Federation's newspaper for free. It's been Edie's habit on Sunday afternoons to help with the print run, operating the huge iron treadle press in the basement. It's this that Joyce Millard has taken issue with, Edie feels sure. Despite the Federation's efforts to support women from all walks of life, in Joyce Millard's eyes Edie is a mere servant of the lowest class with no right to pen pieces for their flagship paper.

Edie forces a smile. 'Good morning, Mrs Millard.'

'Good Lord.' Joyce Millard grimaces. 'I thought you were in Holloway, Miss Lawrence.'

'I was,' Edie says, removing her straw hat for maximum effect. 'Is Miss Pankhurst in?'

Joyce Millard ignores the question, eyes flicking from Edie's head to the bag at her feet. 'On the run, are you?'

Edie bites her tongue. *None of your bloody business.* 'I must speak with Miss Pankhurst. Is she here?'

Joyce Millard jerks her head towards the door leading to Sylvia Pankhurst's private office. Edie hoists her bag, and gives Joyce a cold nod.

She finds the founder of the East London Federation of Suffragettes writing at her cluttered desk. The windows are open, yet the room smells strongly of turpentine, with a note of sewage from the drains outside.

'I'm so relieved to see you, Edie.' Sylvia greets her with a welcoming smile. 'I saw your picture in the paper, and hoped you might come straight here.'

'I would've, ma'am, but I had something to do first.'

Sylvia Pankhurst shunts a pile of *Dreadnought*s off a chair, and gestures for Edie to sit. 'How are you?'

Edie finds herself momentarily unable to answer, blinking away the hot prickle of tears. You simply didn't cry in front of a Pankhurst. The older woman gives a small nod of acknowledgement, a gesture of sympathetic understanding.

'Let's have some tea,' she says gently. Edie notes the stiff way she rises from her desk, as though she's in her seventies, not her thirties. And then Edie remembers: Miss Pankhurst has only recently been released from prison, too, having endured her own hunger strike.

Over tea, Edie briefly outlines her situation, explaining that she's lost her position at Mr Stead's, and now finds herself homeless.

'Of course, you must stay here,' Sylvia says. She is aware of Edie's workhouse origins, and Edie is supremely grateful that she doesn't suggest a return to that hell.

'It'll be temporary,' Edie assures her. She longs to confide in Sylvia, give voice to the plan taking root in her mind, but caution stays her tongue. Plans spoken aloud seldom come to fruition. 'I can do some cleaning for you,' she adds, as an afterthought.

'Well, that would be helpful, Edie.' Sylvia gestures at her desk, the surface covered with sheets of paper, ink bottles and dirty paintbrushes.

'Thank you so much, Miss Pankhurst.' Edie resists the urge to grasp her saviour's hands in gratitude, knowing she wouldn't appreciate an overt show of affection.

'If there's anything else I can do, you have only to ask.' Sylvia picks up her pen again, Edie's cue that their meeting is over.

'You've been more than kind enough,' Edie replies. 'Thank you.'

Sylvia smiles. 'The blue bedroom is free at present. Make yourself comfortable, and let me know if you need any extra bedding.'

Avoiding Joyce Millard, Edie lugs her bag up the back stairs. She sinks down on the neatly made bed, contemplating her new home. The walls of the spare room are painted the pale blue of a winter sky. After resting for a moment, she gets up again to investigate the narrow wardrobe in the corner, finding it empty but for a few dusty hangers. In the drawer of the rickety bedside table, she finds a dog-eared Bible and a pencil, presumably left by a previous occupant.

She counts out her wages from Mr Stead, stacking the coins on the bedside table, calculating how many meals she can afford. Not many, even if she eats frugally. But, thank God, she has a roof over her head. For the time being, at least.

Lying back on the pillows, she clasps Nate's notebook and closes her eyes, her tired mind drifting. On the face of it, her options as a woman with no money or education, alone in the world, are limited: find another position in service or starve. Edie chews a thumbnail, drawing blood. If she'd been born male, she could enlist, head off to fight for her country, like Nate.

If only he were here.

Her mind drifts back to that pivotal day in July, the day of her arrest. Mr Stead had sent Nate on his first solo assignment to report on the latest suffrage protest meeting in Hyde Park. Risking his father's wrath, Nate had asked Edie if she wanted to come with him to help him interview some of the people involved. Edie hadn't needed any persuasion to abandon her cleaning duties. Together, they'd joined the crowds in the park, listening to various suffragists presenting their arguments on stage. Nate had immediately begun scribbling notes in his pad to write up later, but Edie had stood admiring the pluck of the speakers. How brave those women were, standing up there in their purple-feathered hats, demonstrating for the right to vote.

A substantial number of people had gathered in the

park that day, and Edie's gaze had swept over the various suffrage placards bobbing above the sea of heads. There were brightly painted cardboard signs held aloft on poles, six-foot-long banners fashioned from sheets daubed with boot-black, and colourful fabric flags stitched with slogans such as 'VOTES FOR WOMEN'; 'NO SURRENDER'; 'DARE TO BE FREE'.

Most of the crowd that day had consisted of women, but scattered among the throng were a few husbands, fathers, sons, families showing their support. Others, such as the group of young men Edie had spotted approaching from the direction of the bandstand, laughing and swigging from ale bottles, looked merely curious. She'd watched the gang with a wary eye as they lurched ever closer.

Don't let women's rights get left behind!

The voices of the women on the stage mixed with the shouts and clapping of the crowd. Nate was so intent on recording the words of the speakers that only Edie had noticed the drunken interlopers pushing their way into the throng. A bottle had suddenly sailed up and over the heads, followed closely by another. Then someone had screamed, and within seconds, the peaceful protest had descended into chaos.

As the crowd began to surge, Nate had grabbed Edie's hand, and together they had tried to escape the press of bodies. In the scramble, Nate dropped his notebook. Edie stooped to retrieve it, and as she rose again a young man lunged at Nate, swinging a punch, sending him sprawling on the grass.

Surrounded by mayhem, Edie had tried to help Nate to

his feet, only for him to be grounded again by another punch.

'Get off him!' Edie had cried, seizing the attacking youth's arm, only to be rewarded with a violent shove that sent her staggering. A shrill whistle blasted in her ear, and a strong hand gripped Edie's shoulder from behind. Reacting instinctively, she'd twisted round, lashing out, her fist connecting with the solid, brass-buttoned gut of a policeman.

Nate had tried to help her, pleading with the policeman not to arrest his assistant: she was only defending herself. But it was to no avail. Edie had been dragged to a nearby police station, charged with assault, and thrown into a cell.

From that moment, Edie now realizes, her luck had begun to desert her.

Joyce Millard's distinctive, grating laugh permeates through the floorboards, setting Edie's teeth on edge. She closes her eyes briefly. Even without that hostile presence, she can't stay here long term: Sylvia Pankhurst's charity won't last for ever.

A memory of Holloway surfaces, of a rare visit from a chaplain who'd counselled the prisoners to forge their own paths. *God helps those who help themselves.*

The chaplain had meant well, Edie can see that now, but at the time she'd longed to scream in the man's face. Only the threat of punishment at the hands of the sadistic wardens had stilled her tongue. God had never helped her in all her life. Even dear Nate had abandoned her, signing up and heading off without a backward glance.

The only person who can help Edie is herself.

It is this realization that finally galvanizes her. She has nothing left to lose.

Her reflection in the mirror above the washstand comes as a shock. She looks like one of those back-alley thugs, with her shaved head and bruised eyes. Perhaps it's better she hasn't seen Nate: he'd be horrified at her transformation.

Yet her ugliness may play to her favour.

Dragging the bag on to the bed, she empties out the contents. Nate's clothes lie in a crumpled pile. Of average height for a man, he was a few inches taller than Edie, and broader across the shoulders. Would his clothes fit her? She quickly undresses, then pulls on the shirt and suit, finding that the clothes hang on her thin frame well enough, although the trousers bag around her ankles a little. It feels strange wearing men's garb. Freeing. No complicated undergarments, no tight corsetry. She strides about the room, marvelling at the ease with which her legs move, finding herself walking taller. She's always been indifferent to frills and feminine fashion, but it still surprises her how much she enjoys the feel of the trousers on her legs.

Could she pass as a man? She barely needs to bind her chest, her recent hunger strike diminishing her already meagre breasts. She runs a hand over her scalp. The plan percolating in her brain is beginning to sharpen.

To be a reporter, like Nate, Mr Arnold, Mr James and all those other freelancers Mr Stead used to employ, is her dream. Journalism is all she's ever wanted to do, and for years she's nurtured the hope that Mr Stead would one day recognize her abilities, her love of words, and promote her to the role of reporter. But now she sees how pointless that ambition has been.

If she's going to follow her dream, she'll have to make it happen herself.

If she could somehow get to France, somehow reach the battlefields, she could be the first female war reporter the country has ever seen.

Nate is already on his way to war. If she could enlist, too, get out there in the midst of the action, record her experience, Mr Stead would surely pay attention. The risks were high, of course, but the pay-off would be worth it. Her name in print!

What a stunt that would be.

Courage calls, Miss Lawrence, and it finds you ready.

4

Lucinda: August 1914

Upstairs in her bedroom, Lucinda hurriedly dresses. She chooses a fresh white blouse, her best skirt, and her smartest shoes with a low heel. As she tugs a comb through her unruly hair, she wonders if she's wise to leave Sister Bryony alone to cope with the stream of sick women and children this morning. She pictures the queue no doubt already forming outside the clinic. But almost as soon as Lucinda has this thought, she dismisses it. Sister Bryony is the most capable nurse she's ever worked with. Nothing fazes her. Even the unexpected birth of twin babies at the clinic last week – an emergency delivery Lucinda and Sister Bryony had dealt with alone, as Florence had been at the New Hospital for Women – hadn't daunted the nurse. Besides, it shouldn't take long to convince the War Office, Lucinda hopes. She'll be back at her surgery by midday at the latest.

Returning downstairs, she presents herself to Florence, feeling mildly bashful. She's unaccustomed to dressing smartly, abhors feminine fashion, would much rather live in a surgical gown if she could.

Florence's gaze travels the slender length of her, and a smile twitches at the corner of her mouth. 'You are the handsomest woman in London,' she declares.

Lucinda flushes, unused to such a compliment. She knows she isn't conventionally pretty: her shoulders are a fraction too broad, her auburn hair rather messy, her figure too angular for most men to appreciate. But what need has she of a man when she has Florence? Dear, dependable, darling Florence, whose friendship means the world, and whose capable skills as a doctor easily match Lucinda's own.

Florence brushes a loose thread from Lucinda's sleeve, as Lucinda plucks at the tight collar of her blouse. 'Do you think this get-up will impress the bigwigs at the War Office, Flo?'

'I'd feel a wee bit more confident if we gave ourselves time to write what we're going to say.'

'You know how I stumble over my words if I read something prepared,' Lucinda replies. 'I'm much better off the cuff.'

'You are,' Florence has to concede.

'Anyway, we don't have the time to craft a speech.'

'Well . . .'

'Let's strike while the iron's hot, Flo.'

'Your iron is always hot, my darling,' Florence says, rather ruefully. But then she smiles, and squeezes Lucinda's hand. Lucinda's heart tumbles.

∞

The sun beats down from a flawless blue sky as they set off to walk the short journey to Whitehall. On reaching the War Office, Lucinda registers their names with a clerk, who directs them to a plain, stuffy waiting room. They join a dozen other visitors, and a space is made for them on a bench along one wall. But Lucinda can barely sit.

'Will you relax?' Florence says, when Lucinda asks her for the third time how long she thinks they'll be kept waiting. 'I expect whoever's in charge of these things has been inundated with offers of help.'

'Do you think Sister Bryony is managing?' Lucinda frets.

'She'll be fine,' Florence replies, with a sigh. 'I'm rather more worried about you at the moment. Will you sit down? You're making *me* nervous, now.'

After half an hour, just as Lucinda is fearing they must have been forgotten, the same clerk returns to fetch them. They follow him through a maze of corridors, eventually arriving at the offices of the deputy director of the Army Medical Services, Lieutenant General Walton.

'Thank you for taking the time to meet with us, sir,' Lucinda begins respectfully, shaking the officer's hand.

'My secretary was vague as to what this is about, Miss Garland,' Walton replies, smoothing his greying moustache with a barely suppressed sigh.

'*Dr* Garland,' Lucinda corrects him politely. 'My colleague Dr Maberry and I would like to offer our services to the government.'

'In what capacity, Miss – my apologies, *Dr* Garland?'

'Well, as military doctors, sir.' *What else?* 'We can provide references, of course,' she goes on. 'My mother is Dr Eleanor Garland, a qualified surgeon, though now retired.'

'And what relevance is your mother's past profession?' Walton asks dismissively.

Lucinda swallows her annoyance at the man's arrogance. 'My mother's career, as one of the first female doctors to qualify in this country, is of considerable relevance, sir.'

'I repeat my question.' Walton sighs. 'What relevance has your mother's past profession on your offer of service now?'

'Both Dr Garland and I trained at Dr Garland senior's New Hospital for Women,' Florence interjects, with a smoothness Lucinda envies.

'And you believe this qualifies you for military surgery?' Walton asks bluntly.

'We're skilled and keen,' Lucinda replies curtly, 'and *believe* we could be of use to our fighting men at the front.'

'We don't seek glory, or to better ourselves, sir,' Florence adds. 'Only to do everything we can for Great Britain and the Empire.'

Walton's shrewd eyes travel from Florence's calm, serious repose, to Lucinda's flushed, earnest face, and back to Florence. He says nothing.

'Our training and sympathies fit us for such work, sir,' Florence forges on. She briefly explains her post as house surgeon at the Belgrave Hospital for Children in south London, and her role as anaesthetist at the Chelsea Hospital for Women.

Walton listens without interruption.

Lucinda then describes her time as house surgeon at the Royal Free Hospital, omitting to mention that she'd been prevented from treating men, and confined solely to the women's ward. She tells Walton about her visit to America, training at the Johns Hopkins School of Medicine in Baltimore. 'I returned to London to work at the New Hospital for Women,' she concludes, 'first as surgical assistant, then as senior surgeon, during which time Dr Maberry and I also set up our clinic.'

She waits for Walton to acknowledge their eminent suitability. There is a long moment of silence.

'Very commendable, ladies,' Walton says at last. 'However,' he continues, 'I cannot accept your offer. You are welcome to take on some of the duties of our departing doctors, of course.'

Lucinda can only stare at him. Next to her, Florence clenches her long fingers in her lap, her knuckles blanching. 'With respect, sir,' Florence replies, 'we are both qualified doctors and surgeons. There is no greater ennobling field for our energies and professional skills than in helping our gallant soldiers who are facing daily mutilation and death –'

'Military surgery demands the highest talent and skill,' Walton interrupts, without apology. 'It requires extreme mental and physical powers. These do not belong to women.'

Furious, Lucinda feels her cheeks burn. 'I beg your pardon, sir –'

'Your services are required here, at home, ladies,' the officer asserts, 'among the women and children you serve so well.'

'But, sir,' Lucinda's voice is thick with fury, and she has to swallow, 'surely it's sensible that in a war such as this, trained women doctors, like ourselves, should join in the care of the wounded?'

'I appreciate my answer is not one you wish to hear,' Walton replies, rising from his desk and moving to the door. 'My apologies, ladies, but my time is sorely limited, and I have other meetings to attend. I advise you to go home, where you will be safe.'

Out on the street, Lucinda takes several deep breaths, as Florence tries to calm her. 'Such a response to the female surgeon is not new, of course,' Florence reminds her.

'How can you defend that man?' Lucinda cries. 'You must agree that after proving ourselves for so many years, and having gained the acceptance of most of our colleagues, rejection of our skills, when our country is crying out for experienced doctors, is impossible to take.'

'Compose yourself, Lucie,' Florence mutters, as a couple pass them on the pavement. 'I hate to say this, but perhaps the man has a point. Perhaps it would be better to stay at home.'

'I will *not* stay at home,' Lucinda retorts. 'I will *not* stay safe. Damn the War Office. Damn them all.'

'But what else can we do?' Florence dabs at her brow with a handkerchief. 'If they don't want us . . .'

'Walton might not want us,' Lucinda says, 'but surely the French *will*.'

At the French Embassy, twenty minutes later, a clerk admits them into an anteroom, and Lucinda prepares herself for another interminable wait. The temperature in the windowless room is oppressively warm, made worse by thick red damask wall hangings. Florence perches on a chaise-longue, its upholstery the colour of dried blood, but Lucinda remains on her feet, pacing the small room, until Florence begs her to sit down. 'Your nerves are infectious, Lucie,' she says. 'And one of us at least must remain calm.'

After a short while, a man appears and introduces himself as an embassy secretary. He listens politely as Lucinda puts forward their proposal.

'You are doctors?' the Frenchman asks, his face a mask of confusion. Lucinda's heart falls. Medical women are clearly off this man's horizon, and though he speaks decent English, he appears to be struggling to understand that she and Florence intend to go to the aid of French and British soldiers.

Lucinda finds herself wishing she possessed more than woefully basic schoolgirl French, at least then she could get her meaning across.

'*Mesdames*,' the secretary says at last, 'please call upon the president of the French Red Cross, Madame Marie Brasier de Thuy, and she will discuss the matter further.' He gives Lucinda a card of introduction and the directions to the president's house.

On the street again, Lucinda scrutinizes the card. 'L'Union des Femmes de France,' she reads aloud. 'Redcliffe Gardens . . . We'll have to take the bus.'

'What about the clinic and Sister Bryony, Lucie?'

'We can't give up now,' Lucinda replies, with a brief, determined smile.

Madame Brasier de Thuy, a stout woman of mature years, instantly beguiles Lucinda and Florence with her warmth and charm. To Lucinda's profound relief, she also speaks excellent English, and listens carefully to their proposition.

'I'm terribly worried for the safety of France,' Madame Brasier de Thuy earnestly confides to the two doctors. 'Our organization is doing its best, but your offer of assistance is much appreciated, *Mesdames*.'

'We can offer a fully equipped surgical unit,' Lucinda hears herself say, 'staffed by ourselves and a team of other women doctors and trained nurses. A gift to France in her hour of need.' She can feel Florence's eyes on her, can almost hear her friend's voice. *And who's going to pay for all this?*

'An indescribable gift, *merci*.' Madame Brasier de Thuy pours fresh coffee into Lucinda and Florence's bone china cups. 'We will, of course, recompense your staff, *Mesdames*,' she adds.

Lucinda senses Florence relax somewhat next to her.

The conversation moves on to how many doctors may be required to run a unit – Lucinda thinks five or six, including Florence and herself, will suffice.

'We'll need more nurses and orderlies,' Florence warns. 'It will take time to recruit the right women.'

'I will transmit your offer, and its consequent financial requirements, to our Paris headquarters *immédiatement*,' Madame Brasier de Thuy replies. 'We must go forth with hope in our hearts, *oui*?'

'*Oui, Madame*.' Lucinda finds she's barely able to contain her excitement, her cup rattling in its saucer. She longs to squeeze Florence's hand, but must content herself with a smile.

∞

Several days go by, and Lucinda and Florence return to their clinic, as they wait to hear the decision of the French Red Cross. After a week has passed, and still there is no news from Madame Brasier de Thuy, Lucinda begins to worry. Had their offer of help been similarly dismissed by the French? Yet Madame had been so keen to enlist them.

Florence, usually the more optimistic, begins to wonder if the War Office was right, and their efforts should be concentrated on their patients in London, instead of interfering in military business.

Florence's loss of faith shocks Lucinda. 'I thought you were as committed to this as I am, Flo,' she hears herself snap. 'I can't do it without you.' *I never want to do anything without you.*

'I'm only voicing my concerns, Lucie.' Florence taps the newspaper by her plate. 'Things are heating up across the Channel, if the reports are true.'

'I'll visit Madame Brasier de Thuy as soon as I can after clinic and see if there's been any progress.'

'And what if there's been none?'

Lucinda is saved a reply by the arrival of their housekeeper, clutching a handful of letters to her shelf of a bosom.

'Post was late again.' Mrs Fairweather sniffs, as Lucinda riffles through the small pile of envelopes.

'This looks promising.' Lucinda holds up an official-looking envelope with a Paris postmark.

'I've made you a fruitcake,' Mrs Fairweather tells Florence, as Lucinda tears open the letter, scanning the contents. Dimly, she hears Florence thanking the housekeeper, but all she can think is . . .

'They want us!' Lucinda leaps to her feet, causing Mrs Fairweather to gasp and almost drop the breakfast plates.

'Oh, Lucie!' Florence rises too, and folds Lucinda into a hug.

The housekeeper looks on in bewildered indignation. 'Who wants you?' she demands.

'Oh, Mrs Fairweather!' Lucinda feels a sudden urge to pull the housekeeper into their embrace, but she manages to resist. Despite her cuddly, if grumpy, appearance, Mrs Fairweather wasn't keen on physical shows of affection. 'The very best news has come at last! We're going to France!'

'France?' Mrs Fairweather's mouth drops open, and she sets down the plates.

Florence begins to explain their plan, but the housekeeper wants none of it. 'France? With a war on? You've both lost your senses,' she mutters. With a flap of her hand, she retreats to the sanctuary of the kitchen.

The letter from the French Red Cross is now somewhat crumpled in Lucinda's fist. Florence plucks it from her unresisting fingers, reading it for herself.

'I suppose this means it's official,' Florence says. 'They're promising to help us find premises in Paris, and to fund staff salaries. That's a relief!'

'All we have to do is gather the equipment we'll need,' Lucinda says. 'Mother will help, no doubt, and donations will cover the rest.'

'Donations . . .' Florence mutters.

'Don't frown, Flo,' Lucinda pleads. 'France wants us after all!'

'Are you sure this is what *you* want?'

'Only if you're by my side.' Lucinda wills her cheeks not to betray her. Never has she spoken more truly from the heart. With Florence, she can face anything.

'Always,' Florence says softly. She smiles, and Lucinda feels the tension in her shoulders ease for the first time in days.

5

Edie: August 1914

As August drags on, Edie's plight becomes ever more urgent. Her pennies are almost gone, and Sylvia Pankhurst's goodwill won't last for ever: there's only so much cleaning a small office needs. But who else will employ a workhouse-educated maidservant fresh out of prison, with shaven hair and a broken nose? She'll end up back in the workhouse if she doesn't act soon, Edie fears.

As the month draws to a close, Sylvia asks Edie what her plans might be. 'You're more than welcome to stay, my dear,' she says. But Edie knows her friend is being kind, and her charity cannot continue indefinitely.

On the morning she makes her decision, Edie comes close to confiding in Sylvia, but at the last moment suffers second thoughts. What if she tries to talk her out of it?

No, it was better not to tell anyone, she decides.

Edie's nerves are thrumming as she slips past Sylvia's office, thankfully empty at this early hour, and out of the back door.

The army's central recruitment office is at Old Scotland Yard. Dressed in Nate's old suit, sweat prickling beneath her tight linen binder, a cap pulled low, Edie balks at going there. Instead, she hurries east along Roman Road, following painted wooden arrows in the street, and eventually reaches a military village under canvas at Victoria Park. Despite the alarming number of people milling about, it feels less intimidating, less illicit somehow, to commit fraud in a tent.

Head down, she joins a queue of men waiting to enlist in Kitchener's army. Her initial fear that she'll be there all day is quickly dispelled: the line is moving briskly. All too soon, an army clerk ushers her through the entrance of Recruitment Tent A, and she finds herself standing before a desk.

'Name?'

The recruitment officer glances up at Edie, pen poised, and she feels the blood drain from her face. Last night, in the privacy of her bedroom, she'd practised talking in a low, gruff mumble until her voice was hoarse. On her journey here, tense and sweating in Nate's ill-fitting suit, she's willed herself to be brave. But now she's arrived in this sweltering tent, the air thick with stale sweat and brittle bravado, she's fast losing her nerve.

Remember, you're just another young man, here to do his bit for King and country.

Except, of course, she isn't.

The officer frowns as he eyes Edie's broken nose. She should remove her cap, she knows, but she can't bring herself to move.

If this man sees through her disguise, he could have her arrested for fraud or, worse, treason. Everyone knows it's a crime against the King for a woman to enlist as a soldier. The prospect of returning to Holloway softens her knees.

'What's your name, boy? I haven't all day.' The officer flexes ink-stained fingers. At the neighbouring desk, a new recruit begins to stumble his way through the oath.

'I swear by Almighty God that I will be faithful and bear true allegiance to His Majesty King George the Fifth . . .'

Soon it will be Edie's turn to accept the King's shilling. A knife twists in her gut at the thought.

'Ed-Eddie, sir,' she mumbles. For the space of two heartbeats, she stands outside herself. How can she have hoped that adding a single letter to her name would alter her whole identity?

The officer glares up at her. 'Eddie what?'

She swallows what feels like a stone lodged in her throat. 'Lawrence, sir.'

'What was that? Lawrence, did you say?'

Edie nods. Will the officer demand to see identification? She has none, of course, but the excuse she'd thought up earlier is ready on her tongue.

I left home in such a hurry this morning I forgot my papers, sir.

The demand for recruits is so high, Edie hopes she won't be challenged. She thinks of the latest news reports, of the plucky men of the British Expeditionary Force facing down the might of the German Army. The government needs every able-bodied person they can get.

'Date of birth?'

'Fourth of June, eighteen ninety-five,' Edie rasps.

The officer notes her age, his pen nib scratching the paper. Edie tries to breathe.

'Place of birth?'

Edie has a sudden mental image of the workhouse, its

looming grey façade pierced by narrow, soot-streaked windows that the sun struggled to shine through, even on the brightest of days. Though she hadn't been born within its dank walls, she'd spent the best part of her childhood there, Ma working in the laundry all hours. The place haunted her dreams still, but she'd never call it home.

'Roman Road,' she lies, and is relieved when the officer doesn't query this.

'You are a British subject.'

Was he asking her a question? But the officer doesn't seem to require a response, as he marks a cross on his form. He glances up at Edie again. 'You are hereby warned,' he intones, 'that if after enlistment it's found that you have given a wilfully false answer to any of the following questions, you will be liable to a punishment of two years' imprisonment with hard labour.'

The urge to bolt threatens to overcome her, and it takes everything she has to meet the officer's eye. She must not lose sight of why she is here.

The officer consults his papers. 'Are you apprenticed?'

'Yes, sir.' Edie's lying tongue cleaves to the roof of her mouth. 'Local newspaper.'

'Are you married?' The officer is staring at her again.

Edie shakes her head, her face warming.

'Have you ever been sentenced to imprisonment by the civil power?'

She shakes her head again, cheeks burning now.

'Have you ever served in the Royal Navy, the army, or any other force?'

'No, sir.'

'Have you ever been rejected unfit for the military?'

'No, sir.' She tries to square her shoulders, lost though they are inside Nate's jacket.

The officer makes a note on his form. 'Are you willing to be vaccinated?'

'Yes, sir.' Her knees threaten to give, and she prays he's nearly finished.

'Repeat after me,' the officer sighs, clearly bored. 'I, Eddie Lawrence, swear by Almighty God . . .'

Edie falteringly recites the oath, making such a shambles of it she's certain the officer will demand she do it again. But instead the man thrusts his pen at her. 'Sign here.' He pushes the form towards her. In her panic, all she can see is a thick black line next to the date.

She holds the officer's pen in numb fingers, somehow managing to scrawl her initials.

Before the ink has dried, the officer snatches the form back, and now he takes a thin booklet from a pile at his elbow. He scribbles something on the cover, hands it to Edie, at the same time pulling open a drawer beneath his desk.

'One shilling,' he mutters, producing a silver coin, almost flinging it at Edie in his haste to be rid of her. 'All finished here.' He glances beyond Edie to the man she can hear breathing nasally at her back. 'Next tent for uniform and medical.'

She can't move her feet.

'Next!' the officer barks.

On legs that feel fragile as straws, Edie stumbles out of the tent. She joins the end of a restless line of men, a knotted ache cramping her belly now, like phantom monthly pains. She clutches the notebook in her pocket, tries to imagine the blank pages filled with her words, a true record of the war as she experiences it, like nothing ever written before.

The line moves relentlessly forward, the men at the head of the queue disappearing one by one through the flaps of the medical tent. All too soon, Edie reaches the entrance, where a yawning nurse with a clipboard stands guard. Edie mumbles her false name, avoiding the woman's eye as she crosses the threshold.

'Breathe in, lad.'

The doctor presses a cold stethoscope against Edie's breastbone, as she stands paralysed, unable to breathe at all. She prays he won't inspect her any closer, won't demand she remove her shirt. The binder, tight around her chest, is barely an inch below the doctor's invasive fingers.

But the man's attention is elsewhere. He stares over Edie's shoulder, a vacant look clouding his red-rimmed eyes.

'Breathe out.'

Edie tenses, braced for what is surely about to come. Her bound chest and cropped hair have fooled people so far, but to deceive a medical man, even one with only half his mind on the job, is another matter entirely. Any moment now the doctor will blanch, draw a sharp breath, shout for assistance.

A woman! There's a woman here!

But instead, the doctor withdraws the stethoscope and takes a step back. Only now does he seem to register Edie's face, her broken nose. 'How did you come by your injury, lad?'

'Fell, sir.'

The doctor frowns. 'Read that.' He points to a large sheet of paper tacked to a folding screen. A corner of the poster is ripped and hangs down, partly obscuring the letters of varying sizes printed on it. Edie begins to stammer her way down the lines, but the doctor isn't listening. He's dragging a wooden pole on a stand towards her, and Edie's heart lurches at the realization it's a measuring stick. Is she tall enough to pass?

'Five feet five,' the doctor mutters, jotting numbers on a form. He rubs his chin, sighing as he eyes Edie's narrow frame.

'How old are you?'

'Nineteen, sir.'

The doctor stares at Edie for the longest time, his eyes boring right into the dark of her. It takes every ounce of courage she possesses to hold his gaze. At last, he tugs a coil of measuring tape from his pocket.

'Take that off,' he snaps, indicating the suit jacket.

Before it has fully left Edie's shoulders, the doctor steps close and wraps the tape around her chest. She stands frozen, enduring the man's acetose breath as he takes his time squinting at the faded numbers on the tape.

Something is wrong. It's all taking too long. Edie can't breathe. The game is surely up.

The doctor slips the tape back into his pocket and steps away, not meeting Edie's eye, and she tries to think how to explain her presence here without being arrested as an imposter. As she pulls Nate's jacket back on, she waits for the doctor to launch his challenge, but instead he yawns, pencilling more numbers on a slip of paper.

'For the uniform,' he tells Edie, handing her a receipt. He gestures to a nearby nurse, who ushers in the next recruit.

Released at last, Edie escapes outside again. Before she can change her mind, she ducks into a tent signposted 'UNIFORM', to find trestle tables laden with piles of clothing. Edie takes her place among a group of young men waiting to be served. Clearly pals, the men jostle and tease each other good-naturedly, their faces flushed with excitement.

Two uniformed men are serving behind the tables, issuing shirts, tunics, trousers to the waiting recruits.

Edie's turn comes, and she relinquishes the receipt the doctor gave her, receiving in return a khaki-serge tunic and trousers, a collarless flannel shirt, two rolls of brown bandages and a service cap. Arms laden, she emerges blinking into the sunlight, and is immediately apprehended by an officer wielding a clipboard. 'Regiment?' he barks, and Edie fumbles her pay book from a pocket to show him.

'Sixth London,' the officer notes. 'Report for training at Hurst Park.'

Edie stumbles away, desperate to put some distance between herself and all these military men. But it only now occurs to her that if she returns to the sanctuary of the Society offices, she risks being seen by Sylvia and the other women.

It's a risk she'll have to take.

Returning to Roman Road, Edie lets herself in through the back entrance, and dashes up the stairs. There's no lock on her bedroom door, so she wedges the chair under the handle.

It will have to do.

Safe for the moment, she draws the deepest breath she's taken all day. She contemplates the pile of uniform on the bed. She puts on the shirt first, fumbling with the metal buttons – they're on the wrong side. The trousers are a couple of inches too long, but at least they disguise her narrow waist. Last, she dons the rough serge tunic, squaring her shoulders beneath the unaccustomed weight. There are two deep pockets on the front, into which she stows Nate's notebook, a couple of pencils and a spare handkerchief.

Nate's shoes are a size too big, and even wearing two pairs of socks Edie's toes still have inches to spare. But there's nothing she can do about that. She considers the rolls of brown bandages, then begins laboriously to wind one roll around her left calf, tucking the loose end into her socks. She repeats the process with her right leg, and at last she is dressed.

Setting the peaked cap on her head, she wishes there were a full-length mirror in the room so she could see what she looks like.

Through the open window, she can hear rival cats yowling in the yard. In the distance a man is singing drunkenly, but she can't make out the slurred words.

Slowly, she takes off the uniform again, stripping down to Nate's long johns. If he could see her now, what would he think? Would he try to talk her out of her plan? But then, she thinks, he has his own plans.

The thought of Nate firing a gun, fighting off enemy soldiers on some distant battlefield, sends ice surging through Edie's veins.

She mustn't think of it: she'll only lose her nerve.

She takes out the booklet the recruiting officer had thrust at her earlier: *Soldier's Pay Book for Use on Active Service* is printed on the cover, along with her new identity: *Pte Eddie Lawrence. 6ᵗʰ Ldn. Reg. No. 4791*

She flicks idly through the pages. All contain empty tables, presumably for recording payments, apart from the very last page, which is completely blank and simply titled: 'WILL'.

6

Lucinda: September 1914

At the beginning of September, another missive from the French Red Cross arrives in the post. 'They write here that the funds are in place for staffing,' Lucinda tells Florence at breakfast, sharing the letter with her. 'They want to know when we'll be ready to leave.'

Florence reads the letter carefully, as Lucinda bites a ragged fingernail, a childhood habit that's come back to haunt her recently.

'Their urgency is understandable,' Florence says. 'Things are moving fast in France.' She drains her cup of tea. 'At least we've gathered the majority of the equipment, although we still need more donations.'

'Our priority must be staffing now,' Lucinda replies, her fingernail throbbing. 'Do you think we'll find enough women in time?' *However did I think we could manage this?* she wants to cry.

'Have we ever balked at a challenge?' Florence says, and Lucinda wants to hug her. 'We're doing everything we possibly can.'

'I suppose we oughtn't to blame the French for being impatient,' Lucinda mutters. She can hardly bear to read the newspapers any more, their pages full of the nightmare happening across the Channel and beyond. The reports are terrifying, the casualty numbers rising by the day.

She tries to stay calm, like Florence, whose method of coping seems to consist of drawing up long lists of tasks, and methodically ticking off each one as it's completed.

Purchase 3 dozen bales of gauze.√

Despite all the hectic preparations, they're continuing to manage their clinic, treating an ever-increasing number of sick women and children. It's exhausting, and Lucinda is finding it harder by the day to keep a straight thought in her head.

Her evenings with Florence are spent writing countless letters to potential benefactors and lobbying rich friends and relatives, begging for extra funds or medical equipment. Lucinda's mother and her younger brother Ambrose, along with Mrs Gingham, a wealthy friend of Florence from Scotland, were among the first to donate, soon followed by many others. They've succeeded in raising almost two thousand pounds already, enough to purchase a hundred portable camp beds, and enough sheets and blankets for another fifty, as well as a range of dried foodstuffs, and the most important surgical instruments. But still they need more money.

Lucinda has contacted Messrs John Barker and Company, a Kensington firm she uses to supply the clinic, and they've agreed to pack the equipment and oversee the shipping of all the boxes and crates to France.

Letters of encouragement continue to pile up on the dining-room table, much to Mrs Fairweather's consternation. She remains baffled by Lucinda and Florence's desire to help 'the Frogs' when they could be here at home.

But time is running out, and Lucinda's steadfast determination, despite Florence's composure and optimism, is beginning to wane. There is so much still to organize.

The clinic will have to be temporarily closed, they decide. Their existing patients will transfer to the nearby women's hospital, and as soon as the war is over – it can't last much beyond New Year, Lucinda hopes – they will reopen the clinic.

The recruitment of the remaining staff is now of utmost urgency. Lucinda and Florence have appealed to their medical colleagues, three of whom immediately offered their services to the new Women's Hospital Corps.

The week before, Dr Gertrude Jameson, a soft-spoken twenty-nine-year-old surgeon, had signed up. Gertrude had worked with Florence and Lucinda at the New Hospital for Women, and was keen to further her surgical skills.

Dr Grace Cook, a determinedly able doctor in her early thirties whom Lucinda has worked with before, is the next to offer her services, along with Dr Hazel Sydenham, a medic in her mid-thirties with as much surgical experience as Lucinda and Florence.

'Will there be a pathology lab on site?' Hazel had wanted to know.

'We intend to create one, yes,' Lucinda had assured her. 'Would you like to take charge of it?'

Hazel would like nothing more, and Lucinda gratefully entrusts her with sourcing the loan of a couple of microscopes, and other related equipment.

Lucinda and Florence spend a day choosing their nursing

team with care, selecting only women they've worked with before, or who come with trusted recommendations.

'We require nurses with gumption and stamina,' Lucinda tells each applicant she interviews, 'who are not liable to faint or panic, who are physically fit and, above all, able to get on with the job at hand with minimal direction.'

The nursing interviews take hours, but by the end of it eight trained nurses have been appointed, all of whom are keen to be involved in such an exciting new venture.

They'll need a chief nurse, Lucinda realizes, as she opens the clinic with Florence one morning.

'Sister Bryony,' Florence says, without hesitation. The Irishwoman is the most competent and experienced nurse she and Lucinda have ever worked with. Lucinda agrees: she'd be perfect for the role.

'Sure, I thought you'd never ask,' Sister Bryony replies, when Lucinda puts the suggestion to her.

With the appointment of the chief nurse, the medical staffing is complete, and Lucinda and Florence turn their attention to the orderlies. Three women are recruited, the first of them the younger sister of Dr Hazel. 'I'd like to help,' Galantha Sydenham tells Lucinda and Florence during her interview. 'I nursed our mother through consumption last winter, and I realized I'd like to help others. I'm not clever enough to be a doctor, like Hazel, but I'm a hard worker . . .'

'We have all the doctors we need,' Lucinda replies, with a smile. 'The role of an orderly is quite as important, in its own way, and will suit only hard workers. Welcome aboard.'

Mardie Hodgson, at twenty-two the youngest member of the W.H.C., is a self-confessed daredevil. 'I can sail a boat, drive a motor-car and ride a horse,' she informs Lucinda at interview. 'But not at the same time.' She grins, revealing a missing incisor.

Lucinda contemplates the wiry young woman with untidy red hair before her. She can't help but be amused by her youthful spirit. 'I'm not entirely sure that sailing will be required,' she replies, pressing her lips together in an effort not to laugh.

'I'm also fluent in French and German, ma'am.'

'Really?' Lucinda hadn't expected that. 'Rather more useful skills, Miss Hodgson. Welcome aboard.'

Perhaps, Lucinda ponders later, the girl would make a decent quartermaster's assistant. They'll need someone to take charge of the stores in France, someone able to negotiate with the locals for supplies, and if Mardie speaks the language it will make the job so much easier.

Olga Campbell, the third and final orderly to be appointed, can also drive, she informs Lucinda. During the interview, Lucinda discovers that Olga is firm friends with Mardie, and the pair often enjoy adventures together, such as swimming in Hampstead Heath Ponds. Lucinda can't understand the appeal of this, but Olga strikes her as energetic and practical, both attributes useful for the challenge ahead.

'We're going to need some men,' Florence remarks to Lucinda out of the blue one evening over supper. 'Only two or three. For the heavy lifting.'

Lucinda swallows a mouthful of toast, a crumb scratching her throat. 'I thought we were going for an all-female team,' she replies, when she can trust her voice. 'We don't need any men.'

'As I said, we require only a few,' Florence says smoothly. 'We can't expect our girls to heave all the furniture about, can we?'

Why ever not? Lucinda wants to snap. *How many times have we had to lift patients twice our size on and off operating tables, no men about to help.*

'How do you suggest we find these men?' Lucinda asks, repressing her lack of enthusiasm.

'The St John Ambulance Association, in Clerkenwell,' Florence replies. 'I've made some enquiries already.'

'You have? When?'

'The other day, when you were busy writing to Barker's, I sent a letter asking if there were any able-bodied men spare. They replied by return, saying to come in person.'

Lucinda smiles weakly. Florence is right, of course. It would be easier if they had a couple of men, at least to start with. But they will have to be chosen carefully.

They find the St John's Gate hall thronging with people, and eventually push their way through to the administration office.

'I wrote to request some men,' Florence explains to a harried young clerk. 'We were told to come in person.'

He looks at her askance. 'You requested some men?' he repeats, clearly baffled.

'For our military hospital in France,' Florence explains. 'I have a letter here.' She waves it at the clerk, who blanches.

'Just a moment, madam.' He calls for his colleague, and a grey-haired man joins them at the desk.

'A military hospital?' the senior clerk queries. 'In France? By what authority?'

'The French Red Cross,' Florence replies.

Lucinda duly hands over the most recent missive from the *Croix-Rouge française*, and is gratified by the brief look of surprise on the clerk's face. 'We need male porters, for the heavier manual tasks,' Florence presses.

'Our staff are not a commodity, madam,' the senior clerk replies. 'You can't march in here, demanding we hand over our men to you, as though they were *things*.'

'I wouldn't dream of demanding anything of you,' Florence replies coolly, and Lucinda has to suppress a smile. Beautiful, brilliant, brave Florence is not to be trifled with, as the clerk is discovering. 'This letter expressly states that we should come in person, which Dr Garland and I have done, as you can see. And now that we are here we politely request the loan of three men, ideally, to help us with perhaps the most life-affirming endeavour they've ever experienced.' She takes a breath. 'Sir.'

'I see.' The senior clerk reluctantly succumbs, as Lucinda had known he would, and summons three members of his staff.

The first, Richard Figgis, a stocky widower of some fifty years, frowns as Lucinda and Florence briefly explain their plans to him.

'Kitchener'll never let you go,' Figgis says, with a sniff. 'He won't let any women over there. Except nurses, and even they're not allowed near the front.'

'We have full endorsement from the relevant authorities,' Lucinda replies, bristling. 'Our venture will not be without risk, granted, and as such we require staff who are not afraid of hard work and danger. Can we count on you, Mr Figgis?'

'I'm fit as a butcher's dog, Miss,' Figgis replies, returning Lucinda's level stare. 'You won't find a harder worker.'

Lucinda exchanges a glance with Florence, who gives an almost imperceptible nod. 'Thank you, Mr Figgis,' she says. 'Consider yourself appointed.'

The second man, Edmund Tozer, a veteran soldier of indeterminate age, shakes Lucinda and Florence's hands. 'I'm honoured to help,' he tells them. 'There's life in this old goat yet.'

Lucinda smiles at the white-haired, stoop-shouldered man, hoping her doubt doesn't show on her face.

The last appointment is a tall twenty-five-year-old Quaker with a stutter. John Penhaligon tells Lucinda and Florence that he joined St John Ambulance as his religion, coupled with chronic asthma, prevented him from enlisting.

'Would you like the opportunity to make a difference in France?' Lucinda asks him. 'The chance to save lives?'

'I – I would be honoured, ma'am,' Penhaligon replies. Lucinda marks a tick against his name. Their contingent of men is complete.

A week has been lost in securing the staff, but Lucinda writes to the French Red Cross, informing them that they are almost ready. It remains only to finalize the design for their Women's Hospital Corps uniform, which Florence's good friend Mrs Gingham has generously offered to sponsor. After much discussion, a dark green, ankle-length skirt has been decided upon for the female staff, daringly short in Florence's opinion, but Lucinda is secretly pleased. In truth, she wishes she could attire herself in trousers, so much more practical. But, of course, that is out of the question.

The skirt is matched with a belted button-through tunic in khaki. Doctors and nurses will have red shoulder straps on their tunics, the orderlies will have white, and all will display the embroidered initials WHC on the breast. The whole ensemble is finished off with a neat cloth hat complete with veil that reaches just past the shoulder.

'Our fellow suffrage supporters can wear their rosettes on their lapels,' Lucinda decrees. The purple, green and white badges will brighten the functional uniforms, she hopes. 'After all, we mustn't lose sight of our ultimate ambition.'

The three male porters will wear their St John Ambulance uniform.

The time has come at last, and Lucinda sends word to each member of the Corps: they will depart for France the day after tomorrow. In the meantime, she makes a final visit to the premises of Messrs John Barker, to check the supplies are ready. She brings along her mother, Eleanor, who has travelled up from Somerset expressly to see Lucinda safely off.

Eleanor Garland, though retired from medical practice, still possesses the vibrancy of a woman half her age. As mother and daughter make their way by hansom cab to the Kensington store, Eleanor questions Lucinda at length, seeking reassurance that her daughter hasn't forgotten anything essential.

'Did you remember gauze? You can never have enough gauze.'

'We have bales of it, Mama.'

'Carbolic acid? You'll need plenty of that.'

'Florence has ordered two crates, I believe.'

'Scalpels, forceps, bistouries, tourniquets, catlin knives. Have you remembered catlin knives, Lucinda?'

'And tenaculums, rongeurs, and tissue retractors, Mama.'

'Needles? Suture? Cotton wool?'

'It's all in hand, Mama,' Lucinda replies, giving her mother what she hopes is a confident smile. In truth, she's suffered sleepless nights worrying that she's forgotten something crucial.

The cab rattles round a tight bend, and Eleanor steadies herself with a hand on Lucinda's knee. 'Ambrose and Muriel send their love,' she says. 'Muriel is looking rather tired, but she let me listen to the baby's heartbeat the other day, and all seems well.'

'That's good to hear,' Lucinda replies, feeling mildly guilty that she hasn't visited her brother and sister-in-law in months. Life is simply too busy. 'When is she due? I forget.'

'November,' Eleanor replies. 'Not long before I'm a grandmother at last.'

Lucinda bites her lip. Despite all evidence to the contrary, her mother still holds out hope that Lucinda will marry and produce a brood of grandchildren. After all, as Eleanor has often commented, *she* managed to have a family as well as a medical career, so why shouldn't her daughter?

The hansom drops the two women at their destination, and Lucinda helps her mother out of the cab. Together, they survey the crates and boxes stacked high along the pavement beneath the shop's striped awning. Someone has diligently labelled each container in chalk: *Women's Hospital Corps, France*. The crates are filled with packages of dried food, cleaning provisions, bales of blankets and bedsheets, and padlocked cases of surgical equipment, some of it loaned from the Red Cross, the rest from various London hospitals.

Somewhere among the boxes, hopefully packed safely in sawdust and newspaper, are Lucinda's two most cherished possessions: her new binaural stethoscope, engraved with her initials, LG, and an ancient, yellowing fox skull – her good-luck talisman. She'd found the skull while walking with Florence on Hampstead Heath one summer's day, during their early medical studies. To Florence's amusement, Lucinda had insisted on taking the skull home with them, where she'd cleaned it carefully, and christened it Yorick. It usually lived on a shelf in the clinic, overseeing proceedings. Now it was on its way to France.

Mr Barker wheezes out of his shop to greet Lucinda and Eleanor. 'All is ready for shipping,' he declares, shaking Lucinda's hand. 'The paperwork is ready in my office for you to sign, but I'll let you check everything is to your liking first.'

Lucinda's breath shortens as she gazes at the heaps of provisions. The endeavour is suddenly real.

A small crowd is gathering, drawn by the presence of so many interesting boxes. Eleanor begins proudly explaining her daughter's impending expedition to all who will listen, and Lucinda finds herself fielding questions from strangers, abashed at her sudden minor celebrity status.

'How brave of you,' a middle-aged woman wearing an enormous plumed hat says, patting Lucinda's hand.

'Oh, well, thank you,' Lucinda stammers, but the woman talks over her, enthusing about the wonderful thing Lucinda is doing, how proud the country should be that women such as her are helping their dear fighting men in their hour of need.

Not everyone is quite as enthusiastic. Just as Lucinda is persuading her mother to join her in withdrawing to a nearby teahouse, they are waylaid by an elderly man brandishing a cane and a scowl. The man seems unable to accept that Lucinda and her female colleagues will be running the hospital in France, not some cohort of medical men. Women shouldn't interfere in war work, the old man blusters. They should stay at home, where they belong.

'You're one of those infernal suffragettes, aren't you?' the man demands of Lucinda, glaring at her lapel badge. 'You'll never succeed, you know.'

Lucinda flounders for a suitable response, and is saved by her mother.

'My dear sir,' Eleanor addresses the man, her voice clipped and cold, 'I have every reason to believe my daughter and her staff will succeed in France, and when they do, they will advance the women's Cause by thirty years.'

I, EDDIE LAWRENCE, swear by Almighty God that I will be faithful and bear true Allegiance to His Majesty King George the Fifth, His Heirs and Successors, and that I will, as in duty-bound, honestly and faithfully defend His Majesty, His Heirs, and Successors, in Person, Crown and dignity against all enemies, and will observe and obey all orders of His Majesty, His Heirs and Successors, and of the Generals and Officers set over me.

So help me God.

7

Edie: September 1914

She opens the bedroom window, and takes a deep breath of the balmy morning air. Though the sun has barely risen, she's sweating beneath the linen binder wrapped around her chest. September is here at last, yet the oppressive heatwave shows no sign of breaking.

Turning back to the bed, Edie contemplates the collection of garments piled there. Nate's flannel long johns are the last thing she wants to wear in this heat, but she drags them on – at least they help to bulk out her thin frame. Next, she dons the heavy, ill-fitting khaki shirt, trousers and tunic, then laboriously winds the cloth bandages around her calves. Finally, she laces Nate's shoes as securely as she can.

Dressed at last, she runs a hand over her rough scalp.

Her military training is about to begin, and she's as ready as she'll ever be. From downstairs comes the sound of the front door opening, and Edie's heart stumbles. Sylvia Pankhurst has arrived unusually early to open the offices. Edie hadn't reckoned on her friend being here at this hour. The plan had been to slip out of the house, returning later when everyone had gone home. Now she'll have to pass Sylvia on her way.

Perhaps it's for the best. With no mirror in her room,

Edie can't see what she looks like done up as a soldier. Sylvia's reaction will tell her all she needs to know.

She finds Sylvia in the kitchen, filling the kettle, humming to herself. It takes a moment for recognition to dawn in her friend's eyes. 'Edie?' Sylvia abandons the kettle and approaches her in the doorway, gingerly touching the sleeve of Edie's tunic as though Edie might be a ghost. 'I thought for a moment you were . . .' Sylvia falters, falls silent.

Edie swallows. 'I've joined up, Miss Pankhurst. I start my training today, over at Hurst Park.'

'Joined up? I don't understand . . .'

'I need to get to France. To the front.'

'The front? What on earth do you mean?'

Edie's mouth has dried. Spoken aloud, her plan suddenly seems ludicrous. 'I want to do my bit, and report on the war.' It's the only way anyone's going to take me seriously as a journalist, she almost adds.

'Oh, Edie.' Sylvia sinks down on a chair. 'What are you thinking, dear?'

'P-please,' Edie stammers. 'Don't try to stop me.'

'Stop you?' Sylvia gives a wry laugh. 'I'm not in the habit of stopping a woman on a mission, even if that mission is the most audacious I've ever heard.'

Edie bites her lip. 'Thank you,' she whispers.

'Have you considered the dangers, Edie? And I don't just mean on the battlefield. If you're caught as a woman . . .'

'I won't let them catch me, ma'am.'

72

Sylvia gives a small shake of her head. 'How long will they train you? Before they send you to France?'

'I don't know,' Edie admits. 'Can I stay here until I go?'

'Of course.' Sylvia rises. 'You almost fooled me,' she admits, giving Edie an appraising look. 'Quite the soldier. If a little on the small side.'

Edie pulls her shoulders back, trying to stand taller.

'That's better,' Sylvia pronounces with a smile.

To Edie's surprise, her friend envelops her in a warm hug. 'Stay safe, won't you, dear?'

Peaked cap pulled low, Edie sets off along Roman Road, heading west towards Farringdon station. By the time she reaches Cowcross Street, some forty minutes later, the sun has burned through the haze, and the stench of Smithfield livestock market lies heavy on the air.

The city is coming to life. Head down, she almost stumbles over a pavement shrine – she's noticed a few appearing on the streets of late. A creased, sun-faded portrait photograph of a soldier rests against a cracked vase containing a wilting bunch of garden pinks. The sight of the personal tribute makes Edie suddenly think of Nate, and she falters.

Men were dying in their hundreds, thousands even. And Nate was out there somewhere, fighting too. Wherever he is, Edie hopes he's safe. She slips a hand into the pocket of her tunic, where the notebook is safely tucked:

Keep writing, Edie

with love,
N

Farringdon station is swarming with military folk and civilians, and Edie suffers a moment of crippling doubt. If someone challenges her, she'll surely be arrested? But no one pays her any heed, and she manages to purchase a third-class ticket to Hurst Park. While she waits for her train to arrive, she reads a discarded newspaper she finds lying on a bench, hiding behind its pages. If the reports are to be believed, every bridge and railway tunnel in the country is mined, German spies are rampant in the capital, and the entire Royal Navy has been sunk. Edie folds the paper and drops it back on the bench.

She can't bring herself to enter a packed train carriage, choosing instead to spend the hour and a half journey standing in the corridor. Through the grimy window, she watches the London landscape gradually change from grey to green, as the train jolts slowly westwards. She's never travelled further than Battersea before, but she tries not to think about this.

Disembarking at Hampton Court an hour and a half later, Edie follows a stream of men, most of them dressed in some semblance of army uniform, who she hopes are also bound for Hurst Park.

'You've done all right, son.' Edie glances up from beneath her cap, to find a man has fallen into step alongside her. She meets his affable eye. 'Lucky you've got most of the kit,' he remarks.

Edie gives him a brief nod, unable to speak. She notes he's wearing a khaki tunic like hers, but over ordinary trousers. His brown flat cap and scuffed boots give him the look of a labourer. He strides ahead, and she breathes again.

After walking perhaps ten minutes, Edie is relieved to finally reach her destination, a former horseracing track requisitioned by the army. Military guards direct the arrivals towards a white-painted Victorian grandstand, the place overrun with army personnel. A drill sergeant proceeds to herd Edie and the other forty or so newcomers into rows; their names and ages are to be recorded.

Lined up among the men, Edie tries to stand tall. She squares her shoulders, widening her stance, willing her shaking legs to bear her. There are men here of varying statures, she's noticed. She's not quite the smallest, thank God.

A trio of officers mounted on the biggest horses Edie has ever seen are approaching. As they draw near, she sees sweat foaming on the animals' chests. She's never ridden a horse, finds their size and strength intimidating ever since she was almost trampled as a child. She gazes up at the officers, imagining how it must be to sit up so perilously high.

'Attention!' the nearest officer barks. The brass buttons on his tunic shine like tiny suns. 'I am Major Pryce. You will be under my charge during your training here at Hurst Park.' Briefly, he explains to the recruits that they are to receive instruction as laid down in the Field Service Regulations. They will be taught drill, marching discipline, field craft and weaponry. 'Skill cannot compensate for want of courage, energy and determination,' the major concludes. 'To question is to doubt, and to doubt is fatal. You will follow orders to the letter.' Major Pryce hands over to the staff sergeant on his left.

'Fitness for war is the only thing that counts,' the staff

sergeant begins. His voice is deeper, slower, but no less terrifying to Edie. 'Your first duty here is to acquire a soldierly spirit.'

'I for one'd like some spirit,' a man next to Edie mutters.

'You must learn to bear fatigue, privation and danger cheerfully,' the sergeant continues. 'Discipline is the living force by which recruits such as yourselves will be turned into a successful fighting army.'

Edie senses the men around her shifting, feet scuffing the dusty ground.

'The essence of discipline is instant obedience,' the sergeant forges on, 'not just to commands given, but to all rules and regulations duly issued by authority.' He pauses, the ensuing silence broken only by the jingle of bridles, restless hoofs crunching on the ground. A rhythmic stamp of boots reaches Edie on the soft breeze, and she looks across the park to where a long column of soldiers is marching along the perimeter of the grass track.

'Your second duty,' the sergeant resumes, 'is in the training of the body in strength, activity of mind and good health. Drill will develop these qualities, but the preservation of health will depend on you. Every man must stand or fall by his own actions.'

For the remainder of the morning, a drill sergeant has them marching the circumference of the racecourse, admonishing anyone who falls out of step. Edie soon learns the order to 'form fours', how to march in step with forty others, how to turn on command as one. The movements are repeated over and over, as the sun climbs higher, and Edie is dripping with sweat, lightheaded with thirst, by the time the drill sergeant calls a halt.

Granted a brief refreshment break, the recruits seek the shade of the stands, where Edie gulps an enamel mug of water issued from a field canteen. Surreptitiously, she observes the other recruits, many of whom seem to know each other. One man, sitting slightly away from the others, is manipulating a small box in his lap. Edie recognizes the object as a pocket camera – an Ensignette, from the look of it. One of Mr Stead's reporters, Mr James, had one, she recalls. Took it everywhere with him in case a road accident or some other newsworthy catastrophe occurred.

The man catches Edie watching him, and flashes her a grin. He's about her age, perhaps a little older, with smiling eyes and curly dark hair cut close to his scalp. 'This little beauty's going to earn me some cash,' the young man tells Edie. 'D'you want a look?'

She nods, not trusting her voice, and the camera is handed over for inspection.

The young man fumbles in a pocket, pulling out a page torn from a newspaper. He thrusts the scrap at Edie. 'See?'

'WAR SNAPSHOTS WILL WIN £100: AMATEUR'S CHANCE,' she reads.

'The *Sphere*'ll pay hundreds of quid for the right picture,' the man goes on. 'Enough to get me own place, I reckon. Stanley, by the way. Stanley Chay.' He thrusts a hand at her.

'Eddie,' she manages to croak. 'Lawrence.'

'Nice to meet you, Lawrence. You local?'

Edie shakes her head. 'East London,' she hears herself say.

Stanley nods. 'You been in the wars already, have you?'

'What?'

Stanley indicates Edie's broken nose. She brings a hand self-consciously to her face. The bruising has faded, but she still looks as if she's been in a fight. An officer begins bawling at the recruits to 'fall in', saving Edie from answering.

The recruits are marched to a canvas shelter on the far side of the course, where long tables laden with all manner of military equipment have been set out. Edie collects a kitbag, a clasp knife and water canteen, a mug, a spoon and a mess tin with a cloth cover. She's never owned so many things in her life. Around her, men are remarking on the kit, criticizing the length of the knife blade, the size of the mess tin. They talk like clerks, tradesmen, shop assistants, and Edie suspects many have lived an indoor life, their faces paler than hers, their nails clean, hands soft. At least she's used to hard physical labour, she thinks. Her workhouse upbringing and the years of charring for Mr Stead have roughened her edges.

A field kitchen has been assembled in front of the grand-stand, with trestle tables for the recruits to eat at. As they line up to receive their meal, a staff sergeant informs them that training is over for the day, and they must return tomorrow at oh nine hundred hours. Edie contemplates the return journey to Roman Road, hoping that by the time she gets there everyone will have left for the day and the house will be empty.

Sitting with Stanley and the other men, she wolfs down

an unidentifiable meat stew, and immediately regrets her haste as her stomach gripes. Conversations swirl around her, and she listens to tales of jealous sweethearts, worried mothers, bastard employers. Only Sylvia Pankhurst knows she's here, and this knowledge gives Edie a strange, numb feeling.

If only Nate were training with her. She wonders if he might have come through Hurst Park, if he sat at this same table.

'What do you do?' Stanley asks, breaking into Edie's thoughts. 'For a job, like.'

'I'm apprenticed,' Edie replies, her voice low and gruff. Her head swims to speak the lie aloud. 'Newspapers.'

Stanley nods, seemingly impressed. 'Mate of mine's in that line of work,' he says. 'Writes for the new *London Journal*. Do you know it?'

Edie knows it only too well. She's witnessed Mr Stead run the *Journal* down on numerous occasions, but she keeps this to herself.

'Worked, I should say,' Stanley goes on. 'Got kicked in the head by a horse last year, poor sod.'

'I'm sorry,' Edie mutters.

The man on Edie's left leans across her, breaking into their conversation. 'Got a light?' He waves a roll-up in Edie's face. She recoils, shaking her head, resisting the urge to push the man away.

'Easy,' the man sneers.

'Here, Caldwell.' An older man across the table throws him a box of lucifers.

'Cheers.' Caldwell lights his fag, blows smoke from his nose. Edie tenses, as he leans close to her again.

'You're a young 'un,' he murmurs. 'Fool the brass hats, did you?'

Edie can't breathe. Is she about to be exposed?

'Pretty boy, too,' Caldwell mocks, and Edie's heart slams in her chest. She's never felt more vulnerable or alone.

'Leave off, Caldwell,' the man opposite growls. 'He's not your sort.'

Caldwell gives a bark of laughter, and to Edie's relief he moves away, losing interest in her. Gradually, she realizes Stanley is saying something to her.

'Smashed his nose.'

'What?' Edie blinks at Stanley.

'My workmate. The one what was kicked by a horse. His nose was broken, you know, like yours.'

'I wasn't kicked by a horse.'

'Hit by an omnibus, then?'

Edie shakes her head, and before Stanley can ask more, she makes her excuses and escapes to the latrines.

The washhouse, situated behind the grandstand, is thankfully deserted. Squatting in a rough wooden cubicle, the bolt safely shot, Edie takes a shuddery breath. She can feel a headache threatening. For a moment, she imagines herself back in the privy at Stead's, the walls pasted with newspaper clippings and adverts. But the walls of this toilet are bare, the only newspaper a pile of torn sheets in the corner, a handful of which she uses to dry herself.

As she makes her way back to Stanley and the others, worries crowd her mind. How long can she maintain this deception? During her training, she will sleep at Roman Road each night. But when she's sent to France, what then?

She can only face each challenge as it comes, she counsels herself. Everything will be worth it in the end, when the world reads her first-hand account of the war, and she becomes the first woman to report from battle.

At last, her dream of becoming a journalist is coming true.

8

Lucinda: October 1914

The morning of their departure dawns overcast. Lucinda wakes early, having suffered a restless night, and hastily dresses in her new Women's Hospital Corps uniform. Her father's old Gladstone bag sits, packed and ready, at the foot of her bed. She strokes the leather, thinking of her father, a man she'd barely had the chance to know.

Thomas Garland had been an excellent medical man – everyone who had known him said so. Calm and patient, with an empathetic bedside manner, he was a doctor people could trust.

He'd been taken too soon, dead of a heart attack at only forty-two, a few months after Lucinda's younger brother Ambrose was born. All her working life, Lucinda has striven to emulate her father. He'd be proud of her today, she thinks.

'Wish me luck, Pa,' she whispers.

Joining Florence for breakfast, she can barely manage a few mouthfuls of the porridge Mrs Fairweather serves.

'You must eat more, Lucie,' Florence urges. 'It's going to be a long day.'

'I'm too nervous.'

Lucinda can hear the housekeeper banging and crashing about in the kitchen. Mrs Fairweather has made it clear that she fails to understand why Lucinda and Florence want to go to France, declaring the place far too dangerous for two young women.

'I'm nearly thirty, Mrs Fairweather,' Lucinda had reminded the housekeeper, several times. 'Hardly young.'

'Precisely,' Mrs Fairweather had retorted. 'You should know better.'

Despite the housekeeper's lack of enthusiasm for their adventure, Lucinda notes a glistening in the older woman's eyes when she comes back into the dining room.

'Finish your porridge,' Mrs Fairweather grumbles at Lucinda. 'What are you going to do out in France when I'm not there to keep an eye on you?'

Eat my breakfast in peace, Lucinda thinks, as she manages to force down two more spoonfuls of thick porridge.

'Are you looking forward to staying at your sister's?' Florence asks Mrs Fairweather, in a blatant attempt at distraction. 'She still lives in Battersea, doesn't she?'

'That she does,' the housekeeper mutters.

Lucinda professes how glad she is that Mrs Fairweather has her sister for company, while they're away. 'I wouldn't have liked to think of you here alone, Mrs F.'

Florence flashes her a look, as if to say: *Don't overdo it.*

'I've packed you sandwiches,' the housekeeper says, as Lucinda and Florence gather their luggage at the door. 'Don't like to think of you travelling on empty stomachs.'

'Oh, Mrs Fairweather.' Florence smiles, as the housekeeper presses a weighty package wrapped in greaseproof paper into her hands. 'You do love us, after all.'

'Be off with you both.' Mrs Fairweather sniffs. 'But just you make sure you come back.'

∞

At Victoria station, Lucinda and Florence are reunited with the Corps, and the doctors, nurses and orderlies, seventeen souls in all, gather on the platform. Lucinda collects passport papers from everyone, leaving Florence to deal with Mr Figgis's concern that this confidential paperwork might be lost en route to France, and shouldn't one of the menfolk be entrusted with such important documents?

Soon the group are joined by friends and family members, as well as several colleagues from various hospitals, who have come to see them off. Dr Craddock, Lucinda's old medical professor, sends his apologies, unable to attend due to ill health. But to Lucinda's delight and gratitude, he has sent the useful gift of a large fruit cake, sustenance for the journey.

A doctor friend of Lucinda's from her days at the Royal Free Hospital presents Lucinda with a leaving gift wrapped in brown paper. 'Thought this might come in useful,' Alice says, with a wink. Lucinda unwraps it, expecting gin perhaps, but finds instead a bottle of anti-seasickness medicine.

'I used to pride myself on having a cast-iron constitution,' Lucinda laughs, 'but I fear I may need this. Thank you.'

She hears her name called and turns to find Madame Brasier de Thuy and her husband beetling towards her. Lucinda is relieved to see them: the transport of their luggage and equipment has been entrusted to the French couple, and she's keen to check all is well.

'*Oui, oui,*' Monsieur reassures her. 'The supplies were sent on yesterday, to be loaded on the boat you will be travelling on. HMS *Winifred.*'

'And the trucks?' Florence asks. 'They've been arranged, *Monsieur*?'

'All ready for your arrival, Doctor,' the Frenchman assures her.

'*Merci beaucoup, Monsieur,*' Lucinda says, breathing a little easier.

Madame Brasier de Thuy dabs at her eyes with a lace handkerchief. 'I just wish we could go with you,' she says, crying softly. 'I do so miss my beautiful France.'

The Frenchman places a hand on his wife's shoulder, and gives it a tender pat. The gesture brings a tear to Lucinda's eye, and for a moment she teeters, only to be saved by the arrival of Ambrose and his pregnant wife Muriel. The couple are moving slowly towards them, Muriel with a hand pressed protectively to her huge belly.

'My dear, you shouldn't have come,' Lucinda gently admonishes Muriel. In truth she's glad to see her beloved brother and his wife.

'I wouldn't miss this for the world,' Muriel replies. 'It's not every day one has a sister-in-law going off on such an adventure. I'm incredibly jealous of you, Lucinda. You and Florence are so courageous.'

Lucinda feels the heat of a blush. 'I'm hardly on the battlefield, Muriel.'

'We would have arrived earlier,' Ambrose apologizes, 'but some German fellow has been trying to erect a wireless

86

station on the roof of the Ritz Hotel, can you believe? There was a commotion outside when we passed earlier, and we had to divert the carriage through St James's Park.'

'What happened?' Lucinda asks, enthralled.

'Oh, he was arrested, of course,' Ambrose says dismissively.

Lucinda turns to bring Florence into the conversation, only to find her further along the platform, talking with an elderly couple. Her eyes moisten again; Florence has only her aunt and uncle to see her off.

Train doors are slamming, and a shiver ripples up Lucinda's spine. Soon, she and Florence will have to board, as the others are already doing.

'I brought you something for the journey, Lucie.' Ambrose digs in his pocket and flourishes a single green apple, which he places ceremoniously in Lucinda's palm. 'An apple a day . . .' He winks.

'I'm not sure how that works if one is a doctor . . .' Lucinda can't help but chuckle.

Her brother clears his throat. 'We're so proud of you, Lucie.'

'Please don't say any more, Ambrose.' Lucinda blinks back tears. 'You'll make me cry, and I can't be seen to be weak.'

'Of course. Stiff upper lip and all that, sister dear,' Ambrose says, with mock solemnity. 'Ah, here comes the mater. I've been wondering where she'd got to.'

Lucinda follows her brother's gaze, to see their mother making her way towards them, wielding a walking stick. The sprightly, fiercely independent septuagenarian looks her years this morning, Lucinda thinks. What's going through her mother's mind? Does she truly approve of the task her daughter has set herself? So far, Eleanor has expressed only pride in her endeavour, yet she must be worried, frightened even, for the unknown challenges Lucinda faces.

Lucinda feels a sudden pang of guilt. Should she be abandoning her widowed mother to risk her life in a foreign country in the midst of a terrible war? She gives herself a mental shake. No: her mother is proud of her, and wants her to go. And, besides, all Lucinda is doing is continuing the medical journey her mother began so many years ago.

'Shouldn't you be getting on, Lucinda?' Eleanor says, gesturing with her walking stick to the last of Lucinda's staff boarding the train.

Lucinda spots Figgis and Tozer climbing into a carriage, Penhaligon's gangly form following them. That all these people have put their trust in her and Florence, that they are willing to travel across the Channel, leaving their safe homes and beloved families, makes Lucinda's chest tighten. She can never let them down.

A movement at the far end of the platform catches her eye. Two men, one carrying what looks to be a camera on a tripod over his shoulder, are approaching.

Figs! Who invited the press?

To her relief, she recognizes the taller of the pair as her journalist friend Harry Levinson, and her heart lifts.

'I've caught you in time, my dear,' Levinson greets Lucinda warmly. 'Room for one more in your party?'

'I'm rather surprised you're not out there in the thick of it already, Harry,' Lucinda replies, as she shakes his hand.

'I was until recently,' Levinson replies, removing his hat and running a hand through his silver hair. Lucinda finds herself thinking, not for the first time, that the journalist's handsome, confident bearing would just as easily have fitted him to be an actor, or a politician perhaps. But as a writer of newspaper columns, not to mention a staunch supporter of women's suffrage, Levinson's chosen career has been of much more use to Lucinda and other female doctors.

'I was in Berlin until only a few weeks ago,' Levinson says. 'When I returned, the *Daily News* asked me to go over to France with the BEF.'

'You've been out with our boys?' Ambrose says. 'That's quite a scoop, Harry.'

'But Kitchener has changed the rules, the damned interfering old . . .' Levinson presses his lips together as he sets his hat back on his head. 'He considers us correspondents a thorn in the flesh of the military. But never fear, this knight errant of the pen will be hot on your trail, my dear,' he promises Lucinda. He turns to his companion, a sandy-haired young man busy setting up his camera on its stand. 'Are you ready yet, Charlie? This lady has a train to catch.'

'Almost, Mr Levinson.'

Lucinda swallows, glancing around. Where was Florence? She was the photogenic one, calm and confident when faced with a camera.

'You didn't think you'd slip away on the quiet, did you, my dear?'

Lucinda turns back to find Harry Levinson, Eleanor, Ambrose and Muriel gazing at her. 'I hadn't given it much thought, Harry . . .'

To her immense relief, at that moment Florence re-appears. 'Hello,' she greets Lucinda's family. She shakes Levinson's hand. 'Are you here to see us off, Harry? That's sweet of you.'

'The world will want to know about your endeavour,' Harry Levinson says. 'Two beautiful lady medics heading overseas to rescue our dear boys. The scoop of the year, wouldn't you agree?' He and Ambrose exchange a look that Lucinda interprets as amused admiration.

Look at what the ladies are doing!

'We ought to have all the team assembled for the shot,' Levinson muses, 'but there isn't time so it'll just have to be you two gems.'

Lucinda feels her cheeks warm, as Florence comes to stand next to her. They face Charlie and his camera, and Lucinda forces a brave smile, feeling oddly self-conscious.

Just as they are finishing, a shrill whistle blows, startling Lucinda. A guard shouts: 'All passengers to board now!'

'Oh.' She turns to Florence. 'This is it, then.'

'This is it, Lucie.' Florence's nervous smile mirrors her own.

'Goodbye, Mama.' Lucinda gives Eleanor one final brisk hug. 'Wish us luck.'

'If I were only twenty years younger,' Eleanor says, 'I'd be coming with you.'

'I hope I'll make you proud, Mama.' Lucinda is dismayed to hear the catch in her voice. 'I hope I'll succeed as well as you would have done.'

'I have no doubt you will, my darling,' her mother says, dabbing her eyes. 'I wish you all the luck in the world.'

9

Edie: October 1914

After roll-call each day, Edie gathers at the mess tent with Stanley and the other recruits for a hurried breakfast of stewed tea and burned bacon rolls. Most of the men are also commuting from their homes, Edie learns. Some have even further to travel than her, but no concessions are given to those with a long journey. When their training begins, it continues all day until the light begins to fade, by which time Edie is ready to drop.

One morning, she, Stanley and the other recruits have barely finished their breakfast when they're ordered on to buses. They're to be driven to the rifle ranges, for weapons training.

Crammed on to the open top deck beside Stanley, Edie's stomach clenches at the prospect of firing a gun. Around her, the excitement of the other recruits is almost palpable. As the bus lumbers along on its interminable journey, Edie tries to block out the men's boastful chat and raucous banter. No one seems to know exactly where the bus is taking them, but after a while the busy city streets narrow to quieter rural roads.

Stanley lights a cigarette and offers Edie his crumpled pack. She shakes her head.

'All right, Lawrence?'

Edie manages a nod.

'You look a bit green,' Stanley says. 'Bringing back memories, is it?'

'What?'

'When you fell off the back of a bus.'

'*What?*'

Stanley waves his fag at Edie's nose, grinning.

Oh, God, not that again. 'I didn't fall off a bus,' Edie mutters.

'Well, if it weren't a horse, and it weren't a bus, what was it mashed your conk, then?'

But now the bus is shuddering to a stop at the edge of a field, and Stanley's teasing is curtailed as the recruits are ordered off. Edie has lost her bearings, has no idea where she is. Can these meadows browned by sun and bordered by distant copses really be the firing ranges? It's a peaceful, almost bucolic scene, and the only flaw in Edie's eyes is a nearby open-sided wooden structure packed with guns and boxes of ammunition.

The weapons instructor, a sergeant with a vivid scar bisecting his left cheek, lays down the ground rules of the firing range.

No rifles to be loaded or fired until the commanding officer has given the order to do so.

Always keep weapons pointed in a safe direction.

Stop firing immediately on hearing the order to 'Cease fire.'

An accompanying non-commissioned officer distributes rifles among the recruits, and Edie marvels at the solid weight of hers, the wooden stock shiny as a conker, the metal barrel gleaming in the sun. The rifle is an object of strange beauty and terror, and she has no idea what to do with it.

'These are Short Magazine Lee-Enfield Mark Threes,' the scarred instructor begins. 'What you're holding in your hands is your best friend.' He raises his own rifle to chest height. 'Care for it like it's your sweetheart. She may well save your life one day.'

Holding out the rifle before him, he proceeds swiftly to name the various parts: butt, stock, barrel, bolt. 'She weighs just less than nine pounds, with the magazine empty,' he tells the recruits. 'With the bayonet attached, you can add another pound to that. A serious piece of kit, gentlemen.'

He rummages in one of the many pockets of the webbing belt criss-crossing his body, extracting a brass object. 'Your charger clip.' He waves it above his head for everyone to see. 'Holds five rounds – ball cartridges we call them.' He pulls back the bolt on the rifle with practised ease and slots the charger clip into the space. Edie watches closely, desperately trying to commit his instructions to memory.

The sergeant gives his scar a brief scratch, the skin of his cheek flaring red. 'Next,' he continues, 'push the bolt forward and down, like so.' He brandishes the gun. 'It's now ready to fire.'

Edie tries to imagine Nate wielding a weapon like this, but the image won't come. She remembers something she overheard a man on the bus say: *The army's hungry for men. It doesn't matter if we don't know one end of a gun from the other.*

The instructor is talking on, his voice dragging Edie back to the field. She glances across at Stanley, busy inspecting his rifle with a rapt expression. What did he find so alluring? The gun does nothing but chill Edie's blood.

'Right, pay attention,' the instructor announces. 'I shall fire five rounds, so you can see how it goes.'

He hefts his rifle. 'Safety comes off.' He points along the gun's barrel. 'You take aim by lining up the rear and front sights. They're ranged out to five hundred yards.'

The instructor raises his rifle, aiming at a white-painted target post fifty yards away across the field. The recruits watch in silence as he sets the stock of the rifle against his shoulder, and lines up the sights. A shot rings out, the sudden noise making Edie bite her tongue, and a chip of white bursts from the top of the wooden post.

'It's possible to shoot several times rapidly,' the instructor says, lowering his gun. 'The current record is thirty-eight bullets in a minute.' A murmur of appreciation runs through the group.

The recruits are organized into five lines. Edie finds herself positioned between Stanley and a young man called Jackson, who looks even more nervous than she is.

'On the command to load,' the sergeant instructs, 'bring the rifle to the right side of the hip, like so, grasp the stock, muzzle pointing upwards.'

Edie clutches the rifle, her sweaty fingers slipping, as the sergeant makes his way along the lines, adjusting various stances.

'Turn off the safety and draw back the bolt,' he intones. 'Take a charger and place it vertically between the guides.'

Edie's hands are shaking as she tries to follow the orders.

'Force the charger down with the ball of your thumb. Your *thumb*, Private!'

Edie struggles to insert the cartridges. The clip won't go in. Damn thing! Panic grips her, and she promptly drops the clip on the ground.

Next to her, Stanley has managed to load his rifle. How had he done that so quickly? Edie pushes the charger clip into the breech as hard as she can, willing the bloody thing to go in, and at last it does. Her mind is a blank as to what she should do next.

'Force the bolt home,' Stanley hisses.

The sergeant comes to stand in front of Edie. 'Now, front row only,' he calls. 'Direct your eyes on a target and bring your rifle up to rest on your shoulder.' He places a steadying hand under the barrel of Edie's gun as she raises it.

'Keep your left elbow tucked well under the rifle,' the officer instructs, pushing down on Edie's arm. 'Lower your cheek, close your left eye, and align the sights on the mark.'

Edie concentrates on following his instructions, the muscles in her arms trembling.

'Restrain your breathing, Private.'

Edie holds her breath, relieved when the officer moves away to adjust Jackson's posture.

'All right, men, take aim.'

The instructor steps behind Edie's line.

'And fire!'

A sharp crack comes from somewhere down the line, followed a second later by another shot, and now the whole line is firing. Edie presses her finger on the trigger, and the gun fires, bucking against her shoulder with a painful jolt. Ears ringing, arms shaking, she squeezes the trigger again, then again, each time bracing her shoulder a little more firmly against the anticipated recoil.

At last, with no bullets left, she lowers the rifle, heart hammering.

Somehow she's hit her target, splintering the wood into fragments.

'Well done, kid.' Stanley claps her on the back, causing her to fumble the rifle, almost dropping it in the mud.

She barely hears the sergeant's next order, as a mixture of terror and pride surges through her, pushing all else from her mind.

She has just fired a gun.

∞

Each evening, when Edie returns to the Roman Road offices, beyond exhausted from hours of physical training, she finds Sylvia Pankhurst waiting for her. Edie joins the older woman in her office, where they drink glasses of lemonade and Sylvia questions Edie about her day. What was the training like? Did she go to the firing ranges again today? How much longer will her training last? Edie gets the sense that Sylvia is a little envious, that perhaps if things were different, she might want to do what Edie is doing.

When at last the lemonade is drunk, and Sylvia leaves for the night, Edie washes in the pantry, then drags her tired body up to bed. Fighting her exhaustion, she manages to write a few lines in her notebook, before dropping into a deep and dreamless sleep.

It's a huge relief to Edie that Sylvia has agreed to let her stay on at Roman Road. At least now Edie can pay her a nominal rent from her army wage. As the month draws to a close, Edie continues to travel back and forth to Hurst Park every day, leaving the house at dawn to avoid people, and returning after the offices are closed, when only Sylvia remains.

By mid-October, Edie has learned to march with full kit in the oppressive heat of the day, and the relative cool of the evening. She has learned how to dig a defence trench deep enough to shield her body from a blast. She has learned rudimentary first aid, and how to construct a bivouac from canvas ground sheets and lengths of rope. Her fitness has gradually improved, and the regular and plentiful army food helps provide her with the strength to face the physical drills. It takes her a long time to get to grips with firing the heavy, cumbersome SMLE rifles yet somehow she's able to hold her own among the men at the ranges.

The pages of her notebook slowly fill with her observations, and pencil sketches of officers and fellow recruits: Stanley with his camera, young Jackson and his lanky frame, Bembridge, the 'father' figure of their platoon, Caldwell with his shifty expression, Sergeant Ratigan. She intends to write up her notes more fully later. One day, Stanley catches her scribbling in the notebook during a brief rest break and asks if she's keeping a diary. 'You want to hide it,' he warns her. 'The brass hats don't like it when people like us write things down.'

Edie heeds his warning, tucking away the notebook, resolving to write in it only when she's alone. She can't risk having Nate's precious gift discovered and confiscated. It would be almost as devastating as having her identity revealed.

No one knows how much longer the training will go on. The same question haunts every recruit: when will they be sent to France?

And then, one morning in the third week of October, the moment Edie and the rest of the platoon have been waiting for finally arrives.

10

Lucinda: October 1914

Rough sea conditions in the Channel hinder *Winifred*'s passage to France, and dusk is falling by the time the steamer finally reaches Dieppe. The harbour is crowded with ships bearing troops to the battlefields, and Lucinda, Florence and the team disembark on to a dimly lit jetty bustling with dock workers and military personnel.

An English consul is due to meet the Corps for the next stage of their journey, but there's no sign of them yet. Unsure what else to do, Lucinda gathers the group together to wait, their bags piled around their feet. A few are still suffering from seasickness, and Lucinda monitors them, hoping they'll rally soon. She and Florence had spent much of the journey doling out Lucinda's anti-seasickness medicine.

The Corps wait in near silence. No one, it seems, has much energy left for conversation. Lucinda finds herself swaying slightly, the low rumble of the ship's engines continuing to vibrate through her bones. She can taste sea salt on her dry lips, and her windblown hair feels rough as straw, as she pins her hat more firmly. This wasn't at all the start she'd imagined.

'You sure we're expected, ma'am?' Figgis asks her, for perhaps the third time.

Lucinda bristles at the man's doubtful tone. 'Of course, Mr Figgis.'

The porter raises bushy eyebrows, looking as though he might challenge her, but Lucinda musters a confident smile. Grumbling to himself, Figgis rejoins Tozer and Penhaligon.

Several minutes pass, and Lucinda is beginning to seriously worry that Figgis may have a point, when a stocky figure is spotted hurrying towards them along the quay. The man breathlessly introduces himself.

'I do apologize for keeping you waiting,' the consul says, as Lucinda hands their paperwork to him. 'I assume you'll be staying in Dieppe.'

'No,' Lucinda replies, frowning. 'The Red Cross are expecting us in Paris.' She exchanges a glance with Florence. Surely the consul should know this.

'Oh, I see, but it would be beneficial to us if you could stay in Dieppe for a short time, Doctor,' the consul replies. 'We're in dire need of medical aid in the hospitals here.'

'I'm sorry, but that isn't possible,' Lucinda replies, a knot of guilt forming in her gut. 'We must go to Paris.' Her awkward apologies are cut short by the arrival of a second man, who introduces himself as Monsieur Guérin, an agent appointed by Monsieur Brasier de Thuy. The Frenchman gestures over his shoulder, and Lucinda sees three trucks parked in the distance, presumably for them. He begins speaking in rapid French, and Lucinda calls for Mardie Hodgson, the multilingual orderly, to join them. She needs the girl's skills already.

Between translations, Lucinda gleans that the trucks are waiting with their drivers, ready to receive the medical supplies off the ship. The boxes and crates will then be transported to the Red Cross offices in Paris, where they will remain until the team are ready to move into their premises.

'*Merci*,' Lucinda says to the agent, wishing not for the first time that she'd paid more attention in her French lessons at school. 'Will our equipment be transferred off the ship soon?' she asks the English consul hopefully.

At that moment, a boy dashes up to the group. He seeks out Guérin, thrusting a slip of paper at him, gasping something in such rapid French Lucinda can't understand a word.

Guérin snaps a reply, then turns to address the English consul in French, gesticulating at the ship and the trucks.

'What's the matter?' Lucinda asks.

A look of distress warps the Englishman's bland features. 'An unfortunate mistake has been made,' he relays. 'This telegram is from England, sent by Monsieur Brasier de Thuy. Your equipment has apparently been loaded on to the wrong vessel.'

'I don't understand,' Lucinda stammers. 'What do you mean, the wrong vessel? Where are our supplies?'

The consul hands Lucinda the telegram, and the truth hits her like a fist to the stomach: all their precious things are somewhere at sea, on an unknown ship, destined for God knows where.

In the space of seconds, the entire endeavour has been thrown into doubt. 'But our medical equipment is essential,' Lucinda protests, voice rising in pitch, sounding to her own ears like a kettle reaching boiling point. 'Are we to be expected to perform surgery with a kitchen knife?'

Florence places a calming hand on Lucinda's sleeve.

'Please don't worry, Dr Garland,' the consul replies. 'There will be a solution.'

'Monsieur Brasier de Thuy promised he had everything arranged,' Florence interrupts. 'What can be done about this?'

Before the consul can answer, Guérin turns on the boy, gripping his arm and berating him. Tears well in the child's eyes.

'It's not his fault!' Lucinda cries. She bites down on the fury threatening to erupt, the telegram from England crumpled in her fist. The boy breaks away from Guérin's grip, sprinting off into the night.

'These mistakes happen more often than you'd think,' the consul says, with a small sigh. 'The matter will be resolved, I have no doubt.' Lucinda garners little solace from his words.

Guérin mutters a French expletive, and strides away towards his fleet of trucks without a backward glance.

A murmur ripples through the group, and Lucinda can only look in mute despair at Florence. *What on earth should they do?*

'Please, you must come to the Customs Office now,' the consul says, ushering Lucinda and the group along the quay. 'Will this turn of events alter your plans at all, Dr Garland?'

'What do you mean?' Lucinda feels weary to her bones.

'Well, perhaps while you wait for the other ship to turn up, you and your staff could assist us.'

Lucinda is unable to form the words to reject his plea again.

'Much as we'd like to help, sir,' Florence interjects, coming to Lucinda's rescue, 'our plans mustn't deviate. The French Red Cross are expecting us in Paris tonight. They have premises they need us to inspect so that's where we must go.'

'Of course. You must do as you see fit.'

At the Customs Office, the paperwork is finally authorized, and the consul promises Lucinda and Florence that he will contact them through the French Red Cross headquarters in Paris, as soon as he hears word of the lost equipment.

'Should me an' Mr Tozer stay here?' Figgis suggests to Lucinda. 'Make sure the Frenchies transport the right stuff onwards?'

Lucinda grits her teeth, declining Figgis's offer. 'I'd rather we all stay together, Mr Figgis,' she says, sounding to her own ears like some overwrought schoolmistress losing control of her class.

'All due respect, ma'am,' Figgis argues, 'these Frenchies are a tricky lot. They might take notice of us blokes.'

Lucinda draws herself up to her full five feet six and a half inches, her glare almost on a level with the porter's belligerent chin. 'I don't think it's the French who are responsible for this turn of events, Mr Figgis,' she answers. 'The mistake was made in England, was it not? Now let us proceed.'

The group boards one of the last trains to Paris, the onward journey painfully slow through a dark, obscure landscape. From Pontoise onwards, the train stops at seemingly every branch station, where railway workers and the occasional dubious-looking woman press their faces to the carriage windows.

'We could be aliens from another planet,' Grace remarks, with a nervous laugh.

Lucinda, no stranger to unwanted attention in her years working in a male-dominated profession, smiles wryly at the young doctor's comment. But the eyes of these strangers staring through the glass are unsettling, nevertheless.

As the train reaches the outskirts of Paris, the clear night sky is lit up with sweeping searchlights. Through the window, Lucinda watches the piercing beams, listening to the distant rumble of what she wants to believe is thunder but knows must be guns.

She locks eyes with Florence, sitting opposite, and tries to muster a smile. Her dear friend hasn't spoken more than a few words since leaving Dieppe. 'Are you all right, Flo?' *Are you regretting this?*

'That's not a storm, is it?' Florence replies faintly.

'No, I don't think it is,' Lucinda says.

Florence breaks eye contact, turning to stare out of the window again, and Lucinda longs to close the gap between them. If only she could swap places with Grace, and fold Florence into her arms. Hold her.

But, of course, she can't. Florence may as well be on the other side of the Channel, not a mere two feet away, for all she can reach her.

They arrive at the Gare du Nord to find the station in semi-darkness. Apart from a couple of tramps wandering the platform, the place is eerily deserted. Lucinda prays that the room reservations Monsieur Brasier de Thuy promised to make on their behalf at the Station Hotel haven't also been lost. She longs to lie down in a soft bed and close her eyes. Wake up to a new day.

To everyone's consternation, it is soon discovered that the entrance from the concourse to the Station Hotel next door has been locked, presumably in response to some curfew.

'Told you the Frenchies couldn't be trusted,' Figgis grumbles, loudly enough for Lucinda to overhear. 'We'll be stuck in 'ere till morning now.'

'There must be a solution,' Lucinda declares, trying to remain calm. But there are practically no railway guards on duty, and when one is finally located he appears to be no more than sixteen and professes not to understand Lucinda's attempts to speak French. Even Mardie's efforts are met with blank confusion.

Figgis and Tozer find a couple of abandoned luggage trolleys, and load the team's bags on to these. At least their personal belongings are safe, Lucinda thinks.

'Dr Garland?'

Someone is calling her from further along the platform. Lucinda spots the slight figure of one of the orderlies, Olga Campbell, waving. What on earth was the girl doing all the way down there?

'Miss Campbell? Kindly stay with the group,' Lucinda warns, her voice feeble in the echoing station.

'I've found another way out,' Olga shouts back.

Figgis and Tozer begin shunting the luggage carts towards the girl, closely followed by the rest of the group.

'I wish the ground would stop moving,' Florence

remarks, as she and Lucinda follow in the team's wake. 'It's really quite disconcerting.'

True, Lucinda thinks, though it's not just the effect of the sea crossing that's making her queasy. Already she feels dangerously out of her depth.

To Lucinda's relief, Olga has indeed discovered another way out. At the Station Hotel next door, a sleepy night receptionist receives the party of exhausted travellers, confirming reservations have indeed been placed.

Thank the Lord, Lucinda wants to cry.

'Your rooms are on the third floor,' the receptionist informs the group. 'The lift is broken.'

Of course it is.

Bags are heaved up three flights of dimly lit stairs, and Lucinda allocates rooms. With no kitchen open at this late hour, no way of cooking anything substantial, Lucinda and Florence distribute the last of the sandwiches and fruitcake donated by well-wishers in London. They will have to picnic in the bedrooms. Tozer has brought a little portable stove with him, and offers to make tea for those who want it, though there's no milk or sugar.

Drawing on the last of her strength, Lucinda visits each room briefly, wishing the occupant a good night. Too tired to eat anything, she returns to her own room, and is unbuttoning her tunic when there is a tap at the door.

What calamity has happened now?

'It's only me,' Florence says, as she comes into the room.

Lucinda fumbles to do up her buttons again. 'I thought you'd gone to bed, Flo.'

'I wanted to say well done for today.' Florence's face is

pale, her eyes tired, but her smile is bright as sunshine and, *oh, Lord*, Lucinda loves her. The thought winds her, and she can't catch her breath for a moment.

'I'll let you sleep.' Florence turns to go. 'Wait.' Without thinking, Lucinda snatches her friend's sleeve, tugging her back. Immediately, realization hits, and she releases Florence, stumbling back a step.

'I'm sorry,' Lucinda stammers. 'I didn't mean to . . .'

Florence blinks, a hesitant smile hovering on her lips. Lucinda drags her eyes back to meet her friend's bemused gaze.

'I only wanted to say,' Lucinda forges on, 'I'm glad you're here . . .'

There follows a moment of silence, during which Lucinda struggles to gather herself. Should she apologize for grabbing Florence's sleeve? But too late, Florence is retreating into the shadowy corridor, wishing her a good night.

Lucinda closes her door again, and collapses on to the narrow bed. She gives up the thought of undressing, pulls the thin blanket over her legs, and waits for sleep's oblivion to claim her.

Madame Pérouse, of the French Red Cross, arrives at the Station Hotel shortly after breakfast. Lucinda and Florence receive her in the shabby lounge. The middle-aged woman has a small lapdog lodged snugly in the crook of her plump elbow, as though she's nursing a baby, Lucinda thinks. Madame Pérouse is accompanied by an American expatriate doctor in his forties, who enthusiastically shakes Lucinda and Florence's hands.

'Lewis Johnson,' the Texan doctor introduces himself. 'Welcome to Paris.'

Lucinda thanks him, wanting to know what his experience of the city has been, and where he's practising medicine, but Madame Pérouse is already speaking.

'Our city, it is in pain,' she says. Her English is precise but heavily accented, and Lucinda must concentrate to understand her. The Frenchwoman explains that the government and the National Assembly had left Paris some weeks ago, transferring to Bordeaux where it's deemed to be safer.

'How far away are the Germans?' Florence asks.

Her question provokes a memory for Lucinda. She'd read in the newspapers the previous month something about Paris taxis transporting troops fifty kilometres from the city to the Marne battlefields.

'Not far enough,' Dr Johnson replies grimly.

'Official *communiqués* tell us little,' Madame Pérouse adds. 'We look to the *colonnes* for news.'

'*Colonnes*?' Lucinda asks.

Dr Johnson explains how news posters are displayed on the Morris columns that pepper the city streets. 'It's the French method of communicating speeches, announcements and call-ups,' he says.

The method sounds worryingly haphazard and unreliable to Lucinda.

'Madame Pérouse tells me you're aiming to set up a hospital here.' Dr Johnson's perceptive gaze radiates unspoken admiration, and it occurs to Lucinda that this man, with his dark skin, is no stranger to prejudice and discrimination. Just as she and her female colleagues constantly struggle to be taken seriously in the patriarchal field of medicine, Lucinda suspects that Dr Johnson has faced comparable challenges and obstacles in his medical career.

'That's the plan,' Lucinda replies, 'although our equipment is currently still en route.'

'Are you practising here in Paris, Dr Johnson?' Florence asks.

'In Neuilly,' Johnson replies. 'The hospital's been operational for just a short while, but the casualties we've seen so far . . .' He gives a low whistle, shaking his head. 'Like nothing I've experienced back home, let me tell you. Be prepared for the worst injuries you could ever imagine.'

The American doctor's words render Lucinda momentarily speechless.

'Madame Pérouse thought you might welcome some assistance,' Dr Johnson continues. 'I can help steer you away from some of the pitfalls I've encountered myself.'

'We would very much welcome that,' Lucinda replies, exchanging a glance with Florence. 'Pitfalls' sounds ominous.

'Have premises been found for us?' Florence asks Madame Pérouse.

The woman shifts position on her chair, and her dog emits a surprisingly deep growl for its size.

'Ssh, Bijou,' Madame Pérouse admonishes the animal, tapping it on its twitching wet nose. 'There has been a . . . how do you say? . . . a setback.'

'A setback?' Lucinda says. 'In what way?'

'Please, you must not be worried. It will be resolved.'

'What will be resolved?' Florence presses. 'Is there some problem with the premises, Madame?'

'We had secured the perfect location,' Madame Pérouse replies, 'but this morning, it is no longer available.'

By her own admission, Madame Pérouse is uncertain of the current situation regarding other suitable vacant premises in the city. She explains that there are three separate branches of the Red Cross, as well as the Army Medical Department and the military governor of Paris, all of whom are actively searching for properties to turn into hospitals.

'I've heard the Grand Palais is even being considered,' Dr Johnson adds.

As Madame Pérouse apologizes, in her careful English, for the dearth of potential premises, her grey-muzzled dog regards Lucinda with a baleful expression, as if it's heard its mistress's blather many times before.

Just as Lucinda is beginning to lose hope, Madame Pérouse remembers one place that might suffice. 'The Hôtel Clarens is currently empty,' she explains. 'It is closed at present to guests, and might suit your needs.'

'*Completely* empty?' Lucinda queries.

'*Oui*,' the Frenchwoman replies. 'Only the hotel manager remains there, I understand.'

'Is he the caretaker?' Lucinda says.

'The manager is more the hotel owner's representative,' Madame Pérouse clarifies.

'Is the owner happy for us to appropriate their hotel, do you think?' Florence asks.

Madame Pérouse considers the question, then nods. '*Oui*,' she replies.

'How soon can we see it?' Lucinda looks from Madame Pérouse to Dr Johnson. 'Are you free to come with us, sir?' It would be useful to have the American doctor's opinion on the place.

'I'd be honoured to give my assistance, ma'am,' Dr Johnson replies, flashing her a smile.

Madame Pérouse strokes her lapdog's little head and, to Lucinda's relief, agrees to take them to the hotel *immédiatement*. The dog blinks its beadlike eyes and yawns.

Leaving the rest of the group to finish their breakfast and complete their ablutions, Lucinda and Florence follow Madame Pérouse and Dr Johnson out into the muggy morning heat of the city. A passing motor-cab is hailed, and they set off towards the wide, tree-lined Champs-Élysées. The avenue is already busy with pedestrians, cyclists and sinister grey military trucks. To Lucinda's surprise, there are almost no motor-cars, buses or horse-drawn vehicles to be seen.

Most have been requisitioned by the army, Madame Pérouse informs the women. 'My brother had all his horses taken last week,' she tells them sadly.

The cab deposits them outside the Hôtel Clarens, and Lucinda's first impression of the elegant, seven-storey building is promising. There are no doormen, and Madame Pérouse leads the way into the hotel's huge mirrored foyer. Crystal chandeliers cast a glittering light, and Lucinda gazes about, overcome by the unexpectedly grand surroundings.

'The *surveillant*, Monsieur Cassard, I must find him,' Madame Pérouse tells Lucinda and Florence. She bustles off down a corridor with her dog, leaving Lucinda wondering what it must be like to have this place of marble staircases and diamond chandeliers entirely to oneself.

While Madame Pérouse is searching for the manager, Lucinda, Florence and Dr Johnson explore the downstairs salons, four spacious rooms that Dr Johnson pronounces ideal as potential wards. 'Plenty of space,' he says. 'For now, at least,' he adds ominously.

Florence points out the evidence of recent renovation. The windows are covered with whitewash, while empty paint pots and used brushes litter the floor.

'There's some clearing up to do,' Lucinda concedes. 'But it's almost perfect, don't you think?'

Florence agrees. It's far more luxurious than either of them could ever have hoped for.

Their discussion is cut short by the return of Madame Pérouse. She has a short, dark-haired man in tow, but it's not the hotel overseer, whom she's been unable to find. Instead, Lucinda and Florence are introduced to the hotel's chief engineer, Monsieur Perrin. The engineer wipes oily hands on his stained overalls, and greets the women with a baffled look.

'You make a hospital here?' he asks, in broken English.

'That is our intention, yes, *Monsieur*,' Lucinda replies. 'My colleague Dr Maberry and I have come from England. We're both doctors.'

'We want to help France,' Florence adds.

Monsieur Perrin considers this, frowning. He looks at Dr Johnson. 'And you, *Monsieur*?'

'I already have a hospital, thanks,' the Texan drawls.

'The light,' Perrin gestures to the chandeliers, 'not always working.'

'The electricity supply can be patchy,' Dr Johnson adds helpfully.

Lucinda exchanges a glance with Florence.

'The water,' the engineer continues, 'not always hot.'

While this isn't exactly welcome news, it's not insurmountable, Lucinda thinks. 'As long as we have some means of heating water, I'm sure we'll manage,' she says, and Florence nods. They've managed before, in far less salubrious circumstances.

Madame Pérouse says something to Perrin, who responds in rapid, unintelligible French, punctuated with vigorous hand gestures. 'Monsieur Perrin says he is fixing the water problem,' the Frenchwoman translates. 'But it may take a day or two. He works alone here.'

'We understand,' Florence says, smiling at the engineer.

Lucinda takes a breath, meets Florence's eye, and some unspoken understanding pulses between them. It's a look they've so often shared across an operating table that it needs no words. Lucinda knows, without having to confirm aloud with Florence, that her friend feels as she does: that this magnificent shell of marble and gilt, though presently without consistent heating or hot water, and despite the work that must be done to make it ready, is perfect.

'This hotel more than suits our needs,' Lucinda says to Madame Pérouse. 'If permission is given, when do you think we may move in?'

'I see no reason to delay,' Madame Pérouse replies.

Paperwork must be signed, of course, but Madame Pérouse surprises Lucinda with her administrative efficiency. The very next day, Lucinda and Florence are given permission to start their preparations, with the lease of the hotel funded by the French Red Cross.

The rest of the Corps are summoned from the Station Hotel, and Lucinda gathers everyone in the foyer. The morning has barely begun, yet already she can feel sweat sliding down her back beneath her tunic. She decides to allow everyone to work in shirtsleeves today, though Florence will doubtless keep her tunic on: however hot it gets, she seems to have a preternatural ability to remain cool.

'Welcome to our new hospital,' Lucinda addresses the group. 'As you can see, the hotel is quite large enough for our purposes, with plenty of bedrooms for us to board here. Dr Maberry and I have met the resident engineer, Monsieur Perrin, and he has promised that the hot water will be working as soon as he can make the repairs.'

'I'm a plumber,' Figgis pipes up. 'Tell me where this bloke Perrin is, and I can give him a hand.'

'That's very helpful of you, Mr Figgis,' Florence replies.

'You never said you were in the plumbing trade,' Lucinda adds.

Figgis crosses his arms. 'You never asked.'

Fair enough, Lucinda thinks. 'Has anyone any questions?' she asks the group.

Dr Hazel returns Lucinda's brave smile. 'I have a question, Doctor. How will we manage if our equipment doesn't arrive?'

'Good question,' Florence replies, shooting Lucinda a look that speaks volumes. *How indeed will we manage?*

Lucinda reassures them that if she hasn't had word from the Customs House at Dieppe by tomorrow, she will telegraph to Monsieur Brasier de Thuy again. 'I'm hopeful our equipment will be returned to us very soon,' she says, sounding to her own ears more confident than she feels. To her relief, no one presses her on what will happen if the equipment never materializes, or if Monsieur Brasier de Thuy is unable to help.

Galantha, standing alongside her sister, Hazel, raises her hand shyly. The siblings, though close in age, don't look alike: Hazel is petite and olive-skinned, Galantha long-legged with straw-blonde hair. The young orderly suffered terribly from seasickness on the journey over, and still looks wan.

'Will you need us to cook for everyone, Dr Garland?' Galantha asks.

'Another good question.' Lucinda glances at Florence.

'We haven't properly investigated the kitchens yet,' Florence answers, 'but we will do so this morning. The French Red Cross is finding supplies of food for us.'

'We've been informed a chef will be loaned to us,' Lucinda adds. This is according to Madame Pérouse's information, but when the chef is likely to appear is anyone's guess. 'Rest assured, it's at the top of my list to address the issue of meals.'

Lucinda's gaze moves swiftly on to Dr Grace, whose slight build belies an enduring strength. Lucinda has worked alongside her at several exhausting operations at the New Hospital for Women.

'Doctor, when are we expected to be operational?' Grace asks.

'I hope within a few days,' Lucinda replies. 'Meanwhile, all we can do is prepare as best we can, until our equipment arrives.'

*

Once the group have been given a brief tour of the hotel, Florence allocates bedrooms. She's already chosen adjoining rooms on the first floor for herself and Lucinda. 'We need to be close for ease of communication,' she says.

Lucinda's heart stutters.

Gertrude, Hazel and Grace are on the same corridor as Lucinda and Florence.

'I wasn't expecting to have my own room,' Gertrude comments. 'It's awfully plush.'

'Thought we'd be packed in together like sardines,' Grace says. 'This is far nicer than I ever dreamed.'

'We're certainly fortunate to have the entire building at our disposal,' Lucinda agrees. A dream come true.

'Even the sheets are made of silk,' Hazel points out.

The bedding is indeed of the highest quality cotton and silk. Will they have to use this for the patients? Lucinda wonders. If the bedding from home doesn't turn up soon, they'll have no choice, though the thought of this pristine material soiled with blood and other bodily fluids doesn't bear thinking about. The French Red Cross will have to bear the cost of replacing any ruined bedding.

Sister Bryony and her team of seven nurses have been allocated rooms on the second floor. Lucinda leads the way up the rear tradesmen's staircase, and the nurses siphon off to their respective rooms. Sister Bryony's looks out over an enclosed courtyard at the back of the hotel. The space is filled with round tables and ornate chairs, the white-painted metal glinting in the morning sun.

'All to your liking, I trust, Sister?' Lucinda asks. She's worked with the Irishwoman for many years, and has as much respect for Bryony as for any of her fellow doctors.

'Sure, I've never stayed anywhere so grand, Doctor.' Sister Bryony's eyes sparkle. 'I'll no doubt get used to it in time.'

Leaving her to unpack, Lucinda travels up to the third floor, where the orderlies are sharing one large suite. She finds Galantha, Mardie and Olga gathered in the bathroom, exclaiming over what looks to Lucinda like a second lavatory.

'It's a bidet,' Mardie informs everyone. 'For washing your . . .' She pats her small behind. Olga snorts. Galantha's face turns puce.

Lucinda presses her lips together, swallowing her mirth. She senses more than a hint of devilry in Mardie and Olga, and suspects they'll need precious little encouragement to misbehave. She'll have to keep a close eye on them.

Finally, Lucinda pays a visit to the three men. Florence has given them individual bedrooms located on the fourth floor, and Lucinda finds Figgis and Tozer drinking tea and smoking cigarettes in Penhaligon's room. The young Quaker himself is sitting on his bed, looking close to tears.

'Look sharp, lads,' Figgis says throwing a mock salute in Lucinda's direction. 'Boss is here.'

Lucinda squares her shoulders. 'Everything all right, gentlemen?' She will not allow a plumber to ruffle her.

'Lad's feeling a bit sick,' Tozer informs her.

She looks at Penhaligon on the bed. 'Are you still suffering from the ship?' she asks. He certainly looks a little green around the gills.

'Homesick,' Figgis corrects her, stubbing out his cigarette in the hearth.

Lucinda crosses to the window and tugs it open. 'Some fresh air might help,' she says pointedly. 'Is there anything I can get for you, Penhaligon?'

'I'm – I'm sorry, ma'am,' Penhaligon stammers.

'No need to apologize,' Lucinda assures him. 'Why don't you rest for a while?' she adds, with as much patience as she can summon. 'When you're settled in, and have had something to eat, you'll feel better.'

'Thank you, ma'am.' Penhaligon sniffs.

'I'll see you downstairs in an hour, gentlemen,' Lucinda says, at the door. 'There's much to do.'

II

Edie: October 1914

The recruits are granted a mere few hours to bid their families and loved ones goodbye. Perhaps it's a blessing, Edie thinks, to have so little time to dwell on the dangers ahead.

While Stanley and the other men dash home, or write hasty letters to their wives, girlfriends and families, Edie scribbles a note to Sylvia Pankhurst, promising to be in touch again as soon as she's able. She wishes she could say a proper goodbye to her friend, thank her for everything she's done, but there's no time.

That night, Edie and the rest of the platoon are ordered to remain at Hurst Park. The stable blocks and a rear section of the grandstand have been turned into rudimentary barracks, and Edie tries to prepare herself for a night among the men.

The windowless stables have been fitted out with rough-hewn wooden bunks, an aisle the width of a stride separating them. Straw carpets the floor, a smell of horse manure lingering in the air, and Edie's knees weaken as she follows Stanley into the gloomy space. Childhood memories of the workhouse assail her, and all she can think of are ranks of utilitarian beds filled with ragged bodies reeking of destitution and despair.

A sudden memory of her mother comes to her. Ma's days were spent in the workhouse laundry, toiling for hours in the scalding steam. This meant Edie's bedding was changed more often than most, but the price her mother paid was high. How many times had Ma suffered punishment at the hands of the governor for the crime of giving her daughter a clean sheet?

Someone shoves Edie in the back, and she stumbles. 'Out the fucking way, boy,' Caldwell snarls, as he pushes past.

Edie forces herself to move, joining Stanley at the back of the stables, where she finds him stowing his kitbag beneath a bunk.

'Take the top, Lawrence,' he tells her. 'Skinny as a barber's cat, you are.'

Edie hoists her kitbag on to the upper bunk, then sets a foot on the rickety ladder. The wooden frame creaks as she clambers up. Her bed for the night is a thin straw mattress laid over a base of misshapen chicken wire. The whole structure sags alarmingly beneath her meagre weight.

Banter and curses fill the air, and Edie tries to shut out the men's filthy talk, but it's impossible. Beneath her, Stanley is whistling quietly to himself. She lowers herself on to her back, staring up at the slatted, cobwebbed roof pressing down on her, like a coffin lid. Worries swirl through her mind. What if she talks in her sleep? How did she ever think she could keep her sex concealed in France?

Will she ever see Nate again?

She slips the notebook from her pocket, fumbles for a stub of pencil.

Oct '14 she scribbles. *Last night on home soil. France tomorrow.*

'You ever been overseas, Lawrence?' Stanley's voice drifts up through the chicken wire. Edie tucks away the notebook again, as the question brings a long-forgotten memory floating to the surface of her mind. One of the workhouse guardians, old Mr Shorrock, had once given a magic-lantern show in the dining hall when Edie was eight or nine. He had just returned from one of Cook's circular tours through Europe, and he proudly described where he'd been, leaving such an impression on Edie that she could remember every place name even now: Dover, Ostend, Brussels, Lucerne, Genoa, Rome, Monte Carlo, Calais. She remembers asking her mother if they, too, could go to Europe, one day. Ma had smiled, but the smile hadn't quite reached her eyes, and she'd given her usual answer, the one she gave to all Edie's fantastical questions: 'Where there's breath, there's hope, Edie.'

But hope had run out for her mother in the end.

A tide of grief sweeps over Edie now, and she roughly wipes her eyes with a sleeve. 'No.'

'Me neither,' Stanley says.

He goes quiet for a time, and then, 'Reckon I've got it, Lawrence.'

'Got what?'

'You was nicking some sausages, and the butcher punched you in the snout.'

Edie smiles up at the cobwebs. 'Nope.'

'Or – hear me out, kid – you was running away from the butcher, and you ran into a lamp post.'

'Way off.'

'Bollocks.' Stanley resumes his tuneless whistle, and Edie closes her eyes.

Moments later, Caldwell's voice, loud and close, jolts her alert.

'Get your arses down here, boys!'

Edie tenses, barely breathing. If she stays quiet and still, a mouse in the shadows, perhaps Caldwell will forget she's even here.

'Hey, Lawrence.' Stanley's voice, again.

'What?' she whispers back.

'You coming?'

'What for?'

'Crown 'n' Anchor.'

Edie knows this sailor's game: men in the workhouse used to play for matchsticks sometimes. 'Nah.'

'Let's see the colour of your brass, you bastards!' Caldwell hectors.

The ladder creaks, and Stanley's head appears. Edie stifles a curse, as he pokes her in the ribs.

'Come on, kid.'

There's nowhere to hide.

Dread curdling in the pit of her stomach, Edie joins Stanley and the rest of the platoon clustered around Caldwell's bunk. On the floor is a square foot of white material, divided into six sections, each containing a simple shape daubed in black and red paint. In the gloom, Edie can just make out the four suits of a deck of cards: spades, clubs, diamonds, hearts. The fifth section contains what looks like a crown, and the sixth a roughly drawn anchor.

'I dunno how to play,' young Jackson whines. His wide, anxious gaze meets Edie's, and she gives him a surreptitious smile of sympathy. She doesn't really know how to play this game either, or at least how to play to win. She'd tried to keep clear of the gambling men in the workhouse.

'You've got six pictures, see?' Caldwell explains to the boy. 'Crown's the sergeant major, spade's a shovel, diamond's a curse, anchor's a meat hook, heart's a dart, and club's a shamrock. Got that?'

Jackson stares down at the images, rubbing his pimply brow.

Caldwell holds a clenched fist towards the boy, gives it a rattling shake, uncurls his fingers. 'Three dice, each with different pictures on 'em, see?' Jackson peers at the little hand-carved cubes of wood in Caldwell's dirty palm.

'Bet on a picture,' Caldwell says, 'an' if it comes up trumps on the dice, you get your stake back. Easy.'

The rules are clear enough, Edie thinks. Jackson, however, is still rubbing his brow.

Caldwell fists the dice again. 'Gather round, lads.' His voice lowers to a sinister purr. 'Who's bold, then?'

Bembridge is the first to bet, setting a silver shilling on the image of the anchor, and a further two coins on the shamrock.

Caldwell kneels in the straw, shakes the dice in his hand, releases them to tumble over the cloth. 'Two darts an' a sergeant major. Unlucky.' He scoops the shillings off the board, and the game continues.

Edie watches closely, as money is lost and won and lost again. Caldwell's pockets fill, coin by coin, but still the game continues. The dice are likely loaded, Edie thinks. She's seen it all before.

After a while, an elbow jabs her ribs. 'I'm skint,' Stanley mutters. 'Stand us a coupla bob, kid?'

Edie has precious few coins left to squander. Every fibre of her being screams at her to refuse Stanley and walk away. Yet he's her only friend here. She needs him on her side.

'Cheers, kid.' Stanley sets Edie's shilling on the red-painted heart. Other bets are placed, and Caldwell rolls the dice.

'Double dart,' Caldwell spits. He tosses two shillings at Stanley, who grins and claps Edie on the shoulder.

'Once more for luck, eh?' Stanley sets his coins on the heart again, and urges Edie to place two of her shillings on the black club.

Caldwell rolls, and the dice turn up in Edie's favour.

Luck of the devil, a voice whispers in Edie's ear. She meets Bembridge's shrewd eye.

Within half an hour, Edie has won ten shillings off Caldwell. Most of the other men have lost money. Stanley and Jackson have nothing left, and Jackson looks on the brink of tears. Edie hopes he's learned his lesson.

A bugle blasts from outside, the signal for lights out.

Edie pockets her winnings and is about to escape to her bunk, when Caldwell grips her arm. 'You want to be careful, boy.' Caldwell's face is in shadow, his voice low with menace. 'Luck never gives. It only lends.'

Edie suffers a restless night, waking with a thick head, her back aching. An ominous sky, heavy with cloud, presses down as she follows the platoon out to the parade ground. Each man must pack his kit before the eagle eyes of the officers. Edie contemplates her pile of equipment: a hundred and twenty rounds of ball ammunition, a spare pair of socks and a shirt, a mess tin, a spoon and a knife, a rolled groundsheet, a first-aid field-dressing kit, a seven-inch bayonet in a leather scabbard and a rifle. Thirty-five pounds of dead weight she must carry on her back. She tries not to think about this.

Preparations continue after a hasty breakfast: equipment is checked and rechecked, pay books filled in, identity discs issued, rifles cleaned, boots dubbined, and typhoid inoculations administered, after which Edie's arm throbs as though someone has punched it. Finally, they are given their marching rations, comprising a tin of bully beef and a packet of plain biscuits.

'Save them for later, boys,' Bembridge advises, when a few of the men immediately rip open the biscuits. Edie stows hers in her pack.

After dinner, the platoon is granted an hour's rest, and Edie retreats to the bunkhouse. To her dismay, she finds Caldwell prowling, trading cigarettes for tins of bully beef.

'A packet of fags is a fair swap,' Edie hears him arguing with Jackson.

'But I don't smoke,' the boy whines.

'Time you fucking started, then.'

All too soon, the platoon is ordered to form up on the parade ground, ready to depart. Edie takes her place in line, the weight of her kit pulling on her shoulders. A thin rain begins to fall. Major Pryce arrives, accompanying Sergeant Ratigan on a final inspection of the troops.

'You'll embark from Southampton,' Major Pryce informs the platoon. 'By this time tomorrow, God willing, you'll be on French soil.'

Murmurs ripple through the ranks.

'Silence in the lines!' Sergeant Ratigan roars.

'In your hearts,' the major continues, when the men are quiet again, 'each one of you is ready to fight. It is your duty to preserve the principles of freedom and sovereignty, to defend those unable to defend themselves. You are fighting men, and you will not cease to fight until this war is won.'

The men are listening now.

'Like those who have gone before, you face the biggest challenge of your life,' Major Pryce concludes. 'Go forth with courage, men. Go with fire in your hearts. God be with you.'

12

Lucinda: October 1914

With Monsieur Perrin's assistance, Lucinda sketches a
rough floor plan of the hotel on the back of a large sheet
of wallpaper left by the workmen. They need to decide
where best to situate the operating theatre, the dispensary,
the stores and more. Once the sketch is complete, the
engineer hurries back to the boiler room, a place of baf-
fling valves and alarming steam that he'd shown Lucinda
earlier. He'd also taken her to the electrical room, full of
panels of levers that Perrin promised could illuminate far-
flung rooms, or plunge whole sections of the hospital
into darkness.

Florence joins Lucinda at the reception desk in the deserted main foyer, and together they study the map of their
new hospital as though scrutinizing a board game. Lucinda
mentally moves furniture and equipment from one room
to another, each item a chess piece.

The spacious downstairs ladies' cloakroom, with its
pavement access, hot water supply, tiled walls and floor,
washbasins and light-reflecting mirrors will provide an
ideal operating theatre, they decide.

'The stores should go in the basement,' Florence says.
'There's plenty of cool space down there, at least.'

Lucinda agrees this would be a good place to store

perishables, spare medicine and suchlike, should they ever receive anything from England. The missing equipment plays on her mind, but there's little she can do about it.

'Mardie Hodgson,' Florence remarks. 'Didn't we say she'd be good as a quartermaster's assistant?'

'What about Tozer for the role of quartermaster?' Lucinda suggests. 'Would those two work well together?' She pictures the young orderly with the glint of mischief in her eyes, and tries to imagine her taking orders from the affable older man. 'Perhaps if we put them both on a short trial?' she adds. 'That way, if it doesn't work out, we can move people about.'

Florence agrees this is wise.

'The four salons off the foyer,' Lucinda says, pointing them out on the map. 'Do you agree these are sufficient in size for the main wards?'

'Dr Johnson estimated there should be capacity for at least a hundred men.' Florence pencils '25 beds' into each of the quartet of rooms. 'There's a lot of furniture to shift first, though,' she muses.

'I was also thinking,' Lucinda ventures, 'perhaps we could name the wards after female saints?'

'What a wonderful idea!' Florence smiles, touching Lucinda's hand, sending a shiver up her arm.

'How about St Abigail for Ward One?' Lucinda suggests. 'She's the patron saint of honeybees. Did you know? I'm imagining this hospital as our hive, and we its worker bees.'

'And you're our queen bee, Lucie,' Florence teases.

Lucinda can't help but laugh, her cheeks warming. She ploughs on. 'Ward Two could be named for St Bernadette, patron saint of the sick. What do you think?'

'We shall have need of her mercy in the days to come,' Florence agrees. 'How about St Cecilia for Ward Three?'

'I don't think I know that one . . .'

'I'm sure I read somewhere she's the patron saint of music.'

'I wonder if there's a gramophone somewhere.' Lucinda makes a mental note to send the orderlies on a hunt for one at the first opportunity. Music in the wards would lift everyone's spirits.

'And for the last ward . . .' Lucinda ponders, 'St Dymphna?'

Florence gives her a questioning look.

'She's the patron saint of nervous afflictions,' Lucinda explains, with a knowing smile.

'I rather think we'll need her beneficence,' Florence concedes. 'Excellent choices, Lucie.'

The X-ray equipment, when it finally arrives, will require darkness for the plates to develop. Lucinda agrees with Florence that a large windowless storeroom situated near the kitchens and currently containing spare cutlery and crockery is the best place for it.

Lucinda suggests that the rather grand grill room, with its skylights and marble columns, lends itself to a suitable chapel and a temporary mortuary. Florence marks it on the map with a simple cross.

'What are we going to feed everyone for lunch today?' Florence asks.

'Oh, figs!' Lucinda curses. 'I meant to ask Madame Pérouse when her chef might arrive.' She glances at her wristwatch, alarmed to find it's almost midday already. It's an age since she ate a hurried breakfast at the Station

Hotel, but she doesn't feel hungry, only a strong urge to roll up her sleeves and start work.

Monsieur Perrin appears at that moment to report, by a combination of rudimentary English and hand gestures, that he's fixed the hot-water problem.

'*Bravo! Merci.*' Florence smiles at him, and he blushes beneath his layers of grease.

How much is the engineer's work costing? Lucinda frets. She has yet to establish with Madame Pérouse who will pay any workmen they might employ. '*Combien, Monsieur?*'

Monsieur Perrin gives his customary shrug. '*Gratis,*' he replies, with a look as if to say, Why do you ask? Before Lucinda can react, he hastens away.

Florence heads off to investigate the prospective X-ray room, and Lucinda decides to visit the kitchens. Perhaps she'll find some food the orderlies can rustle up for lunch.

As she approaches the kitchens at the rear of the hotel, a rhythmic chopping sound greets her. She pushes open the mahogany and glass doors, revealing a cavernous room. A corpulent man in a white uniform, a towel tucked in the waistband of his apron, is working at a far counter. He appears oblivious to Lucinda's arrival, and she's forced to clear her throat loudly. '*Bonjour, Monsieur,*' she ventures. *Please, God, let this man speak English.*

The chef looks round. '*Oui?*'

'*Bonjour,*' Lucinda says again, keeping a wary eye on the enormous knife gripped in the man's fist. 'I'm Dr Lucinda Garland.' The chef's glare doesn't alter, but to Lucinda's relief he sets his knife down. Did he understand her?

'*Comprenez-vous l'anglais, Monsieur?*'

'A little,' the chef concedes gruffly.

'Oh, good,' Lucinda breathes. 'Madame Pérouse mentioned a chef, but I didn't realize you'd arrived already, Monsieur.'

'Madame Pérouse asked me to begin today.'

'That's wonderful,' Lucinda replies. 'Will you need to know numbers of staff, Monsieur?'

'I know already.'

'I see,' Lucinda replies, rather thrown by this response. 'And what about menus and food choices?'

'It is all agreed, Madame.' The chef takes up his knife again, sets to chopping another huge onion.

Lucinda can't think what to say to this. What does the chef mean, it is all agreed? She makes a mental note to contact Madame Pérouse, find out what exactly she's told this man.

'I beg your pardon, Monsieur, but can I ask your name?'

'Achille,' the chef grunts.

'Your services are being paid for by the French Red Cross. Is that right, Monsieur Achille?'

'*Oui.*'

'And you're happy to cater for my staff and the patients when they arrive?'

Achille grunts, and Lucinda decides to take this response for assent. She wants to ask who he's chopping the onion for. Perhaps he's feeding the mysterious manager she's yet to meet.

Lucinda lets her gaze travel around the kitchen, noting the gas ovens, capacious sinks and extensive marble counters. Copper pans of all shapes and sizes hang from hooks in the ceiling, and Lucinda's roving eye alights on four large silver fish kettles, lined up along one counter.

'These would make ideal sterilizing units,' she tells Achille, lifting the lid of the nearest one.

The chef pauses in his chopping, fixing Lucinda with another glare. 'Do not touch my equipment, *s'il vous plaît*.'

Lucinda hesitates. 'Monsieur,' she tries again, 'some of our medical supplies have been delayed from England. We may have to find our operating instruments elsewhere in the meantime. Could we perhaps borrow a couple of your fish kettles for disinfecting purposes?'

'Absolutely not, Madame,' Achille replies, with an undisguised shudder. 'That will not be possible.'

'I see.' Lucinda suppresses a sigh. 'Well, in that case, I shall have to speak to the manager. Do you happen to know where he is, Monsieur?'

Achille doesn't know where Cassard is, but he thinks his suite of rooms might be on the top floor.

'*Merci*.' Lucinda swiftly retreats.

Tracking down Florence, Lucinda relays her brief encounter with Achille and his alarming knife.

'He sounds delightful,' Florence says. 'Did you ask him about menus and budgets?'

'He wasn't very receptive, Flo.'

'What about meals, then? You did ask him about lunch, Lucie?'

'I quite forgot.'

'Lucie!'

'I'm sorry, but he was most unhelpful. I'll speak to him

again, as soon as we've found Cassard. He appears to hold the keys to everything here, or so it seems.'

They follow the chef's directions to the manager's suite, and Lucinda is grateful for Florence's company as she knocks.

The door opens, and a young woman wrapped in a silk dressing-gown pokes her head out. '*Oui?*' The garment barely brushes her knees, her slim bare legs emerging from its folds. Lucinda doesn't know where to look.

'We're sorry to bother you,' she stammers in English. Her limited French has entirely abandoned her. 'Is . . . is Monsieur Cassard here?'

The young woman frowns at Lucinda and Florence, and retreats into the room, closing the door in their faces.

Lucinda exchanges a glance with Florence. What on earth should they do now?

The door is abruptly reopened, making both women start. A portly, moustached man in a shiny dark grey suit fills the doorway. '*Bonjour,*' he greets them. 'You must be the Englishwomen.'

Lucinda stares at the man's raven-black hair, oiled slick to his scalp. Was it dyed? Or was it a toupee?

'*Bonjour, Monsieur,*' Florence says. 'I'm Dr Florence Maberry and this is my colleague, Dr Lucinda Garland. We're here on behalf of the French Red Cross.'

'Come in, come in,' Cassard says, in smooth, barely accented English. 'I've been expecting you.'

He ushers them into his sizeable suite, opulently furnished with chaises-longues and armchairs upholstered in purple velvet, oil paintings adorning the walls. The young woman in the dressing-gown is nowhere to be seen, though Lucinda thinks she hears the gush of a tap beyond what she presumes is a bathroom door.

Cassard crosses the room and opens a window. The suite is at the front of the hotel, and the window looks out over the bustling avenue below. Lucinda wonders if her own little balcony beneath is visible from Cassard's room above.

The manager spins on his heel to face the women. 'Please, sit.' He gestures to a pair of armchairs.

A musty floral fragrance lingers in the air, but Lucinda can't identify the scent. It's like nothing she's smelt before. 'You knew we were here, Monsieur?' she asks. *Why didn't you come and speak to us?*

'*Oui*,' Cassard replies, taking a seat opposite the women. 'I was preparing to introduce myself, when here you are!'

Here we are, indeed. Lucinda's eye is caught by a gilt-framed painting of a hunt hanging above the fireplace: a pack of hounds ripping at a stag's flanks and throat, the creature's eyes full of fatalistic terror.

'So, you intend to open a hospital in my hotel, *Mesdames*?'

'That's right,' Florence replies, and begins to explain the purpose of their newly formed Women's Hospital Corps.

'How many are you?' Cassard interrupts her.

'We have five doctors,' Florence replies, 'including ourselves, eight nurses, three orderlies, and three male porters.'

'I see.' Cassard smoothes his moustache. 'And who is supplying the necessities to maintain your hospital?'

'The French Red Cross are funding us, but we have a source of private income from donations –'

Cassard cuts Lucinda off with a wave of his hand. 'The Red Cross have no authority here,' he says. 'All decisions regarding the Clarens, they must come through me. Do you understand?'

Lucinda senses a subtle shift in the atmosphere, an almost imperceptible drop in temperature, and wonders if Florence feels it too.

Before Lucinda can ask any further questions, Cassard is surging to his feet and moving to the door.

'Ladies.' He smiles only at Florence. 'I welcome you to the Clarens. Treat this as your home, and anything you need, please ask.'

Lucinda looks at Florence, and they rise. The meeting is clearly over.

At the door, Cassard seizes Florence's hand and kisses it several times. 'A delight to meet you,' he says.

'And you, Monsieur Cassard,' Florence murmurs, her cheeks flushing.

'We will talk more anon,' the Frenchman promises. '*Au revoir.*'

Lucinda and Florence are politely but firmly ejected into the corridor, and the door closes smartly behind them.

'There goes someone used to having his own way,' Florence remarks, as they return downstairs.

'Especially with certain ladies,' Lucinda mutters.

'What do you mean?'

'Well, the way he was fawning over you . . .'

'Don't be ridiculous,' Florence scoffs.

Lucinda rolls her tense shoulders.

'Nevertheless, I think it best you deal with him from now on,' Florence says. 'Don't you, Lucie? You seem immune to his . . . flattery.'

That's because his charms are wasted on me, Lucinda wants to reply. But she can't be so sure about Florence. 'Probably for the best,' she agrees.

After a brief lunch of bread and hard cheese, grudgingly supplied by Achille, Lucinda gathers everyone in the foyer. The time has come for them to set to work.

'Sister Bryony,' Lucinda begins, 'will you and some of your nurses clear up the workmen's debris on the ground floor, please.'

While the nurses are busy, Lucinda directs the orderlies to prepare the four main wards. With the men's help, coffee-tables and sofas are removed from the salons, chairs and sideboards are brought in from various ante-rooms, and bookshelves are cleared of ornaments.

The quartet of salons is divided by floor-to-ceiling glass walls, the panes covered with a thin layer of white-wash. This provides a modicum of privacy, but Lucinda asks Galantha to paste spare sheets of wallpaper to the bottom half of the glass walls, creating further seclusion.

Florence designates a trio of vacant bedrooms on the first floor as a storeroom, a dispensary for medicines and other medical supplies when they arrive, and a steri-lizing room. Lucinda sends Mardie to the kitchens in an attempt to borrow two of the fish kettles she spotted earlier. Will the girl be able to work her charm on the chef?

'Monsieur Achille may appreciate your language skills, Hodgson,' Lucinda tells Mardie. 'But if he becomes belligerent just come straight back.'

She considers warning Mardie about the chef's big knife, but the orderly is already dashing away.

As no word has come about the missing medical supplies from England, the women are restricted in what they can do to prepare the ladies' cloakroom as a surgical theatre. But Hazel and Grace find pails, mops and cloths and set to cleaning the floor and the washbasins, as Figgis and Tozer drag a couple of narrow buffet tables from the dining room to function as operating tables.

'The bed situation is worrying me,' Lucinda confides to Florence, during a brief tea break.

'Our beds may never turn up,' Florence responds, 'but that doesn't matter, does it? We have hundreds at our disposal here.'

'But Figgis is dragging his heels. He informed me earlier that it will take days to dismantle the frames in the bedrooms and bring them down to the wards.'

'That man is a ray of sunshine.' Florence sighs. 'Do you want me to speak to him?'

'No. I'll appeal to Tozer. He's much more receptive.'

Lucinda goes in search of the porters, at last locating them in a bedroom on the fourth floor, grappling with mattresses.

'Here she is,' Figgis mutters. 'Our esteemed leader.'

Lucinda ignores his mocking tone.

'How are things progressing, gentlemen?' She directs her question at a worryingly out-of-breath Tozer.

'A cup of tea wouldn't go amiss,' Figgis mutters.

'How many beds have you managed to move so far?' Lucinda continues to ignore Figgis, addressing Tozer. From the corner of her eye she sees Figgis shake his head at Penhaligon.

'Not many, ma'am. Maybe six?' Tozer answers hoarsely. 'It's just that the bases are solid wood, see . . .'

'Oh.' Surreptitiously, Lucinda assesses the older man's flushed features. The last thing she needs is a casualty on her hands before the hospital is even open. 'Perhaps you require more help. I shall send up the orderlies, Mardie and Olga, once they've had their tea.'

'All right for some.' Figgis coughs wetly.

'Did you say something, Mr Figgis?'

'I said, it's all right for some. Dying of thirst up here, we are.'

'Well, I'm happy to show you where the kitchens are, Mr Figgis.' *You'll get on with the chef like a house on fire.*

The porter glares at her, and Lucinda suddenly worries she may have voiced that thought aloud. She forces herself to smile at the porter. She needs these men.

Muttering under his breath, Figgis returns to shifting a mattress, and Lucinda decides to leave them to it.

'I'll send the orderlies up to help,' she says again, and hurries away.

They work through the day and into the evening. As the sun sets over Paris, Monsieur Perrin switches on the electric lights, and the chandeliers bathe the wards in a glittering, silvery glow. Lucinda surveys St Dymphna Ward, marvelling at the transformation of the salon. Despite Figgis's warning, the men have managed to dismantle twenty-five beds, bringing each base and mattress down the service stairs, then reassembling them in the ward.

With the beds in situ, Lucinda and Sister Bryony discuss the linen. The hundred and fifty cotton sheets and blankets, so carefully packed in England, are somewhere in transit still so they decide each bed will have to be made up with linen taken from the hotel's supply, until their own bedding arrives.

Sister Bryony discovers a store of waterproof mackintosh base sheets in a cupboard, and the mattresses are swiftly covered with these, followed by lower and upper sheets. Each bed is finished with a colourful linen bedspread.

Monsieur Cassard appears as the orderlies are tucking and smoothing the last few sheets. Although the manager is suitably impressed with how much the English ladies have achieved in a single day, he is less enthused by their use of the hotel's bedding. 'You should have consulted me first, madam,' he tells Lucinda.

'I didn't want to bother you with such a trivial matter,' Lucinda apologizes. In truth, it had slipped her mind that she should check with the manager.

'I will be the judge of what is trivial or not, madam.' Cassard stalks off, before Lucinda can respond.

'Doctor?'

Lucinda turns to find Mardie and Olga approaching, each struggling to carry a large silver container. Lucinda's eyes widen at the sight of Achille's fish kettles. 'Well done,' she says. 'How did you manage to persuade the chef to part with them?'

'He was no trouble.' Mardie grins. 'A bit grumpy, though, wasn't he, Olga?'

Olga nods, biting her lip, and Lucinda has the sudden feeling that Mardie isn't telling her the whole truth. 'You did ask him, didn't you, Hodgson?'

'Yes, ma'am,' she says. 'I asked him *very* nicely . . .'

'Well, as long as you did,' Lucinda says, wondering whether she should press Mardie further. 'Thank you, Hodgson, Campbell. Extra hot chocolate for you both tonight.'

'Thank you.' Mardie beams.

Lucinda watches the pair continue on their way, wondering if she'll suffer the chef's wrath in due course.

Early the following morning, a telegram from Dieppe Customs arrives. The equipment from England is awaiting transportation at the docks.

Lucinda telegraphs to Madame Pérouse, requesting her to contact Monsieur Guérin: the agent's trucks and drivers will be required to bring everything to the hotel.

In the meantime, all Lucinda and her team can do is wait, and continue to prepare the hospital as best they can. In the afternoon, there is a flurry of excitement as a truck pulls up outside the hotel. But it hasn't been sent by Monsieur Guérin. Instead, Lucinda takes delivery of an X-ray machine, on loan from Dr Johnson's hospital. She reads the note the French driver hands her.

Thought you might need this, in case your own is delayed.
It's our spare, so no rush to return. Dr J.

'How thoughtful,' Florence remarks.

It is, Lucinda agrees, with a frisson of envy. Fancy having a *spare* X-ray machine to loan to any old Tom, Dick or Harriet.

Florence and Perrin set up the machine in the windowless room previously used as the hotel's crockery store. When Lucinda comes to inspect their work, she finds Florence and the engineer examining a box of glass plates. 'They came with the machine,' Florence tells Lucinda. 'I'm just showing Monsieur Perrin what the human ribcage looks like.'

Lucinda joins them to peer at the blurred image on a glass plate the engineer holds, and after a moment she sees the shadowy shape of a thoracic embolism. She meets Florence's eye, and knows without having to ask that her friend has spotted the same thing.

'*Incroyable* . . .' the engineer marvels, gazing from the plate, to his own torso.

Lucinda smiles to herself. It *was* incredible to be able to see inside the human body without ripping it open. A true marvel. She won't destroy the engineer's wonder by revealing what the plate in his hands really shows.

Early the following morning, trucks carrying the lost supplies from England finally arrive at the hotel. To Lucinda's relief, when the crates are unloaded only one box of glass phials is found to be damaged. Yorick the fox's skull is intact, nestled safely in his box of straw, and Lucinda sets her good-luck talisman on a shelf above the mirrors in the ladies' cloakroom.

*

Over the next two days, the final preparations are completed, and at last the wards are ready to receive patients. A hundred beds are neatly made up with fresh sheets and blankets. The operating theatre in the cloakroom has been thoroughly cleaned, and is now fully equipped. The medical supplies have been stored, ready for use, and the microscopes have been carefully assembled in a bedroom on the first floor designated as a pathology laboratory.

Lucinda grants the Corps a day off, but no sooner has she done this, than an urgent telegram from the French Red Cross arrives.

The single sentence sends ice through Lucinda's veins.

Casualties en route.

'Call everyone to the foyer, please,' she instructs Mardie. 'Immediately.'

While Florence conducts a roll-call, Lucinda tries to project an aura of calm. She tells herself this is precisely why they are here, to treat war casualties, and whatever happens they will cope. She must draw upon all her training and experience now, lead by example, and show the world that her women are up to the task.

She takes a breath, her gaze traversing the expectant faces before her. 'The time has come,' she begins. 'We've had notification that casualties are on their way.'

No one moves or speaks, all attention focused on Lucinda.

'We're as ready as we can be,' she continues. 'Dr Maberry and I have every faith in you. Whatever this war might throw at us, we will meet the challenge.'

'Do we know how many casualties there are?' Hazel asks.

'Unfortunately not,' Lucinda replies.

'The Corps will be split into two shifts,' Florence says. 'Dr Garland and I will finalize a timetable shortly, so you can prepare yourselves.'

Lucinda straightens her spine, arranges her face into what she hopes is a reassuring expression. One by one she meets each team member's eye, receiving a range of taut, nervous smiles in return. She takes another breath. What she says next will be crucial. She must choose her words with care. 'Whatever we're faced with from now on,' she says, 'all I ask is that each of you does your best.'

13

Edie: October 1914

The sun has set by the time Edie's company reaches Southampton docks. The troops are marched through a darkened wharf, busy with dockhands and military, past a long line of tethered, saddle-less horses waiting to be loaded on to ships. Edie envies the animals' ignorance.

Despite the late hour, the docks are a maelstrom of activity and noise: the stamp of hoofs, the tramp of soldiers' boots, the shouts of stevedores working their ropes and chains.

A bloated moon hovers over the sea, and a knot forms in Edie's throat at the sight of glittering waves stretching away. Ships at anchor loom out of the dusk, their hulks filling her with fearful awe. She's entering another world.

'Halt! Fall out!'

The platoon assembles beneath a blacked-out lamp under the watchful eye of Sergeant Ratigan. A strict censure on talking, singing and smoking is issued.

Edie crouches on her pack, rifle gripped tight between her knees. A salt-laced breeze whips along the quay, and she shivers. Around her, men are whispering among themselves. Next to her, Stanley is grappling with one of his boots, cursing under his breath as he struggles to untangle the lace.

Edie feels for the notebook in her tunic pocket.

A journalist writes but for the day. Something Mr Stead once said. *And when the day is done, his words are wiped out, like sums upon a slate.*

Not her words, Edie thinks. One day soon, the world will read them.

An hour crawls by, and Edie's legs grow stiff from sitting on the ground. Stanley passes the time surreptitiously checking his pocket camera, careful to do so only when Ratigan's back is turned. To Edie's bemusement, he's still trying to guess the origin of her broken nose.

'You was walking through town, and a builder carryin' a plank came out of a doorway and whacked you in the hooter.'

'Not even close.'

At last, the order comes to board their ship, HMS *Marguerite*. Edie follows Stanley and the others up a steep gangplank, the wood undulating alarmingly beneath the stream of boots. Water, black as oil, laps against the steamer's rust-streaked hull, and the stench of rotting fish grows stronger as Edie enters the ship.

Stewards direct the troops towards a set of metal steps, and the men climb up to the top deck, open to the elements. 'Keep your equipment close,' a steward barks. 'Rifles loaded. No smoking. No talking.'

The deck is soon crowded, but Stanley has found a free space by the stern rail. Edie grips the cold iron, as a thought strikes her: there must be hundreds of men on this ship, but how many can it safely hold?

Stanley props his rifle upright against the rail, looping

the strap round to secure it in place. Edie copies him, trying not to think about the ship sinking, and what might be lurking in the depths.

A flicker of white far below on the inky water snags her eye: a lone gull, floating like a speck of salt on broth. The thought of broth makes Edie's stomach clench. They've been given nothing to eat since their last meal at Hurst Park, hours ago.

The steamer's turbines rumble into life, vibrating through the decks. Ropes are released, and as the ship slowly begins to move, a small group of men across the deck defy the order for silence and begin to sing, their voices rising above the throbbing engines.

'Eternal Father, strong to save,
Whose arm hath bound the restless wave . . .'

More join in, and the words of the hymn make the hairs on the back of Edie's neck prickle.

'Who bidd'st the mighty ocean deep,
Its own appointed limits keep;
O hear us when we cry to thee,
For those in peril on the sea.'

Edie leans on the railing, watching the dirty white bridal train flowing in the ship's wake. By the time the men have reached the hymn's concluding verse, Southampton port has dissolved into the darkness. Was this the last she'll see of home? The thought gives her a queasy feeling, a toxic mix of thrill and dread.

She turns back to face the deck, spots a steward pushing through the crowd, trying to make himself heard over the noise of the engines. 'Life-vests on the lower deck!' the man yells. 'Going quick!'

'I'll nab us a couple,' Stanley says, and moves off after the steward. Edie turns back to the rail, her eye caught by a dark shape bearing down on them off the port bow. Others have also noticed the approaching ship, and men crowd the rail. The vessel displays no sailing lights, but on its funnel is painted a giant red cross.

A murmur ripples through the men. It's a hospital ship, returning home.

The men clap solemnly as the vessel slowly passes, heading into harbour. Edie can just make out shadowy figures gathered on the upper decks, before they are swallowed by the night.

After a while, Stanley returns, bearing two bulky cork jackets. 'They'll do as pillows,' he tells Edie. 'Bloody hope our boys in blue are awake tonight.'

It takes Edie a moment to work out what he means, and then it hits her. This steamer is no more than a floating target for the Germans, at risk of being torpedoed at any moment. The Navy might be vigilant, but the menace from enemy submarines is real, as she knows all too well from reading the newspaper reports.

Stanley offers Edie a cigarette, but she shakes her head, stomach roiling with the waves. They spread their groundsheets, positioning their packs as windbreaks. Edie doubts she'll sleep at all on the crossing, but some of the men are already lying shrouded beneath their groundsheets, others sitting with blankets wrapped around them. She tries to make herself comfortable, as Stanley slumps next to her, an unlit cigarette in his hand.

'I'm British,' he moans, grey-faced in the gloom. 'The sea's in my blood.' He spits through the railings. 'So why do I feel so bloody sick?'

Edie makes a sympathetic noise, wondering how long the crossing will take. But with the vagaries of tides, weather, the threat of German attack, it's impossible to estimate. She leans back, staring up into the velvet-black of the night sky. Closing her eyes, she sends up a prayer to a God she's never believed in to grant safe passage to this ship of fragile souls.

∞

HMS *Marguerite* reaches Le Havre early the following morning, her precious human cargo intact. Edie has managed a scant two hours of disturbed sleep, and she sags under the weight of her pack as the platoon disembarks on to a rain-slick quayside. Horses are being winched, one by one, over the side of the ship, their shrill neighing tangling with the shouts of men.

Edie's bladder aches, but there's no chance to piss, as reinforcement conducting officers corral the troops on the bustling wharf.

Sergeant Ratigan conducts a roll-call, then gives the order to form up. The platoon marches from the port, towards the suburbs of Harfleur, three miles away to the east. They reach the infantry base depot an hour later, and Edie shudders at the sight of the bleak, sprawling camp of tents and huts. Somewhere to the north, terrifyingly close, comes the relentless whine and thump of heavy artillery.

The platoon assembles on a muddy parade ground, where they're issued with black tea and bread and cheese from a mobile field kitchen. Ravenous, Edie bolts hers, then joins a queue for the latrines. The canvas enclosures are as primitive as she'd feared, each containing a hole in the ground over which a short plank has been laid. The stench makes her eyes water and her throat tighten but at least she has privacy.

The men are allotted billets in numbered grey marquees. 'Ten men to a tent,' Sergeant Ratigan orders. 'Draw your blankets from the quartermaster.'

To Edie's relief, she's billeted with Stanley, and they claim pallet beds next to each other. Edie sinks down on her bed roll, the ground continuing to tilt as though she's still on the steamer's rolling deck. She closes her eyes, but it doesn't help.

'The light in here's shit, Lawrence.'

Edie forces her eyes open again, to find Stanley aiming his pocket camera in her direction.

'What are you doing?'

'Smile, kid.' Stanley fiddles with the Ensignette, and the shutter clicks.

'Ratigan'll have your guts if he catches you,' Edie mutters.

'Don't worry about him, the old bastard.'

Edie looks on, as Stanley aims the camera and snaps another picture of the tent. For a teetering moment, she considers confiding in Stanley, showing him the notebook, sharing her dream. Stanley's photographs would corroborate what she's writing, and together they could report on the war from the ordinary soldiers' perspective. Something never attempted before.

'Post!' A shout comes from the entrance, and Stanley shoves the camera back into his tunic pocket.

Sacks of letters and parcels have arrived from England. Edie is surprised to be handed a small package wrapped in brown paper, labelled 'To a Soldier Friend'. It contains a poorly knitted woollen scarf in a muddy shade of maroon. As she unfurls it, a tightly folded square of paper drops into her lap: a letter.

Dear Soldier, Edie reads slowly to herself, trying to decipher the childish handwriting. *We are thinking of you here in old England, and my classmates and I are knitting as fast as we can to make you warm clothes for the cold weather that is coming.*

Edie wraps the ends of the scarf around her neck, the wool soft against her skin.

We have knitted so many loving thoughts and wishes among the stitches, she reads on. *Do try to shoot the Kaiser in the legs, but not fatally, as he must have time to repent before he dies.*

Laughter rises in Edie's chest, and she clamps a hand over her mouth, passing the letter to Stanley.

'Cheery little blighter.' Stanley chuckles. 'Shit at knitting, though.'

Edie buries her face in the scarf. It smells of soap, and safety, and home.

The rain arrives in the early evening, gathering strength as darkness falls. Soon, the ground is saturated, the paths through the camp transformed into mud slicks, canvas sagging beneath the weight of water.

Edie can't sleep. She lies listening to the rain pelting on the roof of the tent, the men snoring and moaning. Alongside her, Stanley slumbers under blankets and a groundsheet, unmoving.

Her mind churns, as she conjures imaginary newspaper headlines.

Female soldier fights in France.

She thinks of the photograph Stanley took of her earlier. If only she could tell him the truth.

She wakes to a grey morning light, and untangles herself from damp blankets. The rest of the tent is coming to life, and she quickly dresses in her tunic and trousers. It still feels odd to sleep in most of her clothes, but if she thinks of herself as a traveller, ready for anything, she finds it helps. She pulls on her boots, tugs her cap low, and follows the rest of the platoon outside for roll-call.

After breakfast, Sergeant Ratigan leads the platoon out of camp. Returning to Le Havre, the men march in near silence, and Edie is glad to be leaving the camp with its all-pervading atmosphere of tension hanging over it, like invisible fog. At Le Havre station, cattle trucks are waiting to take the men on to the reserve zone. Ragged children flit about the platform, offering the soldiers pieces of French chocolate in return for coins, biscuits, cigarettes. Edie watches the children, and her heart aches to witness their desperate poverty, but she has nothing to give them. She shows them her empty hands, trying to convey sympathy with her smile, feeling guilty relief as she boards a truck and can turn her eyes from the children's plight.

As the train shunts from the station, stones ricochet off the carriage windows and doors.

'Fucking little devils!' Caldwell snarls, as a pebble hurtles through the truck's open doorway and glances off his shoulder. He scoops the stone up, and lobs it back at the retreating crowd of small, bedraggled figures.

14

Lucinda: October 1914

She's lost count of the exact number of wounded men they've so far received. Fifty or more must have graced Lucinda's operating table, each injury worse than the last. Just as Dr Johnson had warned, the carnage from the battlefields is beyond anything any of them have experienced before. Shattered limbs, horrific burns, abdomens ripped open, entrails exposed to mud and filth, flesh destroyed by shrapnel and bullets. Bodies mangled beyond belief.

At last, a chance of respite. Lucinda staggers back to her bedroom to lie down for a couple of hours, but no sooner has she tugged her shoes from her aching, swollen feet than there's a knock at the door.

Oh, God, what now?

She sits on the edge of her bed, massaging her heel, hoping whoever it is will go away again. This is the first opportunity she's had to rest since early this morning, when the latest cohort of casualties arrived. The flood of wounded men seems destined never to end, a relentless deluge of suffering and horror.

It feels to Lucinda as if the hospital has been running for far longer than just a few days. She's spent almost every moment toiling in the makeshift surgery, extracting shrapnel from flesh, amputating gangrenous limbs, swabbing blood and suturing wounds. Now, at the edge of endurance and desperate for sleep, her legs are stumps of lead, the soles of her feet aflame.

More rapid taps on the door, louder now. 'Doctor? Ma'am?' Mardie, sounding uncharacteristically panicked.

Lucinda pushes herself to standing, takes a moment to steady herself. 'Come in.'

The door swings open, and the young orderly trips over her feet in her haste to enter the room. 'Doctor, you have to come.'

'Dr Maberry is on duty, Hodgson.' *Please, let me have just one hour's peace.*

'Dr Maberry sent me to get you, ma'am. She said to tell you there's a bad 'un.'

Lucinda doubts Florence used those precise words, but she understands Mardie's gist, and a shudder runs through her. Someone's injuries are more complicated than Florence can deal with alone. Her message is a plea for help.

The knowledge that no one else can go in her stead gives Lucinda the strength to pull her shoes on. She hurries downstairs to the operating theatre, a place she'd hoped not to have to think about at least for a short while.

'I'm sorry, Lucie,' Florence mutters, as Lucinda scrubs her hands at the sink. 'I had to send Grace for a rest, she almost passed out, but then this one came in, and I couldn't tackle it alone.'

'It's all right.' Lucinda sighs, fumbling with the strings of her surgical gown. She's so tired her fingers are slow to obey. She pushes her hair beneath her cap, and follows Florence to where her patient is waiting.

She's grown used to most of the casualties arriving at

the hospital semi-conscious, clinging to life by such a tenuous thread it's a wonder they survived the journey from the clearing stations.

By contrast, the patient Lucinda is confronted with now is fully awake, sitting upright on a wooden chair appropriated from the dining room.

'Private Nichols,' Florence briefs Lucinda. 'Twenty years old, traumatic head injury. Clearing station patched him up, and sent him here.'

Lucinda takes her first proper look at the young soldier. His uniform is stiff with dried mud, his head swathed in filthy, bloodied bandages, and a familiar rancid reek emanates from him: the stench of the battlefield. She turns to Florence, raises her eyebrows. What is so unusual about this case?

Florence gestures towards the back of the young man's head. The sight that greets Lucinda is like nothing she's ever seen before. Adrenaline surges through her veins, and she feels the familiar tightening in her muscles, spurring her to move. She resists the urge to rush with every fibre of her being: it's imperative she remain calm, even though her nerves are blazing.

She moves to face the soldier again.

Shining, trustful brown eyes meet Lucinda's, and she forces her features into a smile she hopes is encouraging. 'Hello,' she hears herself say. 'I'm Dr Garland. You've been in the wars, haven't you?'

The young man's cracked lips pull apart in an answering smile. His composure unnerves Lucinda. In her experience, the conscious patients are often the worst, noisy and prone to physical violence in their agony and terror.

The poor boy can have no notion of the severity of his injury, she presumes. It is by far the most horrific she's encountered yet – how is he still alive? His apparent calmness must be due to shock, Lucinda fears. The quietest, deadliest killer.

However calm he may appear, though, the fact remains that his life hangs in the balance.

Sister Bryony has already fitted a blood pressure cuff around the soldier's bicep, and is checking the tube attached to the box containing the mercury manometer. She has the man's wiry wrist in her grip, monitoring his pulse. 'Slowing, Doctor,' the nurse reports, before Lucinda can ask. There's a rare sharpness to Sister Bryony's voice. Time is not on their side.

Lucinda senses a cold presence at her shoulder. The threat of death is with her at every operation: one tiny mistake, a thirty-second lapse of concentration, and Mr Morton – Lucinda's name for death, though she has never told a soul apart from Florence – will swoop, eager to claim his prize. Lucinda fights the spectre of Mr Morton with everything she has, every single time. But sometimes the patient is too weak, the stakes too high.

Nichols blinks up at Lucinda, and the fearful hope in his eyes almost undoes her.

'What else do we know?' Lucinda asks Florence, in a low voice.

Florence pauses in her preparation of the local anaesthetic, and shakes her head. 'The tally tag's illegible.'

Lucinda scans the medical label attached to the soldier's uniform sleeve. The card is smeared with mud, and the only marking she can make out is a thick red stripe, indicating danger of haemorrhage. Lucinda needs no scribbled tag to tell her this.

'Are you in pain anywhere, Nichols?'

The young man makes a noise in his throat. 'No, ma'am,' he manages.

Lucinda peers at the label again, frustrated at the lack of information from the casualty clearing station. She needs to know what pain relief this man has already received. How much more can his body withstand?

She tugs on a fresh pair of rubber gloves. 'Do we have the anti-tetanus serum ready?'

Florence shakes her head. 'We've run out.'

Sister Bryony swathes Nichols's upper body in a sheet stained with a previous patient's blood, but at least it conceals his soiled uniform.

'I'm going to look at your wound now, Nichols.' Lucinda gives Sister Bryony a nod, and the nurse begins to unwind the sopping red bandages wrapped loosely around the soldier's head. Lucinda braces herself, and her mother's familiar mantra comes to her: *Be strong, be true, be brave.*

As the bandages are unwound, the full horror of Nichols's head injury steals the breath from Lucinda's lungs.

Oh, dear God.

Around her, the activity of the operating theatre fades to a dull and distant thrum.

'Pulse slowing, Doctor.' Florence's voice snaps Lucinda back.

Florence grips Nichols's wrist, her eyes fixed on the ticking hand of her watch. Lucinda quickly examines the back of the man's head, noting where a chunk of lower skull is missing. Her mind blanks, all her training deserting her. She desperately dredges her memory, but all that comes to her are the names of the three layers of meninges, inside the skull. *Pia mater*, *arachnoid mater*, *dura mater*: pious mother, cobweb mother, hard mother. Useless, utterly useless knowledge.

Florence holds up a syringe of Novocaine, primed and ready, and Lucinda gives a nod to proceed. The supply of local anaesthetic is uncertain, until the next shipment arrives from England, but for now they have enough.

Lucinda stoops to address Private Nichols again. 'We're going to administer an anaesthetic to numb you, but you mustn't go to sleep.' How to explain to this poor, frightened young man the mortal danger he's in? 'You must stay awake, Nichols. Do you understand?'

The soldier gives a slight nod.

'Try not to move,' Florence cautions gently. 'I'm going to give you an injection, but you won't feel anything.'

'And then . . .' Lucinda falters, takes a breath. 'Then I can see to your injury.'

Nichols gives a small noise of assent.

'Ready the site, please,' Lucinda instructs Sister Bryony.

The nurse gingerly tips Nichols's head forward a degree, deftly shaves the remaining tufts of hair from around the wound, then swabs away dried mud and blood with cooled boiled water.

Lucinda selects a small pair of artery forceps from the gurney of instruments, readying herself as Florence applies the syringe of Novocaine.

Sister Bryony peers at the mercury manometer, monitoring the soldier's vital signs, and Lucinda notes the young man's dirt-engrained hands gradually unclenching in his lap, his shoulders sinking beneath the sheet.

Across the room, someone drops a metal implement on the tiled floor, a jarring clatter that makes Lucinda start. Nichols barely reacts.

'Blood pressure rising,' Sister Bryony reports, her voice low and tense.

This is bad news, but there's little Lucinda can do about it.

She returns to the devastation of Nichols's skull. With a less than steady hand, she gingerly peels back a flap of skin.

'Five foreign objects . . .' she mutters haltingly '. . . likely iron nails of varying lengths and sizes . . . two embedded in the lower left occipital bone . . . the rest penetrating brain matter . . .' She'll have to talk her way through this, step by step, and she's sorry if Nichols can hear her. 'Missing skull fragments, but no pus in evidence, no visible inflammation of the *dura mater*. Depth of penetration . . . unknown.'

The soldier gives a weak cough, and Lucinda meets Florence's eye over the young man's head.

I don't know what to do, Lucinda wants to scream.

The nails will likely have carried infection into the soldier's brain, and all her instincts are telling her to remove them immediately. But can the young man survive such a trauma? Would death from infection be better than the almost certain risk of permanent paralysis if Lucinda makes a mistake?

Nichols coughs again, and Florence bends to his ear. 'Try to relax,' she murmurs. 'Think pleasant thoughts if you can.' If Lucinda does nothing, Nichols will never survive the journey home in his present state. She must take a chance and operate now.

Lucinda prepares her forceps, wondering if there is more damage to the soldier's brain that she can't see — other projectiles embedded so deeply they're invisible. Somehow the nails she can see haven't damaged the brainstem. If they had, the man wouldn't be able to speak or indeed breathe.

'What's your favourite poem, Nichols?' Lucinda asks, her mouth dry.

How can he still be breathing?

'"Invictus", ma'am,' the soldier mumbles.

Lucinda recognizes the title, but she's hazy on the poet. 'Henley?' she ventures.

'Yes, ma'am.'

'Know it well, Nichols?' Lucinda applies the forceps to the head of the largest nail. Somehow she must keep the young soldier talking while she pulls it out.

'By heart, ma'am. Learned it for school.'

'Away you go, then.'

'Pardon, ma'am?'

'Recite it for me, if you will.' Lucinda tightens the forceps around the nail, willing her hand not to tremble.

'Out loud, ma'am?'

'Nice and clear.'

'*Out of the night that covers me,*' Private Nichols begins hesitantly. '*Black as the pit from pole to pole . . .*'

'Blood pressure dropping rapidly, Doctor,' Sister Bryony reports.

It was rising a moment ago, Lucinda thinks, glancing at

Florence for her reaction. Florence nods to continue and Lucinda marvels, not for the first time, at her ability to remain calm no matter the crisis. With her nerves of steel, Florence is the best anaesthetist Lucinda has ever worked with.

'Keep going, Nichols,' Lucinda prompts, as Florence injects more anaesthetic.

'*I thank whatever gods may be,*' Private Nichols continues, '*for my unconquerable soul.*'

Beads of sweat escape Lucinda's cap, trickling into her eyebrows. Sister Bryony, ever vigilant, dabs at her forehead with a cloth.

Across the room, the door to the street opens, admitting a cool evening breeze. Lucinda hears the distinctive clop of horse's hoofs, the familiar clatter of metal wheels on stone, and her pulse skids. *Not another ambulance, please God, not now.*

'*In the fell clutch of circumstance, I have not winced nor cried aloud.*'

'You're doing so well, Nichols.' Lucinda's fingers tremble, the forceps threatening to slip. She grips them harder. She must not lose her nerve.

'*Under the bludgeonings of chance,*' Private Nichols stumbles on, '*my head is bloody, but unbowed.*' The poem suddenly strikes Lucinda as horribly apt. Her vision blurs again, and she madly blinks sweat from her eyes. The temperature in the room seems to be rising.

The noises from outside have ceased, but as Lucinda begins to pull tentatively on the nail, a familiar voice carries through the open doors, shattering her concentration.

'Get him in here . . .'

Figgis.

She tries to ignore the slam of ambulance doors, the scuffing of boots, the stomach-churning sound of a grown man crying out in pain. She turns to see Figgis and Tozer coming through the doorway, bearing yet another mangled body on a stretcher.

'Put him over there,' Florence calls out to the two porters, indicating Grace's vacant operating table.

'This one's a DI,' Figgis grunts.

They're all dangerously ill, man! Lucinda wants to scream back at him.

'Pulse critical.' Sister Bryony tugs Lucinda's attention back to the patient in the chair. She can still hear Figgis arguing with one of the nurses, but she shuts out their voices. She can deal with only one crisis at a time.

'The next line, Nichols, if you please.'

'*Be-beyond this place of wrath and tears,*' Nichols whispers, '*looms but the horror of the shade.*'

'Stay with me, Nichols.' Lucinda senses Mr Morton's creeping presence in her peripheral vision, and her veins thrum as she pulls with less caution on the nail, feeling it begin to shift.

'*And yet . . . and yet . . .*' Nichols falters, and Lucinda ceases to breathe for the space of one heartbeat, two, three.

'*And yet,*' Nichols resumes, his body twitching, '*the menace of the years finds and shall find me unafraid.*'

Lucinda exhales, her arms aching, the muscles in her wrists burning under the strain of holding the forceps steady.

She can feel Mr Morton closing in.

'Slow and steady,' she hears Florence murmur, and Lucinda can't tell if she's talking to her or Nichols. Her concentration is waning, exhaustion weighting her bones, sapping her strength. Mr Morton looms closer, and all she can do is bite her lip hard, the pain re-sharpening her focus.

'Nearly there, Nichols. Stay with me . . .'

'*It matters not how strait the gate*,' Private Nichols recites, slurring his words now, '*How charged with punishments the scroll . . .*' His body spasms, and he lapses into silence.

Lucinda pulls at the nail, fingers cramping around the forceps, no longer concerned about potential nerve damage, or infection, or paralysis. She has to finish this, before Nichols collapses.

At last, the nail begins to yield.

'I can't detect a pulse, Doctor . . .'

Fight, Nichols. Stay with me.

'*I am the master of my fate*,' Lucinda prompts him. The nail is coming, coming . . .

Slow and steady.

She so nearly has it . . . 'The last line, Nichols.'

At the precise moment Lucinda pulls the nail free, Nichols's head slumps to his chest. Sister Bryony grabs the man's shoulders, but though he's slight, it's all she can do to keep him from sliding to the floor. Florence is beside her in a heartbeat, holding the soldier in place, as Lucinda discards the forceps. 'Lower him slowly.'

Working together, the three women manage to ease the young man on to the floor, and Sister Bryony cradles his bleeding head in her lap, as Lucinda searches for a pulse, wrist, neck, wrist again. Nothing.

'Nichols? Wake up, Nichols . . .' Lucinda prises an eyelid apart with a blood-slick finger. 'I'm waiting for that last line, young man,' she croaks. Was that a flicker of an eye? 'Lay him flat,' Lucinda snaps. 'Can you hear me, Nichols?' She pinches the man's cheeks. If he can hear her voice, he has a chance. But even as she has this thought, she knows it isn't true.

Florence meets Lucinda's eye, and something cold clutches the back of Lucinda's neck.

She tears off her rubber surgical gloves, readying herself for what she must do. She has a sudden image of Mr Morton in his frayed black suit, hunched over Nichols's body, long, cold fingers splayed over the soldier's heart.

No.

She blinks, and Mr Morton's figure is replaced by Florence's, as she begins resuscitation, raising the soldier's arms over his head to expand his lungs, then crossing his arms back over his chest, applying expiratory pressure. Her movements are vigorous, practised. She has done this too many times before.

'Come on, Nichols,' Lucinda urges. 'Don't give up now.'

Work for the patient till the ultimate moment of life. Her mother's voice comes to her, and Lucinda takes Nichols's jaw in her hand, tips his head back, blows air into his slack mouth.

One breath.

Two breaths.

Three breaths.

Come on, Nichols.

'Lucie . . .'

Blood surges in Lucinda's ears.

One breath.
Two breaths.
Three.

Lucinda becomes aware that Florence has ceased her manoeuvres, and has sunk back on her knees. 'Why have you stopped?'

'He's gone, Lucie.'

Lucinda feels a chill whisper on the back of her sweat-drenched neck. 'No.'

'He's gone.'

Sister Bryony lifts the sheet over Nichols's lifeless body.

After a moment, Lucinda drags herself to her feet, clutching the back of the chair as the room spins. The sickening reek of death fills her nostrils. It's a smell she's come to associate with the battlefield, a smell that lingers on the soldiers' uniforms, on their bodies, in the air. Her vision blurs, as voices ebb and flow around her.

He's at peace now.
Come and sit down a moment.
You did all you could for him.

Florence is asking her something, but she can't make sense of what she's saying, and there's no strength left to respond. She's never felt so tired.

Hands guide her down on to the chair. The seat is still warm.

Figgis and Tozer appear with a stretcher. Lucinda can only look on as Nichols's body is rolled on to the wood and canvas frame, and heaved away.

'Lucie?'

Florence crouches at her side, her eyes troubled. 'Are you all right?'

No, I'm not, Lucinda wants to cry, but no words come. She'd tried her best, but it hadn't been enough.

Mr Morton had won again.

Her vision darkens, strength waning like a guttering candle flame, as the last line of the poem comes to her.

I am the captain of my soul.

15

Edie: October 1914

They march for miles along paved roads and rough tracks, across fields etched with drainage ditches, through a monotonous flat landscape scattered with remote farms and isolated villages. As the hours drag wearily by, a feeling of deadness, a walking paralysis, creeps up Edie's limbs. It takes concentrated effort to keep her legs moving. Her hands feel as if they are swelling, the blood pooling in her fingertips, oozing beneath her nails. Her shoulders slump under the weight of her pack, and her skin feels clammy, her face itchy, her tongue twice its normal size.

She wills her feet to keep moving, each laboured step an effort. Artillery rumbles in the distance, an advancing storm, but sensations have lost their sharpness, and sound reaches her as an indistinct drone.

At first, the men sing marching tunes, but after a while few have spare breath left to hold a tune.

The stamp of a hundred pairs of boots fills Edie's head.

'That's not one of ours.' Stanley's voice jolts Edie from her stupor.

She follows his gaze, noticing for the first time a lone plane, circling above them. Its white wings are almost invisible against the blue of the morning sky, but Edie recognizes the pair of sinister dark crosses painted on the undersides. It's a German Taube, watching them.

'Bloody bastards,' Stanley mutters.

They march for hours, pausing only once for a brief rest break. The day wears on, and as the men grow more tired some discard items from their kit, chucking mess tins, canteens and broken boots into the ditches. Edie contemplates dumping some of her rations, she has no appetite, but Stanley talks her out of it.

'You'll be hungry later, kid.'

A French cavalry corps on bicycles passes them, travelling in the opposite direction. The Frenchmen's sabres glint dully at their hips, bicycle wheels skidding in the mud. Brief greetings are exchanged, *bonjour, bonjour,* and then they are gone.

Edie staggers on, struggling to keep up. Each time the column stops, it takes longer for her body to begin moving again. The roads are congested with refugees, families fleeing with nothing but the clothes on their backs and whatever they can carry. Edie barely sees them, her eyes slits, dazed with fatigue.

The wind picks up as evening arrives, and a chill creeps into Edie's bones, despite the continual marching. She's lightheaded with thirst, her canteen long empty by the time they stop for an extended rest break. Crouching in a shallow ditch, Edie forces down a dry biscuit while Stanley refills their canteens at a transport kitchen. The water is tainted with petrol, but Edie no longer cares. Her temples are pounding with a sickening headache, and she longs to lie down and sleep.

'Stay awake,' Stanley urges, sharing the last of his sweets

with her. The sugar hits Edie's bloodstream, sharpening her focus briefly. Only now does she notice there are houses, a village perhaps, burning like a beacon on the horizon. The boom of guns has quietened at last, the night air charged, like the lull between thunder and lightning.

Sergeant Ratigan grants an extra tot of rum to each man: a concession, while smoking is forbidden. Edie downs hers in one, the rum burning a fiery path to her gut. It does nothing to dull the throbbing pain in her head, nor the ache in her bones, but it warms her insides for a time.

The squeal of ungreased transport wheels cuts through the men's exhausted talk: the dreaded signal that the rest break is over, and it is time to proceed once more.

Edie drags herself up, takes her place alongside Stanley.

'You was playing cricket,' he says, as the column moves off again. 'And someone bowled one right in your snout.'

A noise escapes Edie's lips, sounding more like a sob than a laugh.

They march, then rest, march, then rest, deep into the night. Until at last, as the rose-hued promise of dawn lightens the horizon, they reach a village. The order is given to halt, fall out, and Edie staggers after Stanley and the others into the shelter of a disused stable. There are few villagers awake at this ungodly hour, but one or two early risers emerge from their homes to offer the soldiers what little provisions they can spare: bread, fruit, hot water for tea.

Edie's whole body aches as though someone has set about her with a club hammer. She longs to curl up in the straw and sleep for ever, but her feet must be attended to. She tugs off her boots, to find the skin of her heels rubbed raw, her toes swollen and sore. How much more can they take? She submits to her blisters being powdered and bandaged by a medical orderly, and counts herself lucky. Her feet have held up surprisingly well, compared to a lot of the men's.

Sergeant Ratigan is unsympathetic to their pain. 'If it hurts, it's not serious,' he says. But he permits them to smoke.

The flesh of Jackson's left heel is stuck to his sock, and as the medical orderly peels away a swathe of skin, the boy whimpers, choking back tears. Edie watches as Bembridge lays a heavy arm around Jackson's shoulders, murmuring in his ear, offering his ration of rum. Jackson takes the mug from him, downs it in a single swallow, wiping his mouth with a shaking hand.

Edie hopes the rum dulls the boy's pain, at least for a while.

Roused from a fitful slumber, Edie struggles up, blinking in the dim light.

'We're moving off again,' Stanley tells her. He's already shouldering his pack, and Edie hurries to follow him.

Outside, a thick fog shrouds the village. Ratigan takes a roll-call, then gives the order to load rifles and form up. There is no time for breakfast.

The whine and thud of artillery grow steadily louder,

but no one knows quite where the enemy is. Are they marching towards danger, or away from it?

As the sun slowly rises, the fog lifts, revealing a bleak landscape. The troops march on, skirting hamlets and farms, passing fewer and fewer refugees on the roads. A nearby copse of woodland blazes, ash settling like dirty snow on discarded petrol cans and broken bicycle wheels. The bloated corpses of horses litter the verges. Soot coats the inside of Edie's mouth, and her throat burns. When her canteen runs dry, Stanley shares the remains of his water with her. His gesture of kindness brings fresh tears to her smarting eyes.

Ahead, figures emerge from the hellish nightmare of dust and ash, ominous apparitions approaching along the road. Word filters down the line: *They're our own boys.* The returning soldiers troop past, heads bowed, many staggering as though punch drunk. They look half dead to Edie, the whites of their eyes stark in their mud- and blood-streaked faces.

Questions are asked. *What's it like up there? Are we winning?*

Slaughter, is the only reply.

∞

After a full day of marching, they reach the reserve line late in the afternoon, and the order to 'dig in' is immediately given. The thunder of artillery is ever louder, a constant drum roll punctuated by an occasional echoing blast. With the last of her strength, Edie follows Ratigan's orders, unclipping her entrenching tool from her pack. The men begin to scrape a shallow depression in the earth, and Edie's blunt trowel makes heavy work of the claggy ground. Her arms are soon trembling with exhaustion.

They dig, grunting and cursing, burrowing into the Flanders clay like so many moles, gradually carving out a ditch in which they will sleep tonight.

As the light begins to wane, officers conduct an inventory of the men's equipment. Greatcoats, boots, canteens, rations, spades: so much has been lost en route. Field punishments are meted out, but everyone knows the true punishment is yet to come.

Orderlies appear with sandbags of rations. Bully beef and biscuits are distributed, and Edie extracts her spoon from the top of her puttees where she'd tucked it for safe keeping. She wipes the mud-encrusted pewter on the underside of her tunic lapel, the least filthy part of her uniform, and it occurs to her that she hasn't taken off a single item of clothing since leaving Harfleur. Everything is covered with mud. The only clean thing in her possession is her rifle. If a speck of dirt finds its way inside it, she doesn't fancy her chances with Ratigan.

Devouring the meagre meal, Edie's mind drifts back to her gutter-scraping, starving workhouse days, a past life she'd thought she'd left behind. But the griping of her belly is an old enemy from that time, a cruel hunger that's followed her here.

She huddles in the dark of the trough, gleaning morsels of information from the snatches of conversation around her. But no one really knows anything, and rumours are rife: the Germans are pulling back, the Germans are closing in.

Sporadic rifle fire cracks overhead, bullets ricocheting off the hastily built breastworks. Ratigan orders the men to stay low. Along the defence lines, unwary souls from other companies are picked off with relentless, ruthless efficiency by enemy snipers hiding in the wasteland, their aim deadly.

As night falls, it begins to pour with rain, and the shallow trenches soon fill with water. The already soft clay dissolves into a quagmire of slime, and the roughly laid planks and duckboards vanish below the waterline. There is no shelter from the wet.

There is no hope of sleep.

A message arrives from HQ: a few men are needed to investigate a newly located trench, situated some fifty yards out beyond the Allied line. The enemy is likely using it as a listening post.

'It's suspected the Germans are pulling back,' Sergeant Ratigan tells the platoon, 'leaving only a few snipers to harass our line.'

'If they're wrong, this is suicide, sir,' Bembridge says.

'Are you questioning your superiors, Private?' the officer snaps.

'No, sir.'

'Bloody glad to hear it. You're our first volunteer.'

When no others step forward, Ratigan picks three more for the mission: Stanley, Edie and Caldwell.

'Fucking madness,' Caldwell spits, barely out of

Ratigan's earshot. 'I'm not doing this. He can go himself, the bastard . . .'

'Shut up, Caldwell.' Bembridge sighs. 'Do you think any of us wants to do this?'

'It doesn't matter to you, does it?' Caldwell says. 'You don't give a shit. No one at home to miss you, is there, old man? No one –' His words are cut off as Bembridge's hand clamps round his throat. Before Edie can blink, Bembridge has shoved Caldwell into the side of the trench, pinning him against the slimy sandbags. Caldwell makes a choking sound, fingers scrabbling against Bembridge's fist.

'Shut the fuck up,' Bembridge hisses in his face.

'Leave him, Bembridge.' Stanley shoves himself between the two men. 'Don't do this, man. He's not worth it.'

Bembridge eases back, and Caldwell grabs his chance.

'You fucker!' Caldwell jerks from Bembridge's grip and launches himself at Stanley, punching his head repeatedly. They fall to the mud in a frantic ball of fists.

'No!' Edie cries, but before she can move, Sergeant Ratigan is back.

'Stop that!' Ratigan bellows, and at the sound of his voice the two men cease their fight, and struggle to their feet. Blood oozes from a cut on Stanley's muddy cheek, and one of Caldwell's eyes is puffing up. He spits a tooth into the mud, glaring at Stanley as though he'd like to rip out his throat. Edie can barely bring herself to look at Caldwell: he revolts, angers and terrifies her in equal measure.

'You're both on a charge for fighting in the ranks,'

Ratigan snarls. 'You.' He points at Caldwell. 'Latrine duty. Now. Go.'

'What about the raid, sir?' Bembridge asks. 'Caldwell's on that with us.'

'Not any more,' Ratigan snaps. 'Jackson can take his place.'

Edie exchanges a glance with Stanley. Had Caldwell orchestrated this whole thing?

From the smirk on Caldwell's face as he slopes away, Edie knows he'd done just that.

Jackson's face is so pale with terror Edie wants to plead with Sergeant Ratigan to let him stay behind. How much use will the boy be if he's so scared already? But there's no chance to argue, as Ratigan orders them to remove their insignia, ditch their cumbersome packs, smear their faces with mud.

'Leave any identifying papers, letters and photos here,' the officer tells them. 'Don't want the Hun getting their dirty hands on anything.'

Edie tucks her notebook inside her shirt, hoping Ratigan doesn't check. She stows thirty rounds of ammunition in her pockets, and fixes the bayonet to her rifle.

They have no hand grenades, no mortars, but a small contingent of men from another company is constructing homemade bombs. This, Edie discovers, involves packing old cans with shards of stone and empty cartridge cases, gun cotton, a detonator and a four-inch fuse. Bembridge takes possession of a satchel full of these primitive grenades and Edie, Stanley and Jackson stuff their remaining pockets with spare tins.

Ratigan pours a last tot of rum for each of them. 'Don't assume the Huns' trenches are empty,' he warns. 'Remember, those bastards could be anywhere.'

His final piece of advice sends a chill down Edie's spine: 'Don't stop for anyone. If one of you falls, the rest must carry on. The body-snatchers will pick up the fallen.'

16

Lucinda: October 1914

The incoming tide of casualties is relentless. Soon the hospital is full, a hundred beds taken, yet every day more wounded men arrive. Lucinda feels as though she's taken charge of a lifeboat filled with desperate survivors, in the midst of a raging storm, and none can swim.

She prepares to operate on her fifteenth, perhaps sixteenth, patient of the day. She's lost count. Once more into the fray, she thinks, as Figgis and Penhaligon lift a semi-conscious soldier on to her operating table. The man reeks of the battlefield, his uniform stiff with mud and blood. But Lucinda barely notices now.

'This one's only just stopped screaming,' Figgis grunts. 'Right racket he was making.'

The soldier gives a weak groan, one arm flailing, and Florence deftly catches his wrist. Lucinda meets her colleague's eye across the soldier's body, as the porters return to the waiting ambulance to collect the next patient.

'Ready to go again?' Florence asks, with a weak smile. They have been working since early this morning, with no break.

'Of course,' Lucinda lies. What choice have they? She's so tired, she barely has the energy to think straight.

Yet think she must.

'Who do we have here, Sister?'

'Corporal Wright.' Sister Bryony reads off the soldier's tally tag. 'Broken leg. Morphine given, but it doesn't say how much.'

'Useless, as ever,' Lucinda mutters. If the War Office could see them now, she thinks darkly, fighting to save the lives of so many men, with no information to go on, limited supplies, and precious little time . . .

While the nurse cuts away Corporal Wright's trousers, Lucinda quickly readies herself. Securing a fresh cap over her hair, she snatches up a pair of clean rubber gloves, all the while wondering at the resilience of the human body, how frankly incredible it is that she's still functioning after hours of unrelenting surgery.

Sister Bryony drops the soiled clothing into a bucket, and now Lucinda has a clear view of the soldier's injuries. His left leg is shattered from the knee down, the tibia and fibula bones both broken, jagged ends protruding from his flayed shin. Why hadn't anyone at the clearing station attempted to splint the limb? It's irredeemably damaged now, and Lucinda feels a familiar flare of anger, but she no longer fights it. She needs this fire within her heart – it's all that's keeping her going.

She turns to the instruments, and as she does so her gaze flicks across the room, to where Grace and Hazel are wrist deep in a soldier's ruptured abdomen, grappling to repair intestines that resemble a punctured bicycle inner tube. Both her colleagues look exhausted, but there's nothing Lucinda can do to alleviate their burden. She has enough to deal with: this will be her fourth amputation today.

Corporal Wright gives another faint groan, as Florence rests an anaesthetic mask over his face. Lucinda sends up a silent prayer of thanks for Florence and her well-thumbed copy of Gardner's *Surgical Anaesthesia*. The flimsy wire mask containing a wad of gauze infused with chloroform and ether will keep the soldier under while she operates. Acrid fumes leach into the air, making her eyes itch.

'Pulse erratic,' Sister Bryony reports.

'Blood pressure?'

'Holding.'

It's now or never.

The soldier's arms flop heavily on to the table.

Lucinda glances at Florence. 'Ready?'

'Yes.'

Lucinda selects a scalpel from the tray. 'Prepare the tourniquet, please, Sister.'

All you need is a strong stomach and a steady hand. Her mother's advice comes to Lucinda, as it so often does, in that liminal moment before she makes her first incision. She positions the razor-sharp blade on the soldier's leg, a few centimetres below his knee. The noise and tumult of the operating theatre drop away, as Lucinda's focus narrows.

Eyes smarting, she takes a breath. Her next move must be swift, precise, bold.

To Lucinda's profound relief, the operation goes off smoothly, with no complications. Sister Bryony places the amputated leg on a sheet on the floor, deftly wrapping it and calling for an orderly to take it away. All amputated limbs are destined for the boiler room to be incinerated, though Monsieur Cassard has been haranguing Lucinda about this, objecting to her chosen method of disposal. 'It is a risk to health,' the manager argues. 'The smoke, the fumes, it is not good for the lungs.'

'Would you rather we leave body parts lying about the place, Monsieur?'

What else are they supposed to do with them?

Cassard has no solution, yet his attitude has grown increasingly disagreeable, Lucinda has noticed. It's been reported to her that the Frenchman has taken to lurking in corridors, pouncing on Lucinda's staff for the smallest transgression. Yesterday he'd upset Galantha, accusing her of leaving a slop bucket in a walkway, which Cassard had very nearly stepped in.

Lucinda wishes he had.

Whenever she encounters the manager, he's invariably accompanied by a young woman, never the same one, it seems to Lucinda, and these women are also unpleasant to her staff. She'd confided her dislike of Cassard to Florence. 'I wish there was some way of getting rid of him.'

'Ignore him, Lucie,' Florence had replied. 'He's just an officious little man. Pay him no attention.'

But how can she ignore him, Lucinda thinks, when he has the power to complain to the hotel owners, and potentially close down their hospital? He's oily, and interfering, and obtrusive, and Lucinda wishes she could report his behaviour to someone above him, give him a taste of his own medicine.

Galantha appears, responding to Sister Bryony's

summons to remove the soldier's leg. To Lucinda the girl looks somewhat ill, but perhaps it's just the light in here. There's no time to ask her if she's feeling all right. Sister Bryony is already fetching a basin of picric acid solution, preparing to clean and bandage the man's stump.

Lucinda tugs off her rubber gloves. As she turns to drop them into the pail for sterilizing, the room suddenly swoops and darkens. She clutches the edge of the operating table her legs threatening to give.

'Lucie?' Florence is at her side.

'I – I'm fine,' Lucinda lies. 'I'm fine,' she repeats, a little more firmly.

'Truly?' Florence keeps her voice low.

Lucinda nods, locks her knees. She simply can't succumb.

The porters are back, bringing an empty stretcher. The men lift Corporal Wright's supine body off Lucinda's table, and she watches them ferry him away. If the soldier survives the next few days, he'll recuperate in the hospital until Lucinda can arrange his journey home. His injury is serious enough to be classified a 'Blighty' and for that, at least, Lucinda is grateful. This young man, unlike many she has treated, will not be sent back to fight.

'Doctor?'

Lucinda glances up from washing her hands at the sinks. Mardie Hodgson has appeared, capless and wearing a filthy apron. 'Yes, Hodgson?'

'Two gentlemen to see you, ma'am.'

Lucinda's exhausted brain is slow to process the orderly's words. 'Gentlemen?'

'One said he was Lord Egham, and the other's a doctor from London, but I can't remember his name.'

'Egham? *Lord* Egham?'

'That's what he said, ma'am.'

The cogs in Lucinda's mind begin to spin. Lord Egham, a man whose notorious opposition to female doctors has, at various times, obstructed Lucinda's career, a man who is close friends with King George, and military adviser to Lord Kitchener, was in her hospital! She turns to Florence, but she's disappeared.

'She went to check an X-ray, I think,' Sister Bryony says.

'Go and find Dr Maberry,' Lucinda directs Mardie. 'Tell her I need her now.'

Lucinda fumbles to untie her surgical gown, and Sister Bryony comes to help her. 'Hodgson, wait!'

'Yes, ma'am?'

'Where have you left Lord Egham?'

'Lobby, ma'am. They wanted to go straight into the wards, but I said I'd fetch you first.'

'Well done, Hodgson. Find Dr Maberry as quick as you can.'

Lucinda hurries to the lobby, drying her hands on her skirt in a manner that would shock her mother, if she was here. She suddenly wishes her mother *was* here: she could do with Eleanor's stalwart refusal to be intimidated by men in authority. Lord Egham and whoever his companion was were unlikely to have obeyed young Hodgson and stayed put. They'll no doubt be strutting about the wards, interrogating her staff, recording their findings to take back to the War Office. How dare they waltz in here without warning?

She reaches the lobby to find the two men waiting for her. Lord Egham and his companion turn at the sound of Lucinda's footsteps, and her heart lurches.

Dr Byers. What on earth was he doing here?

'Dr Garland.' Egham proffers a gloved hand, and Lucinda forces herself to smile and shake. 'I hope you don't mind this impromptu visit. Byers and I were in the area.'

'Not at all, gentlemen.'

Egham gestures to his companion. 'Do you know Dr Byers? Senior anaesthetist at the Radcliffe Infirmary in Oxford.'

Byers removes his hat, revealing a bald pate that gleams beneath the chandeliers. 'We do indeed know each other,' Byers says, eyes roaming over Lucinda's rumpled tunic and disordered hair.

Regrettably, Lucinda thinks.

'It's been a long time since I had the pleasure of Dr Garland's company,' Byers says.

Not nearly long enough.

'What brings you here, gentlemen?' She addresses her question to Egham.

'Don't you know? Your hospital is the talk of the town, Dr Garland.' Egham's expression is grave. This is not a compliment, Lucinda fears.

Her hands clench into fists at her sides. 'I trust the talk is favourable, sir?'

'One should never trust talk,' Byers mutters, with a strange smile.

Lucinda does her best to ignore the comment. 'So, you've come to inspect my hospital, Lord Egham?'

'An inspection sounds rather more formal than is warranted,' Egham replies. 'You're likely unaware, but the War Office is currently considering opening more base hospitals further north, some near the coast – Le Havre, Calais, Wimereux and suchlike. Byers and I offered to visit some of the more established hospitals, gather some examples of best practice and so on, and when we heard talk of yours, well, we couldn't resist dropping in.'

'You'll be sending a report to the War Office?' Lucinda presses.

'You've gone rather pale, Dr Garland,' Byers remarks. 'Are you feeling well?'

'I'm perfectly well, thank you,' Lucinda replies curtly. Oh, God, if Florence should find out Byers is here – Lucinda shuts off the thought. She must get these men out of the hospital as fast as possible. It takes her a moment to realize Egham is speaking to her.

'You're not in sole charge of this place, are you, Dr Garland?'

'My colleague and I manage the hospital together,' Lucinda replies, not looking at Byers. She mustn't utter Flo's name. 'We have an entirely female team, except for three male porters, a chef and an engineer.'

'Your colleague,' Dr Byers says. 'Would that be Dr Maberry?'

Lucinda's heart capsizes. How did the man know Florence was here? Has he tracked her down? Was he intending to resume his seduction of her?

She manages a nod, braced for the inevitable, but to her surprise Byers doesn't ask after Florence's whereabouts.

'Well, madam,' Egham says now, 'we very much disapprove of this endeavour.'

Lucinda glares at him, unable to answer for fear her voice comes out as a roar.

'I could never bring myself to fully trust a woman doctor,' Lord Egham blusters on. 'What morbid specimens of womanhood actually desire to be surgeons?' He gives another dry laugh.

Lucinda detests the man with every fibre of her being. In the theatre of her imagination, she kicks him in the shins. Hard. 'I'm proud to be a surgeon, sir.' Cold fury clips her voice. And then she has a sudden paralysing thought: Egham could close down her hospital.

'We would like to know what patients you have here,' Lord Egham says, as if Lucinda hasn't spoken. 'Their numbers and injuries and so forth.'

'At least a hundred soldiers,' Lucinda manages. 'Though that number is increasing by the day.'

'British soldiers?' Byers interjects.

'British, French, some Belgian.'

'All ranks?'

Lucinda nods. They don't discriminate in her hospital.

'I trust the officers are treated separately, Dr Garland?' This from Egham.

'We operate on the officers alongside the regular soldiers,' Lucinda replies shortly. 'They recuperate in separate wards.'

The men digest this information, and Lucinda prays Hodgson hasn't found Florence.

'We should like to see the hospital now,' Egham declares.

It's not a request. She can't refuse the man.

'This way, please, gentlemen.' Lucinda leads the men across the foyer, and into St Abigail Ward.

'We have four wards at present,' Lucinda tells Egham and Byers, as they enter the spacious, glass-walled room, filled with twenty-five occupied beds arranged in a horse-shoe configuration. A trio of nurses are at work, tending the patients. Standard lamps spaced throughout the salon bathe the ward in a soft, warm glow, and Lucinda suspects by their silence that Egham and Byers are rather impressed by the scene of calm order.

'We named the wards after female saints,' Lucinda explains. 'St Abigail contains private soldiers at present. Let me introduce you to one of my most experienced nurses.'

Sister Bryony glances up from adjusting a patient's bandages, as Lucinda and her two unwelcome guests approach.

'Sister, may we interrupt you for a moment?' Lucinda says.

'Of course, Doctor.' The nurse rises, with a polite bob of her head, catching the warning look Lucinda flashes her from behind the men's backs.

'Lord Egham, Dr Byers, this is Sister Bryony, my chief nurse.'

'Good evening, gentlemen.' Sister Bryony greets them smoothly. 'Welcome to our hospital.'

'Tell me about your work, Nurse,' Egham says, as Byers stalks away, lifting a clipboard of medical notes hanging from the end of a neighbouring bed. Lucinda watches him with a wary eye.

'Our nursing team is small,' Sister Bryony answers, 'but

we have the support of orderlies.' Just at this moment, Lucinda notices Galantha passing through the ward, lugging a bucket of soiled dressings.

'Orderly Sydenham is one of our youngest team members,' Lucinda adds.

Hearing her name, Galantha falters, turning shyly to the group, and Lucinda flashes her a smile. 'Carry on, Orderly,' she says. Galantha is still worryingly pale, she notes. Was the girl ailing? But no one has time to be ill here.

'How are the intimate needs of the patients met?' Egham wants to know.

'Our nurses are highly trained,' Sister Bryony replies. She explains the process of admission to the hospital, how the casualties are divested of their filthy, lice-infested uniforms, then given a good wash, if there is time.

'Those not requiring emergency surgery are put to bed on a ward,' Lucinda expands.

'You make it sound as though you're dealing with infants.' Egham frowns.

'On the contrary,' Lucinda retorts, 'we're dealing with badly injured, traumatized, frightened adults, sir.'

Byers returns, wanting to know what injuries Lucinda has dealt with.

'All manner of trauma,' Lucinda replies, wondering where to start.

'Any skull fractures, perhaps?' Byers presses. 'I have a particular interest in head injuries.'

An image of Private Nichols flares in Lucinda's mind. *I am the captain of my soul.*

'Gas gangrene is our most common challenge,' she replies, deflecting the question.

'Gas gangrene?' Egham barks.

'Nothing interesting, then,' Dr Byers mutters.

'We've found that the men are often suffering from very high temperatures, rapid pulse rates, accelerated respiration,' Lucinda explains. 'When we've extracted fluid from their wounds, we've found purple-crimson froth with a foul smell, and on further investigation this has indicated anaerobic infection and sepsis, a serious threat to recovery –'

'How did you discover this?' Egham interrupts.

'A swab of every wound is taken during the admission process,' Lucinda explains. 'The swabs are sent straight to our laboratory, and –'

'What laboratory?' Egham snaps.

'We have a room, with a couple of microscopes set up. They've proved invaluable in spotting the bacteria in time.'

In so many cases, gas gangrene has been detected, revealing the presence of invisible bacteria lurking in a shell wound or a shrapnel injury. If the harmful bacteria are not completely eradicated, the patient will likely die, however successful the preceding surgery.

'Gas gangrene harbours multiple bacteria,' Lucinda continues, warming to her theme now. 'We've discovered *B. perfringens* present in almost every case, as is *Streptococci* and *Vibrion septique . . .*'

Egham wants to visit the so-called laboratory, so Lucinda leads them out of St Abigail Ward.

'What about an X-ray machine?' Byers asks, as they cross the foyer again, footsteps echoing on the marble. 'You have one, I trust?'

They do indeed, Lucinda tells him. She's about to explain how temperamental the machine can be, when Monsieur Cassard appears.

'Ah, Docteur. I have found you.'

Lucinda groans inwardly. This is not what she needs. '*Bonjour,* Monsieur Cassard.'

'I wasn't informed we have visitors,' Cassard says, glaring at Egham and Byers.

Lucinda introduces them.

'You are in charge of this hotel?' Egham asks the Frenchman.

'I am merely the eyes and ears of the owner,' Cassard replies.

'Are they happy their premises are being used as a hospital?' Egham wants to know.

'*Oui,*' Cassard replies, with a Gallic shrug.

'Are they aware it's run by women?' Byers asks. Lucinda bites her lip.

'*Oui.*' Cassard gives another shrug.

'I see,' Egham says. 'Well, I'm afraid we're rather pressed for time, Monsieur, so if you'll excuse us . . .'

With relief, Lucinda hurries her visitors on.

17

Edie: October 1914

A hunter's moon hangs in a charcoal sky. Edie waits with Bembridge, Stanley and Jackson, crouched in a shallow trench that's little more than a ditch at the furthest forward point of the defence line. If Edie were to raise her head above the sandbagged parapet, a suicidal move, she would see nothing but wasteland stretching away into the night. They must cross it to reach another trench that may, or may not, be in enemy hands. Huddled in the darkness, they listen to the murmur of voices drifting from the trenches behind them, the faint clinks of metal spoons on mess tins, a distant, hacking cough that goes on and on.

'Ready?' Bembridge whispers hoarsely.

They answer him with silent nods, eyes wide. They can never be ready for what surely lies ahead.

Bembridge drags himself up and over the lip of the trench, body flat in the mud, and one by one, Edie, Stanley and Jackson follow him. Edie had imagined they'd have to crawl on their bellies across the wasteland, but now she sees it would take far too long, and already Bembridge is on his feet, crouched low in a stumbling run.

A flare bursts overhead, briefly illuminating the ravaged landscape, and Edie glimpses a warren of trenches extending far into the distance.

She staggers after the others, her rifle heavy in her hands, boots tripping and sliding through the mire. Any second now, she expects to hear the distinctive crack of rifle fire – they're an obvious target for enemy snipers, wherever they're lurking.

By some miracle, no shots break the quiet of the night, only the rasping of Edie's breaths, and the frantic pounding of blood in her ears.

Ahead, Bembridge suddenly drops to his stomach. Has he been shot? No, he's crawling along the ground now. Edie shoulders her rifle and drops too, dragging herself over the rutted earth. Cold mud seeps through her trousers, up the sleeves of her tunic, the stench of manure filling her nostrils.

The group inch their way the final few feet to a shallow ditch marking the outer boundary of the German line. Along the jagged parapet, a tripwire of tins has been strung, hanging limp in the still night.

With a nod from Bembridge, Stanley lobs a clod of earth at the wire, setting the tins rattling. The men and Edie lie frozen, hands over their heads. Edie ceases to breathe, braced for the inevitable rat-tat-tat-tat-tat of answering machine-gun fire.

But there is only silence.

After a few seconds, Bembridge gives a short, low whistle. The signal to go on.

They crawl forward, and one by one slide down into what appears to be a deserted listening post.

Edie's legs are trembling. They are in enemy territory, and every second they linger here, the risk of being discovered increases.

There are no signs of life in the trench, no glimmers of light, no sounds, no voices. Bembridge gestures to the others to follow him, and they set off into the darkness, stumbling over discarded empty bottles, food tins and petrol canisters littering the ground. Edie flinches at the sight of a leather glove poking from the side of the trench, like a macabre severed hand.

'Bloody hell, look at this.' A few steps ahead, Stanley is hunched over a leather case. He opens it to reveal a medical kit filled with dressings, phials of drugs, surgical instruments neatly wrapped in gauze. A lucky find. But the case is bulky and cumbersome. Should they take it, or leave it behind?

'It's too bloody good for the Hun.' Stanley hefts the case up, and they stagger on after Bembridge.

It feels to Edie as though they're descending into the earth. The sides of the trench loom over her, and a fear of being slowly buried tightens her chest.

A low warning whistle comes from up ahead.

Edie slows to a stop. She can make out Stanley's motionless figure a little way in front of her, can hear Jackson whimpering somewhere behind her. But she can't see Bembridge at all.

Pressing herself into the side of the trench, Edie barely breathes. She's adept at making herself invisible, a skill honed from her time in the workhouse, years spent avoiding the older, rougher children, the groping hands of certain men, the thump of the governor's cane. But this is worse than anything in that place.

She fights the urge to turn back. To hell with orders. They've proved this trench is deserted. There are no

Germans lurking in the shadows. Every minute they remain here is suicide.

A second low whistle. Was Bembridge giving the all-clear?

Before Edie can react, a sharp crack rends the quiet of the night, followed by a second gunshot, terrifyingly loud, terrifyingly close. From somewhere in the dark ahead, men are shouting, in what language Edie can't tell.

'Move!' Stanley is suddenly dragging her back down the trench, Jackson stumbling ahead, and Edie can't feel her legs, her body numb from the neck down. A stitch tears into her side, a knife between her ribs.

'Move!'

But she can't run any faster.

In a moment of awful clarity, Edie pictures herself as if from above, a hunted fox desperately fleeing hounds, moments from being ripped to shreds. Her heart punches in her chest.

A further volley of gunshots bursts behind them, and Edie stumbles, looks back. Grey figures are bearing down on them. Another shot, and Stanley cries out, crashing into Edie, felled like a tree.

Edie staggers, lifting her rifle as she twists, firing blind. The nearest figure drops, but Edie fires again, and again. And someone is screaming, but the sound is far off, and there's no time to run now, as the second soldier lunges at her.

Time slows. Edie senses a shift in her core, a rising tide of fear and fury that wrenches a cry from deep within her, as she plunges her bayonet into the German soldier's torso. A howl rips from the man, and with a strength born of terror, Edie pushes the bayonet deeper. And now time speeds up again, as her attacker swings a fist, connecting with Edie's jaw, knocking her back, and he's surging at her, pulling her to the ground.

They grapple, Edie's rifle lost to the mud, and everything is forgotten as Edie fights for her life. The soldier's bulk, his sheer muscular strength is far greater, and even as he bleeds out he manages to pin Edie, grinding her body into the earth.

His face looms above her, eyes blazing, teeth bared, and Edie struggles beneath him, unable to breathe, the man's hands gripping her throat now, pressing down on her windpipe. Warm blood spills from the German soldier's mouth, spattering Edie's cheeks, chin. Her senses are dimming, the world turning black.

Where there's breath, there's life.

But there's no more breath.

18

Lucinda: October 1914

Lucinda hastens Egham and Byers towards the pathology room, hoping the men won't demand to see the X-ray machine, where they might encounter Florence.

They arrive at the makeshift laboratory, to find Dr Hazel busy preparing microscope slides. As Lucinda introduces her visitors, she tries to warn her colleague with her eyes of the danger these men represent.

Egham fires questions at Hazel, wanting to know where she studied pathology, who instructs her now, how the results are analysed.

Hazel fields his questions as best she can, but Lucinda can tell she's struggling to retain a polite composure.

'Dr Sydenham has been instrumental in discovering various strands of bacteria,' Lucinda interjects, when she can bear the interrogation no longer. 'There are many types we've never come across before.'

Hazel takes this as the cue to produce a box of neatly labelled slides.

While the men inspect them, peering down the lenses of the microscopes, Lucinda explains to them how bacteria is rampant in the men's wounds, possibly due to manure in the soil. 'The worst of it is, we often have no time to clean the injuries properly,' she tells the men. 'No time to search out every shrapnel or metal fragment. The pressure is too great to operate quickly.'

Egham nods, looking interested, and Lucinda begins to hope he is coming round to the idea of women undertaking surgery.

'Where's Dr Maberry?' Byers asks, as they bid goodbye to Hazel, and Lucinda leads the men out of the lab.

Lucinda's step falters. 'She's on her rest break, I believe.' The lie trips off her tongue.

'I would like to speak to her,' Byers insists. 'Pick her brains about what kinds of anaesthesia she's using here.'

'Ether and chloroform, mainly,' Lucinda answers. 'Supplies are patchy, so it's sometimes a question of improvising.'

'Improvising?' Byers pins Lucinda with a look of scorn. 'I hardly think Dr Maberry would appreciate you describing her expertise in such a fashion.'

'I can't disturb Dr Maberry's rest,' Lucinda hears herself say. 'Where else would you like to visit?'

'The X-ray machine,' Byers says.

Lucinda feels the blood drain from her head. She tries to think. 'We'll go via the officers' ward,' she says, and strides off before either man can protest.

To Lucinda's relief, the patients endorse the hospital, every last one expressing their gratitude to Lucinda and her team of women.

'They can't do more for us, sir,' an officer with a broken collarbone tells Egham. 'Not a jot more. All our needs are cared for. They're angels.'

But despite the affirmation of her work, Lucinda feels

as though she's aged a decade by the time Egham and Byers declare they've finished with their tour. There's no time left to visit the X-ray machine, so Lucinda leads the men back to the entrance foyer, unable quite to believe she's survived the ordeal.

'Dr Garland?'

Florence is suddenly there, her appearance freezing the blood in Lucinda's veins.

'Dr Maberry!' Byers swoops, a bird of prey. 'Where have you been hiding?'

Florence blanches, as Byers plants a lingering kiss on the back of her hand. Lucinda wants to wrench the man away, twist his arm behind his back, march him off the premises. How dare he even touch Florence, after what he's put her through?

'You didn't tell me we had visitors,' Florence says, pinning Lucinda with a sharp look.

'You were resting,' Lucinda stammers. 'I didn't want to disturb you.'

Florence turns to Egham. 'Are you here to see our hospital, sir?'

'We have indeed seen your hospital, Dr Maberry,' Egham replies. 'It's been a most interesting experience. Wouldn't you agree, Byers?'

'Indeed.' Dr Byers is staring at Florence with the focus of a hawk. 'Very interesting indeed.'

'I hope you're reassured by our work here, gentlemen,' Lucinda manages.

'Very much so, Dr Garland,' Egham replies.

Lucinda is momentarily lost for words.

'We're both very impressed, aren't we, Byers? Your

hospital clearly has an important role to play. We shall ensure that the War Office is fully apprised of your endeavours.'

'I'm glad your visit was fruitful, sir,' Florence says coolly.

'Made all the more fruitful for seeing you, Dr Maberry,' Byers says.

The skin on Lucinda's arms prickles.

'Thank you,' Florence answers, gracing Byers with a fleeting smile. Lucinda wants to grab her by the shoulders and shake her. *Don't smile at him!*

'Was that everything, gentlemen?' Lucinda hears the terseness in her voice, can sense Florence's eyes on her.

'Let us leave these good ladies to their work, Byers,' Egham says, heading for the door.

Dr Byers steps closer to Florence. 'I shall be in touch.'

'Why on earth didn't you tell me he was here, Lucie?'

'I had no warning, Flo.' Lucinda feels a familiar tightening in her chest, and fights the urge to seize Florence in a hug, here in the shadowy courtyard behind the hotel, with the dusky-blue sky arcing above them.

Oh, God, why did Byers have to turn up again, like a bad penny?

'That man.' Florence sighs, her eyes shining in the soft light spilling from the ward windows.

Lucinda waits for her to say more, but she falls silent. There is so much Lucinda could say but fear, decorum and concern for Florence stay her tongue. If Florence doesn't want to talk about Byers and his obsessive, sinister pursuit of her in London, what good would it do for Lucinda to drag it up again? The whole sorry affair is in the past, after all, and Florence is here with her. Byers, the bastard, is gone.

Thank the Lord.

Lucinda takes a sip from her small glass of gin. 'Medicinal,' she'd reassured Florence. 'To settle our nerves.'

The unexpected visit from Egham and Byers had been more than troubling.

But they'd survived.

Lucinda breathes in the still, peaceful evening air, the rumble of distant artillery quiet for once. A full moon, bright as a silver coin, winks from behind lacy clouds. She smothers a yawn with the back of her hand. 'I feel as if I've gone twelve rounds with Billy Wells today,' she says.

'You're a wee fighter, Lucie,' Florence murmurs. 'Ever the victor.'

'Victor? I don't feel like a victor. Those two nearly knocked me senseless.'

Florence lifts her glass, gestures for Lucinda to do the same. 'Egham and Byers came,' she intones, in a mock-grave voice. 'Egham and Byers saw.' She lifts her glass a fraction higher. 'Lucie and Flo conquered.' She brings her glass to touch Lucinda's in a toast, and they down their gin in one.

'Goodness.' Lucinda coughs, and Florence laughs. The backs of Lucinda's knees are softening, and although she finds she rather likes the sensation, she's afraid she might fall asleep, right here in the courtyard, if she doesn't take herself off to bed soon.

And yet, she realizes helplessly, all she wants is to stay out here with Florence until the dawn.

19

Edie: October 1914

The seeping chill of dawn finally rouses her. For one long, petrifying moment, Edie has no idea where she is, how she's come to be lying in freezing mud. Rough walls of earth rise on either side of her, shored up with planks and sacking, and the sight triggers a memory at last.

She's in enemy territory.

At the back of her mind, a voice begins urging her to *get out*. But as in a nightmare, her body is numb, her limbs unresponsive. It takes a supreme effort just to lift her head, her neck painfully stiff. At last, she manages to push herself up on one elbow, finally struggling to her knees. Her arms and legs are heavy as lumps of wood, her thoughts sluggish. She can feel the last vestiges of warmth leaching from her body, and her teeth begin to chatter. She's colder than she can ever remember being in her life, unable to feel her feet. Her hands, she discovers, when she tries to rub grit from her eyes, are frozen. She blows on her fingers to warm them. With no warning the world tilts on its axis, and her vision darkens. She slumps, forehead colliding with the trench wall. The shock of reeking wet sacking against her skin jolts her alert again.

A single thought pulses in her brain: *Move.*

Her leg muscles, drained of strength, refuse to support

her; she can do no more than kneel. The trench stretches away on either side of her, bodies strewn the length of it. Next to her is the German soldier she'd stabbed, the body a tangled mass of grey serge stained dark with blood. Edie can't bear to look at the man's face, his dead, staring eyes.

She turns away, only to be met with a sight that freezes her heart anew. Two feet from her, Stanley is lying curled against the trench wall.

With a muted cry, she crawls to his side.

'Stan!' She grasps his arm, and his eyelids flicker. She can see the effort it costs him as his lips crack apart, but no sound emerges.

'Stan!' She's crying now, tears blurring her vision. 'Wake up, please, wake up.'

Don't leave me.

She can't lose him – he's been her north bearing all this time. Without him, she is lost.

Stanley's eyelids open, and he blinks up into Edie's terrified gaze.

'Stan . . .' She tugs on his arm. 'Can you hear me? We've got to get out.'

'Go . . .' Stanley coughs the word, dark liquid trickling from the corner of his mouth.

For the space of one heartbeat, two, three, Edie can't move, can't think.

From somewhere beyond the trench she hears the distant sound of men shouting.

'I'm not bloody leaving you.' Terror fractures her voice. 'I'm not.'

And then her gaze falls on Stanley's blood-drenched

trousers, his shredded puttees sodden with gore. One of his legs is twisted at an unnatural angle, and the sight of it sends Edie's mind into freefall.

'Go . . .' Stanley grips Edie's wrist with a strength that shocks her. His fingers briefly tighten, then fall limp.

'No, don't leave me . . .' Edie sobs. She desperately scans the trench for Bembridge and Jackson, but there's no sign of them. From the depths of her mind, her meagre training comes back to her. She fumbles her field dressing from a pocket, trying to recall the single lesson she'd had on first aid, back at Hurst Park, a lifetime ago. A world away from this nightmare.

Stem the blood. Keep the casualty talking.

'Stan!' She needs him to stay awake. His eyelids flicker again, and Edie's heart lifts. She dredges her mind for something to say that will keep his attention, but all she can think is *Don't die, don't die.*

For the longest moment, she clasps the package of bandages to her chest, paralysed.

Stanley groans, coughing up more blood, and Edie is jerked from her torpor. From somewhere deep in her numb brain, it comes to her what she must do. She tears open the dressing, intending to wrap the length of bandage around Stanley's broken leg. But at her touch he cries out, pushing her away.

Edie hesitates, torn between causing Stanley more pain, and trying to save his life. 'I have to stop the bleeding.'

Stanley collapses back into the mud, bloody spittle glistening on his chin. His eyes close again, and through a haze of panic Edie realizes he's passed out.

'Stan!' She grabs his shoulder, and with the last of her

strength shakes him as hard as she can. But despite her best efforts, she can't wake him.

She slumps against the wall, defeated, and Sergeant Ratigan's voice comes to her. *Don't stop for anyone, lads. The body-snatchers will collect the fallen.*

But where are the fucking stretcher-bearers? No one's coming to help. She's on her own.

Stanley offers no resistance, as Edie binds his legs, cinching the bandages as securely as her trembling hands can manage. Just as she's fumbling to tie the last knot, he lifts his head, mumbling nonsensically, and hope flares in Edie's chest.

Water, she thinks. *He needs water.*

She has none with her. She casts about the trench, and her gaze snags on the German's corpse; a canteen hangs from the dead man's belt. It takes everything she has to unclip the enamel bottle. Before she can change her mind, she wrestles off the cap, brings the bottle to her mouth. Cool water slides down her raging throat like balm.

Crawling back to Stanley, she brings the canteen to his cracked lips, watching helplessly as precious water dribbles from the corner of his mouth. At last, he manages to swallow a mouthful, then another, and his head slumps back against the trench wall.

Edie takes another swig, the burning sensation in her throat gradually easing.

They can't stay here, she knows. Stanley is mortally wounded. If she doesn't get him to an aid post very soon . . . Her mind falters at the thought.

Had Bembridge and Jackson made it back to the reserve line? Will anyone come to find her and Stan?

In her heart, she knows the answer. No one is coming.

'Lawrence . . .' Stanley moans, shivering now. 'Go . . .' He can barely get the word out, his teeth rattling in his mouth like dice, his blood-streaked face alabaster-white in the dawn light.

'I'm not leaving you.' Edie grips his hand, and is rewarded with a weak, answering squeeze.

Only now, Stanley's eyes are closing again, and Edie is gripped with fresh fear as his shivering gradually ceases. Even in her dazed state, Edie knows this is bad news. She searches the immediate area for something to cover him, a piece of tarpaulin, a torn empty sandbag. But there's nothing, only the German corpses, and she hasn't the stomach to touch those again.

Understanding sinks through her: Stanley will die if she doesn't do something.

She can't lose him.

I love you.

The words crowd her tongue, but she can't quite spit them out. How can she admit this sudden, overwhelming feeling, when they are only friends?

Stanley would laugh at her. Tell her to bugger off.

A sudden high-pitched whine pierces the air, growing rapidly louder. Before Edie can register what's happening, the end of the trench explodes, blasting planks and sandbags into the air. Edie flings herself across Stanley's body, face buried in his tunic, as chunks of stone and earth beat down, pummelling her back, her shoulders, her unprotected head.

She can hardly breathe as shellfire rages around her, the ground shuddering. Bullets sear across the top of the trench, mud spitting as they strike the ramparts, the metallic smell of cordite filling the air.

How long she lies huddled against Stanley's body, Edie has no idea. Eventually, the sound of the guns diminishes, and she rolls off, astonished to find she's still breathing. When she tries to sit up, a burning pain rips up the back of her right thigh and she cries out. But there's no one to hear her. With a shaking hand, she feels for a wound site, her fingers coming away tacky with blood.

Oh God, oh God, oh God.

She gropes for Stanley's hand.

His fingers are cold and unresponsive, and even as she grips harder, a wave of terror bears down on her.

∞

Rainclouds advance steadily across the darkening sky. Edie lies curled against Stanley, his hand cold in hers. She tries to recall his voice, his funny little quips, his theories of how her nose had come to grief.

You been a naughty boy, ain't you, Lawrence?

You been dipping your wick where you shouldn't, eh, kid?

Some jealous husband landed one on you, didn't he?

She misses Stanley's gentle teasing, the silly jokes he told her to wile away the time.

Here, kid, this is a good 'un. Who was the greatest chicken-killer in Shakespeare? Macbeth, cos he did murder most foul. D'you get it?

Hours pass, unmarked but for the gradual fading of daylight. Edie listens to the diminishing thump of far-off guns, until she can no longer distinguish the sound from her own erratic heartbeat. If only she could light a fire to warm them, but everything is damp or covered with mud, and she has no matches.

As dusk falls, a thick mist descends. A yellowish haze, like tobacco smoke, fills the trench, obliterating everything beyond Edie's outstretched arm. The knowledge that she's stranded, alone in enemy territory with the darkness creeping in, loosens her bladder. Hot piss soaks her legs, a moment of fleeting warmth that soon grows uncomfortable.

Her mouth is parched, but there's no water left in the German's canteen. She tries to sit up, but after so long lying on the unforgiving ground her legs feel oddly boneless, her muscles powerless. Moving brings on a bout of coughing, and pain racks her body. Her shoulders cramp as she flexes her arms, trying to get the blood flowing again. She wipes her gritty, sore eyes and a sickly-sweet stench reaches her, a putrid smell of rotting flesh and latrines. Movement in the fog brings a strangled cry to her lips, but it's not the German corpses coming back to life: rats are scrambling over the bodies, gnawing at any exposed flesh. She can see their black furry backs writhing, long pink tails twitching.

She turns away in revulsion – and it hits her then: if she doesn't get out soon, she will die here tonight.

She'll be food for the rats next.

And no one will mourn her passing.

Fury flares in her breast. This was never meant to happen. She wasn't supposed to die like this, trapped and helpless. She fumbles the leather notebook from her pocket, thinking of all the words she's yet to write, all the truth she must try to convey. If she dies, her story dies with her.

She finds a stub of pencil, prints her real name and date of birth on the first page.

Edie Lawrence, 4 June 1895

And then she begins to write.

The surge of energy fuelled by anger quickly subsides, and after only a few lines she can no longer hold the pencil to the page. She has no strength left to waste on anything but fighting for her life now.

She stows the notebook away, then leans over Stanley's inert body. His eyes are closed, mouth slack. 'Can you hear me? Stan?'

Nothing.

Edie brings her lips to his ear, whispering. 'I'm sorry.'

It's too late, she knows. She lets her head fall on to Stanley's chest, too exhausted and terrified to cry, and feels the shape of a small box against her cheek. Lifting her head again, she prises Stanley's camera from his tunic pocket.

And now she tastes the salt of tears.

∞

With the arrival of night, the guns fall quiet, only the occasional distant flare piercing the darkness.

Once, a shout, close by.

Anyone there?

Edie has no voice to answer. She lies, staring up into a depthless void, and the stars unfix themselves, trembling in the black.

How is she still alive?

Perhaps she isn't. Perhaps this is Purgatory. She tastes copper on her lips, and as her tongue works a loose back molar free of its moorings, something low in the sky catches her eye: a strange light, bigger than a star. She blinks as it pulses brighter, then dimmer, then brighter again. It begins descending, dropping through the black, somehow falling towards her, and as it falls it grows larger, soon blazing like a small sun. Edie lifts a weak arm to shade her eyes against the glare, wrapping her other arm across her chest, over Stanley's camera and the notebook.

The light is overwhelmingly bright now, and Edie is forced to close her eyes. An odd feeling of warmth engulfs her, flowing up through her legs and into her torso, along her arms. Her fingers tingle. It's akin to being submerged in hot water, although Edie can't recall the last time she enjoyed anything resembling a bath. A moment later, she senses the intensity of the light begin to fade, allowing her to crack open one eye, then the other.

What she sees makes no sense to her.

The sphere of light hovers on the parapet now. It could be the setting sun, except this is no sun. An intense glow radiates out, pulsating a golden light too strong for Edie to look at directly.

She narrows her eyes, and the breath stutters in her throat as a form begins to emerge from the light. Whatever the creature is, it's larger than a human: limbs long and slender, face luminous, eyes glowing. Its curvaceous body is clad in a strange silvery armour that shimmers like distant starlight.

The angel – for surely it can only be an angel – hovers over Edie, its huge, iridescent wings spread wide. Each feather-tip glistens sharp as a bayonet blade.

Paralysed with fear, Edie can only stare as the creature

from the sky beats its wings once, twice. A warm breeze glides over Edie's body, bringing with it a sensation of such profound peace that her eyes fill with tears. She's transported back to a long-ago memory, of lying in the shelter of her mother's gentle embrace.

The angel's mouth opens, and Edie hears its voice as a thousand bells chiming inside her head.

And then she hears no more.

20

Lucinda: November 1914

Hôpital Auxiliaire, Hôtel Clarens, Paris

Dearest Mother

*Your letter came this morning. Much has happened since your last.
We now have French, Belgian, Scottish and Irish wounded. All
the main wards are full, and the English officers are having to
share half of St Dymphna Ward with their foreign counterparts.*

Lucinda dips her pen into the inkwell.

*The surgery is never-ending. We're in theatre almost round the
clock, and the injuries are more complex and traumatic than we've
ever faced before. Many of the wounds we see are already septic,
causing serious complications in terms of gas gangrene. Our X-ray
machine is proving a boon, when it chooses to cooperate. The
bacteria in the wounds manifest as white patches on the slides,
quite easy to spot once you get your eye in. We would be most
grateful for a back-up machine, if that could be arranged. Would
you enquire of the Hospital Board, to see if they could spare one
for us to have on loan?*

    *Domestic arrangements leave something to be desired, but we
do have a chef, Monsieur Achille. He certainly lives up to the*

stereotype, but I must say he's rather impressed us with his
repertoire of dishes made from little more than potatoes and
onions.

Lucinda dips her pen into the ink again, stomach growling. Writing of food makes her think of Mrs Fairweather, how the old housekeeper had despaired of Lucinda and Florence's working lifestyle and erratic mealtimes, treating them like a pair of hapless bachelors in need of feeding up.

The pen trembles in Lucinda's hand, ink dripping, as she conjures in her mind's eye a bowl of Mrs Fairweather's apple crumble and custard, golden and steaming. She can almost taste it. What would Achille say, if she asked him to produce such a dish? Lucinda makes a mental note to ask Mardie to broach the request – the chef seems to have taken a shine to the young orderly.

With an effort of will, she turns back to her letter.

The surgery is intense, with many severe fractures and amputations.
Four staff are needed to dress some of the more major wounds, and
even then it can take the best part of an hour to perform, so you
can see we are hard up against it. Luckily, the nurses and orderlies
are proving to be more than satisfactory workers.

There have regrettably been a number of deaths, but so many
of the men are already on the brink by the time they reach us,
there's sometimes little we can do for them. The Red Cross have
sent over a chaplain, Father Stevens, and he writes letters for the
men, and conducts funeral rites when required.

The desk lamp flickers in the draught coming through the partly open door. Lucinda adjusts the flame, thinking of the tall, hollow-cheeked chaplain who'd arrived unannounced a week ago. She can't deny it was a relief to hand over the responsibility of the funerals to a man of the cloth. Before Father Stevens had appeared, there had been no opportunity to mark the passing of a patient, save a hasty prayer spoken over the coffin before it was taken away by the French Red Cross.

Despite his competence in performing the last rites and conducting services, the flint-eyed chaplain hasn't instilled much confidence in Lucinda so far. When she'd asked him about his experience of comforting the war wounded, Father Stevens had avoided her eye, blustering evasively about serving with the Red Cross back in Southampton.

Our engineer, Monsieur Perrin, has worked a miracle with the hotel's grill room, transforming it into a chapel. It comes with stained-glass moon-shaped ceiling lights, which let in filtered sunlight, and marble pillars flank the room, lending the place a rather cathedral-like air, in miniature, of course. Perrin has constructed a low wooden stage at one end, and has fashioned a cross from some off-cuts of wood he found, which he's suspended above the dais. The engineer really has been a godsend, Mama, turning his hand to anything we ask of him.

Lucinda looks up, tensing as rapid footsteps patter along the corridor outside. What emergency needs her attention now? To her relief, they pass her door without pausing, and her shoulders relax a notch.

Lord Egham came to inspect us recently, bringing with him Dr Byers, whom you may remember practised for a time at the Royal

Free, where Florence briefly worked under his direction. The gentlemen fired questions in an aggressive, military manner, which of course they had no right to do, as we are financed by private donations and the French Red Cross. But we answered all their queries, and showed them round the wards, and the officers and men were all most appreciative of our hospital and made their views known. And, would you know, Egham's manner rather changed, and he was almost friendly by the time he left. If he does as he promises, and puts in a good word for us at the War Office, perhaps they will rethink their attitude and lend us their support.

Any offers of help with clothing are most appreciated. Shirts, socks, small towels, handkerchiefs, these sorts of things are desperately needed.

Please give my fond regards to Ambrose, Muriel and the family.

Very much love, dearest Mother,
Yrs, Lucinda

She seals the letter, thinking of its long onward journey to reach Eleanor, miles away across the sea. Her mother may be frailer in body, but she possesses an indomitable spirit and a core of iron. Lucinda won't be at all surprised if her mother requests to visit soon.

For a moment, she contemplates the pile of paperwork on her desk. The last few days, she's begun to feel more clerk than physician and surgeon, spending every spare minute writing letters, filling in forms, completing dockets. She's all too aware of the need to keep an eye on the accounts, so that there can be no criticism of her hospital management. To that end, she's entrusted Tozer with the responsibility of taking stock of equipment and supplies. The porter is diligently recording every last roll of gauze used, so that those in authority – she's thinking of Madame Pérouse and the French Red Cross – continue to support them. But even though she trusts Tozer, still Lucinda must check and check again, and it is a drain on her time and energy.

The bell in the foyer rings out, three resounding chimes calling all those who are free to make their way to the chapel for the evening's funeral service. Lucinda rises from her desk with a sigh, her legs stiff, and joins Florence and two orderlies, Galantha and Olga, already seated in the temporary chapel.

The room has a gloomier atmosphere than usual, autumnal rain drumming on the skylights. Lucinda slips into the seat next to Florence, who graces her with a smile.

'Shouldn't you be sleeping?' Florence murmurs.

'I may well fall asleep before this is over,' Lucinda whispers back, her eye drawn to the trio of coffins raised on trestle legs, lined up along the low stage. Lucinda's gaze skitters over the rough-hewn boxes, not wanting to think about the bodies of the young men they contain. Her eyes drift up to the plain wooden cross that Monsieur Perrin has suspended from the wall. She tries to take some comfort from it, but her heart beats in a hollow void. What benevolent God would allow this nightmare of war?

She hears murmuring from the chairs behind, and half twists in her seat. From the corner of her eye, she can see Galantha and Olga, white-capped heads tipped together. Olga's hands are carving invisible marks in the air, Galantha's shoulders shaking with silent laughter. Lucinda suppresses a sigh. She should reprimand the girls for their lack of respect in this place of worship, but she hasn't the will to deny them a moment of relief.

'Are you all right?' Florence asks softly, as Lucinda turns back to face the coffins again.

'Yes, of course,' Lucinda lies. She's saved from further questioning by the arrival of the chaplain.

'Good evening.' Father Stevens greets the tiny congregation, barely glancing at the women as he steps up to the lectern. There's something about the man that makes Lucinda uneasy. Yesterday, she'd confided her reservations to Florence, who immediately dismissed her worries as unfounded.

'He can't look me in the eye,' Lucinda had insisted. 'He seems . . . shady . . .'

'Perhaps he's simply overwhelmed by you,' Florence had replied.

This comment had utterly confounded Lucinda. To her knowledge, she'd never overwhelmed a man in her life, intentionally or not.

'Just imagine yourself in his shoes,' Florence had tried to explain. 'He's been sent to an all-female-run hospital, in a foreign country, in the middle of a war, and the first person he meets is the formidably intelligent, disarmingly handsome Dr Lucinda Garland. Can you blame the poor man for being a little nervous?'

Lucinda had been about to object that, on the contrary, it was Father Stevens who made *her* nervous when she'd caught the merest twitch of Florence's lips. Her friend was teasing her.

Lucinda stares at the chaplain now, but the man

continues to avoid her eye. She wonders if he's been sent here on sufferance. Anyone in their right mind would be leaving Paris by now, Lucinda thinks. The Germans are encroaching day by day, if the irregular news reports are anything to go by. Certainly, the city is a shadow of its former self, although Lucinda has seen little of it lately. She's banned her team from leaving the hotel without permission, yet few have shown any interest in exploring, and those who have – Mardie and Olga – returned with reports of shops and cafés shut, rendering outings rather futile.

Lucinda's attention snaps back to Father Stevens, who is opening his Bible now. The sight of the holy book brings childhood memories of church flashing through her tired brain: hard pews and soporific sermons, time slowing to an unbearable crawl. She begins to wilt in the chair, her eyelids feeling as though they're made of stone. Florence casts her a quick glance, and Lucinda has a sudden overwhelming urge to rest her head on her friend's steady shoulder, close her eyes and sink into blessed oblivion for a short while.

'Welcome,' Father Stevens begins, his voice jerking Lucinda alert. She looks up to see the chaplain gripping the lectern as though at the wheel of a ship. 'We have come together today to rejoice over the bravery of three men who have died fighting for us . . .'

As the chaplain drones on, Lucinda's attention is pulled inexorably back to the trio of coffins. She can't help but picture the men they contain, lives that she and her team couldn't save, though God knows they tried their best.

'Please rise for our first hymn,' Father Stevens intones.

Lucinda pushes herself up from the chair. As soon as this service is over, she'll have a few hours to rest. And then the surgery will start again.

For now, she knows she should take this brief opportunity to relax. A rare moment to breathe.

'*O God, our help in ages past, our hope for years to come,*' Father Stevens sings out. The first time she'd heard the deep richness of his voice it had taken Lucinda by surprise. She'd expected a rather reedier tone, given the man's stork-like frame. One by one, Florence, Olga and Galantha join in the hymn, their singing hesitant at first, their varied voices a melodious accompaniment to the chaplain's bass.

'*Our shelter from the stormy blast, and our eternal home . . .*'

As the women's voices rise around her, Lucinda finds herself unable to utter a sound. She can't rid her mind of all the men they have lost, their light extinguished far too soon. A waste of truly epic proportions. Too many of the soldiers were frighteningly young, mere adolescents, and she was almost old enough to be their mother. At nearly thirty, it's practically too late now to consider motherhood, of course, and in truth the urge to bear children has never been strong in her. It would involve a man, in any case, and that has never really been on the cards. And yet here, among these young soldiers, surrounded by her largely youthful staff, a latent maternal urge is rising. It unsettles her.

She can't keep mourning every single death here, she berates herself. These soldiers are not her sons. Losing patients is something every doctor must face and accept. After all, who among her colleagues was without a grave mistake or heartrending loss on their conscience?

She remembers as though it was yesterday the first thing

old Dr Craddock had taught them in their medical training: not every life can be saved.

Yet knowing this doesn't make it any easier.

The hymn ends, and the women sink on to their chairs.

'We must not mourn their passing . . .' Father Stevens continues, but Lucinda barely hears him. Her thoughts have turned to her mother, who lost her fair share of patients over the course of her long career. Each death left a mark, a shadow on the soul, Eleanor had once admitted to Lucinda. But the loss of a young patient is always doubly hard to bear.

Lucinda thinks of Private Nichols, barely twenty, with his whole life ahead of him.

I am the captain of my soul.

Her fists clench of their own accord, nails digging into the clammy flesh of her palms.

'Psalm twenty-three,' the chaplain says. '*The Lord is my shepherd, therefore can I lack nothing.*'

Lucinda steals a glance at Florence, her profile etched in shadow.

'*He shall feed me in a green pasture . . .*'

Lucinda drinks in the soft curve of Florence's cheek, the perfect slope of her nose. Whenever Lucinda looks at her dear friend, it's like putting her eye to the gap in a curtain and glimpsing daylight beyond.

'. . . *and lead me forth beside the waters of comfort. He shall convert my soul . . .*'

Lucinda turns her gaze back to the chaplain, clasping her trembling hands in her lap. A moment later, she feels Florence's cool fingers settle on the exposed skin of her wrist.

'. . . and bring me forth in the paths of righteousness, for his Name's sake . . .'

Florence's gentle touch sends a tingle along Lucinda's arm.

'Yea, though I walk through the valley of the shadow of death, I will fear no evil,' Father Stevens drones on. 'For thou art with me . . .'

Beneath Florence's fingers, Lucinda's pulse gradually steadies. The tightness that has gripped her chest at last begins to relax its hold, and she finds she can breathe again.

21

Edie: November 1914

'Bloody hell, this one's alive!'

Edie surfaces to the sound of a man's voice, close and clear. She feels hands on her, lifting her arms, lowering them again, then both her ankles are seized, and now her body is being shunted sideways. She tries to open her eyes but can crack only one lid, the other gummed shut. A face in shadow hovers over her. 'All right, lad. We've got you.'

Edie's head sways as she's lifted out of the cold mud, away from Stanley. Panic grips her, and she struggles against the tugging hands.

'Come on, lad, work with us.' A different voice, this one harsher than the first.

And she has no more strength to resist, as she sinks down, down, back into the black.

The world returns to her in fragments. When she next comes round, she finds she's lying down but somehow moving, and slowly she understands. She's being carried on a stretcher, four Stygian figures surrounding her, groaning and grunting in the quiet of the night. The air is thick with a sour stench that burns Edie's throat. The bearers mutter and curse, their voices hoarse and low.

'Mind out 'ere . . .'

'There's another fuckin' 'ole . . .'

'Easy, boys, easy, there we go . . .'

The stretcher dips from side to side, as Edie is jolted across a hellish landscape. Around her stretches a quagmire strewn with countless bodies, shell craters brimming with stagnant water, the rising moon a silver eye, watching.

She's carried by the body-snatchers for what feels like hours, and then, at last, they stop, and now there are new voices, acrid petrol fumes, the revving of an engine. Faint lamplight illuminates a scene of chaos. She's loaded into the back of an ambulance, the truck's canvas roof rent with holes, and another stretcher is shunted in alongside Edie's. Rasping breaths in her ear, an animal sound that takes Edie straight back to the trench, back beneath the German soldier, his hands on her throat, and she cries out in terror, but nobody hears her above the rumble of the engine.

Someone has tied her arms and legs to the stretcher, but she can still turn her head, and she forces herself to look at the figure next to her, a figure with no face, bandages swathing its head. Each wheezing, laboured breath sounds to Edie like a death rattle.

Her world darkens as the ambulance doors are slammed shut, and the vehicle begins to move. The bandaged figure moans, as the ambulance lurches through a series of potholes. Though her limbs are loosely strapped, the stretcher offers no support or cushioning, and Edie's right leg throbs with pain. Each time the vehicle hits a rut, it feels as if someone is digging a knife into her thigh, twisting the blade.

Soon, she can no longer think for the pain. Her bandaged companion has fallen silent.

Gradually, the road levels, and the passage is smoother. The pain in Edie's leg eases enough for her to gather her wits. The last thing she remembers with any certainty is tucking her notebook inside her tunic, with Stanley's camera. She can't move to check if they're still there.

She closes her eyes, and an image of Stanley lying in the mud flickers behind her eyelids. Had the body-snatchers collected him too?

She's lost all notion of time. At last, the ambulance judders to a halt, and the rear doors are opened. Warm lantern-light sweeps over her. She can hear disembodied voices, tangled with urgency, as the bandaged soldier is pulled out of the vehicle feet first, and swiftly borne away.

And then it's Edie's turn. Hands lift and slide her stretcher, then lower it to the ground, and a grey-faced man in a blood-smeared apron is crouching next to her, saying something, and she catches the word 'morphine', but the rest of what he says is lost to her.

Then she's being moved again, and the man keeps pace at Edie's side as she's carried into a large tent-like structure, filled with countless stretchers, and Edie can't hear anything the man is saying to her now for the cries and groans and screams of the wounded.

She's deposited in a corner, at the edge of a sea of pallets. The medical orderly kneels beside her with a grunt, quickly releasing Edie's straps.

'Don't go wandering off, lad.'

Edie's limbs prickle with pins and needles, as the blood begins to flow again. She wants to ask the medical orderly where she is, but her mouth won't obey, and the man is already hurrying away. She lifts her head, managing to glimpse a few people in white gowns moving among the rows of stretchers. But no one comes near her.

Abandoned, she drifts for a time in a semi-conscious haze of pain. Her throat feels as though she's swallowed gravel, and when she tries to call out for water she can only produce a rasping whisper. No one hears her.

She longs to sleep, but the pain in her leg is growing ever stronger.

Where there's breath, Edie.

She hears her mother's voice. Ma had never given up hope. Not even at the very end.

Edie's mind drifts back to her dark workhouse years, to her mother, who fought every moment to keep them both alive. She thinks of how Ma somehow managed to keep her enemies at bay, often by sharing their meagre provisions with the other inmates in the workhouse in the hope of protection or reciprocal help. Her mother would have made a wonderful military general, it strikes Edie now, if only she'd been born a man.

Where there's breath . . .

'There's hope,' Edie mutters to herself, as her eyes begin to close.

A hand grips her arm, gently shaking her, bringing her back. Someone leans over her, and a woman in a white nurse's cap slowly comes into focus.

Kind eyes, Edie thinks.

'You must drink some water,' the nurse says. 'Can you lift your head for me?'

The nurse sets a metal cup to Edie's lips, and water spills as Edie gulps, dousing the fire in her throat with each swallow.

'Slowly . . . slowly . . .'

Edie drains the cup, and the nurse refills it from a canister nearby. Thirst sated at last, Edie relinquishes the cup, and the nurse smiles, well done.

Edie rubs her sore eyes, expecting the vision of the woman to disappear, for surely she must be hallucinating, or dreaming, and in a moment she will wake.

'Are you in any pain?' the nurse asks, and her touch on Edie's thigh sears her flesh like a firebrand. Edie cries out, and now her chest is on fire too, and this sets off a racking cough. The nurse holds the cup to her lips again, and she drinks.

'You need more morphine,' the nurse says, when Edie is calm again. 'I'll come back.'

Edie drifts in and out of a shallow sleep, her rest disturbed by a man on a pallet nearby who writhes and shouts, threatening anyone who tries to come close.

'Get off me! Don't you fucking touch me!'

The man's terrified cries cleave through Edie's brain, and she clasps her hands over her ears, but it's no good.

Gradually, the man's cries diminish to choked whimpers, and after a time he's carried away on a stretcher.

Edie wonders if the nurse will ever return. There is nothing she can do except wait, and hope.

Later still, a different orderly, this one with an unlit pipe hanging from the corner of his mouth, appears at her side.

'Hold still, lad.' The man's pipe barely moves between his lips. He's holding a syringe. Morphine, he tells her. 'It'll help with the pain.'

No sooner has Edie submitted to the injection, than the orderly turns his attention to her legs. 'Can you move them?'

Edie manages to shift the left one an inch, but the right refuses to comply.

A different nurse is summoned.

'What's your name, lad?' the man asks.

The morphine is beginning to work. Edie can't make her lips move.

A nod from the orderly, and the nurse opens the neck of Edie's shirt, searching for her identity tag. The metal disc on its cord is stuck to her collarbone with sweat, mud and dried blood. The nurse extracts the disc, wipes the sliver of metal on her apron. 'Lawrence,' she reads.

'All right, Lawrence,' the orderly says. 'Let's have a look at that leg of yours, shall we?'

He examines Edie's blood-soaked trousers and puttees, but doesn't attempt to remove anything. 'Shrapnel wound, looks like,' he mutters, and the nurse scribbles on the tag. 'Gram of morphine.' The pipe dangles precariously.

'Injured anywhere else, son?'

Edie moves her head, no, and the orderly sends the nurse away.

'Back soon, lad,' the orderly says. He rises, and is gone too.

Heat radiates up Edie's legs, and she closes her eyes. Stanley's face floats in her mind's eye, and she tries to hold it, but the darkness is swallowing her again.

22

Lucinda: November 1914

The menacing rumble of guns to the north of Paris grows louder every day, a thunderstorm of artillery creeping ever closer. All the while she's rushed off her feet in the operating theatre, wrist deep in blood and gore, Lucinda has largely managed to push away thoughts of the Germans closing in on the city. But recently it's become impossible to ignore what's happening beyond the hospital.

The latest news reports warn of an added threat: German airships. In the last fortnight, Zeppelins have been spotted with increasing frequency, sinister shadows drifting over the Seine.

It's only a matter of time before the Germans drop a bomb, Lucinda fears.

As a result of the new Zeppelin threat, a few days ago she and Florence had taken the difficult decision to impose an evening curfew on their staff. Not that anyone seems to mind, with hardly any theatres or even bars left open in the city now. It feels to Lucinda as though a lifetime has passed since they'd first arrived in Paris, and she and Florence had taken a reconnoitring walk along Avenue Marceau, down to the Seine. They'd crossed the Pont de l'Alma, admiring the engineering feat of the Eiffel Tower, and later learned from Madame Pérouse that the tower was now a transmitting station, with technicians busily intercepting German radio messages. Lucinda finds this strangely unnerving and comforting at the same time.

But although pedestrians remain able to roam the city freely if they wish, vehicles are now permitted to enter or leave Paris by only fourteen of the fifty-five gates, and these select portals are open for just a set number of hours each day. Lucinda is finding it hard not to think of the city as under siege.

The threat of invasion is real.

One afternoon, soon after Lucinda has finished a particularly complex operation, suturing a soldier's abdomen ripped open by a mortar shell, she returns to her office to write up her medical notes, but is interrupted by the arrival of Mardie. The orderly has brought an urgent message from the French Red Cross.

'When did this come, Hodgson?'

'Just now, ma'am. The lad who delivered it said he'd wait for your reply.'

Lucinda reads the note, and it confirms her worst fears: German troops have advanced to within a few miles of the city's northern defences. The risk of attack is now so high that the hospital must evacuate to a safer location.

'Ma'am?'

Mardie's voice brings Lucinda back to the room. 'It's not quite the news I was hoping for, Hodgson.' There's little point in withholding information: the girl will find out soon enough. 'We must evacuate.'

To her credit, Mardie accepts Lucinda's announcement with a calm nod, then waits patiently as Lucinda dashes off a reply, requesting an urgent meeting with Madame Pérouse, here in the hospital, as soon as is convenient. She hands the note to Mardie, but as the orderly opens the door, she calls the girl back. 'Tell the other doctors I need to speak with them in my office as soon as their duties are finished,' she says, 'and that it's important.'

'Yes, ma'am.'

'And, Hodgson?'

'Yes, ma'am?'

'I need you to be discreet. I don't want anyone else to know about this yet. Do you understand?'

'Yes, ma'am.'

The orderly dashes away, and Lucinda suddenly wonders if she should have told the girl to notify Cassard too. But she hasn't seen the Frenchman since the visit from Egham and Byers, she realizes. And she'd rather tell her colleagues about this development before she involves the interfering manager.

The five doctors gather in the privacy of the office, and Florence closes the door.

'I'm sorry to disrupt your work,' Lucinda begins, 'but I couldn't delay.'

'Is everything all right?' Grace asks.

'I'm afraid I have some bad news.' Lucinda briefs her colleagues on the situation.

There follows a moment of silence, and Lucinda waits for the inevitable questions to begin. Hazel is the first to speak: 'How close are the Germans?'

'I don't know the exact distance,' Lucinda admits. 'Perhaps within twenty miles?'

'How much time before we must leave?' This from Grace.

Lucinda glances at Florence. There's been no chance to discuss any details. 'We'll know more when Madame Pérouse gets here,' Lucinda replies. 'The note from the Red Cross was marked urgent.'

'Did it say where we'd be moving to?' Hazel asks.

'No, but I'm sure the Red Cross have other premises, outside the city.' Lucinda tries to sound confident, but in truth she has no idea if Madame Pérouse will have a safe building for them to transfer to.

'Until Dr Maberry and I speak with Madame Pérouse,' she goes on, 'I think we should keep this to ourselves, for the time being. By tomorrow we'll have a better idea of what's happening I hope, and can start our preparations.'

Her answer provokes more questions.

'What about those patients we can't move?' Grace asks. 'Those men in traction, for instance. How are they supposed to be shifted somewhere that's maybe miles away?'

Before Lucinda can formulate an answer, Gertrude asks a further question: 'Where can we go? I mean, surely nowhere in France is safe.'

'The Red Cross will know of other suitable places to set up our hospital, nearer the coast, perhaps,' Lucinda says, recalling what Byers had told her. 'Paris is a chief target, and we don't want to be caught in the eye of the storm, if the Germans break through. There are more hospitals opening in the Pas-de-Calais area, I've heard, and it's possible we could relocate to one of those, at least in the short term.'

'But what if the Germans don't break through?' Hazel says. 'Why can't we stay here, and brave it out? We've been at risk up to this point, in any case.'

'The risk has become untenable,' Florence replies, meeting Lucinda's eye.

'I can't in all conscience put you, or the rest of the staff and patients, in such jeopardy,' Lucinda replies. 'Not when we've been told in no uncertain terms to evacuate.'

The women are silent, each with her own thoughts. The prospect of such a huge undertaking makes Lucinda feel lightheaded.

'Do we have an evacuation plan?' Hazel wants to know. 'I've never worked in a hospital that's had to relocate all its patients before.'

Lucinda has to admit that she's never experienced a complete hospital evacuation either. 'But we can all remember times, I'm sure, when an entire ward of patients has had to be moved, due to a quarantining issue, or some other crisis.'

The women nod. They have indeed witnessed such times.

'So, we must simply treat this on a greater scale,' Lucinda hears herself say. 'We have procedures in place for moving individual casualties. Our challenge is to scale up the process.'

'I still don't see how we can move those critically ill patients, or the ones in traction,' Grace says.

'For those cases who are unable to make the journey,' Florence replies, 'we'll have to maintain their safety here as best we can, with a few select staff.'

'This needs further discussion, of course,' Lucinda

says, catching Florence's eye again. 'No staff should have to remain here if they don't want to.'

They're in the tightest of corners, Lucinda wants to add. At any moment, they could all be blown to pieces. She doesn't have the faintest clue how they're to move everyone out of Paris safely. All she knows is that, whatever happens, she will not abandon a single person.

'I'm not suggesting any of our staff are made to do anything they're not comfortable with,' Florence adds. 'But the fact remains, we have perhaps a dozen men who can't be moved. Not many, thankfully, and therefore we'd need to retain only a handful of staff. I'll volunteer to stay and, with a nursing sister and perhaps Tozer, we should be able to manage.'

'We need to hear what Madame Pérouse has to say, before anyone volunteers for anything.' Lucinda inwardly winces at the bluntness of her words, and notes the answering clench of Florence's jaw.

'You said yourself, Lucie, we can't jeopardize anyone else's safety,' Florence replies. 'So, I'll volunteer to stay.'

'No one is volunteering for anything yet,' Lucinda repeats. 'Please, Flo, we can't make any rash decisions until we know what the Red Cross intend to do.'

'When have I ever made a rash decision?' Florence replies, with a coolness that lowers the temperature in the room by several degrees.

Lucinda shakes her head, dismayed at the turn the conversation has taken. Arguing her case has never come easy – she becomes tongue-tied at the slightest hint of conflict. Which is why she's never envied her brother

Ambrose's legal career. But as for arguing with Florence, it has simply never happened.

Lucinda opens her mouth, with no notion of what she will say next.

'When are you going to tell the rest of the staff?' Gertrude interjects. She looks at Lucinda, but Florence answers.

'There's little point in worrying people tonight,' she says. 'We'll call a staff meeting after we've met Madame Pérouse.'

'What about patients expecting surgery?' Hazel wants to know. 'Will their operations go ahead? Or are we to postpone everything?'

'Any non-emergency procedures will have to wait,' Lucinda says. 'If someone needs an urgent operation tomorrow, we can manage that, I expect, but in the meantime we must prepare for our meeting with the Red Cross.'

'There are patients waiting now,' Gertrude says. 'So, if you'll excuse me . . .'

'Of course, you must carry on,' Lucinda says. 'Please try not to spread word of this to the others yet.'

Gertrude, Grace and Hazel promise to keep the meeting to themselves, and the three doctors hasten from the room.

As soon as the door closes behind them, Florence turns on Lucinda. 'I'd appreciate it if you didn't undermine me in front of the others.'

'What?' Lucinda blinks at Florence across the desk. 'I didn't.'

'It's up to me if I choose to stay here or not.'

Lucinda swallows, her throat suddenly dry. 'We always decide things together, Flo,' she croaks. 'That's all I meant when I said we shouldn't make rash decisions —'

'No,' Florence interrupts, moving to the door. 'It's not what you meant. You've made up your mind that we all have to up sticks, travel to some place on the coast, and never mind what anyone else wants to do!' Florence grips the door handle.

'Wait, please!' Lucinda rises from her desk, takes a step towards her friend. What on earth has she said to upset Florence so badly? They've never argued like this before, always worked in harmony, like the sun and moon, one affecting the other, yes, but in balance. Now they're like two flints striking off each other.

'I have to get on,' Florence snaps. 'There's no time to *discuss things*.'

'Please, Flo, don't be like this,' Lucinda says, straining to remain composed. 'I don't think you should sacrifice your own safety when others may be willing to remain here.'

'That's simply ridiculous, Lucinda.'

Florence's use of her full name sends a warning shot across Lucinda's bows.

'Why?' Lucinda stammers.

'Because I've already decided it will be me who stays.' Florence fixes Lucinda with a determined look. 'No one else need volunteer.'

'Now *you're* being ridiculous, Flo.'

'I'm *not*,' Florence cries, throwing up her hands, forcing Lucinda to take a step back. 'How dare you suggest I am?'

Lucinda raises her own hands in a placating gesture. 'I'm sorry,' she says. 'I didn't intend to be rude.' She's never witnessed Florence's temper quite like this before, never seen her grow so angry so quickly, and it's unnerving, as though her friend has turned into a stranger. 'I'm only worried, Flo. You must see that.'

'You think I'm not worried too?' Florence opens the office door. 'But when we came here, we never expected it to be safe.' She pauses on the threshold, turns back towards Lucinda. 'Every day we risk our lives here. Every single day.'

'Let me stay instead, then,' Lucinda pleads.

'I'm volunteering,' Florence repeats, speaking slowly. 'You must go with the rest of the staff. They need you, Lucie.'

But I need you.

Lucinda's throat is clogged with words she can't speak.

'I'll ask Tozer to stay with me here. You take the other men with you. Figgis will need to be kept busy, and Penhaligon's nerves will never take the strain of remaining here anyway.' Florence talks on, but Lucinda can barely hear her for the dull thrumming in her ears. 'Sister Bryony will no doubt offer to sacrifice herself.'

'No one's sacrificing themselves!' Lucinda cries, meeting Florence's searing gaze.

Least of all you. Please God, not you.

'It's the only answer.'

As the argument circles back to the beginning, an aching chill suffuses Lucinda's bones. 'But you can't stay here, all alone.' She hears the raw despair in her voice.

'I won't be alone,' Florence says, stepping back over the threshold. 'I'll have the patients to keep me company and, besides, I doubt Cassard will leave the luxury of his suite, even if Germans overrun the hotel.'

Cassard. Just hearing the manager's name sends a stutter of electricity through Lucinda's veins. The prospect of leaving Florence alone in the hotel with the Frenchman terrifies her almost as much as the encroaching German Army.

'Florence, please,' she tries once more. 'You must listen to me.'

'There's no more time.' Florence steps away from the door, comes close to Lucinda, tips her head down. Lucinda opens her mouth to appeal, but Florence silences her with a fleeting kiss on her flushed cheek.

And then she is gone.

Lucinda stares at the empty doorway, a hand to her cheek, touching the place Florence's lips brushed.

As if she can seal the kiss on her skin.

23

Edie: November 1914

She dreams of the workhouse. She's seven years old again, helping Ma hang out laundry in the courtyard on a rare dry day in spring. Edie sits in a patch of sun, the pale light bringing with it a promise of warmth to come. Her mother works fast, hefting acres of sheets on to lines taller than herself, smoothing the cotton with the flat of her calloused hand. Ma's arms are wiry, roped with muscle from her work in the laundry, and Edie marvels at their strength.

Edie has been given the job of sorting out the bag of dolly pegs, separating the usable from the broken. As she works her way through the bag, she secretly names each wooden stub for someone in their world.

The weather-damaged pegs, their wooden heads split and swollen, she names for their enemies. 'This one's Mr Gifford,' she whispers to herself, setting a broken peg to one side. 'He's cracked in the head too.'

Edie's hatred of the governor is physical, her veins flooding with hot, mute fury whenever she sees his fleshy face. She hates the terror he provokes, the mysterious things he does to Ma in his office that leave bruises all up her arms. Edie often finds herself fantasizing about seizing the governor's bronze-tipped cane and battering his over-stuffed belly with it.

'Be wary of him, Edie,' her mother continually warns her. 'Keep out of his way.'

'Yes, Ma.' She's always wary.

In her dream, Edie watches her small, grubby child's hand as it reaches into the bag for the next peg. From somewhere behind her comes the distinctive, terrifying rap of Mr Gifford's cane on the flagstones, a tapping that grows louder and louder, and she looks up. The courtyard is gone, and so is her mother. She wakes with a start.

She's still on the pallet, the same figures in white glimpsed among the rows of stretchers. But at some point while she was sedated, she's been moved, and now she's lying beneath a window. The tapping in her dream is revealed to be the tattoo of heavy rain against the dirty pane.

She has no idea how long she's lain here, or what will happen to her next, and yet, for the first time in so long, she isn't consumed with terror. Nurses and medical order-lies move about in the dim lamplight, attending to the wounded, and the sharp odour of carbolic fills the air. To know she's reached the relative safety of a casualty clear-ing station lends Edie some reassurance, but now fresh fear strikes: has she still got her notebook and Stan's camera?

A check of her tunic reveals both items are safe, and she breathes out.

Assailed by a sudden raging thirst, she pushes herself up on to her elbows. A fist hammers inside her skull, and she slumps down again. Slowly, she gathers her frayed strength, lifts her head again. On the floor next to her pallet, someone has left a tin cup, half filled with water. But as she reaches for it, pain stabs her leg and she knocks the cup over. It clatters across the floor, spilling its contents, and a man on a neighbouring stretcher cries out.

Edie looks on in helpless alarm, as the man begins to thrash and shout, until at last a nurse comes to sedate him.

Edie lies, surrounded by crying, moaning, coughing men. Barely able to see in the dim light, she slips her notebook from her pocket, and scrawls a few words.

Nov, date? CCS – where? Many wounded

She has no strength left to write more.

24

Lucinda: November 1914

That evening, Lucinda and Florence meet with Madame Pérouse, two other representatives of the French Red Cross, and Monsieur Cassard. The women are informed by Madame Pérouse, in no uncertain terms, that they must evacuate the majority of their staff, as well as all but the very worst of their patients.

'There is an empty château, in Wimereux, that we've acquired for you,' Madame Pérouse tells them.

Lucinda recalls Lord Egham mentioning the little coastal town. It's a couple of hundred kilometres from Paris, out of the German line of fire. The château, she is informed, is available immediately on a two-month lease. No further discussion is required.

The next day the move begins in earnest. More than half of the patients have Blighty wounds, and are soon sent on their way home. Madame Pérouse proves her worth again by arranging a convoy of trucks to transport Lucinda and her staff, with all the equipment they can carry, and twenty patients deemed likely to survive the journey, to their new home. All being well, the convoy will leave for Wimereux that afternoon.

Working frantically to pack as many supplies as she can

into the last truck, Lucinda barely has time to bid Florence farewell. They must content themselves with only a brisk hug, and a promise to write to each other at the first opportunity.

'Take care, won't you, darling?' Florence says, releasing Lucinda and stepping back.

'You too, Flo,' Lucinda manages, wishing she could stay in her friend's embrace for ever.

But she must go. Which is as well, Lucinda thinks, as her truck leads off, and she watches the figures of Florence, Tozer and Sister Bryony dwindle into the distance. If she'd had more time in Florence's arms, would she have been able to let her dear friend go? At the very least she would have ended up sobbing. And no one needed that.

They arrive at the château as evening is drawing in, tired and hungry after a gruelling three-hour drive. They are met by an agent acting for the town's *maire*, a Monsieur Bataille, who hands Lucinda the keys. Bataille is dressed in the blue serge of a sea-captain, and has a face so creased and craggy Lucinda could quite imagine him on a galleon. But despite his gruff manner and rudimentary English, he welcomes them, and Lucinda soon discovers that he's even hired several local women to clean the place in readiness, and prepare a basic supper.

'*Bienvenue*,' Bataille says, as he leads Lucinda and the others into the château, and gives them a brief tour. There are three floors, with eight bedrooms spread over the first and second. Each floor has several bathrooms with running hot water, and there are kitchens and a laundry room on the ground floor. To Lucinda's delight, the château also boasts a huge south-facing conservatory at the rear of the property.

Bataille brings them back to the lobby, and Lucinda sends her team to begin unloading the trucks.

'*Merci beaucoup*,' Lucinda says to the agent, gazing around the spacious, white-tiled lobby. Someone wealthy must own this place, but there isn't the time to chat with Bataille about its heritage. The patients in the trucks must be brought inside and made comfortable as quickly as possible.

The château's three large, airy ground-floor salons are immediately turned over to wards, and Lucinda names each one after a Greek goddess. She hopes Florence will approve. The officers' ward she calls Elpis, after the goddess of hope, the pre-surgery ward she names for Enyo, a goddess of war, and the main ward becomes Calliope, after the muse of poetry, as she's noticed that many of the men are writing verse.

As furniture in the salons is removed, and the patients are brought in on their stretchers, Lucinda checks each man is stable. Madame Pérouse has arranged for extra bedding to be delivered, and once the patients are comfortable, Lucinda gathers the Corps in the dining room, where they drink lemonade, and eat the bread, cold ham and cheese that Bataille's women have kindly laid out for them.

Refreshed, Lucinda urges on her staff. Their next task is to transform the conservatory into a surgical theatre, the space quickly emptied of wicker chairs, with a couple of deal tables from the dining room requisitioned for operating.

Lucinda positions her own table next to the French windows that open out on to the gardens. Not that she can see them in the dark, but Bataille assures her that the lawns sweep down to flowerbeds, and a kitchen garden. The conservatory is naturally light-filled in the day, he impresses on Lucinda, which is good as the electrical supply here was temperamental. His comments make Lucinda wish Monsieur Perrin had come with them, but the engineer had wanted to remain with his family in Paris.

Lucinda allocates bedrooms to her staff on the two upper floors, but for herself she takes the château's library, situated in an annexe on the west side of the building. The snug, book-lined room is furnished with a rather moth-eaten chaise-longue, which Lucinda will sleep on. There is also a small escritoire.

The empty trucks depart on their journey back to Paris, and Lucinda appoints two of the most awake and alert nurses to supervise the night shift, sending everyone else to bed.

'You've all gone beyond the call of duty today,' she tells her colleagues, pride and exhaustion cracking her voice. 'Get some well-earned rest. We have a busy day ahead of us tomorrow.'

She retreats to the library, and finds someone, most likely one of the agent's women, has thoughtfully left a sheet, woollen blanket, and a pillow on the chaise-longue. But she can't sleep yet.

In a drawer of the escritoire, she finds writing paper and envelopes. She digs for a pen in her Gladstone, and sits down to write a letter to Florence.

Château Mauricien, Wimereux

My dearest Flo,

We are here, in Wimereux, safe at last. Our journey took longer than hoped, but all the patients have fared well. This place is a fraction of the size of the Clarens, but even so it will serve us well, I hope.

Lucinda pauses, pen trembling over the paper, her mind filled with her last image of Florence, standing on the pavement outside the Clarens. The thought of her beloved friend, miles away, being stalked along the hotel corridors by Cassard while bombs drop over Paris is unbearable, like pressing on a bruise.

I trust Yorick is taking good care of you?

Lucinda re-reads the last sentence, tempted to score it out. She'd left Yorick the skull, her precious good-luck talisman, with Florence. Now the gesture strikes her as ridiculously childish, not to mention utterly useless. Even so, something stays her hand, and she can't quite bring herself to draw a line through her words.

I can't wait for you to join us here, Flo.

Lucinda's pen falters again. If only the words flowed, but she's never been one for pretty phrases. Yet Florence, she knows only too well, appreciates a beautiful line.

A sick feeling rises, as she's reminded of Dr Byers, and

his passionate pursuit of Florence through a flood of truly dreadful poetry.

She grips her pen more firmly, and forges on.

I wish you were here so that you might lend me some of your indomitable strength and good sense, Flo. I feel all at sea, surrounded by a rising tide.

Lucinda hesitates again. Was this too much? She doesn't want Florence to worry unduly . . . or perhaps she does.

I hope you're able to leave Paris soon, so that we can be reunited. Until then, I shall imagine you're beside me, and try my best to be content with that.

Her nib stutters on the page.

I love you. I miss you. I want you.

If she can summon an ounce more courage, if she lends her pen a fraction more force, the words will appear, inked indelibly on paper . . .

Her nerve fails her. She writes instead:

I long for news of you.

Yours affectionately,
Lucie

A drop of water lands on the page, ink bleeding into the paper.

No, no, no, she mustn't cry.

But it's too late and, oh, the relief as the tears come. For a moment, she's no longer Dr Lucinda Garland, she's only Lucie, tired beyond endurance, lost and alone, heart breaking.

Pull yourself together, she counsels herself sternly. *Pull. Yourself. Together.*

She grapples a handkerchief from her skirt pocket and blows her nose, noticing only after she's dampened the cotton the FM stitched tidily in one corner. Why is it that everything conspires to remind her of Florence? With unsteady hands, she folds the letter and tucks it into an envelope ready to be posted in the morning.

There's nothing left to do but try to grab a few hours' sleep. She lies down on the dusty chaise-longue, pulls a blanket over herself, and waits for sleep to claim her.

Sunshine filters through the conservatory's opaque glass roof, warming Lucinda's spirits as she greets her surgical colleagues the next morning. On this first day in their new hospital, she'll work with Dr Hazel. In the absence of Florence, Hazel will take on the role of Lucinda's anaesthetist. They'll be supported by a trio of nurses, while the others continue to settle the patients into their wards. The men had slept on stretchers last night, but Bataille has promised that portable beds will arrive later today. Already he has hired a cook, who will oversee the catering requirements, with the help of Lucinda's three orderlies who will take their turn in the kitchens.

More worryingly, a telegram arrived before breakfast from the French Red Cross, warning that the first contingent of casualties from the front was on its way.

Frustratingly, no specific numbers or timings had been given.

'Do you know how long before they get here, Doctor?' Hazel asks, as she helps Lucinda prepare the two operating tables. She checks the supplies of lint and gauze, while Lucinda casts her eye over a tray of surgical instruments, which will have to be shared between both tables.

'I'm afraid I know as much as you.' Lucinda's reply sounds a tad too blunt to her own ears, but there's no chance to apologize, as at that moment Nurse Whiteman, one of the least experienced members of the nursing team, drops a kidney dish full of scalpels on the floor. She bursts into tears.

'There now,' Lucinda says to the nurse. 'There's no need for tears.' Where has that come from? She's prided herself on choosing stalwart young ladies for her nursing squad, and has been rewarded with no histrionics so far.

At a loss as to what to do, and wishing Florence were here as she would know precisely, Lucinda hesitantly pats the nurse's arm.

'I'm so sorry, Doctor,' the young woman sobs.

'Really, Nurse Whiteman, it's hardly the end of the world.'

Dr Hazel and the other nurses are on their knees, gathering up the scalpels to be re-sterilized.

'Do you need to rest, Nurse Whiteman?'

'Oh, no, Doctor,' the nurse stammers. 'I just didn't sleep well last night.'

Lucinda studies the bruised crescents beneath the young woman's eyes. Are the staff falling apart, and she simply hasn't noticed? In the mad dash to flee Paris, had she lost her grip on the most important aspect of this whole endeavour? The wellbeing of her colleagues?

'We can manage here without you for a short while,' Lucinda persists. 'At least until the first patients arrive.'

Nurse Whiteman wipes her eyes with a handkerchief.

Something about the young nurse is coming back to Lucinda now, something Sister Bryony had told her, but though Lucinda racks her brain, she can't recall what the issue is – a sick mother at home, perhaps?

'I'm quite all right now, Doctor,' the nurse says, blowing her nose.

Lucinda considers asking the woman about her family, but she's loath to pry into her staff's personal lives, especially in the operating theatre. In contrast, Florence frequently did, and had once told Lucinda that it was often the only chance she had to catch up on their colleagues' news. Lucinda has happily left that sort of thing to her. Flo is so much better at 'peopling', as Lucinda thinks of it. In Lucinda's world, there is little time for small-talk and pleasantries when she is so busy saving lives.

'But, darling,' Lucinda remembers Florence once saying to her, 'don't you ever wonder about the lives you're so busy saving?'

I only wonder about us, Flo.

'Even so,' Lucinda says to Nurse Whiteman, her gaze straying to the sweeping lawns beyond the conservatory walls, 'why don't you step outside for some fresh air, before surgery starts?'

Nurse Whiteman hesitates, her throat bobbing.

'You could investigate something for me,' Lucinda goes

on. 'Monsieur Bataille mentioned a kitchen garden. I'm wondering if that little path there,' she points through the window, the nurse following her finger, 'leads to a vegetable patch.'

Lucinda opens the French windows, and chill air blows in. The day might be sunny, but there's no escaping the onset of winter. What will this place be like when the weather takes a turn for the worse?

She closes the conservatory doors again, and watches Nurse Whiteman through the glass as she makes her way across the lawn and down the path.

Florence would be proud of her efforts to help the young woman, Lucinda thinks, as she washes her hands in a bowl of water one of the orderlies has brought through. One disadvantage of working in the conservatory is that there is no water on tap, but they'll just have to make do.

Lucinda tucks loose strands of her unwashed hair into her bun. Oh, for a long, hot bath, she thinks. When will she ever have time for that sort of thing again?

'At least the sun is shining today,' she remarks to Hazel. Perhaps this evening, if the weather stays dry, she might have a chance to stretch her legs, even make it down to the sea. According to Bataille, it's just a short walk from the château.

If only Florence was here to explore the area with her.

Mardie Hodgson arrives, arms laden with supplies from the dispensary: more anaesthetic, gauze, bottles of iodine. Hazel helps her sort everything on a side table, then sends her off in search of some clean metal pails.

'Shall I lower the blinds?' Hazel asks Lucinda. 'The sunlight is strong, don't you think?'

'Oh, no,' Lucinda replies quickly, 'that won't be necessary.' She doesn't add that she hopes the natural light will help to soften the tense atmosphere of surgery. Instead, she finds herself sharing how profoundly glad she is to have this space for their new operating theatre. The rainclouds will return soon enough, and the electric lights will no doubt have to be cranked on. But, for now, Lucinda allows herself to savour the winter sun, and breathe a little easier.

∞

The brief moment of calm is cut short by the arrival of the first of the wounded. Ambulance trucks deliver a dozen men, every last one clinging to life by a gossamer thread. The women spring into action, triaging the injured in the foyer, and Lucinda hurries back to the conservatory to begin what will no doubt be a full day of surgery.

Figgis and Penhaligon lift an unconscious soldier on to Lucinda's operating table.

'Little 'un for you, Doc,' Figgis grunts. 'Makes a change.'

'Thank you, Mr Figgis.'

The porters leave, and Lucinda turns her attention to her patient. She swiftly assesses his slight build and smooth cheeks, noting what looks like a broken nose that hasn't healed straight; he looks underage, though. So many of the soldiers who have come under her knife have been barely older than boys.

'Any notes with this one?' she asks Dr Hazel, without much hope.

Hazel is already searching for the soldier's tally tag, but it's missing. All she can find is an identity disc, tied with a grubby, frayed cord about the soldier's thin neck.

'Private Lawrence,' Hazel reads off the disc.

The soldier gives a weak moan, eyelids flickering. Lucinda pulls on her gloves, and nods to the nurse to begin pre-operation checks.

'Can you hear me, Lawrence?'

A faint groan. Was the boy trying to say something?

'It's all right, Lawrence, you're safe.' How many times has Lucinda uttered this lie to soldiers at death's door?

'Pulse weakening, Doctor.' Hazel has the soldier's skinny wrist in her grip, and the look she gives Lucinda says, *Be quick*.

The soldier's eyelids are trembling, but he's fallen quiet, which Lucinda knows all too well is never a good sign.

She's seized with an intense, icy rage. Mr Morton will *not* have this one before she's even started.

'All right, let's see what we've got here, shall we?'

The soldier's right thigh has been inexpertly bandaged over the top of his trousers, the blood-soaked gauze loose and flapping. A hundred questions flash through Lucinda's mind: is this a shrapnel wound, a shell fracture, a broken femur? If the thigh bone is broken, is it transverse, oblique, spiral, compound? When did this boy sustain his injury? How long has he been in transit to her hospital? What medication has he already been given?

'I wish we could X-ray,' she says to Hazel. It's a pointless remark, but she can't help herself. They hadn't been able to bring their machine from Paris, and Bataille may be good at providing beds and cooks, but the Frenchman can't be expected to work miracles and conjure complex apparatus from thin air.

Hazel gives a nod. 'Would be helpful.'

Lucinda swallows her frustration, making a mental note to write to her mother again, see if there is any news on the spare X-ray machine Eleanor was originally going to send to Paris.

Lucinda starts to undo the buttons on the soldier's tunic. Why hasn't anyone taken this filthy thing off him? Moving as one, Lucinda and Hazel remove the jacket, stiff with mud and dried blood, and as they do so, a small leather box falls out. Lucinda scoops it up and, without thinking, slips it into her gown pocket. There's no time to look through the soldier's belongings, to salvage anything precious: that will have to be done later by the orderlies.

'Doctor?' The nurse is poised with a pair of surgical scissors, and Lucinda gives her the nod.

While the nurse carefully cuts off the dressing on the soldier's leg and begins to peel away the torn remains of his trousers, Lucinda removes his mud-caked boots and filthy socks, dumping everything into a slop pail beneath the table.

'Pressure dropping,' Hazel reports, glancing up from the blood-pressure gauge. 'Shall I ready the mask?'

'Yes,' Lucinda answers. 'Keep fighting, Lawrence,' she mutters, more for her own sake than the soldier's.

'Doctor Garland . . .'

Fumbling to tie her face mask, Lucinda doesn't at first hear the nurse.

'Doctor . . .'

Lucinda turns back to the soldier on the table. The soldier's trousers have been removed, exposing the entire lower half of his body.

For a moment, Lucinda struggles to register what her eyes are telling her. 'A woman?' she finally manages.

As if hearing her, the soldier gives a strangled gasp and flings out an arm, clutching at the nurse's apron. The nurse stumbles back, but Lucinda reacts instinctively, seizing the soldier's narrow shoulders, holding steady. 'The sedative now,' she orders Hazel.

'Yes, Doctor.'

The soldier's eyes snap open, and Lucinda finds herself staring down into a pair of startlingly blue irises, bright with life.

Whatever's going on here, Lucinda thinks, Mr Morton will have to up his game if he wants to bag this one.

'You're safe,' Lucinda hears herself say. 'Try to relax now.'

Hazel lowers the mask over the girl-soldier's face. Within seconds Lucinda feels the bony shoulders relax beneath her hands.

Lucinda releases a long, shuddery breath, her mind reeling. How has a woman dressed in British Army uniform ended up on her operating table?

'Doctor?'

The urgency in Hazel's voice pulls Lucinda out of her temporary stupor. In the commotion, the girl-soldier's thigh wound has reopened, blood spreading over the wooden table, dripping on to the floor.

There's no time for Lucinda to question how this injured young woman in a soldier's uniform has washed up on her shore. Taking a breath, she sets to work once more, her single aim to save this life from Mr Morton's clutches.

25

Edie: November 1914

She wakes alone in an unfamiliar room. An oil lamp burns low on a side table, and as Edie's eyes adjust to the muted light, she realizes she's in some sort of storeroom. The wall on her right is lined with shelves from floor to ceiling, each packed with boxes and paper-wrapped bundles. The opposite wall has a small window, a short, tasselled curtain half drawn across it. There's nothing else in the room but the truckle bed she's lying in, a cup and a jug next to the lamp, a wooden stool in one corner.

She can smell something faintly medicinal, a blend of carbolic soap and unidentifiable chemicals, and for a breathless moment, she struggles to orient herself. A charged silence permeates the air, as though some living presence is sharing the cramped space with her, holding its breath too. How did she get in here?

The solid wood door has a keyhole, but there's no key. Is she locked in here? She can hear nothing beyond the door, no voices or footsteps, no evidence of other humans. Groggy and weak, she lies still for a few seconds, gathering her strength. Then, with a grunt of effort she sits up, pushing off the stiff sheets, only to discover that she's wearing a man's blue cotton nightshirt, and nothing else. The clean-smelling material is soft against her skin after so long in rough, filthy khaki, and for a moment this is all she can think.

Until another thought winds her: someone had undressed her.

Someone had washed her.

They will know she is a woman.

She casts about the room for her clothes.

Her uniform is gone.

Her precious notebook and Stanley's camera are gone.

Stanley.

An image of him lying in the trench comes unbidden to Edie's mind. It is this, of all the horror she has witnessed, that remains seared in her memory.

She left him.

She never went back for him.

The thought that he might still be lying there, waiting for her, bleeding into the mud, is unbearable. She has to believe the stretcher-bearers reached him in time and dragged him to safety. He's probably drinking tea in some aid station right now, flirting with a nurse.

He can't be dead.

Her thoughts are mired with fatigue, and a desperate thirst assails her.

The sudden rasp of a key turning in the lock startles her, and she grabs the sheet to her chest as the door opens. A dark-haired woman slips into the room, quickly shuts the door again, and stands with her back pressed to the wood.

Edie lies frozen, barely breathing.

'You're awake,' the woman says, her voice low. She hesitates, then takes a step towards the bed. 'My name is Dr

Garland.' Something about her seems vaguely familiar. Edie grips the sheets tighter.

'Don't be frightened.' The doctor spreads her hands in a calming gesture, a frown line creasing her high brow. 'You're safe.'

Edie has heard those clipped vowels before. She regards the woman warily, as memories of the prison doctors at Holloway return to haunt her. Yet this woman isn't bearing any tools of torture, her eyes shining kindly in the lamp-light.

The doctor pulls something from her pocket, and Edie stops breathing. It's her notebook, its blue leather cover smeared with mud and scarred with dents and scratches. The doctor is gingerly opening it, and Edie can only look on, helpless.

'Edie Lawrence,' the doctor reads aloud. She glances up at Edie. 'That's you?'

Edie nods.

'This is your diary?' The doctor turns the brittle pages, scanning Edie's words. 'You wrote all this?'

Edie's throat constricts. She nods again.

'Dear God,' the doctor murmurs to herself. 'You've been to Hell, haven't you?' Her eyes flick to the door, back to Edie again. 'Why are you here?'

Why indeed? Edie no longer knows herself, and the thought is suddenly so ridiculous that hysterical laughter bubbles in her chest, only to die on her lips.

'How did you come to be here?' the doctor repeats.

Edie can only shake her head, swallowing.

'You can't speak?' Dr Garland's eyes are sharp. 'I've met you before,' she mutters. 'Where have we met?'

Edie wants to say she thinks this too: the woman's face, her voice, everything about her is familiar. But she's so tired, her mind so addled with fear that she can't formulate the words.

'Have you lost your memory?' the doctor asks. 'Is that why you can't answer my questions?'

Edie can no more speak the truth aloud than fly from the room. Silence stretches between them, heavy with expectation.

'I can't help you, unless you tell me why you're here.' A slight edge has crept into the doctor's voice. 'How on earth have you ended up injured in battle?'

Edie tries to ask for her notebook back, but only succeeds in producing a choking cough.

In a second, the doctor is at her side, helping her to sit up, offering a cup, and Edie gulps water.

'You were thirsty,' the doctor says, when Edie has drained the cup.

Edie wants to thank her, but the words refuse to come. She shifts in the bed, gasping as pain stabs her thigh.

'Try not to move,' the doctor says. 'The morphine is wearing off. That's why your wound is hurting.'

If it hurts, it's not serious. Sergeant Ratigan's voice comes into Edie's head, as the doctor draws away the sheets, revealing Edie's bandaged thigh. Blood is beginning to seep through the gauze, and at the sight of the red bloom Edie's vision blackens at the edges and sweat breaks out on her upper lip.

'I can't give you any more pain relief yet,' the doctor says, pulling the sheet over Edie's legs again. 'Your dressing needs changing, though. I'll be back soon.'

And then the doctor is gone, taking Edie's notebook with her.

Left alone once more, Edie listens to the faint murmur of voices coming from beyond the closed door. The voices rise and fall, but though she strains to hear, she can't make out any words. She contemplates dragging herself out of the bed: the door is so close. But her leg protests every time she tries to move, waves of pain pinning her to the thin mattress.

Trapped in the bed, Edie can do nothing but wait, her belly growling. When was the last time she ate anything? She can't remember. Her stomach is so empty, it feels as though it's folded in on itself. Even another cup of water would be something, but there's none left in the jug.

She needs to get out of here.

She rubs her throat. Why can't she speak? Has she only temporarily lost her voice, or has some damage occurred to her vocal cords that means she can't make a sound ever again? How can she make herself understood if she can't speak?

Where has she seen the doctor before?

It's an effort to think, but gradually a memory emerges from the fog in her mind. She remembers being taken to a house once, somewhere in London, and the same doctor was there, but she doesn't know why.

And now darkness is swooping down on her again, and the memory dissolves as she succumbs.

26

Lucinda: November 1914

She closes the library door, turns the key, though it goes against her natural instincts: her door is always open to her staff. But she can't risk being disturbed while she tries to decide what to do with the girl-soldier.

Dr Hazel and Nurse Whiteman have been sworn to secrecy, and Lucinda trusts her colleagues to keep the situation to themselves, at least for a while. But some secrets are impossible to keep, as Lucinda knows only too well.

The most pressing issue is establishing the young woman's motives. Why was she masquerading as a British soldier? Why on earth would *any* woman in her right mind disguise themselves in soldier's garb and fight?

As soon as Lucinda has this thought, her mind fills with memories of suffrage rallies, the violence and brutality she's not only witnessed over the years but also experienced on many occasions. Her own brief, traumatic prison sentence for affray in 1912 has left an invisible scar on her memory that will never entirely heal.

Of course women can fight. They have always had to fight.

But not like this.

Lucinda rubs her brow, reliving the previous day's

shocking discovery on her operating table. Had she been quick enough to conceal the young woman? She'd lied to Penhaligon and Figgis, instructing the men to carry the 'dangerously contagious' patient to the storeroom next to Elpis Ward.

She's locked the room now, to prevent her staff from entering, at least in the short term, but will that make them suspicious?

What's even worse, Lucinda realizes, is that the young woman is conscious and aware of her situation. She's no longer heavily sedated. Hazel had administered the maximum amount of anaesthetic during the operation, allowing Lucinda to clean and stitch the deep wound in the girl-soldier's leg. They'd worried that the amount of ether was enough to knock out someone twice the girl's size, but Lucinda had taken the risk. She'd needed the girl to stay under for as long as possible.

But now the young woman, whoever she is, is awake.

What are you going to do? Florence's voice comes into Lucinda's head.

Oh, God, she wishes Flo were here. She would know what to do.

Lucinda sinks down on the chaise-longue, though there's no chance for sleep yet. Instead, she pulls from her pocket the little leather box the girl-soldier had been carrying inside her tunic, next to her heart.

She opens the box to find it's a pocket camera. An Ensignette. Her brother had had one of these, she thinks. She has no idea how it operates, only that you point the 'eye' at whatever you want to snap. If only Ambrose was here, he could tell her how it works, and perhaps even get the film out.

Lucinda sets down the little camera and studies the notebook again. It's clearly a diary, the handwriting tiny and cramped, the spelling erratic. It looks almost as though a child wrote it.

A sudden knock at the door makes her start. For a second she contemplates ignoring whoever wants her, but she can't. Thrusting the camera and notebook back into her pockets, she unlocks the library door again. Olga is waiting in the corridor, an apologetic look on her face that Lucinda recognizes.

'Sorry to bother you, ma'am, but there's a visitor for you.'

Who on earth was visiting them here? In Paris, their hospital had attracted all sorts of voyeurs, from distinguished military personnel to curious locals wanting tours of the wards. Once, Lucinda had received a letter from the Duchess of Westminster, politely requesting she send six of her doctors to observe Lucinda's experimental surgical procedures.

In addition, the French Red Cross had sometimes brought their own medical people to witness Lucinda and her team at work, which was flattering, Lucinda can't deny, but it had also been rather distracting.

But they'd been in Wimereux barely five minutes. Hardly anyone knew they'd even left Paris.

'Who is it, Campbell?'

'He wouldn't give his name, Doctor. Just said to tell you your knight errant has arrived.'

'Knight who?' Lucinda struggles to make sense of Olga's

words. She has no idea who her uninvited and frankly unwanted visitor might be.

'That's all he said, Doctor.' Olga gives her an apologetic look, and Lucinda dismisses her with a sigh of thanks.

Lucinda finds her errant knight waiting in the foyer. The tall, silver-haired gentleman in a crumpled tan suit is non-chalantly perusing a framed oil painting of the local coastline hanging on the wall. Painted by the château owner's late wife, Bataille had told Lucinda.

The man turns at the sound of her approach, and as he does so, her steps falter. She hasn't seen her friend Harry Levinson since the day she left England, a lifetime ago. Harry's photographer had taken her and Florence's picture on the platform at Victoria station. For the journalist to appear before her now, here at this château in Wimereux, snatches the breath from her lungs.

'My dear Lucie,' Harry says, closing the gap between them and clasping Lucinda's hands. 'Am I glad to find you!'

'What a wonderful surprise,' Lucinda stammers, fighting a sudden, embarrassing urge to throw herself into his arms. Instead, she invites Harry into the library, clearing a pile of medical notes from a chair, gesturing for him to sit. She pushes the blankets to the end of the chaise-longue, and sits down too. Only then does she take a proper breath. 'What on earth brings you all the way out here, Harry?'

The journalist perches on the rickety chair, bracing his long legs. 'It's been a heck of a journey, Lucie.' He sighs, offering Lucinda a tired smile. 'I promised your dear mother that I'd report back if my path crossed with yours. Let her know what's really happening.'

'Mother sent you?' So the letter she'd dashed off to Eleanor hours before leaving Paris must have reached home. Lucinda knows from her mother's that Eleanor would dearly love to come out and lend a hand at the hospital, but her fragile health had so far precluded such a difficult journey. But now they'd settled on the coast, Eleanor might think again.

'She sends her love,' Harry adds, 'and hopes you're truly as well as your letters suggest.' Harry smoothes his moustache. 'Any chance of a cup of tea, Lucie? I've been on the road since, oh, I've lost track . . .'

'Of course, yes, I should have offered . . .' Lucinda opens the library door, and spots Olga Campbell hurrying past with a pail.

'Orderly Campbell, can I trouble you a moment, please?'

'Of course, Doctor.'

'I'd love a pot of tea, if you could rustle one up.'

'I'll bring one as soon as I can, Doctor.'

Lucinda thanks the orderly, closing the door again. She sinks down at her desk with a barely suppressed sigh. It's such a relief to have Harry here, a true friend, someone who may genuinely be able to help. He won't merely gawp at the patients and make meaningless small-talk.

'What are you really doing out here, Harry?'

'I've been hunting an infamous tribe of women,' the journalist says, winking a keen eye, 'headed by the most extraordinary pair of doctors. Would you happen to know of them, Lucie? I'd dearly love to interview them for a piece I'm writing on military medicine.'

Lucinda releases a shaky laugh, her shoulders relaxing a notch. 'Oh, Harry, I'm so glad to see you.' Her voice catches and she hurriedly clears her throat.

'I've taken a lot of trouble to find you, Lucie,' Harry says. 'I consider myself rather clever to do so.'

'Very clever,' Lucinda agrees. 'I'm sorry if you were kept waiting. I hadn't long finished surgery.'

'On the contrary, it gave me time to admire your paintings,' Harry replies. 'I didn't know you indulged.'

Lucinda can't help but laugh. 'The château owner's wife was an artist, so I'm told.'

'Well, I'm sure you could do just as well as this so-called artist, my dear, given the chance.' Harry's eyes twinkle and Lucinda feels herself blush as though she were a girl again. She marvels at Harry's ability to charm even someone like her, a self-proclaimed independent woman immune to male flattery.

'How are you, Lucie?' Harry says softly, breaking the fragile silence.

Lucinda clasps her hands in her lap, considering his question. How was she, really? Exhausted. Overwhelmed. Pining for Florence.

'Your move from Paris, how did that go?' Harry continues, before Lucinda can respond. 'How long have you been here?'

Lucinda tries to think – the days bleed into one another. 'This is the fourth day.'

'Not long, then,' Harry says. 'And your team are all here, are they?'

Lucinda swallows a lump in her throat. 'Florence stayed

behind, with Sister Bryony and Mr Tozer. We had about a dozen patients we couldn't risk moving.'

'That must have been a difficult decision to make,' Harry murmurs.

Lucinda nods, not trusting her voice.

'But a wise one.' Harry holds her gaze.

'I'm so worried, Harry,' Lucinda whispers.

'Understandable.' Harry smiles slowly, knowingly. 'But last I heard the Germans were on the turn.'

This is news to Lucinda, and her heart lifts.

'Florence knows how to take care of herself,' Harry adds, and Lucinda flushes.

She's rescued at that moment by a knock at the door. Olga has returned with a tray of tea things.

'Thank you, Campbell,' Lucinda says gratefully. The girl dips her head, and hurries away again. 'I wish I could offer you something to eat, Harry, but the catering here is rudimentary at best, and the next meal isn't until this evening.'

'Who does your cooking?'

'Local women,' Lucinda replies. 'Food supplies are rather unpredictable at present, but we get by.' She stirs the teapot, thinking of the girl-soldier in the storeroom. She'll have to check on her again very soon, and take her some food. Decide what to do.

The urge to confide in Harry, to share the burden of the dilemma she's facing, threatens to overwhelm her. It's on the tip of her tongue to blurt out what's happened: *I discovered a patient was a woman . . . She was dressed as a soldier . . . I don't know what to do . . .* But she fears it's too soon to drop that incendiary piece of news into the conversation.

Instead, she hears herself ask Harry how he'd got here, when travelling around the area is so dangerous and challenging. 'I thought freelance war correspondents had been prohibited from France and Belgium.'

'Our wings are so damned clipped, Lucie,' Harry replies. He tugs a creased booklet from a trouser pocket, and slides it across the desk to her.

Regulations for Press Correspondents Accompanying a Force in the Field, she reads.

'Kitchener's circulated a list among the BEF,' Harry says, 'of the names of all the British correspondents he thinks are in France, and whose immediate arrest he seeks. Guess who's number one on that list, Lucie.'

'Oh, Harry . . .'

'It's not only Kitchener who's obstructing us, though. The French war ministry have adapted old siege laws from the last century to restrict reports too. They're determined that the only supply of news from the front should come from its own *Service d'Information*.'

Lucinda pours tea, as Harry goes on.

'Correspondents caught in civilian clothes risk being shot as spies,' he says. 'I know of several already who've been arrested on charges of espionage.'

'Surely they don't think you're a spy, Harry!'

'A colleague of mine who works for *The Times*, Morrison, managed to get close to the BEF on their retreat at Mons, back in August. He reported on how fast the Germans were advancing, how their pursuit of our men was relentless, merciless, and how our troops were suffering grievous injuries and unbelievable losses.' Harry accepts a cup of tea from Lucinda and takes a long swallow. 'He was told to go straight back to London, or they'd lock him up for illegally sharing information.'

The following month, Harry continues, another correspondent, a Frenchman called Durand, who wrote for *Le Matin* and whom Harry knew from before the war, cycled into Reims. 'Right into the middle of the German bombardment.'

Lucinda drinks her tea, too shocked to speak.

'He was with his photographer, a chap called Moreau,' Harry says. 'They witnessed women and children fleeing for their lives, the cathedral destroyed, shells falling on the city like rain.'

The deadliest rain, Lucinda thinks.

'Durand wrote up their experience, but they were both arrested, warned they'd be shot if they printed another word.'

'How are you getting your stories back to Britain, if reporters are so restricted?' she asks.

'Couriers in Calais,' Harry tells her. 'That's where I've come from. I'm not the only reporter wandering on the fringes of the action and smuggling their stories back, but there aren't many of us left now. Not since Kitchener deployed his latest weapon against us.'

Lucinda pours more tea into Harry's cup. 'What weapon?' she asks.

'He's appointed a soldier to supply the newspapers with their information.'

'What do you mean?'

'There's a colonel in the Royal Engineers, Swanson's his

name. He's producing the dullest copy, full of military terminology that no civilian can understand. He leaves out place names, the names of soldiers, regiments, details that might identify anything of interest.'

'I didn't know this.'

'No one does. That's the point, Lucie. But I'm not giving in. I'm on the hunt for compelling, human-interest stories that I know the public will want to read.'

The girl-soldier would be just such a story, Lucinda thinks.

'Those at home need to know the truth,' Harry goes on. The teapot is empty now. 'They need to be told that the enemy is advancing, the front lines aren't stable. Day after day, innocent people are being butchered. The strain on our troops is untenable.'

For the sake of a few hundred yards of ground, thousands of lives were being lost. Lucinda knows this only too well.

'The public are aware of only half the story,' Harry says, with a sigh. 'They read of the victories, but the true cost is hidden.'

'Where are you going after here?'

'I'm heading to Paris, I think.'

'Will you visit the Clarens?' Lucinda stammers. 'Will you see if Florence is well? I'm so worried.'

'I know, my dear,' Harry smiles at her in sympathy, 'but I can't be certain they'll even let me through the gates. If I can, I'll pay a visit to Florence, but it will likely be too risky to delay there.'

'She should be here.' Lucinda's teacup rattles in its saucer. 'Please, Harry, I must know if she's safe.'

'I'm sure she's fine, my dear,' he says, 'but I'll do my utmost to make sure.'

'You'll stay here tonight, won't you?' Desperate though she is for news of Florence, Lucinda can't bear the thought of her friend leaving so soon, heading off into the perilous night.

'I was hoping you'd have a bed free, yes.' Harry smiles. 'Will you have time for an interview while I'm here? I want to write about your phenomenal hospital, Lucie.'

Lucinda's eyes prickle. 'I wouldn't call it phenomenal,' she says quietly. 'We only do what we can.'

'I beg to disagree,' Harry says. 'It must have been a *phenomenal* exercise, moving everyone out of Paris.'

'It was quite a challenge,' Lucinda admits, recalling the hasty evacuation from the Hôtel Clarens, the long, uncomfortable, perilous drive to this place. 'We could only move those patients we deemed strong enough to survive the journey,' she tells Harry. 'We packed everything we could into the trucks, but had to leave a great deal behind, of course.'

'Quite a responsibility,' Harry says.

Quite a responsibility indeed. The life of every last person in this place was Lucinda's responsibility. Including that of the strange young woman she's hiding in the storeroom.

She bites back the urge to add that she often feels culpable for her patients' invisible mental wounds, as well as their physical injuries, as though their torments and nightmares are her fault. Which is ridiculous, of course.

And yet the weight of this burden presses down on her relentlessly, as if gravity has multiplied a hundredfold.

She looks up and catches the full force of her friend's scrutiny.

'You must be exhausted, Lucie,' Harry murmurs. 'You're looking rather thinner than I recall . . .'

Lucinda struggles to find an adequate response to her friend's observation. It's true she's neglected her health of late, often forgetting to eat, too busy for proper meals. No Florence to anchor her.

'What will I tell your dear mother, when I next see her?' Harry's mock disapproval aims to lighten the tone, but it only makes Lucinda want to cry. Her friend's concern is almost too much to bear, his gentle teasing threatening to undo her.

'I'm quite well, Harry,' she mutters at last.

The two friends sit in silence, Lucinda trying to think. Could Harry help her decide what to do with the strange girl? She respects his judgement, not least because of his support of female suffrage. She considers the many times he's accompanied her on protest marches back in London. She thinks of the countless news pieces he's published over the years, supporting women and the Cause, criticizing the government's treatment of half its citizens.

He means more to Lucinda than she can ever admit. The affection she feels for him is akin to the love she has for her family.

She chews a thumbnail, thinking of the battered little notebook and the camera in her pocket. It's all so strange and not a little sinister, and she can think of no ethical or logical reason why a young woman would choose to disguise herself as a soldier and endure the squalor and danger of the battlefield.

If only Florence was here. Thinking of her makes Lucinda's sternum ache. She can hardly bear that the woman she loves is alone in Paris at the mercy of the oily Cassard. What dubious suggestions was the manager whispering into Flo's neat ear?

'Is everything all right, Lucie? You've gone quite pale.'

Harry's voice tugs Lucinda back to the library. She contemplates her friend for a moment, and tries to decide what Florence would do if she were here.

She takes a breath. 'Can you keep a secret, Harry?'

27

Edie: November 1914

Time passes, and Edie drifts in and out of a restless slumber. At last, the doctor returns, bringing with her an older man with silver hair, whom she introduces as Mr Levinson.

'Please, call me Harry,' the man says with a smile, dragging the stool to Edie's bedside and sitting down. 'Lucinda tells me you've been in the wars.'

Edie can only stare at the man. Like the doctor, he has a kind smile that reaches his eyes, but his green gaze pierces her.

'I'm a freelance war reporter,' Harry Levinson says, after a pause. 'Lucinda has asked me to help you.'

Edie drags herself up on the pillows. A reporter? Was he telling the truth? With his tan suit and swept-back hair he looked more like some actor from the theatre.

'I think you and I have something in common,' Harry Levinson continues. 'I'm not supposed to be here in France. Journalists like me are banned from fraternizing with soldiers, discovering the truth of war. But you're not meant to be here either, are you?'

An uncomfortable silence settles on the room.

Harry Levinson exchanges a glance with the doctor, who, Edie now notices, is holding a bundle of dressings and other medical paraphernalia. She hovers by the door, as though she can't quite make up her mind whether to stay or leave. Her tangible nervousness unsettles Edie, and she turns her attention back to the man, to find his focus on her hasn't wavered.

'No, I don't think you're meant to be here at all,' Harry Levinson murmurs. 'What's your story?'

His question triggers a sudden urge in Edie to escape the room, but when she tries to move pain rips through her thigh, and she gasps.

'I need to see to that wound.' Dr Garland finally sets down the dressings, and draws back Edie's sheets.

'Of course.' Harry Levinson rises. 'Can I help?'

'When did you last wash your hands, Harry?'

'Good question.' The journalist contemplates his palms. 'Tuesday, I think.'

This elicits a snort of laughter from the doctor. She begins to remove the blood-soaked bandages from Edie's thigh.

Dr Garland and Harry Levinson talk over Edie's prone body as the doctor works, and it seems to Edie almost as though they've forgotten she's there.

'Who else knows about this?' Harry Levinson asks at one point.

'Only Hazel,' Dr Garland replies. 'She's been my anaesthetist while Florence is in Paris. And Nurse Whiteman who assisted with the operation.'

'Anyone else?'

'Figgis and Penhaligon my porters,' Dr Garland says. 'They don't know the full facts, of course, but they suspect something's up. Figgis is a nosy soul, and I doubt he believed my contagion story.'

'Did you find anything else apart from the book?'

'Only the little box camera I showed you.'

A strangled noise escapes Edie's throat. The doctor and the journalist snap their attention back to her.

'Those things are important to you, aren't they?' Harry Levinson asks her.

Edie nods.

'Would you like them back?'

Edie nods fiercely.

Dr Garland exchanges a glance with Harry Levinson, and they seem to reach an unspoken agreement between themselves.

'Just a moment,' the doctor says, and hurries away, leaving Edie and Harry Levinson alone. Edie waits for the journalist to ask her more questions, but instead he takes a notepad from an inside pocket of his jacket, rummages for a pencil and proceeds to write. Edie watches him, wishing she could see what he is setting down on paper.

After a while he glances up, catching her eye. 'You're an intriguing conundrum, young lady.'

Edie has no notion what he means.

'A true mystery,' Harry Levinson muses, tapping his pencil against his teeth. 'Why would a woman dress herself in soldiers' garb, and put herself at such risk? Unless . . . she was following her sweetheart, perhaps?'

Edie's eyes widen at such a ridiculous suggestion.

'I do believe I've hit a nerve,' Harry Levinson murmurs. 'But something traps your tongue.' He tucks his pad and pencil away. 'For what it's worth, I will tell you this. There is no one I would trust more with my life than Dr Garland. All she wants to do is help you. But in order to do that she needs to know everything. You have to tell her the truth, however hard that may be. Do you understand?'

They are interrupted by the return of Dr Garland, and Edie's heart stutters to see her notebook and Stanley's camera in the woman's hands.

Harry Levinson takes the little case from the doctor, and slides the Ensignette out to inspect it. Edie wants so much to snatch it from him.

'You've taken photographs with this?' Harry Levinson asks Edie.

Edie hesitates. It was Stanley who took the photographs, not her. But the camera is hers now, the only thing she has left of him. She wants it back.

Dr Garland frowns. 'It was found in the pocket of the uniform you were wearing.'

'Perhaps it belonged to your sweetheart,' Harry Levinson ventures.

'What are you talking about, Harry?' Dr Garland says. 'What sweetheart?'

'I was just saying to your unexpected guest here,' Harry Levinson gives Edie a conspiratorial wink, 'that it's quite unusual for a young woman to pull such a stunt, to put herself in such a risky situation. I've never come across a woman disguised as a soldier before. But then, people do act rather strangely sometimes, especially in the name of love.'

Harry Levinson gives Dr Garland a knowing look, and the doctor's cheeks flush.

'It seems to me the most likely explanation, Lucie,' Harry Levinson continues. 'This young lady, desperate to be with her beloved, somehow manages to procure herself a soldier's uniform, then gets herself to France, determined to track down her sweetheart and bring him home.'

'I think you've been reading too many novels, Harry.' The doctor chuckles drily. Her brief smile transforms her face, and Edie suddenly remembers where she's seen her before.

London. Mouse Castle. This woman was the doctor who had tended her after she'd been released from Holloway the time before last. Edie had maintained her hunger strike for a fortnight that time, and the prison had eventually been forced to allow her to recuperate in the suffragette safe-house in Notting Hill. Gradually, Edie realizes Harry Levinson is speaking to her.

'I think we can agree that's a possible scenario,' he says. 'Unless you're able to furnish us with an alternative truth.'

Edie tries to corral her fractured thoughts.

'So,' Levinson presses, 'did you find your sweetheart?'

When Edie doesn't answer, he focuses on the camera again, turning it over in his hands, examining it from every angle. 'I've used one of these before,' he mutters. 'I can get the film in this developed, Lucie.'

'We have a darkroom set up here, for the X-ray machine that's on its way,' Dr Garland replies. 'How long will the film take to develop?'

Edie thinks fleetingly of Stanley, and what he'd say if he was here now, listening to this conversation. *Just wait 'til you see what's on it . . .*

'Let me see that notebook again, Lucie.'

Edie looks on helplessly, as the doctor hands it over.

Harry Levinson leafs through the pages. 'So this is your diary?' he asks Edie.

She nods hesitantly.

'Looks like you've kept a pretty detailed log of your adventures . . .' He sounds impressed. 'There's a story here,' he says, turning pages as he speaks. 'An incredible story.'

Edie watches as the journalist peers closely at a particular entry. It gives her a strange, unsettled feeling to have someone else read her scrawled notes.

'How did you keep this secret?' Harry Levinson asks.

'Is there something illicit in here?' Dr Garland says, taking the diary from Harry. 'Is that why you aren't talking to us?'

Edie feels the blood drain from her head.

'If this diary's anything to go by, our guest has been through Hell, Lucie,' the journalist murmurs. 'Is it any wonder she isn't speaking?'

'Are you physically unable to speak?' Dr Garland asks Edie. 'I should check your throat.'

Edie brings a hand to her neck, shrinking back against the pillows.

'Can you write?' Harry Levinson asks her. 'Can you write down why you're here?' The journalist passes her his notepad and pencil.

Edie grips the pencil in an unsteady hand. What was the point of withholding information now? She'd been discovered. Her stunt is over. She's failed.

'Where are you from, Edie?' Harry Levinson prompts gently. 'Why are you here?'

She slowly writes *London*. The letters judder and blur, as a tear drops on to the paper. She wipes her running nose with the back of a hand. Where does she start? These people will surely never believe her, yet she has to tell them the truth.

All I want is to be a journalist, she writes at last. *I lost my job. No one would hire me. I wanted to be the first woman to report from the battlefield.* She passes the notebook back to Harry, and he reads her words aloud.

'Quite the stunt,' he says. 'Tell me –'

He's interrupted by a knock at the door.

Dr Garland shoots Harry a look of alarm.

'Doc? You in there, ma'am?' a man's voice calls from beyond the door. 'They're asking for you in theatre.'

'Figgis,' Dr Garland hisses. 'How does he know I'm in here?'

'You have to go, Lucie,' Harry Levinson whispers.

'I'll be there in a minute, Mr Figgis,' the doctor calls. 'You can return to your duties now, thank you.'

'Can you give me an address in London, Edie?' Harry Levinson says. 'Any names of people who can help you?'

Edie writes on the pad: *Sylvia Pankhurst. 39 Roman Road.*

'Sylvia Pankhurst?' Dr Garland snaps. 'How do you know her?'

A friend from the Society.

'Well, that's easily verified,' Harry Levinson pronounces, as Edie hands back the pad and pencil. 'I'll telegraph Miss Pankhurst immediately, and see what light she can shed on all this.'

28

Lucinda: November 1914

Early the following morning, before surgery starts, Lucinda meets Harry in the library. She'd had no chance to talk to her friend the previous evening, as various emergency cases had arrived, which she'd been called to deal with.

'You look as if you need a drink already,' Harry says with a dry laugh. 'Where do you hide your stash?'

'Don't tempt me,' Lucinda sighs, sinking down at her desk. 'Did you sleep well?'

'Better than you, by the look of it.' Harry makes himself comfortable on the chaise-longue. 'Were you up all night, Lucie? You're terribly pale.'

'I had to amputate a man's right foot,' Lucinda replies. 'He plays football for his town, he told me yesterday. Well, he won't be playing any more.' Lucinda musters a weak smile. 'It doesn't get any easier, Harry.' There's no point in complaining, even to Harry, who, she knows, would listen with sympathy. 'Have you gleaned any more information from the girl?'

'She's quite the little fighter,' Harry replies. He takes his reporter's pad from his pocket, and passes it to Lucinda. The pages are filled with his barely legible scrawl.

'Has a spider written this, Harry?' Lucinda says, with a

smile. 'It's worse than Florence's handwriting.' She passes the pad back across the desk.

'I'll tell her you said that.' Harry's answering smile creases the corners of his eyes. 'Edie told me everything,' he goes on.

'So, her voice has returned?'

'Only a whisper, poor thing.' Harry flicks through his pad. 'She gave me her life story. Poor girl's had it rough. After her father left, her mother had nowhere to go but the workhouse. She grew up there, until she was sent out to skivvy at fourteen, a week after her mother died. She ended up as maid-of-all-work at a local newspaper office. The editor's son saw how keen she was to write, and sometimes took her on assignments as his assistant.'

Harry makes Lucinda laugh, as he recounts how Edie had shared his supper, devouring most of a French loaf, with a generous chunk of cheese, and a pot of tea that Harry had refilled twice.

'I don't think it touched the sides.' Harry chuckles. 'And then she told me she was still hungry!'

'She's making up for lost time,' Lucinda says.

Through skilful questioning, Harry had got Edie to retrace her steps, starting with her release from Holloway, then her subsequent enlistment into the army and her military training at Hurst Park. She'd described her first experience of the sea on her journey to France, the arduous march to the battlefields, and how she'd been trapped in a trench raid, left for dead.

'When she got to that part, she began to tremble like she had the ague, Lucie.'

'I hope you didn't interrogate her.'

'I offered to stop the interview but she didn't want to.'

Edie had closed her eyes, Harry tells Lucinda, clearly haunted by dark memories, and it had taken her a long time to gather herself together to continue her account. 'She lost her friend in that trench raid.'

'Killed?'

'She doesn't know for certain, but fears so. Stanley Chay's his name. This is his camera.' Harry produces the Ensignette from his suit pocket. 'She got rather upset.'

'Understandable.' Lucinda nods. 'She's been through so much, by all accounts.'

'I told her there was nothing she could have done for her friend. She was almost dead herself.'

'She's only here now because the stretcher-bearers found her in time,' Lucinda says.

'She asked if we'd sent word to Sylvia Pankhurst yet.'

'Mardie dispatched the telegram yesterday,' Lucinda replies.

'The world needs to hear Edie's story,' Harry says. 'She's quite an extraordinary young lady.'

'That sounds like you want to tell it,' Lucinda says.

'She can write it herself, even if she is somewhat erratic with her spelling. Which isn't a surprise, really, as she virtually taught herself to read.'

'What are we going to do about her in the meantime?' Lucinda asks, rubbing the back of her neck. Hours of bending over an operating table has caused a permanent dull ache in her spine. Fleetingly, she imagines Florence standing behind her chair, massaging the nape of her neck with her long, cool fingers.

'It frustrates her not to be able to walk,' Harry reports. 'But I gave her some paper last night, and left her scribbling away like the dickens, setting down her version of events. Her determination puts some of my colleagues to shame.'

Lucinda thinks of the girl's mud-smeared notebook, the pages of cramped, barely decipherable script. 'What are we going to do about her, Harry?' she repeats.

'If Sylvia Pankhurst will take her, she ought to go home, don't you think?'

'I'm not sure she's strong enough to withstand the journey. And I'm worried her regiment will be looking for her.'

'She enlisted under a false identity,' Harry says.

'That's an offence, and she could be court-martialled.'

'We can't let that happen,' Harry says, 'which is why we have to send her home as soon as possible.'

'As a Blighty on a hospital ship?'

'Or you could pass her off as one of your staff.'

Lucinda tries to wrangle her thoughts into some sort of order. Nothing seems straightforward. 'I don't know what to do for the best, Harry. My heart tells me to send her home, but what if the military authorities get wind of this? I'm assisting someone who's broken the law, aren't I?'

'It's one heck of a story, Lucie . . .'

'Forget the story for a moment, Harry. You know I can't risk being arrested.'

'But she's not a soldier any more, is she? She's simply one of your people, who's sustained an injury and needs to recuperate at home.'

'Except that's not true . . .' Lucinda tries to think. Could what Harry is suggesting work?

'She won't want to go back to England yet, though,' Harry says, after a moment.

'What do you mean?'

'She's desperate to find out what happened to her chum.'

'Is he her sweetheart, do you think?'

'No. She met him when they were training.'

'Well,' Lucinda suppresses another sigh, 'she's too weak to be moved for a couple of days anyway.'

'She's a strong little thing, Lucie.'

'The staff haven't seen you going in and out of her room, have they? Tell me you've been discreet, Harry.'

'None of the staff suspects a thing. Stop worrying.'

'Figgis is suspicious.'

'That odious porter? The man's clueless.'

'I don't think he's half as dense as we think.'

There's a knock on the library door. Nurse Whiteman pokes her head into the room to remind Lucinda that ward rounds are due to start soon.

'We'll talk more about the girl afterwards,' Lucinda says to Harry, when the nurse has gone.

'If I'm still here.'

'What do you mean? You aren't leaving?'

'I can't remain here much longer, Lucie. I need to get to Paris. Every day I stay in one place, the net closes. If I'm caught, I don't rate my chances . . . and I really don't fancy a stay in a French jail.'

Lucinda tries to think of something to say that will persuade her friend to stay. 'What about the camera?' she says at last. 'You were going to develop the film.'

'There isn't time now, Lucie. And I promised Edie I'd

give it back,' Harry says. 'It's the last link she has to her friend.'

There is so much Lucinda wants to say, but she's all too aware of the huge risk her friend is taking just by being here. If the military authorities should get wind of his presence, they'll arrest him for disobeying orders. At the very least, he'll be sent back to England with a black mark against his name to wait out the war with the rest of the freelance reporters banned from the front.

'I understand,' Lucinda says at last. 'I only wish I knew what to do.'

'You'll hear from Sylvia Pankhurst soon, I hope,' Harry says. 'Then in a day or so, when Edie is well enough to travel, you can send her home.'

Lucinda begins her morning rounds in Elpis Ward, where she finds most of the officers resting peacefully, as far as their injuries permit.

She moves swiftly along the beds, checking dressings, signing off paperwork, making a few adjustments to apparatus supporting broken bones.

'When am I going to the pictures, Doctor?' a young lieutenant asks Lucinda, as she checks his medical notes. His question brings a brief smile to her lips. She finds the men's nicknames for the various ordeals they face, such as going under the anaesthetic on the operating table, quite inventive and often amusing.

'Tomorrow, all being well,' she tells the officer.

'Hope you're showing *A Study in Scarlet*, Doctor,' he quips.

'Very good.' Lucinda smiles. She moves on through the

ward, answering the men's questions about pain relief and recovery times, assuaging their worries and fears as best she can. Eventually she arrives at the bedside of a patient suffering from extensive burns to his torso.

'How are we feeling today, Captain?' she asks, scanning the clipboard hanging from the foot of the officer's bed: *Cpt. J. Wainwright: Refusing food, nervous outbursts.*

'I've been rather better, Doctor,' the captain replies.

Lucinda assesses the man's sickly grey pallor, his trembling hands. 'Is the pain worse?'

'N-not really,' he stammers. Lucinda notes his rapid blinking.

'An improvement then, Captain,' Lucinda says. 'Ah, here comes the breakfast trolley. Ensure you eat something, won't you?' She prepares to move on, but the officer grasps her sleeve.

'It's only . . . I don't know how to tell my wife . . .'

Lucinda hesitates, politely extracting her sleeve from the man's grip. 'Your wife, sir?'

'She'll be so upset, Doctor.'

'Have you written to her, Captain?' *Does she know the full extent of your injuries?*

The officer gives a stiff shake of his head.

'I can ask Orderly Campbell to write for you,' Lucinda offers. The girl has proved herself a true scribe lately.

'She has no idea . . .' The officer's voice cracks, and he can't finish his sentence.

Lucinda hesitates, at a loss as to how to respond. Sometimes, it's better to leave a patient alone with their emotions. At least, that's what she's found previously. To her relief, Orderly Hodgson appears at that moment with the breakfast trolley, offering tea and toast, and Lucinda withdraws.

Her final patient is awake and alert in the neighbouring bed, watching proceedings with a bright-eyed intensity. Lucinda greets the man politely, scanning his notes to see what painkillers he's been given. The officer is in his forties, making him one of the oldest patients Lucinda has treated. His rugged face reminds her unnervingly of the police officer who'd arrested her in Whitehall in 1912. But she refuses to believe he's the same man – it would be far too much of a coincidence. For his part, the officer gives no indication that he recognizes Lucinda.

Instead, while she checks the dressing on his leg, the officer regales her with his experience of battle, and the strange apparition he and his men had encountered.

'I wasn't the only one to witness it,' the officer tells her. 'The Germans had been shelling us unremittingly for hours. My men were losing faith. It looked as if we could never break through their lines. It was as though we were at war with the whole bloody German race.'

Lucinda nods as though she understands, but she can barely bring herself to imagine the horror of the battlefield. It's enough that she has to face the aftermath every day on her operating table.

'It was all up with us, I thought,' the officer goes on, 'and then, the next minute, there appeared this ball of light, and from it came a tall figure in silver armour . . .'

The man is delirious, Lucinda thinks. Although his account isn't the first sighting of an angel or saint she's heard about.

'. . . with wings,' the officer is talking on, somewhat

296

breathlessly now. 'And the angel, or whatever it was, opened its mouth, and the most curious sound came out, like bells ringing . . .'

Perhaps she should adjust the man's morphine levels, Lucinda thinks. 'Are you sleeping well?'

'As well as can be expected in this place,' the officer snaps. 'I haven't finished telling you what happened, Doctor.'

'Please, continue.'

'Thank you. Before I could react, the Germans ceased their onslaught and began to retreat. The apparition simply vanished.'

'A successful outcome, then,' Lucinda says, sounding briskly patronizing to her own ears.

'You think I'm mad.'

'No, not at all, but I do think you may be suffering from exhaustion, and possibly delayed shock.' Lucinda looks round for Sister Whiteman, but the nurse is busy at the other end of the ward dealing with a vomiting incident.

'I'm perfectly sane, Doctor. I know what I saw.'

Lucinda turns back to the officer. 'I'm sure you are and that you do,' she says. After all, who was she to doubt this man's experience, in the thick of battle?

She has her own Mr Morton, after all.

The ward rounds are finally completed. Washing her hands, she wonders if Harry has left already. But before she can go in search of him, she's called to the lobby to oversee the latest discharge of patients.

Signing the paperwork, Lucinda contemplates the five

soldiers departing from the hospital. One is going on leave, two are being transferred to Boulogne and a hospital ship, which will eventually take them home, and two are returning to the front.

Lucinda shakes each man's hand in turn, wishing them luck.

'I can't wait to see my sweetheart,' the soldier going on leave tells her. 'I haven't seen her for two months. I'm going to ask her to marry me. Should have done it before I left.'

'You're wise not to waste a single moment, Private,' Lucinda tells him. 'Be sure to keep your weight off that leg, or it will take longer to heal.' He's among the lucky ones, receiving a shrapnel wound to the knee. Unlike most of the other gravely injured soldiers Lucinda has operated on, this young man has lost part of his kneecap, but it's enough to keep him from the front line for several weeks.

After everyone has gone, and the hospital's doors are closed again, Lucinda lingers in the empty lobby. Seeing off this last group of patients has set her heart aching anew. What was Florence doing right now? Was her dear friend thinking of her?

She listens to the sounds of the hospital, the faint voices of nurses and soldiers drifting from the wards, the occasional cry of pain, a distant tinkle of piano keys — Penhaligon must have found time to tune the dilapidated old instrument in the dining room.

Surrounded by her staff and patients, Lucinda never feels truly alone but at this moment she is so dreadfully lonely she could cry. Tears prick her eyes, and she rubs them roughly away with the heels of her hands. She simply can't be seen to be weak.

This is no good.

Perhaps she should write to Florence again and confess her feelings. But she's hardly any better at expressing her emotions on paper. If only she knew the right words to explain the mysterious alchemy of passion swirling in her breast, the depth of love she feels for Florence.

The hospital without you is like a library without books. I miss you, with all the love my heart can hold.

At least in a letter the words will be clear and calm, not stammered or meandering or full of nervous faltering as they would be if she had to speak them aloud.

The thought of repressing her love for her friend, hiding her true feelings from Florence for evermore, is simply unbearable. It's like trying to conceal a burning candle in a burlap sack: only a matter of time before the whole thing goes up in flames.

And, yet, how can it be any different?

She thinks of the young soldier already on his way home to propose to his sweetheart. If only she were a man, there would be none of this indecision.

If anything should happen to Florence in Paris, if she should die, it would be like losing a vital organ, Lucinda thinks. No, that's not true, because Florence's absence already makes her feel hollowed out, as though she's missing them all.

'Doctor?'

Lucinda turns to find Mardie Hodgson coming towards her.

'Dr Grace said to tell you they're ready for you in surgery, ma'am.'

'I'll be there straight away, Hodgson.'

It's late in the afternoon by the time Lucinda finishes. She's worked through lunch and tea, adrenaline robbing her of appetite, but now as she makes her way back to the library she finds herself wondering if the cook has saved her a plate of anything. If Florence were here, she'd insist Lucinda sit down and eat something.

But Florence isn't here.

To her surprise, Lucinda finds Harry at her desk, writing. 'You haven't gone.' She can't keep the relief from her voice.

Harry glances up as Lucinda closes the library door. 'Lucie, I was just coming to find you.' He sets Lucinda's pen back in its pot, and gathers up sheets of paper.

'Are you staying, Harry?'

'I truly wish I could.' Harry rises from the desk, and offers the papers to Lucinda. 'The top page is a draft of what I plan to print as soon as I'm back on English soil,' he tells her. 'The rest is Edie's account.'

Lucinda stares at the papers in her hand, the words swimming before her eyes.

'I have to go, Lucie.'

'Can't you at least stay until after supper?'

'You know I'd love nothing more.'

Then don't go, Lucinda wants to cry. 'What about Sylvia Pankhurst?' she says instead.

'She'll reply, Lucie, depend on it.'

'Please stay.' Lucinda inwardly winces at the pleading note in her voice. 'I can't face this on my own.'

'You can face anything, Lucie. You're the strongest, cleverest, most competent woman I know.'

'But what am I supposed to do?' she cries, no longer caring if anyone passing the library hears her.

'All you *can* do is keep doing what you do best, and soon Edie'll be strong enough to return home. I'll pay for her passage, if need be. Just send word. And I'll let you know her progress when I'm back on home soil. She'll need help to tell her story.'

Lucinda can think of no reply.

'It's all there, Lucie.' Harry gestures at the paper trembling in Lucinda's hand. 'I must leave now. Take care, won't you?'

Before Lucinda can react, Harry is through the door and gone.

Left alone, Lucinda sinks down at her desk and begins to read Harry's words.

There are to be found in these wards angels of the highest order. An all-female team working tirelessly, night and day, tending our battle-scarred men. This military hospital in Wimereux is an example of how the human spirit can not only endure, but can triumph . . .

She reads on, unable to tear her eyes from Harry's account of how she and her staff had risked their lives treating wounded soldiers in Paris as the German Army threatened to invade. How the Corps had been forced to flee, taking with them as many patients as they could. How they had then set up a second hospital, starting from scratch, in a vacant château on the coast.

Lucinda's eyes widen as Harry goes on to describe how she had discovered a female soldier on her operating table, and had saved the young woman's life.

The soldier of the 6th London Regiment, serving as Pte Eddie Lawrence, was in fact Edie Lawrence, an aspiring journalist. Edie had risked all on a stunt to make her name as the first female journalist to report from the thick of battle, an astonishing act of bravery.

Lucinda turns to Edie's own account, learning how the young woman had dressed in men's clothes to enlist in London, then endured weeks of military training, learning how to march and drill and shoot. In October, when the call had come, Edie had travelled to France to fight alongside her fellow soldiers, during which time she was shot in the thigh.

Lucinda tries to imagine herself wielding a gun, shooting a person, even a German soldier, in cold blood, but the image refuses to come. She sets the papers on the desk, trying to absorb the astonishing account of reckless bravery captured in ink. It's almost too much to take in.

Her eyes begin to blur, and she takes Florence's handkerchief from her pocket and holds it to her face, breathing in the faint rose-soap scent of her friend. The smell conjures Florence in her mind, a fleeting impression she wishes she could bottle like perfume and hold for ever.

All at once, she's assailed by such profound longing for Florence that she can do nothing but sit with the handkerchief pressed to her eyes for several seconds. Never before has she missed her friend with such a deep-seated yearning. Tears threaten, but her eyes remain dry. She's too tired now even to cry.

At last, she pulls herself together enough to move. She suddenly craves the sea, though where this desire has sprung from, she cannot say. Before she can talk herself out of it, before anyone can waylay her, she pulls on her coat, hurries from her office and across the lobby to slip out of the front door.

Outside, she's greeted with a melancholic air, a cold moon rising in a bruised sky. She crosses the empty court-yard, opens the gates and sets off, dimly recalling Bataille the agent telling her that the sea was a few minutes' walk to the west. A stiff breeze blows, but Lucinda is oblivious to the chill as she hurries along the road, turning right at the end, passing houses and chalets shut up for the night. She ought to be checking on Edie Lawrence, she knows. She ought to be supervising the evening ward rounds. She ought to be making sure her staff and patients are all right.

But, for once, she can't face any of it.

As she nears the end of the road, she smells salt on the wind, and hears the sea calling to her, a pulsing roar that draws her on. Shoes crunching over pebbly sand, she makes her way to the foaming shore. The tide is on the turn, and she has a little way to go before she reaches the water. Her shoes sink into soft sand, and if she cared to look back, she would see a single jagged trail of small depressions in the pristine shore stretching away behind her.

But she doesn't look back.

The wind off the sea is brisk, and her hair, loosened of pins, flicks her eyes and grows damp and heavy on her shoulders. Sometimes, she fantasizes about taking her surgical scissors and lopping it off, imagining Florence running her fingers through her neat, short bob, and professing her handsome.

She stands motionless as the waves sweep in and out, the tide surging and retreating, surging and retreating, the sea's eternal heartbeat.

Water laps at the toes of her shoes, as she sucks in lungfuls of brackish air. But however deeply she breathes, she can't seem to fill her lungs. The roar of the surf grows ever louder, penetrating her skull, washing away all thought.

It's strange to be entirely alone, with no one but the scattering of gulls bobbing on the waves to witness her taking off her shoes, her stockings, her bare toes sinking into the cold wet sand.

Hitching up her skirt, she staggers further into the restless, churning surf, each step plunging her deeper into the slate-grey water, ankles pushing against the force of the swell. The water is so cold it burns her skin, the pain so sharp she can barely breathe.

Can barely think.

It brings her peace, unlike anything else.

She keeps her eyes fixed on the moon, floating above the dark line of the horizon.

For a few blissful moments, there is nothing else.

And then a gull's stark cry comes to her, and she finds her thoughts full of Florence again, strong, solitary, brave Florence. Her dear friend reminds her of a gull, always fond of a storm, able to weather anything.

She takes in a ragged breath, releasing her own sobbing cry that's instantly snatched by the wind, blown away like spindrift off the rolling waves.

Something, some dark urge, is luring her ever deeper. If she chose to keep going, wading further and further from shore, the water would eventually close over her head, and her broken heart wouldn't matter any more because nothing would matter.

Freezing water has reached her knees, tugging at her numb legs, and she pictures herself as a piece of sea glass, pummelled by the waves, buffeted by the wind, washed clean.

Eventually, the cold becomes too much to bear, and she stumbles out of the water. Not bothering to replace her damp stockings, she pushes her freezing feet into her shoes and makes her way back up the beach. Legs shaking, she retraces her steps along the dark road, barely able to see the uneven path before her.

The first tingle of alarm is ringing in her head. She's been absent from the hospital for too long. She's tired now, so tired, her body a slack sail. If only she could sleep, but her next shift begins in a few short hours. Besides, in the absence of Florence, sleep has become increasingly elusive, painfully fleeting, like a fish that slips from her fingers every time she tries to grasp it.

Reaching the gates of the hospital, she's slow to notice the front door of the château standing open, light spilling out on to the courtyard. Had she forgotten to close it behind her?

As she draws nearer, she hears a cacophony of voices from inside the lobby, and enters to find half a dozen British military policemen in their distinctive scarlet caps, surrounded by a small crowd of nurses and orderlies, Dr Grace in the centre of the turmoil.

'Oh, thank goodness you're here,' Grace says, hurrying over. 'I've been trying to find you. These men want to search the hospital . . .'

A military policeman bears down on Lucinda. 'Are you Dr Garland?'

'I am. And who are you?'

'Captain Humphreys. I have a warrant to search the premises.'

'A warrant? Whatever for?'

'We have reason to believe you're harbouring a criminal.'

Lucinda's heart stutters. *Someone must have alerted them about Edie Lawrence.*

She's suddenly acutely aware of how dishevelled she must look to these men, her hair a damp tangle, the sodden hem of her skirt cold against her bare ankles. An utter sight. She summons every ounce of remaining strength, standing straight, gaze level.

'What on earth are you talking about, Captain?' she hears herself say. 'This is a military hospital. We deal with casualties of the battlefields here, not criminals.'

'We've been informed you have a woman here who enlisted under a false identity.'

'Who gave you this – this information?' Lucinda stammers.

'Our source must remain confidential, madam.'

'Then I refuse to allow you to disturb my patients at this time of night, sir.'

'You cannot refuse, madam.' The captain clicks his fingers at a fresh-faced policeman standing ready. 'Organize a search party.'

'Excuse me!' Lucinda's voice rises, her mind roiling as she tries to think how to hide Edie before these men discover her. 'As chief doctor here, my duty is to my patients, first and foremost. I demand you desist immediately, and leave my hospital forthwith.'

'My orders come from the provost marshal,' the captain replies, entirely untroubled by Lucinda's outburst. 'If you have an issue, madam, I suggest you take it up with him.'

29

Edie: November 1914

A sliver of mauve sky is visible through the partly curtained window. Dusk is falling, and Edie's thoughts turn again to Stanley, wondering where he is, if he could possibly have survived. Her thigh wound itches as though a million ants are crawling under her skin. If only she could scratch it, but her leg is securely bandaged, and she can't force her fingers beneath the gauze.

Earlier, she'd had to relieve herself, a painful, exhausting exercise that had involved an undignified tussle with the bedpan the doctor had thoughtfully left her.

Afterwards, she'd collapsed back against the pillows, spent.

Her stomach begins to rumble. It seems hours ago that the journalist had brought her a bowl of soup and some bread, when he'd come to bid her goodbye.

Has she been forgotten?

The prospect of remaining locked in this room makes her shudder, and she's wondering if she has the strength in her legs to get out of bed, when she hears voices beyond the door.

'We have orders to inspect the entire hospital,' she hears a man say, his tone clipped and authoritative.

'Now just wait one moment . . .' Edie recognizes Dr Garland's voice.

The door bursts open, and before Edie can react, two armed military policemen in red caps are invading the room. Dr Garland pushes her way past the men, to stand at Edie's shoulder.

'I've told you, Captain Humphreys, my patient is injured and possibly contagious,' the doctor says, her voice laced with anger. 'She mustn't be disturbed.'

'We have orders from the provost marshal,' the captain replies. He glares down at Edie, and she feels the blood drain from her head.

'Under what charges are you arresting my patient?' Dr Garland draws herself up to her full height. She's dwarfed by the policemen, yet her slight build exudes a wiry strength. Edie suspects she would stop at nothing to fight off these men if she had to.

'We've received information your patient enlisted under a false identity,' the captain replies. 'My orders are to take her to Saint-Omer for further questioning.'

'But this is ridiculous,' Dr Garland stammers. 'You can see she's injured . . .'

'She can be moved.'

'Absolutely not. I refuse to allow that.'

'Then you are obstructing us in the course of our duties, ma'am, and you will be arrested too.'

'Please,' Edie rasps. 'I can explain.'

'You can start by stating your name,' the captain demands.

'Edie Lawrence, sir, but I can explain –'

'Save it for the court-martial.'

'Court-martial?' Dr Garland takes hold of Edie's arm. 'There's surely no need for that.'

'Bring me the uniform she was wearing on admission,' the captain orders Dr Garland. 'And any personal belongings.'

The doctor hesitates. 'It's all gone.'

'Gone?'

'We send the uniforms away to be fumigated.'

'Any personal effects,' Captain Humphreys presses. 'Letters or documents, all must be declared.'

'She had nothing with her.'

Edie daren't look at Dr Garland.

'Get her dressed,' the captain orders.

'Dressed?' Dr Garland's hand tightens on Edie's arm, the pressure of her fingers painful now. 'I've told you, Captain, she can't possibly be moved in her condition . . .'

'You have five minutes to get her ready to travel, or we'll take her as she is.'

'There's nothing for her to wear, Captain!'

'This is a hospital run by women, is it not?' the captain replies, with icy calmness. 'There must be spare clothes. You now have four minutes remaining.'

Captain Humphreys and his colleague stalk from the room, leaving Edie and the doctor alone.

'I don't know how to stop them,' Dr Garland says at last, breaking the shocked silence.

Edie opens her mouth, words clogging her throat. 'I have to go,' she manages, her voice a hoarse whisper.

Dr Garland leans closer, her gaze darting from Edie's face to the door, and back to Edie again. 'If Harry was here, he'd know what to do.'

'Please keep my notebook and the camera safe.' Edie has to force the words out.

'They'll never have them,' the doctor mutters. 'I promise you that.'

'Two minutes!' a voice barks from the corridor.

Edie meets the doctor's eye, and an unspoken question passes between them.

What will happen to Edie now?

Threatened again with arrest if she doesn't comply, Dr Garland is forced to lend Edie a spare blouse and her only other skirt. Her shoes are a size too big, so one of the nurses donates a pair.

While Captain Humphreys paces the corridor, Dr Garland helps Edie out of the nightshirt. Naked, Edie shudders at the sight of her thin, scarred limbs, skin grimed with dirt. Moving as quickly as her wounded leg allows, she dresses in the clothes Dr Garland has brought her.

'You're not guilty until it's proven,' Dr Garland reminds Edie, as she kneels and ties her shoelaces.

Dressed at last, Edie slumps back against the pillows.

'I'll fetch you some water,' the doctor promises.

But there's no time for water. Captain Humphreys and his men are crowding back into the room, and Dr Garland is shoved aside.

'For goodness' sake, what difference will another day or two make?' Dr Garland begs the captain. 'There's no chance of her absconding . . .'

Captain Humphreys ignores her, brandishing handcuffs. 'I'm arresting you for impersonating a male and falsely enlisting in the British Army,' he says, seizing Edie's forearm. She twists out of his grasp, coming close to biting his hand. But the captain is quicker, stronger, and after a short grapple he has the cuffs snapped around her wrists.

Edie is hauled from the bed, held between two thickset policemen.

'You can't possibly expect her to walk!' Dr Garland cries.

'If she can stand, she can walk, madam.'

Edie is dragged from the room, and half marched, half carried along a corridor. She can hear Dr Garland somewhere behind her, remonstrating with the policemen. They emerge into a lobby milling with people, and Edie is hurried through a main door, and outside into a dark courtyard. It feels a long time since she's breathed fresh air, and she raises her face to the star-studded night sky.

With a small crowd now in attendance, the police drag Edie out to the road. She can hear Dr Garland shouting at the captain, from somewhere amid the throng. 'Where are you taking my patient? I demand you tell me!'

'Saint-Omer,' Edie hears the captain reply. He refuses to answer any more of the doctor's questions, threatening her with arrest if she continues to obstruct him.

Edie is forced into the rear of a covered truck waiting on the road. Two policemen climb in after her, taking their places on the bench opposite. Moments later, the engine shudders into life.

Sprawled on the bench, Edie tries to brace her body as the vehicle begins to move. One of the policemen lights a cigarette, flinging the match out of the open rear of the truck. Edie considers jumping after it. *Damn her injured leg.* As the truck rounds a corner, Edie glimpses Dr Garland's slim figure standing apart from the crowd, a hand to her mouth.

Dizziness swoops, and Edie drives her fingernails into her palms.

She must not pass out.

The truck rumbles on, and Edie tries to grip the wooden bench with her good leg, her stomach roiling each time the vehicle lurches through a pothole. The moonlit road unravels behind them, and with each mile that passes her courage fades.

The policemen ignore her. One falls into a doze, his head lolling against the canvas side of the truck, while his colleague stares listlessly at his boots, cigarette hanging from his fingers.

Are they taking her to a prison? Edie wonders. She's heard talk of the gaol under the ramparts of Ypres, a hellish place hidden underground, but at least out of range of the guns. Beyond that, she can't bring herself to imagine.

Another thought strikes her. Why didn't she keep her notebook with her? The notes would prove her intentions were honourable. All she wanted to do was report on the war.

But, no, the diary is safer with the doctor, she concludes. The police could so easily see its contents as evidence of her guilt.

The policeman lights another cigarette, blowing smoke into Edie's face. She closes her eyes, grimacing against the pain radiating along her leg, and her mother's voice comes to her.

Where there's breath, there's hope.

30

Lucinda: November 1914

Haunted by Edie's arrest, Lucinda struggles to concentrate on her work. Questions plague her: who on her staff had alerted the authorities? Was it Figgis, as she suspects? What actual proof had she to accuse the porter, apart from his involvement in the concealment of Edie in the storeroom? She'd known Figgis was suspicious from the start, despite Harry's assurances that the porter knew nothing.

But what use was accusing Figgis, or anyone else, when the police have taken Edie away? It galls Lucinda to think that she'd saved the girl's life on her operating table, yet she's failed to save her after all.

She thinks back to what Harry had told her about Edie, and the girl's own written account that was currently hidden in the desk drawer in the library. Harry was adamant Edie's story must be told, and Lucinda feels sure that if he'd still been there when the police arrived the outcome would have been very different. Captain Humphreys would likely have listened to another man. Maybe Harry could have bought Edie more time to recover before she was arrested and carted away.

She should have fought harder on the girl's behalf.

But how could you oppose the military police? Florence's

voice of reason echoes in Lucinda's head, but it fails to reassure her.

All Lucinda can do is focus on the never-ending stream of casualties passing through her hospital. But with half her mind elsewhere, slip-ups are inevitable. She makes a couple of minor mistakes during surgery, and one potentially serious error during an arm amputation, provoking Grace to ask if she is all right.

'Would you like me to conduct the evening ward rounds for you?' Grace offers quietly, as they clean up at the sinks after the last operation.

Lucinda is about to refuse her colleague's tactful offer, when she has a change of mind. Perhaps a short rest would be wise. 'Thank you.'

Grace nods, frowning still, but she says no more, and Lucinda is grateful for her understanding.

Later, ensconced in the library with the door firmly closed, Lucinda slumps at her desk, head in her hands. A profoundly troubling fatigue weighs her down. She's never felt so hopeless and alone. Yet how can she feel like this, when she's surrounded and supported by such a wonderful team?

After everything she's faced so far, all the challenges she's overcome, the incident yesterday has left her shaken, her brittle resolve even more fragile. Yet again, she's reminded of her powerlessness as a woman. The military police rode roughshod over her, ignoring her authority entirely. They wouldn't have treated a male doctor in the same way. Of that she feels certain.

But it's never been easy forging a career in the patriarchal world of medicine, she reminds herself. In the past, she's never let a challenge defeat her, always quietly but doggedly pursuing her path.

So why does she feel so utterly defeated now?

Florence.

Everything feels a thousand times harder without the gentle, steady comfort of Florence at her side.

Enough. Self-pity is useless, she chides herself. Her stomach growls, and it occurs to her that it was a mistake to have missed dinner earlier. She's not eating enough as it is, and she's let herself become too depleted. It's no surprise her mood is suffering. She has only herself to blame.

She reaches for a sheet of paper and her pen. The weekly report to the French Red Cross is overdue, a frustratingly time-consuming task, but essential nonetheless. She sets to work, her head soon aching as she struggles to condense descriptions of complex surgery into simple enough English for the French clerks to understand.

Broken bones, lacerated skin, traumatic burns, shrapnel wounds.

From outside in the corridor she hears a familiar scuttling of footsteps, then a sharp rap-rap-rap on the door.

'Come in.'

Mardie appears in the doorway, bright-eyed and pink-cheeked.

'What is it, Hodgson?' If it's more visitors wanting a tour, they'll just have to come back tomorrow, Lucinda thinks. She can't face sightseers tonight.

'Doctor, you're wanted in the lobby.'

'Who wants me?' Lucinda suppresses a sigh. 'If it's visitors . . .'

'Not visitors, ma'am.'

Before Lucinda can ask for more information, Mardie is dashing away again.

She must have another word with the orderly about her attitude, Lucinda thinks, as she rises and follows the girl back to the lobby.

She finds most of her staff gathered there, and for a heart-plunging moment wonders if the military police have returned, this time to arrest her. Why hadn't anyone come to fetch her sooner? To Lucinda's relief there are no red caps in evidence, no Captain Humphreys. The women are in a buoyant mood, she realizes, smiling and hugging each other. Then she notices the bags and tea chests piled by the entrance.

'What's going on, Sister?' Lucinda asks Nurse Whiteman.

'They're here.' The nurse beams at Lucinda.

'Who's here?'

'Dr Maberry, Sister Bryony and Mr Tozer.'

It takes a second for the nurse's words to sink in. *Florence is here?*

'They arrived a few minutes ago,' the nurse adds. 'They're just bringing the last of their things from the truck.'

Sister Bryony appears at the front door, followed by Tozer, both laden with bags. A few seconds later, another figure materializes.

Florence.

For a moment, Lucinda's legs refuse to move. She meets Florence's searching gaze through the milling bodies, and Florence's smile pulls at her heart, like a compass drawn to north. And now her legs are moving of their own accord, and Lucinda finds herself across the lobby, embracing her friend, holding her close, breathing her in. She can hardly believe this is happening, that Florence is alive and safe in her arms.

She's been so worried for her, terrified that the Germans would break through the Allied defences and take Paris. But none of that matters now that Florence is here with her. Despite the German Army's best efforts, Fate has brought them together again.

Eventually they draw apart.

'I've missed you so much,' Florence says, leaning close to be heard over the hubbub. 'How have you been?'

Lucinda, lost in the glory of Florence's soft Scottish burr, can only open her mouth, and close it again, a floundering fish.

'I didn't quite catch that.' Florence chuckles, her smile teasing.

'I've missed you too,' Lucinda manages. A movement at her feet makes her step back. 'What on earth . . .'

A small dog has appeared, and is licking Lucinda's shoe.

'Oh, he does this sometimes,' Florence laughs. 'Os! Here, boy.'

The terrier mongrel reacts to Florence's voice, ceasing his licking as Florence bends to pat his head. The dog licks her wrist. 'Os, this is Dr Garland, our chief.'

'A dog?' Lucinda can't quite process this development.

'I couldn't leave him behind, Lucie.' Florence gazes down at the dog with a benevolent expression Lucinda has only ever seen her bestow on sick children.

'A dog?' she stammers again. The animal's rough brown

and white fur is patchy in places. Is it mange? The wiry little dog grins up at Lucinda, and she's startled by its different coloured eyes – one blue, one brown. Is he part blind?

'Os can see perfectly well,' Florence says, as if reading Lucinda's mind. She slips a rope-lead around the dog's neck. 'He's a stray,' she explains. 'I found him hiding in the stores. He'd hurt his paw.'

Lucinda nods numbly, and only now registers the near-empty lobby. The rest of her staff have dispersed to their rooms or back to their evening duties, and she hadn't noticed. At her feet, the dog gives a playful yip, as if to remind Lucinda of the conversation.

'His paw?'

'It's healed now,' Florence says. 'But I couldn't abandon him, Lucie.'

'Well, no . . .'

'We decided to name him Os. It's French for bone.'

Of course.

'Can we keep him, Lucie? He's a wonderful ratter.'

'Where will he sleep?' Lucinda asks weakly. 'What will he eat?'

'Our room, and scraps,' Florence answers promptly.

Our room? They've never shared a room before.

'Well, anyway, you can't turn him out tonight,' Florence says, linking her arm through Lucinda's. 'It's cold and dark, and he'll only howl if you lock him outside . . .' She trails off, as they make their way to the sanctuary of the library, the dog trotting beside them.

'When did you leave Paris?' Lucinda asks, closing the library door, sealing them in. 'Where are the patients?'

'We left after breakfast this morning,' Florence replies, slipping the lead over the dog's head. Freed, Os sets off on an investigative sniff around the room. 'Jenkins and Wilkinson both died the day after you left,' Florence adds quietly. 'The remaining nine I deemed well enough to be sent home, and the last went yesterday.'

'I had no idea . . .'

'Didn't you get my letter?'

Lucinda shakes her head. 'I've been so worried, Flo.'

'I did write, I promise . . .'

They regard each other in silence, and Lucinda longs to sink into Florence's embrace once more. Euphoria and relief have buoyed her up to this point, but now her strength is leaching from her muscles. But she can't fall apart: there is far too much to do, and so much to tell Florence.

'Sister Bryony and Tozer deserve a medal, Lucie,' Florence says. 'They went beyond their duty, especially when Cassard –' She breaks off.

'When Cassard what?' Oh, God, what had that dreadful man done? Had he made a move on Florence?

'It's not what you're thinking, Lucie.'

'What am I thinking?' *Please don't say what I'm thinking.*

'I thought I might have a wee problem with him, when you left . . .'

Lucinda clenches her hands together, waiting for Florence to go on.

'But I needn't have worried. He abandoned us, almost immediately.'

'What do you mean?'

'He upped and left. Didn't bother telling us. One day he was there, the next he'd gone.'

'Oh, Flo.' There is so much Lucinda longs to know, but she bites her tongue.

'I'm exhausted, Lucie.' Florence sighs. 'How about a medicinal? Achille gave me this before we left.' She rummages in her shoulder bag, and pulls out a bottle of wine.

'Good idea.'

Lucinda finds a couple of used teacups, gives them a quick wipe with her sleeve, and pours a generous measure of wine into both. They raise their cups to each other in a toast.

'I'm so glad to be back with you,' Florence says, draining her teacup in one.

Lucinda takes cautious sips, the alcohol hitting her empty stomach and flooding her veins with its heat.

'Flo, I must tell you something . . .' She falters, takes another sip. Why did words always fail her at the crucial moment?

Florence sets her empty cup on the desk, her gaze questioning.

'You know you're very dear to me . . .' Lucinda stammers.

'And you're very dear to me too,' Florence replies tenderly. 'I missed you dreadfully.'

Lucinda is suddenly aware of how close they are standing, so close she can see the flutter of a pulse in Florence's long neck.

'I mean to say,' Lucinda tries again, '*very* dear . . .'

Florence's eyes lower, and she makes no reply. For a long moment, Lucinda ceases to breathe. Has she overstepped the mark? Has she offended Florence or, worse, frightened her?

'Forgive me,' Lucinda whispers, 'I only –'

Her words are cut off by the touch of Florence's fingers, stroking her cheek. Florence moves closer, until there is only an inch of breath between them, and Lucinda has to close her eyes, terrified of making a wrong move. And then she feels Florence's hand caress her jaw, followed a heartbeat later by the shocking softness of Florence's mouth meeting hers.

She can't think, can't move, every molecule of sensation centred on her lips. Florence tastes faintly of wine, and as the kiss deepens, Lucinda's heels rise a fraction, and she finds herself being gently eased back against the desk. Her legs feel dangerously unsteady, and she's grateful for the support of the wood beneath her. All other thought is banished, as she relaxes into the kiss, and it's as if she's drowning in warm honey, unable to breathe, but not caring one jot. She only wants this moment to last for ever.

At last, they draw apart, and Florence places both hands on Lucinda's ribs. At her tender touch, Lucinda feels her insides soften, as she breathes in, breathes out, a tide of longing.

'Oh, Lucie . . .' Florence murmurs.

And then they are kissing again, and Lucinda feels the release of tension deep inside her, like a dam breaking, sweeping everything away. Her legs threaten to give. She will melt, right here on the floorboards, if she lets this go any further . . . *Lord Egham*, she thinks desperately. *Lord Egham in the nude.*

But it's no good. Lucinda is falling.

From somewhere by the door, the dog whines, breaking the spell.

They pull apart, and Lucinda wonders if her own cheeks are as flushed as Florence's. 'You make my wee head swim,' Florence says, her laugh uncommonly shaky.

Lucinda sets a steadying hand on the desk, her head swimming too. To think that her kiss can have such an effect on Flo – her strong, calm Flo! The thought is intoxicating.

For so long, she's struggled to maintain an innocent friendship with Florence, a struggle that's only grown harder as time has gone by, wringing the song from her heart. But now it hits her: this moment is what she's longed for.

She takes Florence's hand, as carefully as though cradling a bird, and draws her closer again.

'I love you, Flo.' To speak the truth aloud makes Lucinda's heart sing once more.

31

Edie: November 1914

At last, after what feels to Edie like days rather than hours, they reach their destination. As the truck judders to a halt, the policemen rouse themselves, and Edie is unloaded on to the street like a sack of coal. She can barely stand, weak with thirst, her leg wound aching. Captain Humphreys appears, checking Edie's manacles are secure without speaking a word to her. She tries to gather her bearings, but can make out little of her surroundings in the darkness. Buildings stretch away into shadow. Was this place Saint-Omer?

On a nod from the captain, the two policemen seize Edie, and half drag, half carry her up the steps of a nearby building. An armed guard at the door admits the party into a large, gloomy entrance hall, oil lamps casting ineffectual pools of light. Edie wills her legs to hold her as she takes in the bare walls stained with damp, the lingering smell of sweat and leather. She could have been back in the workhouse.

A man in uniform emerges from behind a desk, greeting Captain Humphreys. Paperwork is produced, and the two men talk while the captain signs forms. Edie catches the words *false enlistment* and *trial*, and clasps her hands against her chest in a vain attempt to stop them shaking.

Two armed guards are summoned, and the captain stalks away. The guards hustle Edie through a doorway into a long, narrow corridor and Edie's legs now fail her.

'Stand up!' The guards haul Edie to her feet, propelling her along the passage to a door. One of the guards produces a key, and Edie finds herself in a room with no natural light, the stagnant air filled with the odour of rotting vegetables.

One of the guards lights an oil lantern, and hangs it from a hook in the low ceiling.

Dread squeezes the breath from Edie's lungs as gradually the shadows retreat, revealing a cave-like room. Wooden crates are stacked along the far wall, and in the darkest corner sits what looks like a marble cutting block.

Edie's manacles are released, and she rubs her sore wrists.

'Where am I?' she croaks.

Neither guard replies, as they close the door behind them, locking her in.

Edie sinks to the floor, a taste of copper filling her mouth, and it takes her a moment to realize she's bitten her tongue.

The oil lantern swings from the ceiling, casting a smoky light. How long until the fuel in it runs dry?

There comes the muffled scrape of footsteps out in the passage, as though someone is approaching the door. Edie drags herself to the nearest wall, clawing her way to standing. If the guards are back, she wants to be on her feet.

She waits for the rasp of the key, but instead a charged

silence descends once more, making the hairs rise on the back of her neck.

Fear twines like rope about her chest.

∞

The sound of a key turning in the lock wakes her. She struggles up to sitting, stiff-limbed and dry-mouthed, to find the lantern has dimmed to a weak, bilious glow.

The door is wrenched open, and the same two guards enter, one carrying a canister of oil, bringing with them the fresh scent of rain. The canister is dumped on the floor, and the guards ignore Edie as they go about refilling the oil lamp.

Movement in the open doorway catches Edie's eye: a figure dressed in a long black robe, a white hood obscuring the face, glides towards her. Edie presses herself against the wall, but there's no escape. The figure draws nearer, and now Edie can see it's a nun bearing a cloth-covered tray, which she silently places at Edie's feet. As the nun straightens and steps back, she meets Edie's terrified gaze. She gestures at the tray on the floor, saying something in French, her voice low. Edie forces herself to move, uncovering the tray to reveal a bowl of soup, half a small loaf of bread and a jug of water.

The guards have finished with the lamp and are now at the door. 'Come,' one says to the nun.

'*Cinq minutes*,' the nun replies.

To Edie's surprise, the guard gives a nod, and both men disappear into the passage, pulling the door to behind them. A moment later she hears the scrape of a match on stone, and catches the scent of cigarette smoke.

The nun upends an empty crate and sits close to Edie, her gaze steady. Her long robes, arranged neatly around her feet, emit a fresh, outdoor smell, and Edie has a sudden longing to feel rain on her face. It could be hailing bullets outside and she would never know, locked away in here.

The nun speaks softly in French, gesturing again at the tray of food, and Edie's stomach gnaws. She begins to eat, the vegetable soup deliciously warm, the bread soft on her sore tongue. After a minute or so, she realizes the nun is staring at her bandaged leg.

Edie mops the last of the soup with a crust, then sets down the empty bowl. She could eat it all again with ease. A faint scratching comes from a shadowy corner of the room — a rat, perhaps. Edie stiffens, but the nun doesn't react. Instead, she lifts the jug from the tray, pours Edie a cup of water. Edie drinks deeply, and is rewarded with a smile.

'Time's up,' a guard calls from the doorway.

The nun gathers up her tray, bestowing a final smile on Edie, and the door is locked once more.

Silence descends, like a shroud, the shadows pressing in on her.

Not since her mother died has Edie felt so wretched, so despairing.

She curls into a ball on the floor, and lets the tears come.

Hours pass, how many Edie has no way of knowing. The nun returns, this time bearing a pail of steaming water, which she sets on the floor. Then, with the guard yawning at the open doorway, the nun hurries away again, returning with a towel and bandages, a tray of bread, cheese and more water.

While Edie devours the food, the nun mutters in French, peering at Edie's leg. And though Edie can't understand a word, she catches the woman's concern. The wound needs to be cleaned and re-bandaged. Edie washes the dirt from her face and hands as best she can, then submits to the nun's ministrations. Her leg throbs with a dull pain, and she can't watch as the nun peels off the filthy gauze, exposing ragged stitches.

'*Vous êtes très courageuse*,' the nun murmurs, as she gently rebinds Edie's thigh.

The nun is clearing away the dirty bandages, when two more guards appear.

'You must leave now,' one snaps at the nun.

Handcuffed again, Edie is dragged to her feet, and taken back to the entrance hall. She glimpses daylight through the partly open door to the street, as she's man-handled into a large, wood-panelled room.

A trio of uniformed officers, one of whom is Captain Humphreys, are seated at a long baize-covered table. Ignored by all three men, Edie is deposited on a wooden chair set before the table. She clasps her manacled hands tightly in her lap, her knees shaking.

This court-martial is a formality, she knows. How can she possibly convince the men of her innocent intentions? She feels as though she's poised on the edge of a precipice, her life hanging in the balance. Whether she's convicted or set free depends on the whim of these strangers.

The officers conclude their conversation, and now their attention is focused on Edie.

The senior of the three, his insignia that of a lieutenant

colonel, removes his spectacles, polishing the lenses with a handkerchief. His dour countenance reminds Edie a little of Mr Stead, but this gives her no comfort.

'As president of this court,' the lieutenant colonel begins, replacing his spectacles with fastidious care, 'on this twenty-seventh day of November, in the year of Our Lord nineteen hundred and fourteen, I declare this trial in session.'

The president shuffles papers, and the trio confer in low voices. Edie glances towards the door, to find her only means of exit secured by armed guards.

The third officer, a bullish, ruddy-faced man displaying the insignia of a major, pulls an open tome towards him. Edie watches as he dips a pen in a pot of ink, hand poised to write an account of the proceedings. The president instructs Edie to swear on the Bible. 'You are now under oath,' the senior officer intones.

Captain Humphreys clears his throat. 'You have been arrested for fraudulently enlisting in the British Army, and contravening military law by concealing your sex. State your name and date of birth for the record.'

Edie presses her shaking knees together. 'Edie Lawrence,' she croaks. 'Fourth of June, eighteen ninety-five.'

'How did you come to be in France, in the dress of a British soldier?'

'I enlisted, sir.'

'Which recruitment office?'

'Victoria Park, sir.'

The officers exchange glances, and Captain Humphreys produces a thin red booklet Edie recognizes as her company pay book. How had they got that?

'You enlisted under the name of . . .' the captain makes a show of deciphering the name scrawled on the cover '. . . Private Eddie Lawrence. Is that correct?'

'Yes, sir.'

'Eddie Lawrence is a false name, is it not?'

Edie swallows. Whatever she says, these men will never believe her. But she has to try. 'The surname is my own, sir.'

The officers confer again, their voices too low for Edie to make out what they're saying. Motes of dust drift in the watery sunlight shining through the windows. Edie's ears prick at the sound of raised voices in the hall, and the distant slam of a door somewhere beyond the room.

'You adopted a male identity, and fraudulently enlisted,' the captain states. 'What was your motive in committing this crime?'

'I'd lost my job, sir,' Edie replies. 'I had nowhere to live, no money . . . I was desperate, sir.'

'Desperate enough to commit such a treasonous offence?'

'I wanted to make my name, sir,' Edie tries instead. 'As a reporter, sir. It was a stunt, to see if I could get to the battlefields. I only wanted to write from the battlefields.'

From the captain's dark stare, Edie is suddenly certain she's made a terrible mistake. She should never have mentioned writing.

'For whom were you writing?' the captain wants to know. 'Was your intention to supply the enemy with information?'

'No, sir!'

'Then who were you writing for?'

'Only myself, sir,' Edie lies. 'All I wanted was to tell my

story. The first woman journalist to experience war from the battlefield. That's all.'

A silence descends, as all three officers stare at Edie.

'How did you keep your sex concealed?' This from the major.

'I – I wasn't barracked during training, sir,' Edie stammers.

The men continue to stare. What else do they want her to say? That she never stripped in front of her platoon, always pissed in private. Kept her head down.

The officers confer among themselves. Edie waits, trying to ignore the burning sensation in her thigh, the wooden chair growing more uncomfortable by the minute.

At last, the officers break apart. 'Have you anything else to say in your defence?' the captain asks.

'I never meant to commit treason, sir,' Edie says. 'All I wanted was a chance to make my name.'

32

Lucinda: November 1914

She wakes an hour late, surfacing from the deepest, most peaceful sleep she's enjoyed for weeks. Her limbs are entwined with Florence's still, their bodies curled together beneath the sheets on the wide chaise-longue. Nebulous sunshine seeps through a gap in the curtains: the start of a new day.

Florence slumbers on, her head resting in the dip of Lucinda's shoulder, her belly warm against her hip. One arm is draped over Lucinda's waist, her soft, even breaths tickling her collarbone.

Last night, under Florence's gentle touch, a profound serenity had suffused Lucinda's whole body, the ghost of which lingers on. After everything she's endured here, the triumphs and tragedies, to lie here with Florence is a heavenly dream.

But time presses, as always, and she really must rise and face the day. Her colleagues will be expecting her in surgery, yet she can't quite bring herself to break this perfect moment. As she lets her eyes drift closed again, an image of Edie lying bleeding on her operating table floats into Lucinda's mind, shattering her peace.

'I can feel your heart beating.' Florence's lips move

against Lucinda's skin in a delicious murmur that makes Lucinda swallow.

'I thought you were asleep.'

'I was.' Florence yawns, lifting her head slightly. 'But someone's heart is drumming in my ear, rather frenetically . . .'

'Oh,' Lucinda breathes.

'Penny for them?'

'What?'

'Something is making your heart race, Lucie.'

You, Flo. You make my heart race. 'There's something I haven't told you.'

'That sounds rather ominous.' Florence sits up with a catlike stretch, releasing Lucinda to sit up too. On the floor by the desk, in a nest of blankets, Os snores on. 'You're not having regrets, are you, Lucie? About us?'

Lucinda's heart stutters. 'How can you think that?'

Florence gives a quiet laugh, her gaze tender.

'You're not . . . ?' Lucinda can't finish the question, can't bear to face the possibility that Florence might harbour misgivings about their union last night.

'Having regrets?' Florence finishes. 'Never.'

Her friend's declaration of love should be reassuring, Lucinda knows, but somehow it only makes her confession harder.

'A lot has happened,' Lucinda tries again, 'since we were parted.'

'Well, that has to be the understatement of the century, my darling.' Florence adjusts the pillow behind her back, the sheets falling away, and Lucinda drops her gaze, concentrating on her hands clasped in her lap. She finds she can't think straight, with Florence so close, yet she needs to.

Footsteps sound beyond the library door, and Lucinda tenses, half expecting someone to knock. How long before the staff discover her and Florence's new sleeping arrangements? Can they keep their relationship a secret from everyone?

As the footsteps retreat, Florence touches Lucinda's hand, bringing her back to the moment. 'What's happened?' she prompts.

'I should have told you before. A soldier came in wounded . . .'

'Well, that's hardly unexpected,' Florence teases. 'We *are* running a hospital, Lucie, darling.'

'He wasn't who we thought he was.'

'Oh?'

'*He* turned out to be *she*.'

'You're not making any sense, Lucie.'

'The soldier was female. That's what I'm trying to tell you.' Lucinda rises from the chaise-longue, and begins hurriedly to dress.

'A female soldier? Are you joking?'

'Something else I haven't told you,' Lucinda says, fumbling to do up the buttons on her blouse. 'Harry Levinson was here.'

'Harry?'

'He was a great support,' Lucinda replies, pulling on her tunic, and dragging a brush through her tangled hair. 'He sat with the girl, listened to her story of how she'd enlisted, travelled over here with her platoon, and ended up injured in a trench raid. I'll show you her account later – there isn't time now.'

'I don't understand. Who is this girl?'

'Her name's Edie Lawrence.'

'Where is she now?'

'Well, that's the problem. She was arrested and taken away, but I don't know where to. The police said something about Saint-Omer. That's where they've moved the British Army headquarters to, isn't it?'

'Slow down.' Florence snags Lucinda's arm, gently tugs her down to sit beside her. 'Start from the beginning.'

Lucinda takes a breath, and quickly recounts the events of the past thirty-six hours.

'How did the police even know the woman was here?' Florence asks, when Lucinda has finished.

'Someone must have tipped them off. I have my suspicions, but I can't prove anything. I couldn't stop the police taking her, Flo.'

'Well, of course you couldn't.' Florence is quiet for a moment. 'Where have I heard the name Edie Lawrence before?'

'I was thinking the same, that I'd met her before somewhere.'

'Could she have been a patient we once treated?'

And then it strikes Lucinda. *Mouse Castle*. Could she have treated the girl at the suffragette safe-house in London, Mouse Castle? The more she thinks about it, she recalls a half-starved waif, in a dreadful state following a stint in Holloway. Had that been Edie Lawrence? It was like some strange dream.

'Before Harry left, we telegraphed Sylvia Pankhurst,' Lucinda forges on.

'Sylvia? How can she help?'

'Edie was part of her suffrage society.'

'Ah, it's starting to make sense.'

'But it was all useless. The police arrested Edie and took her away, and Harry's gone, and what if Miss Pankhurst doesn't reply?'

'Ssh, it's going to be all right.' Florence pulls Lucinda into an embrace, holding her tenderly. 'You did everything you could. If Edie is the girl you once helped, we both know she's a fighter.'

Lucinda wishes she could share Florence's faith.

That afternoon, a reply arrives from Sylvia Pankhurst. In a brief lull between surgeries, Lucinda and Florence retreat to the library to read the telegram in private.

TO: DR GARLAND

THANK YOU FOR SENDING WORD OF EDIE STOP
SHE IS A GOOD FRIEND OF MINE AND A
CHERISHED MEMBER OF THE SOCIETY STOP
PLEASE ADVISE IF FUNDS ARE NEEDED TO
SECURE HER SAFE RETURN TO LONDON STOP

SYLVIA PANKHURST

Lucinda lowers the telegram, and meets Florence's eye.

'You have to find her, Lucie.'

'I can't leave the hospital, not at the moment.'

'You can't leave the poor girl at the mercy of the British military police, either.'

'But what about the patients?' Lucinda worries. 'How will you manage?'

'We can cope for a couple of days,' Florence assures

337

her. 'I've got Grace, Hazel and Gertrude, and we can shoulder your surgical cases in the short term.'

'I'll be parted from you again, and I can't bear it.'

'Only for a few days at most.'

'What if I can't find her, Flo? What if I'm too late, and they've already sentenced her?'

'My darling.' Florence steps closer, and Lucinda can't breathe again. 'You are the cleverest, strongest woman I know. You'll find her.'

But what if I can't? Lucinda wants to cry. As she sinks into Florence's arms, the truth strikes her: she'll never forgive herself if she doesn't try.

∞

She leaves that afternoon, armed with Sylvia Pankhurst's telegram, Edie Lawrence's notebook, and her father's old Gladstone bag, packed with bread and cheese, fresh bandages, carbolic soap and a change of clothes.

Lucinda's first task is to locate Monsieur Bataille, and glean from the agent the quickest way to get to Saint-Omer. She learns that the town is a little more than forty kilometres to the east of Wimereux, but the Frenchman is adamant that the journey is too dangerous for Lucinda to attempt by road.

'Then I shall take the train,' she decides.

The journey takes twice as long as Lucinda anticipated. She spends the entirety of it sharing a carriage with three young French airmen – shockingly young, Lucinda thinks – who are also travelling to Saint-Omer. From their stilted conversation, she learns that there is an active airfield just outside the town, and a pilots' pool where her companions are destined. From here, they will be allocated to a squadron, working with the French Aviation Service, alongside the British Royal Flying Corps. Lucinda thinks of the fragile-looking aircraft she's occasionally spotted in the skies, and can't imagine why anyone would ever want to fly. The mere thought of it makes her knees and elbows tingle unpleasantly.

'*Et vous, Madame*?' one of the airmen asks her, his grey eyes taking in her Women's Hospital Corps uniform. 'Where do you go?'

Lucinda rests a hand on her father's Gladstone, a solid presence on the seat next to her. The leather is warm and smooth, and having the bag with her somehow lends her a modicum of courage. 'British Army Headquarters,' she tells the young airman. 'Do you happen to know where that is?'

They do, and one of the men draws her a rough map of Saint-Omer on the back of a scrap of paper. General Headquarters, Lucinda discovers, is currently located in a château on a hill between the town and the aerodrome. A good walk from the station, according to the airmen.

It's past ten o'clock by the time they reach their destination. Lucinda stumbles out of the carriage on stiff legs, tired and hungry. She'd shared her bread and cheese with the young airmen, in gratitude for their help and information. The grey-eyed one, whose name she now knows is Jean, insists on accompanying Lucinda to a nearby *estaminet* where she's served a meal of greasy fried eggs and potatoes, and orders her first French beer. It tastes like watery dandelions, and she can't bring herself to finish it, much to the *patron*'s bemusement.

By the time she's finished her meal, it's too late to travel up the hill in search of GHQ. She will have to go first thing in the morning. Reluctantly, she pays for a single, shabby room that smells faintly of mould, and falls exhausted into bed.

Early the next morning, thanks to Jean's directions, Lucinda finds the château on the hill with minimal difficulty. Carrying the Gladstone, she makes her way up the stone steps to the entrance, surprised to find the place so busy with military personnel.

'I'm here to see Captain Humphreys,' Lucinda tells the armed guard on the door.

'Your name, madam?'

'Dr Lucinda Garland. He visited my hospital in Wimereux recently, and it's imperative I speak with him.'

The guard calls to a colleague, who tells Lucinda to wait outside while he makes enquiries. She sets her bulky bag on the ground, frustrated that the guard won't allow her to sit inside. Military men hurry in and out of the building, no one paying her the slightest attention. Dark clouds loom over the town, obscuring the sun, and it begins to spit with rain. Lucinda takes shelter by the château's wall, glaring at the guard, who returns her stare with impassive indifference.

Minutes pass, and Lucinda is contemplating challenging the guard again, when the distinctive growl of an approaching car tugs her attention to the road. A Citroën, its tyres mud-splattered but its bodywork shining, rumbles to a stop in front of the château. The guard on the door stiffens to attention, saluting as two men in British officer regalia emerge. Neither so much as glances at Lucinda as they stride up the steps.

Grabbing her chance, Lucinda lunges across the path of the nearest, blocking the man's progress with a strategically placed Gladstone. 'Excuse me, sir.'

The officer is forced to stop mid-stride. 'Madam?' he barks, glaring at her as though she were a vagrant in his way.

'I need to speak with Captain Humphreys,' Lucinda says, before the officer has a chance to object further. 'Please, sir, it's urgent.'

The officer attempts to sidestep Lucinda, but she's quick to react, shifting the Gladstone to obstruct his escape.

'Madam, your bag is in my way.'

'My name is Dr Garland,' Lucinda replies, with as much authority as she can muster, 'and I've travelled from my hospital in Wimereux. I must speak with Captain Humphreys urgently.'

'Is this woman being attended to?' the officer snaps at the guard.

'Yes, sir,' the guard replies.

'I'm not being attended to,' Lucinda retorts. 'I've been left here, outside, in the rain.'

The officer sighs. 'Humphreys, did you say?'

Lucinda fights the urge to grab the man's gold-braided sleeve. 'Please,' she says. 'I need to speak with the captain for just a moment. I have an urgent message.'

'Come with me.' The officer escorts Lucinda past the

guard and into the bustling entrance hall. 'Wait here,' the officer commands, and disappears through a door.

Ignored by the military personnel, Lucinda waits again, her Gladstone bag at her feet, like a faithful dog. She's glad she brought it now. Its bulk has come in rather useful, and its presence makes her feel her father is with her in spirit. She takes Sylvia Pankhurst's telegram and Edie's notebook from her pocket, gripping them with clammy hands. They're all she has. Will they be enough?

Minutes pass, and at last the officer returns.

'Captain Humphreys is busy, I'm afraid, Dr Garland.'

'But I really do need to speak to him urgently!' Lucinda's voice is loud enough to attract suspicious looks from one or two passing soldiers.

'That's impossible, madam,' the officer snaps. 'He's conducting a court-martial, and cannot be disturbed.'

A court-martial. The words stop the breath in her throat.

'Where's the trial being held?' Lucinda presses. 'Is it here? Which room?' The officer's gaze twitches to a nearby door, but it's hint enough for Lucinda to abandon her bag and stumble towards the room.

'Madam, you can't go in there!' she hears the officer shout, but she takes no notice of his commands to desist, and opens the door.

She takes in the scene at a glance. In the middle of the room, the small figure of Edie Lawrence is slumped on a chair, her face ashen. To Lucinda she looks as though she's ready to pass out. Facing her are two British Army officers and a military policeman, seated at a long table covered with papers.

Lucinda recognizes Captain Humphreys.

A guard tries to seize Lucinda's arm, but she somehow slips free, dodging past him into the room.

'Who let you in here?' The captain surges to his feet. 'Arrest this woman!'

Two military guards advance on her, but Lucinda moves quickly, taking refuge beside Edie's chair. The girl stares up at Lucinda, shadows like bruises beneath her eyes, imploring, fearful, hopeful.

Lucinda turns to the officers. She has one chance.

Only now does it strike her how ludicrous this whole situation was. At this very moment, hundreds if not thousands of men were dying in battle. Across the country, medics as dedicated and brave as hers were desperately trying to save the wounded. And yet here these men were, treating a harmless, insignificant English girl as though she was the most dangerous enemy. The brass hats had lost all perspective.

'Get her out of here!' the captain orders.

The guards are almost upon her, as Lucinda lurches towards the officers' table, Sylvia Pankhurst's telegram and Edie's notebook held before her.

'Gentlemen,' she says, breathless, 'you must let my patient go!'

33

Edie: November 1914

'What the devil is going on?'

The president is on his feet, wielding his gavel like a weapon, glaring at the dishevelled woman who has dared to disturb the proceedings. Before Edie can utter a warning, two guards pounce, seizing the doctor's arms and dragging her backwards.

The doctor struggles, crying out to be released, but to no avail. The guards hold her fast.

'Madam!' the president barks, banging his gavel repeatedly on the table. A war tattoo. 'Cease your caterwauling!'

'This is a private affair,' Captain Humphreys adds. 'You have no right to come barging in here.'

'Please, sir, I ask only a moment of your time.' The doctor wrenches an arm free, waving a slip of paper, now crumpled and ripped during the tussle with the guards. 'I have a telegram from Miss Sylvia Pankhurst of the East London Federation of Suffragettes.' The doctor twists round to look at Edie as she speaks, her eyes shining, but Edie can only gape back at her. 'It proves Edie Lawrence's true intentions and good character.'

'If I call the guards off, can I trust you to behave, madam?' the president says, in the manner of a headmaster speaking to a child brought before him for some misdemeanour.

'Yes, sir.'

'Release her.'

The guards let go of the doctor's arms, but remain flanking her.

'Let me see it.' The president clicks his fingers, and a guard plucks the telegram from Dr Garland's hand and passes it to the officer. A taut silence falls, as the president fussily adjusts his spectacles, then scans the telegram. A look of distaste distorts his features, as though a used bandage has been brought for his perusal.

'This is addressed to a Dr Garland,' the president says. 'Who is this Dr Garland? Am I to expect him to invade my courtroom next?'

The doctor draws herself up to her full height. 'I am Dr Lucinda Garland,' she replies. 'Your colleague will vouch for me.' Her glare slides from the president to Captain Humphreys.

'She speaks the truth,' the captain mutters.

'Why are you here, madam?' the president demands.

'To reclaim my patient,' Dr Garland snaps back. 'She was taken from my hospital without my permission, and I am here to request her return to my care immediately. Sir.'

The president finishes scrutinizing the telegram, and now passes it to the captain. The doctor's shoulders are set, and she looks to Edie as if she's ready for a fight.

'What else do you have there?' The president gestures to the book the doctor clasps to her chest. As the item is passed to the officers, Edie tenses as she recognizes the battered blue cover. It's her notebook.

'What you have in your hands is a private record of what my patient has endured, over a period of months,' the doctor begins. 'It proves she had only good intentions, and has served her regiment, not to mention her King and country, with true courage.'

'Your patient masqueraded as a man and fraudulently enlisted,' the president says, his voice edged with steel. 'She has committed a crime against His Majesty's Army, and thus must be punished.'

'But, sir,' Dr Garland persists, 'as Miss Pankhurst's telegram states, my patient is of good character. If you care to read Edie's account, you will see that she was faced with destitution so she took her chance to serve her country.'

'She deceived the authorities, Dr Garland,' the captain interrupts. 'And, what's more, a suffragette's opinion, however much it endorses the accused's good character, is irrelevant.'

The president flicks through Edie's notebook. 'As I see it,' the senior officer intones, 'the matter of the prisoner's guilt comes down to a question of intent. Is the court satisfied that the accused intended to deceive the authorities by fraudulently enlisting as a soldier? And what was her intent in doing so?'

'The prisoner's intention to deceive is self-evident,' the captain says.

'Her intention was to serve her country,' the doctor objects. 'She did that to the best of her ability, as her account will attest. That's all.'

The president removes his spectacles, rubbing the bridge of his nose. 'This character reference from Miss Pankhurst supports your assertion, Dr Garland. I'm inclined to believe that your patient's actions, while reckless and foolhardy, were committed with good intent.'

'With respect, sir,' the captain presses, 'I would like to remind the court that the crime of false enlistment, whatever the intention, carries a punishment of imprisonment with hard labour.'

Edie can't look at the men, can barely breathe. Every fibre of her being longs to flee. Could she make a run for the door, while these officers argue among themselves? As soon as she has this thought, she dismisses it. More guards have appeared, and her leg would never hold her.

She realizes Dr Garland has moved back to stand alongside her, and now the doctor rests a gentle hand on her shoulder. It is so long since anyone has touched her with such tenderness that Edie could weep.

She tries to take strength from Dr Garland's presence, a guardian angel at her side. The officers gather, conferring in voices too low for Edie to hear what they're saying. Dr Garland watches the men, rigid as a statue, and Edie strives to breathe.

At last, the officers cease their discourse, and resume their positions.

'We have considered the evidence,' the president says. 'The court has concluded that the prisoner's actions, although in contravention of military law, were nonetheless undertaken with innocent intent, and therefore the case is dismissed.'

Dr Garland's hand squeezes Edie's shoulder so tightly it hurts. Edie can't move, as she struggles to process what the officer has said. Was he letting her go?

'The court releases you into the care of Dr Garland, Miss Lawrence,' the president continues, 'on the understanding that you will return to England immediately.'

Dr Garland is the first to react. She sinks to her knees before Edie, grasping her arms. There are tears in the older woman's eyes, and Edie feels an answering prickle in her own, but she is too numb with shock to cry.

'You're free, Edie.'

Edie labours to swallow, unable to speak.

The doctor stands again, turning back to the officers. 'Thank you, gentlemen,' she says. But the captain is already striding from the room.

The president and the major are gathering up their papers. Edie's notebook lies discarded, and she forces herself to her feet. The president looks up, but says nothing as Edie staggers to the table and takes back what is rightfully hers.

With Dr Garland supporting her, Edie limps from the room into the crowded lobby. The doctor pauses to scoop up a large leather bag, and then they are pushing their way outside at last. Edie lifts her face to a sky washed clean, rare winter sun warming her skin. The wind, though chill, is blessedly fresh after the oppressive, musty courtroom, and Edie breathes deeply.

Holding tight to Dr Garland's arm, Edie stumbles slowly along the road a short distance, and they rest for a moment on a low wall, the bricks damp and crumbling.

'Even the weather rejoices,' Dr Garland says, her smile bashful as she takes Edie's hand and gives it a brief squeeze.

Edie smiles shyly back. 'I can't thank you enough, ma'am.'

Dr Garland shakes her head. 'You saved yourself in

there,' she says, 'with perhaps a little help from Sylvia Pankhurst.'

The street is busy, military figures everywhere Edie looks. The doctor's expression turns serious. 'We have to get you away from here, before they change their minds.'

Edie glances back towards the château, benign in the winter sun. The rumble of guns in the distance is a reminder that battles are raging on. But for this brief time, the war is elsewhere, and Edie is apart from it. Gradually, she realizes the doctor is talking to her.

'I'll be back shortly,' Dr Garland is saying. 'Don't move from here.'

'Where are you going?' Edie croaks, in a voice that doesn't sound like her own. But the doctor is already hurrying away down the street.

Dr Garland returns a few minutes later, to Edie's enormous relief.

'I've found us a vehicle,' she tells Edie breathlessly, as though she's been running. 'They can squeeze us on, but we have to be quick.'

The military truck, Edie learns, is parked around the corner. They stagger to it, and Edie is helped up into the truck's bed, where she sits amid a contingent of British airmen returning to the station. Dr Garland climbs up after her, lugging her leather bag, and a space is made for her on the bench opposite Edie. The doctor's smile of reassurance is enough to quell Edie's rising panic at being trapped among so many strangers.

At the railway station, Dr Garland finds Edie a seat in the waiting room, an oasis of calm in the maelstrom. Edie longs to lie down on the hard wooden bench and close her eyes, her reserves of energy almost empty. But there are hours, and miles, to go yet.

Dr Garland disappears again, returning with cups of lukewarm tea and a couple of stale buns. Edie has no idea where she's found refreshments, but the doctor reminds her a little of her mother, who would often conjure such things as an egg or a crust of bread for Edie, seemingly from nowhere.

'There's only one train to Wimereux,' Dr Garland tells Edie. 'It leaves in half an hour.'

Edie tries to make her bun last, but she's starving and it's gone in a few bites. Dr Garland smiles, and hands Edie half of hers. 'You need it more than I do,' she says, when Edie tries to protest. 'Once we're safely back, I'll re-dress your leg, and you can rest properly,' she adds.

'This helps,' Edie says, sipping the tea. Despite the shelter of the waiting room, she is shivering in her thin blouse.

Dr Garland removes her jacket. 'Put this on,' she says. Edie wants to refuse, but the tunic is made of thick material, and she's shaking now.

'Won't you be cold?' Edie asks.

Dr Garland straightens her shoulders. 'I have more natural insulation than you,' she replies, with a wink.

'Thank you,' Edie whispers. She slips her notebook into a pocket, and they settle down to wait.

∞

They reach the hospital as dusk is falling, to be greeted by a jubilant reception committee. While Dr Garland is surrounded by her staff, a young orderly with messy red hair wearing a grubby apron guides Edie to a nearby chair.

'You look ready to drop,' the orderly comments cheerily. 'I'm Mardie, by the way. Your name's Edie, I know, cos Dr Maberry hasn't shut up about you and Dr Garland since yesterday.'

'Thank you, Hodgson.' Dr Garland reappears, accompanied by two women.

'I'm Dr Maberry.' The taller woman introduces herself. 'And this is Sister Whiteman.'

'We've met before,' the nurse says, smiling down at Edie, 'but you mayn't remember.'

'You must be exhausted, Edie,' Dr Maberry says. 'Let's see to that wee leg of yours, shall we? I'm surprised it hasn't fallen off.'

Edie is too tired to laugh. A wheeled bath chair materializes, pushed by an older man who reminds Edie fleetingly of Bembridge. She's helped into the wicker seat by Sister Whiteman, and Dr Garland promises to come and check on her, just as soon as she's freshened up.

As she's wheeled away, Edie glances back to see Dr Maberry pulling Dr Garland into an embrace, unfettered joy on both women's faces.

Edie finds herself in a library, a modest room filled with bookshelves, a desk covered with papers, and a generous French-style sofa.

'Let's get you settled,' Sister Whiteman says, helping Edie remove her shoes and transfer to the chaise-longue. The red haired orderly hovers in the doorway.

'Can you fetch some water, Hodgson, please?' the nurse says. 'And perhaps a cheese sandwich, if you can muster one.'

The orderly flashes a smile at Edie, and disappears.

'Right then,' Sister Whiteman says. 'Let's see about this leg of yours.'

∞

Edie cradles Stanley's camera in her lap, her mind filled with memories of his gentle teasing and silly jokes, his ridiculous guesses as to how she'd broken her nose.

She thinks of the cigarettes and sweets he'd shared with her, how he'd mimicked the voices of the officers to make her laugh.

How he'd defended her from the worst of Caldwell's bite.

She'd never told Stanley the truth of who she really was, and the thought saddens her anew.

'Edie?'

She's tugged from her ruminations by Dr Garland arriving with a tray. 'Now, you're to eat this all up, young lady. On doctor's orders.'

Edie's eyes widen at the sight of fried eggs and mushrooms, three pieces of buttered toast and a ramekin of fruit jam.

'This is Harry Levinson's address.' Dr Garland hands a slip of paper to Edie. 'Once you're back in London, go there. If Harry's not back, his wife Mary will welcome you. She's the sweetest woman but, beware, she'll insist you eat a plateful of her jam tarts.'

'I love jam tarts,' Edie says.

'Well, that will stand you in good stead.' Dr Garland smiles. 'Take the camera to Harry, and he'll develop the film. I'll send a telegram today and let them know you're on your way.'

Edie reads the address, a place near Hampstead Heath.

'Now, you'll need some money,' Dr Garland continues. 'Sylvia Pankhurst has already financed your travel, and we have a small contingency fund for soldiers in need. I'm going to give you a little from this to tide you over until you see Harry.'

'I don't know how to thank you, Doctor.' It's all too much. Edie wills herself not to cry. She must be strong now. For Stanley's sake.

Because a plan has begun to seed in her mind.

'You can repay us when you've published your story,' Dr Garland says, with a smile.

∞

Edie's passage home is aboard a hospital ship that Dr Garland assures her sails regularly between Boulogne and Dover.

Whenever she thinks about crossing the Channel again, Edie's guts churn, and she'd been unable to finish her breakfast, despite Dr Garland's orders.

The time has come for her to leave.

'Have you everything you need?' Dr Garland asks.

Edie nods. One of the nursing staff has generously donated a carpet bag, and others have given a spare skirt, a blouse, stockings and a pair of shoes. The orderlies have supplied Edie with a comb, a little bar of soap, and all has been packed into the bag along with Edie's precious notebook and Stanley's camera, wrapped in a cardigan.

'You have Harry's address safe?' the doctor asks.

'Yes.' Edie's hand strays to the pocket of the dark blue pea coat she's wearing – another item of donated clothing, this time from Sister Bryony. Her fingers touch the slip of paper, tucked safe with a letter from Dr Garland that Edie is to post on to the doctor's mother, once she's on English soil.

'All is ready, then,' Dr Garland says.

Mardie arrives with a parcel wrapped in cheesecloth.

'Thank you, Hodgson,' Dr Garland says. She passes the package to Edie, to be added to her bag. 'There should be enough food in there to last you until you reach home.'

Home.

The word sends a shudder down Edie's spine.

Where was home?

To Edie's embarrassment, a small party of staff gather in the courtyard to bid her farewell. Sister Whiteman presses a kiss on her cheek, and the other nurses and orderlies shake her hand.

'*Bon voyage,*' Dr Garland says, as she helps Edie into the back of an ambulance truck. As a nurse helps her find a space among half a dozen Blighty soldiers also returning to England to recuperate, Edie suffers a sudden stomach-plunging flashback to her arrest, and for a moment she can't breathe.

'You can rest your leg on your bag,' the nurse suggests. 'Not too far to the port,' she adds, with a smile of encouragement. 'All being well.'

'Tell Miss Pankhurst she's to let you rest for at least a week,' Dr Garland calls up to Edie. 'Promise me, now . . .'

'I promise,' Edie replies, her voice thick.

The truck judders into life, and they begin to move off. Dr Garland raises her hand in farewell, walking a few steps behind the vehicle, but soon she and the rest of the staff are reduced to dots in the distance, and then they are gone.

∞

Edie limps between rows of stretchers, through a mass of wounded men crowding the decks in tangled heaps of bloodied gauze and torn khaki. Medical orderlies and VAD nurses, red crosses emblazoned on their uniforms, tend the casualties, but no one pays Edie any attention as she makes her way to the top deck, and it occurs to her how much has changed in such a short period. The last time she'd been on a ship, she'd dreaded being discovered as a woman. Now, here she is, a woman among so many men, and nobody cares.

She reaches the upper deck, to find it strewn with walking-wounded, bodies huddled under blankets and greatcoats; the men sleeping, or passed out, or dead. Finding space by the stern rail, Edie grips the cold metal, as the rumble of the ship's engines joins the bass notes of heavy artillery in the distance. The sound rolls like thunder through her head, as she looks out across the sea.

The waves are tipped with silver in the moonlight, and all she can think is that Stanley should be here with her.

∞

A flaming dawn sky heralds the ship's arrival at Dover docks. Edie has managed barely a couple of hours of broken sleep, her leg wound throbbing, the cold wind off the sea keeping her awake.

Exhausted, she transfers to a packed train for the final stage of her journey, eventually reaching Victoria station. She disembarks on to a platform seething with people, a hellish tumult of soldiers and civilians, wounded men, officers and medics, the railway guards' announcements drowned in a cacophony of voices.

Pushing her way out of the station, Edie heads in the direction of Roman Road. Every few yards, she's forced to stop and rest, her leg so painful she fears she can't take another step. She cuts through Spitalfields market, moving so slowly it takes her more than two hours to reach the Society headquarters. To her dismay, she finds the place busy with women. With barely any strength left, Edie stumbles the last few steps to Sylvia's Pankhurst's office.

'My dear girl!' Sylvia cries, as Edie sways with fatigue in her doorway. 'Come in, my dear. Sit down before you fall!'

Edie collapses on to a chair and submits to Sylvia's care.

'Did you get Dr Garland's telegram?' Edie asks, when she can speak again.

'I received it this morning,' Sylvia replies. 'If I'd known you were coming on foot, I would have sent a cab to meet you. I can't believe you walked all the way here with your poor leg . . .'

Several members of the Society gather at the open door, keen to witness the miraculous reappearance of their brave suffrage sister, rumoured to have survived the unthinkable.

Edie is handed hot sweet tea, and a slice of seed cake. Someone wraps a crocheted blanket round her shoulders, and she fights to keep her eyes open, as more and more women appear, all wanting a glimpse of the returning heroine.

'Is it true you've been fighting in France with our boys?' a large woman demands, pushing her way into the room and looming over Edie. 'How close to the front did you get? What's it like there?'

'Please, Mrs Winton,' Sylvia Pankhurst implores, 'let the poor girl get her breath back.'

At last, Sylvia insists Edie is left in peace, and the Society reluctantly disperses. She helps her up to the blue bedroom.

'I hope you sleep well, dear,' Sylvia says, engulfing Edie in a rare hug. 'You can tell me more about your adventures in the morning.'

34

Lucinda: December 1914

Blood everywhere, bright red rivers of it. Lucinda's bare hands are slick with gore, fingers slipping as she grapples with the gaping neck wound. There's been no time to don rubber gloves, or a mask, or to sterilize her instruments. Everything she's ever been taught about sepsis and hygiene is forgotten in her desperate effort to save the soldier on her table.

'More swabs, Nurse!'

'The subclavian artery may be compressed at the base of the neck, opposite to the centre of the collarbone.' Lucinda's spine stiffens at the familiar voice of Dr Craddock emanating from somewhere behind her shoulder. Where has her old medical instructor sprung from? She wants to turn round, appeal for Dr Craddock's help, but if she reduces the pressure on the wound even for a moment she will lose this patient.

Sister Bryony's hands appear in front of Lucinda's blurring eyes, her fingers full of cotton wool.

'Pack the wound!' Lucinda gasps. Why doesn't the woman move faster? They must staunch the flow of blood before it's too late . . .

'By drawing forward the shoulder, the artery will be more easily reached by the thumb pressing downwards against the first rib behind the clavicle,' Dr Craddock's voice drones. He sounds like he's reading from a medical manual. 'Compression can also be effected with the handle of a key wrapped in a soft cloth . . .'

'A key?' Lucinda hears her voice crack. Where did the man think she was going to lay her hands on a key, for Heaven's sake?

'Hurry!' she snaps at Sister Bryony. 'Never mind, just give them here!' She snatches the cotton wool from the nurse, shoving clumps into the ragged slash in the soldier's neck. They disappear one by one, swallowed by welling blood. No matter how many she crams in, the wound continues to pump out a stream of blood, and now her arms and apron are crimson.

Dr Craddock is right, of course. A key might be her last chance. 'Find me a key!' she shrieks, to anyone who will listen. 'A key!'

But it's too late, the soldier's face is greying, his lips turning blue. Too much blood has been lost and his fate is sealed no matter what she does now.

'No, no, no, no . . .' Lucinda presses harder, in one last frantic effort to save the man, but Sister Bryony is grabbing her forearms, prising Lucinda away, and though she struggles to free herself from the nurse's grip, the younger woman is stronger and –

'Lucie, wake up!'

Lucinda surfaces with a gasp, to find the sheet twisted tight about her legs, Florence pinning her arms, gently but firmly.

'Lucie, darling, you're safe . . .'

Florence's familiar Scottish burr brings Lucinda to her

senses at last, and a shudder of relief runs through her. She exhales as Florence releases her, and they lie facing one another on the chaise-longue. Soft morning sunlight filters through the window, bathing the library in a rosy tint.

'Another nightmare?' Florence asks, her voice tender.

Lucinda swallows. 'I couldn't save him . . .'

'Oh, Lucie.'

'I'm sorry if I woke you.' Lucinda lifts a trembling hand, and rests it on Florence's clavicle. The vital heat between their bodies quickens Lucinda's breath, and at the same time soothes her.

'It's all right,' Florence murmurs, placing a hand over Lucinda's. 'I was awake anyway.' Florence's smile reaches her warm, hazel eyes, and all Lucinda longs to do is lie there, drowning in her gaze, for ever.

'I love you,' Lucinda whispers, still trembling inside.

'I love you too.'

And then Florence's warm mouth finds hers, dissolving the remnants of the dream with her caress. And as the kiss deepens, Lucinda can think of nothing but this precious, miraculous moment.

Once morning surgery is over, Florence is called away to speak with Monsieur Bataille about hiring a new cook, a task Lucinda would do herself, but she must complete her weekly report to the Red Cross.

She hurries back to the library, fearing that if she doesn't manage to finish the dreaded report today, she risks jeopardizing vital funds.

An hour later, as she is concluding her summary of the

hospital's surgical procedures, someone knocks at the door and opens it. Mardie has brought her a sandwich from the kitchen.

'Dr Maberry said you'd forget to eat,' Mardie says, setting the plate on Lucinda's desk.

She *had* forgotten lunch, Lucinda realizes.

'And this letter came for you just now, ma'am.' The envelope is postmarked London, and stamped CONFIDENTIAL.

'Thank you, Hodgson.'

'Dr Maberry wants to know if you'll be joining her on the ward rounds, ma'am.'

'I'll be there in a moment, tell her.'

'Will do, ma'am.'

Ignoring the sandwich, Lucinda tears open the envelope, extracting a single sheet of government-issue paper, headed *War Office*.

Dear Dr Garland and Dr Maberry, she reads. Skipping the rest, she checks the signature at the bottom of the page: Lieutenant General Walton, the deputy director of Army Medical Services.

The man who'd summarily dismissed her and Florence's offer of help several months before.

What did the old goat want?

Lucinda absently chews the sandwich, as she properly reads the letter. She's forced to read it twice, before the words fully register.

And then she's on her feet, scattering crumbs, dashing from the library.

She finds Florence in Elpis Ward, conducting morning rounds with Sister Whiteman.

'Can I speak to you outside for a moment, Dr Maberry?' Lucinda says.

Florence takes one look at Lucinda's face, and makes her apologies to the officer whose broken collarbone she's checking, leaving him in the care of the nurse.

Out in the corridor, Lucinda thrusts Walton's missive into Florence's hands. 'You won't believe this.'

Florence scans the letter. 'Is this some sort of joke?' she says, frowning.

'It's no joke,' Lucinda replies.

'So, the War Office is genuinely offering us a vacant workhouse in London, and they want us to turn it into another military hospital?'

'That's about the size of it, Flo.'

'I don't understand,' Florence says. 'The last time we offered our services, Walton told us in no uncertain terms to leave the war surgery to men.'

'Egham must have spoken very strongly to him about our work in Paris,' Lucinda says, taking the letter back. 'See here,' she points at a line. 'Walton says that Lord Egham has revised his opinion of women doctors, and has nothing but good to say about our hospital.'

Lucinda reads the final paragraph aloud: '*As you are no doubt aware, the system of evacuating casualties from the front has significantly improved over recent months. With the increase in the number of hospital trains and ships now available, it's possible to bring our men back to England far more swiftly than before. Sir Alfred Keogh is prepared to give you full command of the new hospital, and only requires that you submit a weekly report to Whitehall.*'

Lucinda lowers the letter, and the two women look at one another.

'Well,' Florence says, at last, 'what do you think?'

'I think before we decide anything we have to consult the rest of the team.' She smiles at the thought of Walton and all the other brass hats, sitting at their tidy desks in their safe offices, finally realizing that her women have proved a success.

'Naturally.'

'Walton's set us a huge challenge,' Lucinda muses, chewing her lip as she scans the letter once more. 'My head hurts just thinking about the logistics of this whole new endeavour . . .'

Could they really do it all over again?

'What does your heart tell you?' Florence reaches for Lucinda's hand, and as their fingers entwine, Lucinda feels a swell of emotion in her chest, the ventricles of her heart filling with love.

'That I can do anything with you, Flo.'

35

Edie: December 1914

Edie's strength gradually returns, her leg wound healing as each day passes. To her relief, Sylvia is happy for her to stay at Roman Road, in return for administrative duties in the office. Joyce Millard is so incensed at Sylvia's decision that she immediately resigns her membership of the Society and leaves.

'Good riddance,' Sylvia declares, assuaging Edie's worry that she's caused a problem for her friend. 'That tiresome woman had nothing positive to say about anything.'

The other women of the Society welcome Edie back into the fold, vying to feed her up on their cakes, plying her with questions about what it was like in France, fighting alongside the soldiers.

She tries to answer their questions honestly, but in truth she finds it impossible to convey the full horror of her experience. There are no words that come close to expressing the depth of her grief and guilt for Stanley.

Every day, she scans the lists of the fallen, but she never finds his name. His loss is like a disease, consuming her from within. No one can understand what she suffers, certainly none of the women in the Society. She knows from talking to them that many have sons, husbands, brothers serving, and some have lost their men. But none can imagine what it's like to fight in the trenches, to be hunted by the enemy and left for dead.

Though surrounded by the love and support of the Society, Edie has never felt so lonely. In her heart, she knows that if she's ever to move on she must confront what has happened, and to do that she needs Harry Levinson.

The journalist's three-storey townhouse is on a leafy street, half a mile south of Hampstead Heath. Edie has never been to this part of London before, and as she steps off the bus, she hears the distinctive *crack-crack-crack-crack* of gunfire. She grips the strap of her satchel, her whole body tensing, until she remembers what Sylvia had told her yesterday: that local soldiers were now using the Heath for rifle training and military exercises. Edie feels sick at the thought of all those men digging practice trenches and filling sandbags, oblivious to the horrors that lie ahead.

She finds Harry Levinson's house, set back from the street within a generous plot. Mature trees border the front garden, and Edie's shoes crunch up the gravel drive. Reaching the front door, she hesitates, doubting her decision to come. Would Harry want to see her again?

She reminds herself of what Dr Garland had told her: that Harry will help get her story out into the world.

Even so, it takes everything she has to pull the bell.

The door is opened by a tall, well-built woman in an apron liberally stained with what Edie hopes is jam. 'Yes, dear?'

Edie grips her satchel tighter. Stanley's camera, her

good-luck talisman, is inside. 'I'm sorry to disturb you, ma'am . . . I'm looking for Mr Levinson.'

'You want Harry?' The woman wipes floury hands on her apron, her gaze astute.

'Yes, ma'am.'

'My husband's out at the moment, but he should be back soon. Is he expecting you?'

Edie doesn't know what to say to this. She should have written to Harry first, arranged a time to meet. She kicks herself for not thinking to do this. 'He helped me in France,' she says at last. 'I wanted to thank him.'

'Why don't you come in?' Mrs Levinson says. 'It's far too cold to wait outside.'

Edie steps inside, acutely conscious of her appearance. She's wearing a borrowed skirt and blouse, which are slightly too big, and the pea coat donated by Sister Bryony, which hangs off her thin frame. At least the knitted beret Sylvia gave her covers her short hair.

'What's your name, dear?' Mrs Levinson asks. Edie tells her, and the woman's eyes widen. She smiles warmly. 'Harry's told me all about you, dear. What a time you've had . . .'

Mrs Levinson leads Edie deeper into the house, the whole place smelling of hot sweet jam.

'I'm baking tarts for the Women's Emergency Corps,' Mrs Levinson tells Edie. 'We're raising funds for refugee children.' She stops at a door, opens it to reveal an office.

'Harry should be back any minute. I'll leave you in here while I see if I can find Susan to make some tea . . .'

Before Edie can respond, Mrs Levinson is hurrying away. Harry's office is like a small library, Edie thinks, the walls lined floor-to-ceiling with shelves, every inch of space crammed with books. A fire crackles in the hearth, and Edie immediately feels safe, as though she's cocooned inside a shell of wood and paper. She could happily live in this room, she decides, as she runs a finger along a book-shelf, reading the eclectic titles. Philosophy, world history, fiction, all muddled together. A slim, gilt-edged spine catches her eye, and without thinking she slips out the volume. She opens the book, to find it's a text on ancient forest myths. Quite fascinating . . .

'Aha! The girl-soldier returns.'

A man's voice from the doorway makes Edie start, and she spins round, almost dropping the book. 'Mr Levin-son,' she stammers.

The reporter crosses the room in three strides. 'How wonderful to see you, Edie.' He takes her free hand, clasps it in both of his. 'I was saying to Mary only this morning, I wonder when I'll see Edie Lawrence again.'

'I've been staying with Miss Pankhurst,' Edie replies.

'Ah, yes, our dear friend. It looks like she's taking good care of you.' Harry notices the book in her hand. 'One of my favourites,' he says. 'Would you like to borrow it?'

Edie feels herself blush. 'It does look interesting,' she says. 'Thank you.'

'My pleasure.' Harry ushers her into a deep armchair, then takes a seat at the desk. 'So, tell me everything that's happened,' he says, without preamble.

Haltingly, Edie gives the journalist a shortened version of her journey back to London, and the welcome she received from Sylvia and the Society. She tells Harry about her work in the office there, expecting him to praise her, but instead the journalist wants to know what she's written.

Edie can't answer him.

Harry leans back in his chair, the wood creaking. He says nothing for a long moment, and then, 'You have your friend's camera still?'

Edie fumbles Stanley's Ensignette from her satchel.

'I can develop the film today,' Harry says, taking the camera from her. 'It'll be interesting to find out what your good friend Stanley shot. Who knows? We may even be able to publish one or two pictures.'

At the mention of Stanley's name, Edie feels the hot prickle of tears. He should be here, talking to Harry about his passion for photography, how he'd hoped to publish his pictures one day.

'Did you ever find out what happened to him?' Harry asks.

At that moment, a maid arrives with tea and some jam tarts on a tray.

'Ah, thank you, Susan,' Harry says, taking the tray from the girl. He pours Edie a cup without asking if she wants one, and pushes the plate of tarts towards her.

'Eat them up,' he urges. 'Lord knows, you need some meat on your bones, girl.'

Edie's appetite has deserted her, but she dutifully takes a warm tart, the jammy pastry melting in her mouth.

'Have you heard any news from your friend?' Harry asks again.

Edie shakes her head. She has no idea if Stanley survived the trench raid, or if he's still lying in the mud.

'I'll make some enquiries,' Harry says, pouring tea. 'Someone will know something.'

They drink their tea in silence for a moment, and then, 'What makes a good journalist, Edie?'

Thrown by Harry's question, Edie struggles to think. There are so many answers she could give, but which is the right one?

'Good writing?' she ventures.

Harry Levinson shakes his head. 'No. Being *interested* makes a good journalist.' He fixes Edie with a steady gaze. 'Life may be dull for many people, but good newspapers are a report of life, so must they be dull?'

Edie shakes her head slowly.

'No, good newspapers are not dull,' Harry goes on. 'The key is finding the interest in mundane phenomena.'

Edie tries to follow his line of thought.

'You want to be a journalist, don't you.' It's a statement, not a question.

Edie accepts another jam tart, her appetite returning. What Harry is saying is true: to be a journalist is all she's ever wanted.

'Anyone can learn to write copy, Edie,' Harry continues. 'Even half-decent copy. But to be a good journalist, you must discern what is *interesting* in life, and that comes not with *tuition*, but with *intuition*.' Harry smiles, raising his teacup in a mock toast. 'And I think you have it.'

'Thank you, sir.'

'Call me Harry.'

'Thank you, Harry.'

'Now, one other thing . . .'

A log crumbles in the hearth, and Edie longs to stay in this snug, book-lined room for ever.

'How's your leg?'

'It's almost back to normal,' Edie replies, touching her thigh. 'Thanks to Dr Garland . . .'

'Repairing soldiers is part of her job.' Harry grins. 'Now the leg's mended, how about going on the music-hall circuit?' Harry helps himself to a second jam tart. 'Vesta Tilley's making a killing, and she's a sham. With you, though, we have the real deal . . .'

Edie stares at Harry. Surely he wasn't being serious. She's still thin enough to pass for a soldier, and her crooked nose and angular face would fool most people, at least from a distance. But Harry can't think she'd be happy on a stage?

'I'm teasing you,' Harry says.

A relieved laugh escapes her.

'But you have to tell the world your story, Edie. Just think how interesting it would be to read now, and in years to come when this war is but a dim memory and life has returned to its usual, dull routine.'

'I'm no hero,' Edie whispers. Who would want to hear her story? She failed to save Stanley, and that will haunt her for the rest of her days.

'I can't agree with you,' Harry says quietly but firmly. 'It's my belief that you can only evaluate a person's achievements by knowing where they came from. And by that measure, your achievements are monumentally heroic.'

Edie thinks of Stanley: he was the true hero. His story should be told.

'People *will* want to read your story, Edie,' Harry says. 'And when you're ready to write it, I'll be here to help you.'

'I'm ready,' Edie says.

And what a story it will be.

Author's Note

In the summer of 2012, I came across the fascinating yet forgotten memoir of a young Edwardian woman called Dorothy Lawrence. I'm drawn to women in history who survived, and occasionally thrived, in a man's world, and Dorothy tried to do both.

Born illegitimately in 1896, Dorothy longed to be a journalist, but her sex, background and lack of education held her back. She wasn't going to relinquish her dream easily, though. In 1915 she travelled to France and managed to disguise herself as a male soldier in the British Army. Her aim was to become the first female journalist to report the truth from the battlefields.

She fought alongside the Royal Engineers for ten days, until an injury brought her identity to light. Arrested on suspicion of being an enemy spy, Dorothy was court-martialled, and finally sent home under strict orders never to return or write about her experiences.

I couldn't get Dorothy out of my mind. What sort of woman had the courage to travel to an enemy-occupied country in the middle of a war, disguise herself as a man, and risk her life in battle? An interesting woman, in my opinion, and one who deserved to be remembered.

So, I began to re-imagine Dorothy's story. At the same time, I came across the incredible achievements of two female doctors. Louisa Garrett Anderson (1873–1943) was a surgeon, a suffragette, and the daughter of the first female doctor to qualify in Britain, Elizabeth Garrett Anderson. Flora Murray (1869–1923) was a Scottish anaesthetist, a suffragette, and the life partner of Louisa.

When war broke out in 1914, Louisa and Flora founded the Women's Hospital Corps (WHC), and offered their services as doctors to the War Office. They were rejected, told that women were not capable of performing military surgery. Instead, Louisa and Flora and their all-female team appealed to the French Red Cross, who gratefully accepted their offer of help.

The WHC established two military hospitals, the first in Paris, the second in Wimereux near Boulogne on the French coast. Casualties from the battlefields flooded in, filling the wards with traumatized men suffering horrific injuries, the likes of which the medical establishment had never faced before.

But the women rose to the challenge, and soon their success came to the attention of the Royal Army Medical Corps (RAMC). By providing exceptional care to wounded soldiers, Louisa, Flora and their team demonstrated that they were equal to their male counterparts.

Women of War is a work of fiction, the characters created from my imagination but strongly inspired by Dorothy, Louisa and Flora. The locations that feature in my novel – the hotel in Paris, the château in Wimereux, the War Office in London – and the challenges my characters face are all taken from real places and events.

Everything else is made up.

Acknowledgements

My heartfelt thanks to the following people for all their help getting *Women of War* out into the world:

Alison Bonomi: thank you for your steady, empathetic, patient support. I couldn't ask for a better literary agent.

Hannah Smith: your enthusiasm for Edie and Lucinda gave me an enormous boost, right when I most needed it. Thank you from the deepest chambers of my heart for giving me the chance to tell their story.

Hazel Orme: thank you for your diligent, eagle-eyed copyediting, and making my sentences shine.

To Nick Lowndes and the entire publishing team at Penguin Michael Joseph for all your hard work.

Julie Ma, your writerly friendship means the world to me. An email a day (from you) keeps fear and stress at bay. One day, you'll come to Hampshire, and I'll buy you a cup of tea and the biggest slice of cake.

Beta readers are the unsung heroes of publishing, and I'm lucky enough to have had a trio of superheroes who helped me from the start: Marian Sweet, Scott Goldie and Lisa Koning, incredible writers all, you deserve my huge thanks for your insightful comments on my early drafts.

William Bodey FRCS: thank you so much for checking my medical facts, and preventing my doctors from inadvertently murdering their patients. All remaining mistakes are mine.

Team Goldfinch: Gary, Jude, Andrea, Ash and everyone

who works in the best bookshop in Alton (and the world), thank you for all your support, and the opportunities you've given me to stretch my literary wings. Here's to our future.

Alton Library: Susan, Hilary, Michelle, Huw, Kevin, Lesley, Scott, Giusy, Sue and all the team, thank you for your continual help with my (sometimes bizarre) book requests, and a friendly, warm chat when I need to escape my desk.

Thank you to the Society of Authors and their Authors' Foundation grant, for helping to fund my research.

Last, but never least, thank you to all my family, especially Andrew, William and Ellen, who keep me real, and Darren, who keeps me from hurling my laptop through the nearest window. I love you.